Ben Reid and Sam Reid are brothers. They both studied English at Brasenose College, Oxford. The brothers are dyslexic: Ben has no apparent sense of direction and Sam can't tell the time – it is a minor miracle that they were ever in the same place at once, let alone wrote a novel. They both currently live and write in London.

GENERATION

BEN & SAM REID

For more information about this and other books
by Ben and Sam Reid please go to
samreid.com

THINGS TO COME

Georgie pressed herself flat against the crumbling wall. All she could hear was her heart beating in her throat and the loud hissing of the rain. It fell in fat droplets, breaking the surface of the shallow lake, puckering it into a large, grey sheet of gooseflesh.

Eight months ago there'd been shops here; she'd done her Christmas shopping *right here*. She almost laughed at the thought. What had she bought? She had no idea; it seemed like a lifetime ago. That was before the fire had burnt the heart out of London leaving this wasteland.

A wasteland that was now rapidly filling with water. There wasn't much time.

She pushed her hair out of her bruised face and tried to catch her breath. Her fingernails were cracked to the quick, knuckles split so badly in places that white bone and yellow fat peeped out from beneath the skin. Georgie didn't even notice.

Far away on the other side of the lake, partly obscured by the drifts of rain and the charred remains of houses, she could just make out the cliffs of unburned buildings. That was where they'd come from, that was where her home was. She'd never see it again now.

A flurry of pigeons burst from one of the broken windows and wheeled off into the darkling sky as if startled by some unseen predator.

Her heart quickened again. What had scared the birds? No, couldn't be *them*, it just couldn't. They'd made a mess when the train had crashed but *they* couldn't see them, not here.

Georgie squinted hard, looking for movement, for the tell-tale white blurs that might mean an attack.

Nothing.

Stillness.

Probably just a feral cat.

She leant her head against the wall behind her and allowed her eyes to close for a moment. She and Sarah had now reached the first building on the easternmost edge of the lake. This was where the danger really began. As soon as they stepped into the deserted streets, crept out between the flooded buildings, then they were at risk again. They knew how *they* found them - they'd learnt that little secret the hard way - but that wouldn't help them right now. She just had to hope that *they* weren't watching this part of the city.

The water was already up to her knees. They had to make it across the bridge before it was too late.

She looked over at her companion. Sarah stood shivering beside her, clothes hanging in heavy drapes from her lean body. Water dripped from the ends of her short, boyish hair and ran in bloody rivulets down her cheeks. There was a cold and violent gleam in her eyes as though Georgie was looking down through turbulent waters at two darkly gleaming flints. Sarah didn't speak, only stared back from those dead eyes while the muscles in her jaw worked rhythmically.

That was another worry: could she trust Sarah? She just didn't know. Almost getting them caught. And then the tunnels… something had happened to Sarah in the tube tunnels. She'd disappeared and come back… changed. The spoilt girl who'd been so difficult to like and the trusted friend she'd become were gone, replaced by…?

Georgie turned and craned her neck cautiously around

the edge of the wall, glad to escape that unsettling thought. The road looked quiet enough; no sign of movement. But then there never was - until it was too late.

How long had those malevolent eyes been watching them all, unsuspected before *they* made their devastating move? And now two of her friends were dead. Two that she knew of – she could only hope that if she and Sarah made it through, the rest of the group would be waiting for them safely at the meeting point. She became aware once more of the patchwork of bruises and scratches that covered her body. Her mind began to drift back to the tunnels, those dark tunnels that had almost taken their lives. Tunnels where so many answers and horrors lay. And something more than the cold made her shiver.

But something in those memories also gave Georgie the strength she needed. She grabbed Sarah's hand, took a breath, and then together they ran splashing into the cracked and ravaged streets of London, determined to escape, determined to survive.

CHAPTER 1.

A greasy white pigeon scanned Leytonstone High Road in quick, jerky movements from its perch on the street's Christmas lights. Clumps of newspaper rustled in the gentle breeze, a burst pipe dripped persistently onto a pile of uncollected rubbish bags with a lazy *plop, plop, plop*. Through the window of a car that sat crumpled against a lamppost, the bird spied what it was searching for. Olive green and yellow, a short length of wire hung from the slack mouth of the dashboard, perfect for repairing a nest. The pigeon fluttered down to rest on the car door, regarding its prize with a jealous eye, when an unexpected noise made it flee in a spatter of wings.

It was a girl that had broken the still of the high street. A girl with mousy brown hair, who wore a thick coat and scarf and carried a large rucksack on her shoulders. She moved slowly and cautiously along the road as though she was unused to the terrain and unsure how it would respond to her footsteps.

When Georgie had first left the house she'd been awed by the silence - silence pounded, buzzed, actually hurt her ears. It was a constant roaring like the sound of waves on a pebble beach. The sheer absence of human voices had become all but deafening. Finally, desperation had overcome her fear and she had begun to shout. She shouted under windows, through letterboxes and up at the sky - at first in the hope that someone would hear her and then just to keep herself company.

She had searched the houses, but finding no one, no one who would answer her call, she had taken whatever she thought would be useful and headed out into this new, silent London. She didn't know where she was going exactly - as yet she had no plan - but the need to find others kept her moving. She let her feet guide her and they nudged her softly along familiar paths until, finally, she had found herself at the high street. Here the strangeness of this new peopleless world gripped her again. A line of a song her father used to sing went through her head – 'streets as quiet as a sleeping army'. She realised the truth of it; there is nothing as quiet as something that should make noise and doesn't. Or can't.

Apart from the wrecked car there were no signs of violence or struggle – just emptiness. Most of the shops were boarded-up in an eternal Sunday morning. A white van that had been carrying paint stood by the crossroads; the tins had tumbled out spreading a rainbow-coloured smear across the pavement. Someone had trodden in it leaving sandy brown footprints. Georgie followed them for a while, hoping, but they petered-out eventually and she was alone again.

She stopped to tuck her scarf back into her coat and close the gap that had opened up, letting in the cold. Where should she go? The radio had long since stopped broadcasting - even Granddad's shortwave. All she got now was static or a repeating request to '*stand by for further transmissions*'; a polite message that had been playing for a week now. There'd been no advice, no emergency centres set up, she guessed there just hadn't been time. So whatever she decided to do it was up to her. No one to ask, no one to blame.

She supposed that the best thing to do would be to head into the middle of town. That was usually the busiest area, so if there was anyone else left, the chances were they'd be there. But how was she going to get to the centre? She'd been there hundreds of times but always in Dad's car or on the tube She didn't even know which bloody direction it was. How long would it take to walk anyway? Three or four hours maybe, if she knew the way. Which she didn't.

If only the tubes were running. Then she stopped. Of course, the tubes. They may not be running but the tracks were still there and they could take her straight into the centre.

She had a plan now. That's what she would do, she would follow the train lines, have a look around some of the bigger stations, just in case, and sooner or later she was bound to find someone.

What if the tracks were still electrified though? She'd have to test them. She sure as hell didn't want to get hurt when there was no one around to help. How should she test them? Hang on, what was she worrying about? Nothing worked anymore, that was the whole problem. No electricity, no heating, no cars, no trains, no planes. Nothing.

* * * * *

The helicopter thumped through the air, banking left before dropping its altitude suddenly. It was gaining speed, its rotors a whining blur, when without warning it crashed headlong into a framed picture of the Queen.

With a resigned sigh, Donnie flipped the controller over his shoulder. He'd have to pick up another one of those things tomorrow. Sooner or later he was going to get the hang of it.

He settled himself back down onto the lilo, careful not to get any of his clothes wet. Donnie was wearing an oversized tuxedo, complete with a bowtie that was draped jauntily about his shoulders – mainly because he wasn't sure how to do it up. His brown hair was slicked back but Donnie's unruly mop was doing its best to spring free and his wind-burnt cheeks spoke more of fresh sea air than cocktail lounges. He'd even got himself a cigar - like his uncle Robert sometimes smoked - but he hadn't bothered to light it since, in Donnie's opinion, they smelled vaguely like horse crap.

He wasn't particularly tall for his age, but there was something about the laughter lines around his green eyes that gave the impression that somewhere – pretty well hidden, admittedly – there was an old soul within Donnie.

The lobby was probably his favourite part of this hotel. When he'd met Sarah they were both staying in a scruffy little place on Russell Square and since they were both new to the city, Donnie had suggested they pack up their bags and make for the swankiest hotel in London they could find.

The lobby of *The Royal* was a sweep of beautiful, shining grey marble. The plant pots, the picture frames, even the penholders and telephone were gold. There was nothing like this in Inverrareigh. The pub where his uncle sometimes took him had a canny pool table and a plump barmaid with a low-cut top - but here? Even the lobby toilets had aftershave and fresh folded towels in them!

Paddling gently, he moved over to the side of the orna-mental pool and heaved himself from the lilo. The fountain had stopped working at the same time as everything else, but it was still nice to float there in the foyer now and again, watching the large goldfish flitting about beneath him in out and out of the oversized water-lilies.

Donnie had to walk to the 22nd floor, of course, but he always had bags of energy anyway, and the views from the enormous room they'd claimed for themselves were amazing. He knocked on the door before going in; Sarah would know it was him, but it seemed polite anyhow, since they hadn't known each other for all that long and besides, girls were always changing in and out of clothes.

Donnie entered the penthouse a little sheepishly. He had said he was going to find some food ages ago, and he knew Sarah would have been worrying. She was that kind of girl.

Pale and skinny, and just like the ones in his class who always sat far too near the front and were always giving orders.

He couldn't hear Sarah, but the parrot was where he'd left it, sitting on the flat-screen TV and following him with its inquisitive gaze.

"Alreet boy?"

As usual, no answer.

When they had changed hotels he and Sarah had come across a large pet shop on one of the backstreets. The place stank when they entered; far more than the usual pet shop smell of dog food and gerbils. The cages hadn't been cleaned for a long while, and the animals that were still alive were filthy and restless.

Donnie had wanted a pet parrot for as long as he could remember – and now who was going to say no?

The parrot hopped from its perch on the flat-screen to his shoulder and seemed content to explore his earhole and eat the prawn cocktail crisps that Donnie passed up to him.

Sarah had insisted that they liberate the rest of the animals. The hamsters and mice disappeared in a wriggle of fur the moment their cage doors were opened, but the smaller birds found perches on the stock shelves or cash register and just sat there, tweeting. Only when Donnie and Sarah left the shop did the birds seem to take courage, presenting the two of them with the sight of dozens of canaries and budgies fluttering up in a colourful cloud of blues, yellows and greens before settling on the bare trees.

Donnie had been doing his best to teach the parrot a variety of the filthiest words he knew, much to Sarah's disapproval. But no matter how many times he called the bird a 'dirty wee bastard' he never seemed to get a response.

Donnie made his way into the plush living room. "Sarah?" he called, doing his best to sound casual and cheery.

She was in one of the bedrooms. He threw the packets of sandwiches he had made over to her. "I wasnae sure if you wanted your foie gras and ketchup on brown or white, so I did one of each. The stuff looks a little poncey, if ahm honest – ah think it's basically just sandwich spread - but it's no bad scran."

Sarah, sitting stiffly on one of the beds, didn't touch them.

"I was worried, Donnie. You were gone absolutely ages. You and I agreed no more than a half an hour and it was a lot more than that."

Donnie sighed. She was a nice girl, but sometimes that whiney, posh accent got right on his pip. She had a point though.

"Am sorry. Ah lost track o' the time ok?"

Sarah still couldn't understand the way Donnie was just able to carry on like nothing had happened. As though he wasn't even bothered that everything - absolutely everything - had just fallen apart.

She'd been in the corridor when they'd met, just sitting outside her room on that filthy, threadbare carpet, crying and too scared to look out of the window again – to find that London had gone from a startling mess of Christmas lights and taxis and shoppers to somewhere as quiet as Hertfordshire. Donnie had just walked up to her and started chatting as though they'd met...well, met *normally*. And before she'd known it Sarah had gone along with his plan, packing her stuff and wandering through the streets until they'd found The Royal.

And now Donnie treated the world as though everything was his. *But you can't do that*, thought Sarah. *Things have to stop somewhere; we have to get back to normal.*

Donnie had finished his sandwiches and now, slapping his lips like a man at a feast declared, "Right then. Time for some pud. One fer me and one fer you," and passed an enormous box of luxury Swiss chocolates over to Sarah, without seeming to notice that she hadn't even started her own sandwiches yet.

"I've been thinking," Sarah began, "we should push on now. Leave here and move on."

"You don't like this place?" asked Donnie.

"It's not that," Sarah persisted, pushing a strand of hair back behind one ear, "it's just this isn't getting us anywhere, is it?"

"Where're we supposed t'be gettin'?" asked Donnie, without paying her much attention.

Sarah knew that wasn't what she had meant to say, but she was finding it hard, just now, to make sense of things. Her father would be waiting for her back at home. He might be worried. Even Amanda might be worried.

"We need to move on," she repeated.

Donnie was working his way through the box of chocolates, concentrating with unnatural care on the contents list and throwing the ones with hard centres out of the open window.

"Something new eh?" he said, mouth full, "sounds alreet, I guess."

It didn't take them long to pack their belongings, although Donnie lingered a little, pausing to nick a bathrobe and a couple of brandy miniatures from the mini-bar.

Outside, the cold January air hit them both. A chill gust of air rose suddenly and with a squawk the parrot took off from Donnie's shoulder, flying towards the horizon until it was lost amongst the grey sky.

"Gone, and never called me a dirty wee bastard once," sniffed Donnie.

* * * * *

The platform was pitch black, darker than any night - no reassuring moon or stars down here, no faint orange glow on the horizon, just blind, terrifying blackness. It lay thick about her, tickling her neck, pressing over her face and mouth. Georgie tried swinging the beam of her torch as quickly as possible to give her a sense of space. The benches flashed into view along with adverts showing bright tropical islands and the huge faces of women with white teeth and glossy hair. She saw yellowed papers headlined *Government Denies Report* and *Global Panic* and glanced away. But the gloom was so vast that her torchlight seemed like a fragile needle, the darkness of the tunnels crowding against her back and stroking her with its sooty fingers as soon as the torch moved on.

A continuous, light breeze sighed through the tunnel, heavy with the smell of grime and dust, still strangely warm like the tube she could remember from before. Her torchlight flashed across the rails, bright amidst the discarded crisp packets and dust balls and Georgie found herself wondering again which one was electrified.

Or is it two that are live? How the hell can I check?

She looked at the shining steel and her mind went to the coins in her pocket. It wasn't much good for anything else now. She took the pile of loose change and began throwing it onto the tracks. The metal pinged loudly through the silence, but there was no sign of any sparks and, feeling strangely reckless, Georgie jumped down from the platform.

A couple of tentative taps with her toe confirmed it: the rails were dead. The beam of her torch seemed to fade into a brown haze in the distance, but somehow the long climb back up the dark stairs to the deserted street felt just as unwelcoming so she began to move forward.

After half an hour the tunnel branched off to the right, but both ways were just as dark and gave no indication of where they might lead so Georgie chose to plough on in the same direction. It was difficult to walk hemmed in between the rails. Drops of cold water dribbled from the arched roof onto her head and back, and it was all she could do not to trip over the wires and electrical transformers littering the ground.

Her eyes stung and watered and her nostrils itched. She stopped to wipe away the soot. Her anxiety was growing, the darkness was overwhelming, it was so complete she felt she could lose not just her way but herself. The lack of senses, is this what it felt like to be…

Something caught her attention. The sound of scratching came from somewhere out in the darkness.

Instinctively she backed against the wall. She couldn't see her feet and when she turned her head there was nothing around her but an ocean of darkness.

She listened.

Her shoulders itched and tickled as though someone were watching her.

Georgie thought she heard more sounds: a thud, followed by the noise of something soft and heavy being dragged. She caught her breath.

That was impossible, wasn't it? There wasn't anyone. There wasn't anyone there and anyway, she was invisible, a shadow dissolved amongst the blackness.

When she listened again there was nothing.

But it had been there, she had heard it. Hadn't she?

In the blackness the long minutes ticked by.

The breeze blew softly over her skin.

Still she heard nothing.

It was just her imagination trying to fill the void, surely. *Focus on what's real*, she told herself, *Try to find a way out of here.*

But what lay in the maze of tunnels ahead? How long would she have to keep walking? Georgie suddenly realised that there was no way she could be sure where she was going and the torch had only one set of batteries.

The breeze blew a little harder down the tunnel, and now she could hear a rasping, painful moan echoing from some hidden place. Fear caught in her chest and she was suddenly gripped by a powerful, unbearable need to get out.

Without caring whether she tripped and fell or where she was even going Georgie bent towards the waiting mouth of the darkness and ran.

She ran that day and she kept running. In the days to come she would remember the all-consuming dark, and the terror of a blackness so profound that it seemed to smother all of her senses - not just her sight but all of her, as though she'd ceased to exist. It would haunt her, shaping her movements and her actions. If someone had told her then that one day she would be heading back into those tunnels gladly, she would have laughed.

If someone had told her what was going to drive her down there, her laughter would have died.

CHAPTER 2.

The boy had curly ginger hair, blobby freckles, and blue eyes which were a little on the dull side. It was hard to call him chubby, since he was tall and fairly broad-shouldered. He swung a rusted crowbar in one hand, and as he walked up the hill he half-carried, half-dragged a battered green kit-bag in the other. The way the sack clanked and rattled suggested it must have weighed a tonne, but the boy didn't seem to notice as he plodded clumsily on.

About halfway up he came to a Mercedes. It was very black and very shiny and, even now, spotlessly clean. The boy took a step back, deposited his bag in the middle of the road, and approached the car with an appraising look. He scratched his scalp, finally nodding as though he'd come to a decision and then, with systematic dedication, began to lay into it with the crowbar for all he was worth.

He shattered each of the windows in neat succession, took out both of the headlights and then battered every inch of the bodywork. He scrambled up onto the roof of the car and jumped up and down, only stopping once he was finally satisfied that the dent was as deep as it was going to go.

He leaped down to the road and, after taking a moment to admire his handiwork, set off back up the hill with his bag, using the crowbar to knock the wing mirrors from every car he passed.

William didn't like these streets of terraced houses. They

had fields where he came from, big forests where you could go and have a proper laugh. He'd known the school trip was going to be rubbish. And then everyone died. Typical.

For a moment his mind drifted. He thought about the shed he and the lads had found, which was full of rusty tools and ancient copies of Razzle. He thought about coming into the house after an afternoon in the cold. He thought about sitting down to his tea and about how it had been made for him. He thought about sausages and about hot and crispy Alphabites.

But he didn't want to think about that stuff anymore.

Anyway, he was at the park. He knew he'd get to one eventually. Stopping by the railings William delved into the huge sack and, squatting down with his profile low, pulled out an air-rifle with mounted telescopic site. For a minute he observed the expanse of park, absently picking at his nose.

There was one of them. Alone, for now, and unaware that it had been spotted.

William let out a little snigger. With his right thumb he slipped the safety catch off and re-sited the crosshairs. Gently, he squeezed the trigger.

The pigeon exploded in a satisfying cloud of blood and feathers.

A crack rang out over the empty football pitches, the deserted benches and litterbins and away over the rooftops. When William stood up, the red hair at his fringe had stuck to his forehead in sweaty loops. He brushed some strands of grass and an old lollypop stick from his jeans, and worked his way over to a new hiding-place.

After an hour of turning pigeons into bird soup William was growing bored, when suddenly he noticed a beautiful, bright green parrot perched on a nearby branch. His eyes lit up.

Another weapon was needed.

William began to pull things from his kit-bag. There was a lock knife. A dozen candles. A Zippo lighter. A hatchet and a lethal-looking antique cutlass. Two types of catapult. An old starter pistol. But he wasn't happy with any of these and flung them onto the grass behind him. Then his hand re-emerged holding a bright orange petrol can. He shook the container, hearing the liquid sloshing about inside.

William grinned.

Then his grin faded.

He could've sworn that parrot just called him a dirty wee bastard.

* * * * *

Farran Alkhaban was bent over panting at the entrance to the tower block that loomed at his back, impassive and empty. A cruel wind blew around the estate, whipping up the rubbish that had collected in the corners into little tornadoes, and moaning round the swings in the play park before rushing across the parking lot to tug persistently at the thin material of the boy's trousers.

He wore a blue salwar kameez; the traditional loose trousers and tunic were covered in mud, which here and there had dried to a flaky grey, and the leather jacket he'd pulled on over the top brought little protection from the cold. He didn't complain, he didn't even notice, his cheeks still flushed hot with shame.

A bead of sweat trickled from his temple.

It ain't my fault, he said to himself, *no one coulda done it*.

No one could say he hadn't tried. No one.

The wind continued to rattle uselessly at the bars of the play park.

He'd tried till his effing shoulders ached. And his wrists. And his back. But that wouldn't 'ave been good enough for the old man, would it? Course not. He could hear him now

– jus' another bloody thing you are screwing up, eh? Jus' another thing that stupid ignorant bloody bast' boy can't do. No tradition him. No idea of family duty. Do you want to be like your goodfor-nothing brother, eh? Do you want to waste your bloody time with those gang boys? Little boys playing at being big men. Do you want to be making your mother cry?

"SHUT UP!"

Farran's voice echoed around the empty estate.

He threw the spade away and rubbed at the blisters on his palms.

It was too damn cold and the ground was just too damn hard.

He straightened up, his back beginning to stiffen now. He lit a cigarette and watched it burn angrily.

He'd leave and come back later.

Later's no good. Don't you even understand your own culture, eh?

He'd come back sometime when it was warmer and he'd do it properly then.

Running away?

But right now he was hungry and sore and cold and the whole thing was impossible.

Same old excuses.

Anyway, when had that old bastard ever lifted a finger to help him? A hand, yes, but a finger? Served him right.

And your poor mother and sisters?

He kicked the door of his block with his heel, once, twice, three times, hard enough to make his heel throb and his knee jolt. He took a pull on the cigarette and then headed out of the estate and up the road without looking back.

He tried the handles on the nicest cars first but they were all locked and too new for him to get into. He came to a beaten-up old Ford that he knew belonged to one of the teachers from school who happened to live nearby. Or rather, *used* to.

Farran smiled to himself and with practiced speed, whipped out a length of straightened coat hanger with a small squared-off hook at the end. From force of habit he looked quickly round, then laughed at his own foolishness. He shoved the coat hanger between the window and the rubber seal and into the door. After a couple of attempts there came the familiar muffled *click* as the lock popped up and in a few seconds he was out of the cold and sitting in the driver's seat.

Laughing again, he was actually in Mr Phillip's car. The most feared teacher in Mile End and he, Farran Alkhaban, was about to nick his car. Man, he wished the rest of the lads were here to see this. Even Abdi would have been impressed. Abdi who always got to drive, who always said where they dumped it after - and now *he* was the one in charge.

"Right, where to?" he said aloud and then paused. Farran checked again - he reached down to pump the accelerator and then looked up. Yep, with his foot on the pedals he could just about see the windscreen wipers, but he sure as hell couldn't see the road. *Shit*, he thought, *that's why Abdi always drives*. He looked at himself in the mirror.

"Right, plan B."

Ten minutes later Farran was speeding down the road with the wind ruffling his short, spiky hair. He swooped under the railway arch, through the deserted streets and up towards the main road. Dropping down a gear he stood up in the saddle to get an extra burst of speed.

Typical, end of the world, no pigs and I'm ridin' a bike.

Just then the hem of his trouser leg snagged on the peddle, the bike wobbled dangerously. He fought for control and reached down to unhook himself. It wouldn't come loose.

He looked down, pulled harder.

Free.

He looked up. Right in front of him was a startled white girl.

Farran swerved at the last moment, lost control and he and the bike thumped hard into a parked car.

"Where the hell were you runnin' to, you daft bitch?" he shouted over his shoulder. He didn't notice how much the girl was shaking.

The girl ran over to him, "I'm sorry, I'm sorry. Are you alright?"

He turned to face her, chest puffed up, "No I'm bloody not. What you playin' at?"

"Me?" the girl said, rising to the fight. "*Me?* There's only two of us left in the whole world and you almost run me over."

Farran's face cracked and he let out a howl, "Oh my days, man you're right, *ha ha.*"

The girl laughed too, overwhelmed to see another human being - "I was beginning to think I was the only one left," she gushed. "I haven't seen anyone else for weeks, and then here you are…someone else. I stayed in my house at first, then I tried going out a bit but I could never find anyone; I called and called, then I just thought to myself *there's no point in just sitting in the house waiting for something to happen. Get out and see what's what* and so here I am; I walked along the tube tracks down the Central Line." She took a breath, "I'm…I'm Georgie, what's your name?" and she extended a hand towards the boy.

Farran's expression drained of the brief sparkle that had filled it when he laughed, as though his face had a slow but persistent leak and couldn't hold any joy for long. It sunk into its usual desiccated sneer – a look that Georgie would come to refer to as the 'Alkhaban scowl'. She would frequently ponder in the coming days just how much effort it took him to screw up his face that way, like he'd smeared something disgusting under his nose.

"Farran," he said at last but left her hand hanging and scanned the distance, avoiding her eyes.

Georgie felt deflated and tousled her already messy brown hair in confusion. "Is there anybody else with you?" she asked hopefully.

"No."

"Have you seen anyone else?"

"No."

"Where were you going?"

"Dunno."

"Do you have a plan?"

"No."

Georgie sighed, this was going to be difficult.

There was a long pause and the silence of the city seemed to seep down from above the buildings into the street, like a valley slowly flooding.

She tried again, "I was going to carry on down the tube lines into the centre of town. I thought maybe there would be other survivors. Do you want to come along?" As difficult as this boy seemed she hoped he would say yes; even bad company was better than no company and the idea of going back into the tunnels on her own was unbearable.

Farran shrugged, "Yeah I guess."

The silence started to trickle in again.

Farran puffed out his cheeks and then moved off in the direction of a row of shops.

"Umm, the station's this way," said Georgie, gesticulating like a slightly manic airhostess. "Hello?"

"I gotta ditch these stupid clothes first. An' get somethin' decent. I'm freezin' my backside off, man," he called over his shoulder.

"I thought that's what, you know, you wore…"

Farran turned round, "What, I'm not some Paki. Yeah I wear this all the time - I jus' got to go find my turban!"

"Jeeze. I didn't say that. Where did that come from? I just meant, well…why are you wearing it if you think it's stupid? Hey, you're the one who said it, not me."

"Well I'm not gonna wear it, am I? I jus' said I'm gonna pick up somethin' else." He continued on towards the shops.

"Oh," said Georgie. "OK then. Glad we could have this talk." She almost wished she were on her own again.

Farran was now outside a slightly scruffy sports shop; he strode up to the kerb and without breaking pace lifted up a bin and put it through the shop's plate-glass window. The window shattered into a thousand pieces, spilling out onto the pavement with a noise that sent birds scrambling into the air.

"Woah," said Georgie under her breath. Then called out, "Done that before have you?"

Farran flashed her a grin.

Ten minutes later they were headed towards the station, Farran now wearing tracksuit bottoms that showed off most of his pants and a bright orange hoody. Georgie wasn't sure that's what she'd have called 'something decent' but it seemed to have made Farran happier, if not more friendly.

Farran stopped abruptly and turned to face Georgie.

"Hey," he said, with a sudden note of interest in his voice. He eyed the girl up and down, "how tall are you?"

CHAPTER 3.

"An' that's why am a genius," said Donnie triumphantly.

"Right." Sarah, a little distracted, continued to look at the crossroads, tucking a long strand of hair behind her ear. She considered the four options.

"*Right*? Is that all y'can say? I tell you my great plan, lassie, an' why am goin' ta be rich an' famous, an' you just say *right*?"

"What do you want me to say? I am *trying* to determine where we are."

"Determine eh? That's a good word. I like that, *determine* - it's a good word is that. So com'on, what d'ya think?"

"You are going to become rich…"

"And famous."

"…sorry. You are going to become rich *and* famous because of pens?"

"No, not just pens, *flavoured* pens."

"Flavoured pens?"

"No, not jus' flavoured pens; honestly, sometimes ah think ya don't listen. Flavoured pens – *pah* - that would be crazy, and wasteful. No, jus' the end of the pen is flavoured - for people who chew their pens. Genius. No more nasty plastic taste, an' sore teeth, an' ink in ya gob. You chew on a long-lasting, flavoured, non-toxic soft end of pen. Fruit flavours ah think."

There was no response, so he added - "*Mmm*, pineapple biro!" enthusiastically; but to no avail. "OK, you win, let's try an' work out where we are and not talk about mah great invention."

"I think this is 'The City," said Sarah.

"The big buildings gave it away, eh?"

"No, I mean we are in *The City*; the financial district of London. My father used to work here…before. This is no good, there's hardly ever anyone here - except during working hours and I think it's still holiday time - so we're unlikely to find help here."

"The fact that everyone's dead doesn't help either."

Sarah shot him a look. "That isn't true. It would be ridiculous to assume that everyone else has died. We'll get back to my father and Amanda's house in the country and everything will be fine, you'll see."

"We can't walk to Hertfordshire."

"No, of course not, nor can we drive there; we are children, which is why we are trying to find someone in authority who will let them know that I'm safe and then drive us to my father's house. Now come on - this way, I think."

Sarah strode off down the road and Donnie had no choice but to trot after her.

Sarah had been Queen Bee and was more than comfortable with giving orders. She was always the centre of attention with a flock of girls swirling and squabbling about her. And teachers simply *adored* her; according to last term's report she was 'polite, confident, punctual, and eager (if not necessarily the most academically able in the class)' – oh, but she had planned to make Mr Eggerton suffer for that! - she was, in short, destined to be Head Girl. Mrs Watkins had whispered this little fact to her with a giggle one day as they were stacking books after class, and the sweet, frumpy woman had blushed conspiratorially. She had suddenly looked 30 years younger and Sarah had told her so, eliciting another, deeper blush and yet another giggle. She was so cute!

That is not to say that Sarah didn't have her self-doubts.

She was often troubled that such-and-such a girl was smarter or more sporty (though seldom prettier), that perhaps they might become more popular with the teachers or the other girls, and this would worry at her. It seemed there were just so many things that she didn't have control over. When it became really bad she would worry so much that she found it hard to eat. Her food would stare unappetisingly back up at her from the plate and the distance between her fork and her mouth would seem to stretch like some camera trick in a horror film.

This was worse at home - not that her father ever seemed to notice. Sometimes *Amazing Amanda* did and would take her father's hand whilst turning a face full of 'maternal' worry toward her and say, "Harry, I'm worried that darling Sarah isn't eating enough. Perhaps she doesn't like my cooking?" And then she would smile at Sarah. Sarah's father would order her to "eatup" as though she were a horse, and go back to his laptop. There was always a distinct difference in her weight at the start of the holiday and at the end of it.

Sarah had discovered, however, that when she had felt fragile at school it wasn't such a terrible thing; there was always someone - one of her friends or one of the younger girls in her house - who had been only too willing to run to the nurse to fetch her ibuprofen for her period pains, or her lucky mascot without whom she couldn't *possibly* do the exam, or a chocolate bar because she felt faint because her doctor had warned her that she had low blood sugar. She would smile weakly up at their concerned, content faces and everything would slide into place again.

For the rest of the morning they walked; Sarah marching up this street and down that one, with Donnie prattling along happily beside her. Donnie tried to engage Sarah in conversation again and again but she always seemed to be only half listening to him. Donnie wasn't sure where she was going or what she was searching for, and, to be honest, he had a sneaking suspicion that Sarah didn't either, but it seemed to keep her calm and besides, he was quite content to do some sightseeing.

At last Sarah led them down one of those strange little roads that exist in The City. A great black, metal and glass monstrosity had been shoehorned between two crumbling walls - remnants of another time - the tired old piles of bricks sagging gratefully against the interloper for support.

At the end of the road an underpass waited, dank and uninviting; here and there plants growing in the cracks, sucking on the wet and slime that ran down the walls.

Sarah paused involuntarily and Donnie fell silent. Something seemed to be moving up ahead.

It was dark, and but for the flashing light of the traffic beacon she wouldn't have been able to see anything at all. The orange light whirled madly, creating a constant play of shadows that swirled along the slicked stone and out towards the far end of the tunnel. There, a black shape, silhouetted against the comparative bright, was definitely moving.

A confused look passed between the two of them before they continued on cautiously. Further into the passage their eyes began to adjust to the intermittent gloom. The distant shape began to coagulate slowly until Sarah thought she recognised it. The domed top of the shape was a hat, a helmet perhaps.

It was a man. A policeman.

She stopped, she couldn't believe it. After all their worrying, all their searching, here was a policeman just standing, waving at them. He was leant nonchalantly against the railings and seemed to be saying something. They were too far away to hear him but his lips were moving.

Sarah ran towards him with Donnie trailing a little way behind. Perhaps they'd been wrong about how bad it had been, or maybe it had been bad, but all of the surviving adults had hidden somewhere, waiting until it was safe to come out. She and Donnie had been sitting in that stupid room all this time, miserable and alone for no reason. This was all Donnie's stupid fault, tucking them away in some ridiculous hotel so that no one could find them, just because he had never been anywhere even remotely posh. She would give him such a talking to when this was all sorted out, and so would her father.

Sarah called out to the policeman as she drew nearer, "Hello, sir? We need help."

She couldn't tell if he had heard her or not. The policeman didn't seem to be replying but he was still talking and he was still waving. There he was, just waving away with the same persistent, jerky motion. His arm must be getting tired by now; Sarah was sure she couldn't wave for that long. A thought entered her mind. *No it was ridiculous, the two things simply didn't add up.*

"Hello?" she called again. But still there was no response.

Maybe he was talking into his radio? He must have been able to hear her by now. Why couldn't *she* hear *him*? Maybe he was whispering, but why? That damned light made it so hard to concentrate.

"Sarah wait," called Donnie. He had a strange urgency in his voice.

Wait, wait for what? This was yet another one of Donnie's silly boy-games.

There was something unnatural about that movement, about that voiceless talking. Sarah felt a strange feeling in her chest like the ground had fallen away from under her and she had fallen with it. It was as though her body knew what was wrong before her brain could process it.

"He's dead, Sarah. Sarah, stop, don't go over there!"

Sarah looked back at Donnie and then back at the policeman. "What? I...I don't understand." She continued to drift forward. "But he's saying something, his lips are moving."

"What? No. It's jus' the light, Sarah."

Donnie rushed over to where the traffic beacon stood and fumbled until he switched it off, but it was too late, Sarah was only a few feet away from the policeman.

The tunnel was plunged into gloom but Sarah could still make out the policeman's face - without the animation of the orange lights she could see that it was still and grey - and quite dead. She stood transfixed by that grey-blue face; skin starting to flake where it had been exposed to the weather, eyes milky, like those of a well-loved doll that has been played with until the paint has scratched off. His right arm was hooked into the railings and took all of his weight; he must have been supporting himself, staggering somewhere when he died. Then Sarah remembered the waving - that couldn't have been just the movement of the light, *what was going on?* With morbid fascination she stepped round the roadworks, out of the tunnel and into the light.

She could see that the corpse's left arm was caught in a tangle of brambles that overhung the wall and to the right of the body, previously hidden by its torso, was a large, greasy-looking fox. It perched on the railings, gnawing at the flesh around the elbow. With every tug of its sharp little teeth it pulled the policeman's arm downwards and every time it let go the spring of the branches snapped the arm upright again.

Sarah staggered backwards, looking blankly at Donnie, her own arms hanging helplessly by her sides.

Donnie hurried over, guiding her down the road and out of sight, leaving the policeman and the fox to continue their sordid dance in private.

"But, but he was…and it was…That was horrible. Oh God, oh God, I think I'm going to vomit." Sarah bent over, supporting herself on weak knees.

"Come on now, jus' calm down, it's all gone." He patted her back uncertainly. "Let's jus' let sleeping policemen lie."

A little burst of laughter exploded from Sarah, and then another, until they were rattling out in quick succession. *OK*, thought Donnie, *at least she's laughing*. But somehow it didn't seem to be the good kind.

"Hahaha, *let sleeping policemen lie*, hahaha." Her laughter rose higher and higher, until all of a sudden she was crying. "They're dead, they're all dead," she said between sobs. "The policemen, the soldiers, the judges, they're all dead. Teachers – they're dead. All those good people are dead. Priests, social workers, office workers, butchers, bakers…"

"Candlestick makers?" added Donnie helpfully.

"…politicians, milkmen, fathers, wives, sons, daughters – THEY ARE ALL DEAD."

"So what you're sayin' is, they're dead," said Donnie.

"How can you joke about this?" screamed Sarah. "How??"

Donnie sat on the cold kerb and sighed.

"How can you joke when everyone you know is dead?" Rising to a crescendo. "Every category of people you can think of is now extinct. EVERYONE BUT EVERYONE IS DEAD."

At this last explosion Sarah's anger seemed to burn itself out and she stood above Donnie, red-faced and breathless.

"Look at it this way, were yer ever bullied at school?"

"What on earth are you talking about?"

"*Were yer* ever bullied at school?"

"Yes, of course."

"Did a teacher ever give yer a bad mark yer didn' deserve?"

"Yes"

"Well *they're* dead too. Did yer ever get into a lift where someone had let one off and not admitted to it? – dead. People who jump queues – dead. People who talk through movies – dead. People who laugh at adverts – dead. Estate agents – dead. Charity muggers – dead. Russell Brand – dead. The Swiss – dead. Murderers – dead. Morticians – dead."

Sarah sat down next to him on the kerb and puffed out

her cheeks. A few moments passed in which the only sound was Sarah's delicate sniffing.

"Do yer know who's not dead?" asked Donnie.

Sarah looked up in the middle of wiping away a tear from her blotchy face.

"Us," he said, "*We're* not dead."

Sarah smiled.

"But where are they all?"

"They jus' died at home in bed. We should be glad it's winter, it coulda smelt a lot worse."

"But all of them? Everyone can't have gone like that. That policeman is the only person we've seen."

Donnie shrugged. "Ah don't know."

She sighed.

"But how can you be so calm?"

"Hey I'm scared too but, ya know, we're alive, a lot of people aren't. For the first time in ma life am a high-achiever. We're both ahead of the curve - we'll get by." He stopped for a moment, not sure how much to say. "I'm also kinda used ta bein' on ma own, an lookin' after maself. I've got kinda good at it. Ma uncle Robert was a bit rubbish really, he had some problems, but that's another story; the long an' short of it is - we'll get by."

"I guess."

"There ya go, that's that spirit." Donnie jumped up. "Come on then, let's get a move on."

"Where to? What's the point? We've pretty well established that apart from you and I and a mangy old fox there *is* no one else. We might as well stay here and curl up." She hugged her knees.

Donnie could tell that it was delicately balanced, it wouldn't take much for her to dissolve into tears again.

"But we were jus' guessin', we don't *know*, Sarah. There could be lots of people still alive, we jus' havnae found them yet. There could be a big welcomin' party waitin' with cardboard hats, burgers an' cake an' hot tea served by buxom nurses wearin' bikinis 'cos all the dry cleaners are dead. OK it's *unlikely*, but there has to be somebody else. It cannae jus' be you an me, lassie; that doesnae make sense – ya said so yerself. Why would we be the only ones to survive?"

He hauled Sarah up onto her feet.

"Come on, let's make a move or the tea will be gettin' cold. Or worse, the nurses." He began to drag her along by the arm. Then he looked left and right in extravagantly exaggerated movements. "OK, I think left."

"Right is better," said Sarah meekly.

Donnie smiled quickly to himself. "That's the spirit, lassie, we'll have you bossy again in no time."

Donnie knew it would take a lot more than that to restore Sarah's spirits - she just wasn't used to a world without adults and people to tell you what to do every minute of the day - but she was moving and that was important. If he could just keep her moving she would be all right in the end. They both would – because Donnie had begun to realise that he needed Sarah's belief in survivors almost as much as she did.

CHAPTER 4.

Tyrone Phillips stopped walking and looked behind him.

The bloody thing was still there. Tongue lolloping out of its mouth. Staring at him and waiting.

"Look, be a good dog and sod off will you?"

The Alsatian didn't come any closer, but it didn't back off either. Just kept the same distance, staring.

This was ridiculous; it had been following him for days now. Every time he walked it followed him, never attacking but not exactly looking friendly either. When he went into a building to get supplies or check for survivors the dog waited outside, the same blank expression on its face. When he stopped to find somewhere to spend the night it disappeared, but was always there the next morning. It should have made him feel less lonely but somehow it did the opposite.

"What do you want from me? I fed you once. Once! And you almost took my hand off. I'm hardly gonna do it again, am I?"

Still it didn't move.

Maybe it was sorry. Maybe it was actually a good dog. Maybe it only looked like a rabid werewolf and was really a sweet little thing.

The dog lowered its head and gave a low growl.

Maybe not.

Whatever, it didn't seem like it was going to attack right now so he'd take a little breather – well, he'd have a fag, anyway.

He took the packet out of his record bag and lit up. As always the first smell of smoke brought back the memories - for a moment he was back in his house as the flaming bottle of petrol crashed through the living room window and the house began to fill up with smoke - the heat - the feeling of terror, of a familiar world, familiar people turned to chaos - then the need for nicotine took over and he took a drag anyway.

As quickly as they'd come the memories were gone again like a…well, like a puff of smoke.

His finger unconsciously stroked over a patch of red, smooth skin on his arm-

It was all so insane, easier to waft the images away than it was to believe they were real. Besides, he'd been smoking since he was twelve and was now on twenty a day, so they could pretty much taste like raw sewage and he'd still spark up.

Smoking since he was twelve; ever since the science lesson they'd had on the dangers of cigarettes. Ever since Mrs McDougal had told him they could stunt your growth. It hadn't worked. Tyrone was now fourteen and 6ft 2. He'd been the tallest in his school since long before that science lesson – and that included the teachers.

He'd been a naturally quiet boy, sensitive even, and would have loved nothing better than to remain anonymous, blend in, be average. Fat chance. Every adult he'd ever met immediately treated him like he was years older than he was and expected more from him than he was ever capable of – he should play basketball, he should know better than to talk in assembly, he'd been spotted acting-up outside the corner shop on his way to school. There was nowhere to hide. If there was a group all messing about in the playground and they were caught, it was invariably *his* name the teacher yelled.

As he got older he could feel this disappointment changing into something else, a new expectation. He knew that he was somehow, through some force he didn't quite understand, being moulded into something he didn't want to be. He was getting a reputation.

The dog growled again and edged a little closer so Tyrone flicked his cigarette at it. It skittered back a moment before taking up its normal position, but now with a slightly louder growl.

Saliva dripped from its tongue.

"Nice one, Tyrone, what you've done there is take the large, starving wolf-dog and pissed it off just that little bit more."

He was actually starting to get worried now. What had started off as being funny had begun to feel serious. If he didn't know better he'd say it felt like he was being stalked. No, wait. He *was* being stalked! That's what it was doing - sizing him up. Jesus, it was working out whether it could take him or not. Waiting till it was hungry enough to risk it.

He looked around. He'd been walking north towards Waterloo and was now probably somewhere around Oval. Thing was, all of the shops on the main road he was on were boarded-up. Sweat started to prickle under his arms. If Fido decided to actually get nasty there wasn't a lot of options - he'd have to run for it. He sort of regretted that cigarette now. Smoking it as well as flicking it.

The dog edged closer, muzzle low to the ground, legs planted wide.

Ignoring his rumbling belly, Tyrone dipped into his bag, got out his last cheese sandwich "Here boy, hope you're not lactose intolerant," and flung it as far as he could.

The dog leaped backwards from the projectile. Then warily made his way back to investigate. He pawed and sniffed at it.

"Go on, bruv, it's got a bit of Marmite in it - not everyone likes it, but it's better than stringy black kid."

The Alsatian didn't seem to agree, because right then he decided to pounce.

* * * * *

Donnie stopped. He couldn't hear anything and that was a bad sign. *No whining*, he thought to himself, *no Sarah*. He looked back and sure enough, there was nobody there. He sighed heavily - *right then, back we go*.

"Sarah? Oh Sarah sweetheart, where are you?" he sang out.

Finally he spotted her sitting dejectedly in the middle of London Bridge with her shoes off, rubbing her feet.

Donnie jogged towards her, mumbling to himself as he went. "How many times does that mek, eh? Ten, maybe twelve? No, ah reckon it's more like fifteen. Don't posh people ever walk anywhere? Maybe she rides a pony when she goes shopping - 'Oh, Smithers, could you just hold Portia's reins for a few moments while I pop into TopShop?' - I mean honestly, how do these people get rich in the first place? Great, now am talkin' t'mahself - ah there y'are, lassie, I was beginning ta think y'd run off an' joined the circus."

"My feet hurt," she said, still rubbing away.

"Och I know, lassie, but we need ta dig deep, be men, be all we can be."

Sarah started to blubber gently.

"Ah come on, I was jus' tryin' ta cheer y'up. We need ta keep movin' if we're goin' ta find anyone else lassie."

"My feet really hurt. I can't walk any further, I am cold, there probably isn't anyone else, and my name is Sarah, not lassie - I'm not a dog!"

"No you're a bi...beautiful young lady. I apologise. It's jus' the middle of the bridge is no a great place ta stop, what with the biting wind, an' the sleety rain an' the hypothermia an'all. What say I get yer some blister plasters or a bandage or somethin'? I'm pretty sure there's a big hospital round here and if the worst comes ta the worst," he said with a smile, "we can amputate. Maybe at the neck."

"OK."

"OK what?" said Donnie a little confused.

"OK, I will get up if we can go to the hospital…"

"I was only jokin' about the hospital. I don't think yer need one."

"I know I don't, but there might be people there; adults." She put her shoes back on gingerly. "But if there aren't we could still get a bandage."

"Well com'on then, let's go. If yer don't come right now I'm goin ta have to leave in a huff," he helped her to her feet, "An' where I'd find a huff at this time of the day I don't know."

Sarah rolled her eyes and they started off again together.

* * * * *

Tyrone's reputation at school had gotten worse no matter what he did. There were a couple of the male teachers… he'd started to sense something else from them, something he couldn't quite put his finger on, something more disturbing. They sort of…bristled. They drew themselves up, puffed out their chests more and the way they talked became sort of clipped. It was as if his height, his presence alone, was some-how a challenge to them. When he was talking to them he felt his heartbeat quicken, his jaw tighten - he felt anxious. But why? He wasn't in trouble, they weren't telling him off and yet - then he realised with a shock what it was. These teachers, these people in authority were barely containing their aggression towards him, a kid. They were seething below the surface and there was nothing he could do about it. Nothing he'd done in the first place. Except. Except that he'd become that legendarily dangerous creature: a big black boy.

The first time he realised this he'd disappeared to the boys' bogs and sobbed his heart out at the injustice of it all as adrenalin caused his outsized hands to shake.

As a result he never blossomed at school. Quite unconsciously he'd begun to wear more neutral, less threatening
clothes and to hunch his shoulders, stooping to disguise his
true height. At the same time his manner changed, becoming less boisterous. In class he was now almost taciturn, his
humour drying up, becoming sarcastic, quickly fending off
any interaction before it even began.

But at home he was a different person altogether. In the
loud hustle and bustle of the Phillips household he could
unfurl. Literally. Here he wasn't expected to be an athlete, or
an adult, or a hard case, here he was just RyRy (as the twins,
and so everyone else, called him). Home was a sacred place,
which made it so much worse when they burnt it down.

At home he squabbled with his older brother and sister
but he helped the twins with their homework; he remembered to set the table but he forgot to do the dishes. He was
an ordinary kid. By the time he went to bed at night he was
a good four inches taller than when he walked through the
door.

Right now he was glad of every inch of that height because
skinny as this dog was, it just wasn't letting up. His legs were
barely keeping him ahead as it was.

He'd managed to dodge its first attack, just moving out
of the way in time - the dog slamming into a car door with
a yelp - but it came at him again and he'd taken to his heels.

He'd run and run, no time to look back. At the roundabout
before Vauxhall Bridge he'd paused, searching desperately
for somewhere to hide but there was nowhere, just nowhere.
Then he'd noticed that the Alsatian wasn't alone any more.
Its barking had drawn more dogs. There was a whole pack
– pugs and Labradors, terriers, dogs of every shape and kind.
But what really disturbed him were the lap dogs; once-cute
pooches with that same vicious, hungry look. They looked

ridiculous and terrifying all at the same time.

"I am not getting savaged by a poodle," Tyrone panted to himself, "I don't care how much my lungs hurt, that is not hapenin'." And he set off running onto the bridge.

It was only a couple of paces across that he'd realised what a truly stupid decision it had been. His lungs felt like he'd inhaled lots of tiny cheese graters, his legs were heavy and now he had absolutely nowhere to go but onwards; there was only the road ahead or the dark unforgiving water of the Thames either side. In the failing light the river looked almost thick, more like molten slag than water. At this height the river would be almost certain death. He needed to get to the end of this bloody bridge and then he needed to find somewhere to hide, fast.

In his mind started to appear images of those teeth biting into his ankles, snapping his Achilles tendon, bringing him down. Of being overpowered, his neck exposed, those yellowed teeth coming down-

There!

A light.

Through the hedges of the estate at the end of the bridge he could see a flickering light in one of the flat's windows and a garden door slightly open, more light spilling out through the crack.

In the quiet of the growing dark he could hear the panting of the dogs and the skittering of their unclipped nails on the tarmac.

He dug deep and ran on.

He jumped the hedge.

The dogs burst through after him, though there was some yelping as some of the smaller dogs didn't make it.

He raced over the tiles of the garden.

His hand was on the long aluminium handle.

He was through, slamming the door hard shut as he fell to

the floor, gasping for air.

There was the sound of heavy bodies slamming into the door and for a moment he thought it'd break, but it held.

Tyrone looked up from the dirty linoleum floor and there, at the table, was a girl his age eating cornflakes from a shoe.

The girl looked up.

"Awright? I'm Joanna."

And then she went back to her cereal.

* * * * *

After some searching among the railway arches and blank-faced warehouses of Bankside, Donnie and Sarah found the hospital. It stood as dark and deserted as every other building they had passed. The two children stood hesitant before it. A light flutter of snow drifted noiselessly down past the chimneys and the ducts, past floor after floor of dead-eyed windows, settling briefly on their upturned faces before evaporating into a wet chill on their skin.

They glanced at each other and then made their way up the stairs to the sliding doors.

They stayed firmly shut.

"Of course," said Donnie feeling slightly foolish. "No electricity."

He tried sliding the doors open, then they both tried squeezing their fingers into the gap to prize them apart, but still they didn't move.

"They're too heavy, we'll never get 'em open. Maybe there's a side entrance."

They scanned the area - to the left of the main entrance a high mesh fence stood and behind it an alley led away into darkness.

"Why don't you try down there?"

"Why don't *you* try down there?" retorted Donnie.

"I can't, remember, I have a sore foot."

"Yer jus' want me to go down there an' get eaten by booglies. No way."

"What's a booglie?" asked Sarah, trying to suppress a smile.

"You know, a *booglie* – a ghostie, a bogey-man, a zombie, anythin' that lurks in the dark waitin' ta eat yer brains – a booglie."

"But there might be people inside. Adults that can help us. An adult that can bandage my foot, make us some hot food, tell us what's happened. We can't just wander around the streets of London forever. Anyway, you promised."

Donnie looked at her seriously for a moment, rested a hand on her shoulder in an impressively adult gesture, then asked, "Have you ever noticed that yer voice goes really squeaky when yer complainin'?"

"Donnieeeeee!"

"OK, OK, I'm goin'."

Reluctantly, he clambered up the fence and down the other side, then pushed his face up against the wires.

"If I get eaten by a ghostie, I'm comin' back ta haunt yer." He smiled a big grin. "Ta Ta."

Sarah watched him grope his way down the side of the hospital until the darkness swallowed him.

Immediately Donnie wished that he'd taken one of the torches. It was dark as night in the shadow of the hospital. He had to let his hands guide him along the building's rough wall, searching for the gap that would indicate a door. He was beginning to think he would have to turn back when he felt a sudden nothingness and a disinfectant smell hit his nostrils. Taking a couple of fumbling steps forward, he heard the unmistakable screech of rubber on lino. Ahead, dimly, could be seen a long corridor that turned eventually to the right, gurneys and upturned trolleys picked out in the weak light. But there was no movement.

"Hello?"

His voice echoed harshly through the building, the sound seeming to make the murky air vibrate like ripples in a stagnant pond. When the sound died away the air settled again, thick and sour and lifeless, but no reply came. Suddenly something made him turn.

Nothing.

Good.

Just the sickly green of the walls and a cluster of crayoned eyes staring out at him from some sickly children's artwork.

But he couldn't shake the itch that crept up his neck and the watery feeling in his stomach.

"Ah for God's sake, Donnie, get a grip will ya. There's no one here. Yu've gone an' spooked yersel'." He had to resist the urge to run out of the hospital. The second he ran he'd be admitting the fear, and that would be worse.

He made himself continue, following a yellow line on the floor until it brought him to a dead end. On the right hand side, above two large double doors, *Leviathan: Temporary Disposal 4* had been hurriedly sprayed in fluorescent yellow paint. It looked out of place in the white hospital corridor and Donnie wondered who'd put it there. And what the hell a 'Leviathan' was.

On the left was a smaller door that seemed to be a store cupboard, he tried the handle and, to his amazement, it opened. Inside were all sorts of neatly packaged medical supplies: razorblades, scalpels, syringes, bags of saline...

"Bandages, hurray - now I can get the hell outta here."

Donnie scooped up a few items and left the room. Pulling the door to, he stopped, looked behind him. The corridor was as quiet as before. He turned to go again. Again he stopped.

The two large swing doors below the sprayed sign stood just as still as before but there was something about them. He walked forward as though drawn by some unseen force. Reaching them he paused, one hand resting on the cold metal plate of the door. Then he entered.

His heart seemed to stop, frozen by what confronted him there. The bandages and supplies clattered to the floor but Donnie never heard them.

* * * * *

"There were dogs chasing me," panted Tyrone. "Big dogs. Hungry dogs."

"Is that what they was?" Joanna slurped from her spoon. She didn't stop looking at him as she did, and a lot of what was on the spoon never made it to her mouth. She didn't seem to notice. "Was wonderin' what was makin' all that noise."

Tyrone looked up at the grubby girl with the pleasant smile for a moment. There was still sweat streaming down his face.

"Them, and me screaming and, you know," he pointed to the rip in the knee of his jeans, "trying not to get eaten. Sorry if we disturbed you."

"S'alright." She wiped soggy cornflakes from her mouth with the sleeve of her parka.

Sarcasm was obviously lost on this girl.

Tyrone looked around at the room he was in, there were wrappers, empty cartons, discarded food and tin cans covering the floor like autumn leaves. Dirty plates and bowls were stacked high in the sink, and on the work surfaces, and on the chairs. And on the couch.

Something in one of the stacks moved.

The place stank.

"You here on your own?" he asked.

"How'd you mean?"

He wasn't sure how else to put it. "Uhm... Is there anybody else here?"

"Oh," Joanna said, as though finally working out a tricky bit of algebra, "y'mean m'I here on my own?'"

Tyrone hesitated. "Yes."

"No. I mean yes. I mean jus' me and my mum."

"Your mum? Where is she?" He hadn't seen a grownup for weeks.

"Bedroom."

Tyrone looked over in the direction of a glass-panelled door.

"She's good wiv sewing."

"Sewing?"

Joanna pointed down at his ripped knee.

"But does she know what's happened? Does she know if there's anyone else?"

"Dunno. Don't fink so."

"Well, can I go and ask her?" Tyrone had got to his feet now.

"No."

"Sorry, is she sleeping?" He stopped. "Is she sick?" he asked both apologetically and with a growing sense of apprehension.

"No, it's cos she's been dead since a week last Wednesday."

"Right." Tyrone slumped back down. "Probably not gonna be much help with the sewing either, then."

"Prob'ly not," agreed Joanna, then by way of compensation asked, "You want a cuppa?"

Tyrone looked round at the furry dishes stacked about the place like an evil game of Jenga and decided he didn't want to risk it.

"I'm good, I had salmonella for lunch. Thanks though."

"'S'no bova," she said cheerfully and went over to another shoe on the coffee table, which Tyrone now realised had a clump of tea bags piled up in it. They were a pair.

Joanna saw his worried look. "Don't worry they ain't my shoes," she said with a laugh, "they're Mum's."

* * * * *

Outside on the steps Sarah shivered. Her bottom had gone numb and she was most of the way to convincing herself that Donnie had found help and was at that very moment enjoying a nice bowl of soup with the busty nurses. But she couldn't have been more wrong.

She looked up - from somewhere deep inside the hospital came a terrible scream. Sarah scrambled to her feet, searched the façade of the hospital, but the dumb bricks told her nothing. She tried to work out where the sound had come from.

"Donnie," almost to herself, then louder, much louder, "DONNIE!"

She waited anxiously, straining to listen, hardly breathing. She was about to look for a way in when she thought she heard another, fainter noise. She did; a rapid *clack clack clack*, that was getting louder. Where on earth was it coming from? What was it? It was louder still. *Feet*, she thought, *it sounds like feet*.

Suddenly the emergency exit burst open and Donnie came tumbling out. He ran right past her and kept going.

"Donnie?" she called after him. "Donnie, what is it?" He wouldn't stop so she had no choice but to run with him.

After a couple of blocks he began to slow his pace.

"Donnie, Donnie what is it? Why are we running? Donnie, I can't run anymore, my feet hurt." She hardened her tone, "Donald…" she realised she didn't actually know his last name, "Donald …Scottishboy, you stop this instant!"

He stopped so abruptly that Sarah almost ran into him.

"What on earth are you playing at? What's going on?" she shouted, hands on hips.

Donnie was doubled over, his back heaving, as he tried to catch his breath. His shoulders moved more violently. No, he wasn't catching his breath. To her surprise Sarah realised that Donnie was crying.

* * * * *

Why was it that Joanna McGillis seemed so comfortable in this new, harsh world? A world without a safety net. It wasn't because she was stoical or brave, and it wasn't because she was too dumb to notice for that matter – though there would have been a whole common room full of teachers that would have been surprised to hear this (had they not all been dead). She lacked imagination, and that certainly helped when it came to not seeing a potential threat in every loose wire and unclean cup of water, but that wasn't it either. The thing that stopped her from curling up into a foetal ball and rocking till it all went away was that Joanna lived in a lovely, warm, insulating blanket of low expectations.

She wasn't unhappy (at least not that she knew), it was just that nothing in her life up to this point (up to and including the death of everyone she knew) had led her to expect anything good to happen. Indeed to expect anything at all.

Things just happened to Joanna. Events occurred around her and she got on with it. As long as there was Monster Munch and sugary soft drinks to get her heart beating a little faster in the mornings then she could carry on – and she had yet to run out of either of them. In fact she had more if anything. In life's menagerie Joanna was a heifer. She plodded, head down, content to graze on whatever grass was on her side of the fence, only dimly aware that there might be another side and knowing that it was certainly none of her business whether or not it was greener. That's just not what heifers did, was it?

Her hide had grown thick enough that she treated both rain and shine alike.

Tyrone looked down at the vase full of murky brown liquid in front of him.

"Sorry, didn' know the milk'd gone off."

Tyrone thought it had looked more like cottage cheese than milk.

"Reckon it tastes alright still."

Tyrone didn't want to hurt her feelings but it wasn't going to taste alright; he could smell how sour it was from here. He smiled weakly and squashed some of the larger lumps with the back of his spoon. There was no way any of that tepid bog water was going in his gob.

"Sorry there weren't no boilin' water neither. Gas went off a week ago. Gets bloody cold at night now. Where you from?"

He'd started to get used to Joanna's random silences and bursts of questions so he hardly hesitated at all before answering, "Earlsfield."

"'S'that far?"

"Yeah, but I've been moving about for a while now. Ever since we got burnt out."

Joanna looked confused.

Tyrone swallowed. "We got burnt out of our house. My family was the first to get sick on our street. Seems like the neighbours didn't want us there anymore. We'd known some of them for years."

"Yeah, we was an all."

"Hey?"

"My sister was the first to get sick on the estate."

"Oh. Sorry."

"'S'all right, weren't your fault was it."

"No. Look, tomorrow I think we should head off."

"What, like you an' me? Leave here?"

Yet again Tyrone looked at the filth that lay about them. "Yeah, it might be for the best. Y'know, see who else is out there. Should be alright - haven't heard those dogs for a while."

"We can go out the front way anyway. The estate's like a big maze, never find us - come out by the chippy blocks away."

"Alright then, sounds like a plan."

* * * * *

Donnie and Sarah walked alongside the river, heading west past the London Eye, towards Westminster. They'd been walking now for over an hour but neither of them had said anything since the hospital. The sun was setting like a burst egg yolk behind the skyline, streaks of yellow dribbling down between the buildings and bleeding into the Thames. Sarah knew that it would be dark soon and was beginning to worry about finding shelter, but she wasn't brave enough to break the silence.

Donnie stopped but continued to look at the ground, "Ah'm sorry...about before."

"What happened?" she asked kindly.

"Ah don't want t'talk about it."

"OK, you don't have to."

Donnie started to walk again, his head low as he scuffed along.

"We will need somewhere to stop soon, we've got the torches, I know, but it will be much harder to break in if we can't see what we're doing properly. Gosh, Daddy would be proud if he could hear me talking about breaking and entering." She looked over at Donnie with a smile but he didn't look up.

They walked on.

"They were all dead," he said simply.

"I know."

Donnie flicked his eyes up at her.

"I mean I don't know, but I can guess. Was it bad?"

Donnie decided right then that he would never tell Sarah or anyone else what it was that he had seen in that heaped hospital ward.

Stacked like meat.

All he said was, "Ah think you were right, there's no one left to rescue us, we're on our own."

Sarah stopped in front of Donnie.

"Maybe there is," said Sarah. "*Maybe* - we don't know anything for sure. There must be some who survived. We did. *Ya said so yerself, laddie.*"

Donnie sniffed.

"Come on, Donnie, look, there's a McDonald's up ahead, why don't we see if we can't get one of the cookers working - they might be gas."

Donnie looked up at her face, still a little self-conscious of the blotchiness of his own.

"You could try to make a triple burger, or a quadruple burger, like that dog in the cartoon," she continued.

A look of confusion came across Donnie's face and then his mouth opened.

"What? You like the idea? We could make a whole stack - wow, you really like the idea. I mean, I'm glad you're happy but - are you mocking me, Donnie? Well, if you don't like the idea you just have to say. There's no need to be rude."

Donnie's jaw had continued to drop and his eyes widen as Sarah talked, until finally he was just opening and closing his mouth like a demented guppy. Above Sarah's head, rising like a glimmer of hope, a spark soared into the twilight.

"Afa…afa a f f f…firework!" shouted Donnie.

Sarah turned just in time to see the ember crack open into a thousand stars and one colossal bang.

"This is it, a sign. We're saved! This must be a rallying signal."

Another firework screeched into the air.

"Who's sendin''em?"

"Who cares? Where are they coming from?"

More and more fireworks were exploding above the Thames, thick and fast now; the boom and retort doubling up in a melee of noise and light that spread out across the skies above London.

"Looks like they're comin' from somewhere near the Houses of Parliament."

"Of course, the government is being restored. We're saved!"

The two of them joined hands and sped off at full tilt towards their salvation.

CHAPTER 5.

As Range Rovers go it was top of the line, but the vehicle was going up Edgware Road like a bumper car that had escaped the fairground. It wove amongst the abandoned cars and piles of rubbish, clipping bins and scraping paintwork as it went. There was the painful crunch of changing gears.

At that moment, Farran wasn't saying a word, which Georgie found worse than anything. She checked the rearview mirror briefly, catching a glimpse of their two new passengers in the backseat.

Tyrone hadn't said much more than his name so far. Thin, black and very tall, he sat there calmly, holding onto the seat in front of him as the car lurched.

"You can change gears now," said Farran.

"This gear's just fine. I *like* this gear," Georgie replied.

In the back, Tyrone's head was ducked down between his shoulders but his head still easily touched the car's ceiling. Joanna was huddled on the other side, almost lost inside her grubby pink parka and staring intently out of the window. Her chubby face was impossibly pale, but dirty in a way which made it seem as though her freckles had smeared.

They had reached the place where the Middle Eastern restaurants thinned out and gave way to dreary modern office blocks. Georgie strayed briefly onto the kerb and swerved back to the road with a clunk just before they hit a lamppost. She could feel Farran's gaze lusting after the steering wheel.

"I feel sick," said Joanna cheerfully, "Where we goin'? Ooh! Look at that cinema. I think I know that cinema! Is that a sweet in my pocket?"

As Georgie came to a crossroads her concentration faltered and she took too much pressure from the clutch. The car stalled and she had to start the ignition again, just like they'd practiced earlier. Georgie managed it first time now, and gave Farran a look which mixed triumph with warning.

Outside, rubbish had settled everywhere. Tatters of newspaper scudded across the street in front of them like snow. Windows were smashed, doors left open and empty cars jutted out into the road at odd angles. Here a pram lay overturned in the gutter, there a solitary shoe sat in the middle of the pavement.

In the back, Tyrone had produced a packet of cigarettes from somewhere and was now lighting one up.

"Uh!" gasped Joanna.

"What?" asked Tyrone, flatly.

"You're smoking cigarettes!"

"They're not as good if I eat them."

"Are you allowed to smoke ciggies?" she asked.

"I don't think anyone's going to mind anymore," Tyrone concluded with a sad smile and went back to looking out of the window, his long body slumping down into the seat.

The road followed the course of Hyde Park. Georgie couldn't remember if this was the place where she'd tried boating a few years ago. She caught a street sign – 'Park Lane' – and found herself thinking about Monopoly. Several coaches still lined the pavement next to the park, but these were completely empty now. Georgie flicked up the control next to the steering wheel.

"Why'd you do that?" asked Farran.

"Because I wanted to indicate left."

"But that turns the windscreen wipers on, man."

"I know that, Farran."

"What's the point, anyway?"

"I want to do it all properly," replied Georgie, tetchily.

"Then try changin' gears."

"I told you, I *like* this bloody gear."

She continued to drive regardless, keeping her eyes firmly on the road and glad that the big car gave her such a good vantage point. She was just noticing how the traffic lights were all dead now, standing dark at intervals ahead, when an arrow smashed through the windscreen.

It missed Georgie's right ear by a centimetre and continued on until it punctured the back window and shot out.

Georgie slammed her foot on the brakes, closing her eyes as she felt the heavy Range Rover spin and slide at the same time, careening across the road before coming to a shuddering halt.

Farran was out of the car before Georgie. It took several seconds for the world to stop spinning before she managed to open the door and follow, legs shaking, onto the street outside.

Ten metres away stood a boy with curly ginger hair, planted firmly in the middle of the road, bow still in hand.

"Freeze," he shouted, his eyes flicking between Georgie and Farran, and then on to the other two as Tyrone and Joanna followed up to join them in a group.

"What the 'ell d'you think yer doin', you fool?" shouted Farran angrily.

"Have you seen the state of my windscreen?" yelled Georgie, "Hang on. Sod the *windscreen*; you nearly bloody killed *me*!"

The ginger boy furrowed his brows. "Don't throw a wobbler, I didn't know it was going to be you, did I?"

"Us?" asked Farran.

"Well, you know, other kids," explained the boy, lowering the bow and walking back a couple of paces towards the large green kit bag on the ground. "I didn't know you was going to be like me. You could've been anyone."

"Like?" asked Georgie, walking forward with the others.

"Y'know," the boy said with a shrug, "You could've been going to rob me or something."

They were all crowded around him now, Farran and Georgie demanding explanations at the same time. The boy eyed them carefully as they advanced. Tyrone had pulled himself up to his full height and was now looking down at him menacingly, his cigarette forgotten. Farran was up close, shouting angrily in his face. Georgie was jabbing her finger in his chest, furious. The boy started to push back, asking questions in turn. The three of them got even angrier with him and shouted more loudly than ever. The only one the boy didn't seem worried about was the short, scruffy girl in the pink parka.

So it must have come as quite a surprise when Joanna kneed him in the testicles.

Hard.

* * * * *

Tyrone looked dispassionately at the boy as he lay on the road, curled up in a foetal position. "Perhaps icepacks would help," he commented.

Georgie shrugged. "We'd have to search a few chemists, but I suppose if his testicles are swollen we could get our hands on them."

"You keep your bloody hands off my testicles," groaned the boy, looking up for the first time, "you've done enough already."

"Where the hell did you get a bow and arrows from anyway?" asked Georgie.

"Sports shop I passed somewhere," the boy replied, "you

should see the other things I grabbed. There's stuff every-where, just for the taking."

"What's your name then?" asked Georgie.

"William."

"I'm Georgie and this is Farran, Joanna and Tyrone."

"Sorry 'bout yer balls," said Joanna, smiling sweetly.

William gave her a reproachful look.

"So what's the story then?" asked Tyrone, hauling him to his feet "How'd you get here?"

"I was on this crappy school trip."

"What, over Christmas?" interrupted Georgie.

"We was supposed to get back before, and then, you know…"

William picked at his ear.

"So you're not from London, then?" asked Georgie.

"Nah, Leicester."

"What's it like?" Joanna piped up, wiping her nose on the back of her sleeve.

"Better'n this place," replied William with a shrug, "I've got a quad-bike, and there are woods, places to go walking and that."

Farran sucked his teeth. "All that hippy shit's for poofs."

"Nicely put," muttered Tyrone.

"I was alone in our flat f' days," put in Joanna, "There was nothin' to drink 'cept water out of the taps an' just Super Noo-dles to eat. Luckily I found a Asda where the doors weren't locked and ate all the pick 'n mix."

Georgie looked about at them all. "I thought it was just me at first."

"We all did," said Farran.

"What if there's more of us?" suggested Tyrone, lighting another cigarette. He looked at Georgie, "Y'know, just hiding somewhere and thinking they're the only ones. Like we all did before we met."

"We can't just search the whole city though, can we?"

William commented, sulkily.

Georgie ignored him. "Maybe we could use something like radio, though," she said.

"Not exactly easy, is it?" said Farran, shaking his head. "Even if someone was listenin'."

"No," Georgie agreed, "but we *could* use a signal – like a flare or something."

William suddenly brightened. "I know exactly what we could use."

"What," put in Farran, "hoist you up on a kite so people could see your ginger bonce for miles around?"

William scowled. "No," he said, then brightening again, "When I was in that park over there," he pointed.

"We gonna go feed the ducks?"

"Maybe we should let him finish, Joanna," said Tyrone.

"D'you mean Hyde Park?" asked Georgie.

"Yeah. When I was exploring the place, I found this sort of shed, packed with hundreds of the biggest fireworks I've ever seen."

"Maybe they were stored there for the big New Year's celebrations?" suggested Georgie.

"Never happened though, did it?" said Joanna.

"Guess not."

"If we piled all of 'em up in a great big heap and lit the whole lot at once you'd see them for miles," finished William, with an unsettling grin.

"He's got a point," admitted Tyrone.

"We'd have to pick the right spot," reasoned Georgie.

Farran nodded. "Somewhere central."

"What's that place..." said William, thinking. "I know! First day of the school trip we went to see Parliament. There's a big square covered in grass right outside it."

"That's not such a dumb idea," said Farran, nodding.

"Right then," said Georgie, with a clap of her hands, "let's get the Range Rover loaded up."

CHAPTER 6.

The fireworks were supposed to be part of a professional display, they had no fuses, no convenient *light the blue touch paper and stand well back* instructions; they were meant to be ignited by an electronic switchboard operated at a sensible distance by experts adhering to strict health and safety codes.

William put his hands on his hips and stared at the massive haphazard pile in front of them. "I reckon we tip petrol on 'em."

"And I reckon that's a good way to get our heads blown off," said Tyrone. The whole thing was starting to make him uneasy. Sure, the signal was a good idea, but he knew better than anyone how dangerous fire could be.

"We want them to last for a while, so people can find us," said Georgie, "we don't want them to all go off at once."

"God, fine. Why don't we make nice safe fuses out of bog roll, put them in a nice safe straight line and light 'em one by one, nice and safely? That'll be lots of fun."

"Good idea."

"I was being, you know, whatsit. I meant it would be boring."

"Well, you don't have to do it, if you don't want to."

"I never said that!"

Now that William was crouched next to the first firework it didn't seem that boring after all, in fact, he was starting to feel a little nervous. The thick plastic tube only had a serial number and some Chinese-looking squiggles so he didn't know exactly what it would do, what colour or pattern it would send shooting up into the air when it exploded. It would be an exciting surprise, he told himself.

The thing was, though, crouched down like this, the bugger was taller than he was. He'd strapped a couple of Roman Candles together before and stuck them down a rabbit hole as part of his one-man war against Watership Down, but nothing like this. His homemade *bunny-bomb* hadn't been a *third* the size of this monster.

He looked along the line of evenly spaced fireworks that stretched off to where the others stood, a worryingly long way away. The girl in the parka gave him an encouraging thumbs-up. There was no backing out now.

He looked at the metre of tightly twisted loo roll that disappeared into the top of the enormous firework. It was getting a little windy now and the makeshift fuse was starting to blow about. What if it went out? He didn't want to have to come back and relight it. You were never supposed to return to a firework, he knew that much. Then he had a great idea - if he put a little, just a *little* lighter fluid onto the paper it would definitely burn. That would be much safer!

He surreptitiously took the tin of lighter fluid out of his back pocket – didn't want that Georgie girl whining at him - and poured a thin drizzle all the way along the trail of loo roll. He took a breath and put his lighter to the end.

For a moment nothing happened, then it caught, perfectly. The flame moved in blue flickers towards the waiting explosive. He watched it for a moment in satisfaction. Look at it go! It was zipping along. The loo roll began to unfurl in the wind. Good job he'd thought of the lighter-

All at once, the whole thing was alight.

He gulped. That wasn't supposed to happen.

He backed away in growing fear, slowly at first and then faster and faster.

In an instant the flame reached the top of the firework.

William realised with sinking dread that he had totally screwed up, he was never going to get away in time. He was just turning to run when the firework went off.

Luckily for William it didn't, as he'd hoped, explode in balls of flame, but rather burst into a dazzling fountain of silver sparkles. Cinders pattered about him; a stinging rain like insect bites on his hands and head. He ran along the line of fireworks until he was just outside its arc and then he turned laughing to look at it.

He looked back at the others, arms spread wide in a grandiose gesture that said *look what I've created!* They clapped and whooped back at him.

The silver sparkles continued to gush up and out in a ten foot spread, when they hit the damp ground they hissed out of existence, but when they hit the flat surfaces of the park railings, stone plinths, and the other fireworks they kept burning, like pretty fireflies. It was like being in his very own music video.

The first of the other fireworks set off by the pretty fireflies exploded not two feet from William. It threw him flat on his back, winding him. A ball of purple flame shot into the night sky along with a flaming bit of the container that whizzed past him, striking another firework, setting it off instantly. It was the start of a chain reaction. Random eruptions sent William gibbering from left to right, never knowing where the next danger was coming from, scurrying desperately towards the group.

The noise in the confines of Parliament Square was deafening, concussive torrents rang out in quick succession. Shadows were hurled crazily against the walls, stuttering and jerking against the stones that were one moment pink, the next a violent green.

William reached the others just as one of the tubes toppled onto its side, spewing blazing rockets in their direction.

They flung themselves to the ground just in time to see them slam into the wall behind them. Scrambling away on hands and knees they sought cover behind an upturned phone box.

Explosion after explosion erupted, fireballs ricocheted off statues or zigzagged crazily into the night sky, window-shattering spheres of stars burst into being, then died, only to be replaced immediately by another and another and another.

"So much for staggering them," said Georgie.

"Nothing we can do about that now, except watch."

So they huddled together in the relative safety of their hiding place and enjoyed the show. They stayed there until the fireworks were just smoking husks, their edges molten and glowing in the winter dark, and the clouds of smoke had all drifted away. And then they sat down to wait for all of the other survivors to come to them.

Two hours later Georgie looked at the five faces around the fire – Joanna and Tyrone, William, Donnie and Sarah. They were alive, but their young faces were gaunt and dirty. Six strangers; all different but each wearing the same troubled expression. Farran was as sullen and remote as ever and she somehow felt that even their brief alliance had faded. An icy gust cut across the square sending a shower of sparks up from the fire. Georgie shivered.

At first they'd all talked incessantly, all at once, not even listening to the others' replies. They had talked about everything, anything, just grateful for the distraction, the noise that proved they were not alone. But it had gradually petered out, damped in reverence to the great silent city that stood around them, watching. And now they talked in hushed tones or sat in silence, waiting.

The spicy smell of cordite had all but evaporated, but apart from the initial excitement at the arrival of Donnie and Sarah, no one else had found them. Perhaps there was no one else *to* find them.

Georgie couldn't work those two out, not that she really knew any of them. The pair had come racing into Parliament Square only twenty minutes or so after the first rockets went up. When Sarah had first reached them she had searched about frantically, burst into tears and then refused to talk to anyone. Donnie on the other hand had started laughing like a madman, so hard it had taken him a full ten minutes just to get his name out. Every now and then he would still mumble, "We're saved!" to himself and start chuckling all over again. The two of them were now sat on their backpacks, together but not: Sarah rigid, her body turned away from the group, hands fiddling absently with a rocket stick, while Donnie – the only one of them who seemed at all relaxed - was engaged in an animated conversation with William about the relative merits of shoelaces versus Velcro.

For Georgie, it felt like her old life was a hundred years ago, when the most she had to worry about was getting her Christmas shopping done or whether her parents would end up arguing over the turkey. Then Christmas day...first Dad, then a couple of days later Mum and Grandpa. Having to stuff coats against the bottom of their bedroom doors, the radio and television going dead until finally the lights had gone out and she had been completely alone. That feeling of helplessness and loneliness, too afraid to go out, pressing her nose up against the sitting room window wondering what had become of the world.

Georgie continued to look around their little raft of light, lonely in the huge sea of darkness. That boy Tyrone was tearing up the supply of cardboard boxes they had collected and was slowly feeding them to the fire. She felt a little calmer when she saw him. Maybe it was because he was so much taller than the rest of them or because he seemed so... self-contained. As he worked he chatted lightly with Joanna about some band or other and it looked more like he was talking for her sake than for his. He listened attentively to her answers, even though they were rarely more than a mumble, delivered when she popped briefly from the depths of her parka like a turtle peeking from its shell.

Tyrone watched the fire intently, propping up a layer when it looked like it might collapse and smother, banking up the ashes, and Joanna watched Tyrone. The fire illuminated the greasy strands of dark hair that had escaped from her hood and cast shadows into the dimples of her plump, grubby cheeks. Georgie had the strange feeling that even if everything were normal those cheeks would still have been grubby.

Georgie turned her attention to Farran who was sitting at the furthest edge of the fire's light and warmth. He was scraping mud out of the tracks of his trainers with angry flicks. Every now and then he would stop his digging and look impatiently around the group and then out towards the darkness. He was doing one of his circuits now. Georgie caught his eye on its way round and smiled; Farran stared at her for a moment and then looked away in one long, disdainful blink.

Was this all there was? Were they the only ones left? Her mind started to drift, to reach out into all of those dark empty places which lurked out there in the city...

Georgie stood up decisively, coughed, and immediately felt slightly foolish. "Umm, shall we get on with it?"

"Get on wiv what?" barked Farran.

"Well, shouldn't we make a plan or something? It doesn't look like anyone else is coming, so we should decide what to do."

"They might," said Sarah weakly.

"What you talkin' about, man?" shouted Farran. "We been all over this town an' we ain't seen nobody. There ain't no one else, just us. They're all dead. This is it." He cast his arm dismissively around the group.

Sarah looked at the ground and said nothing. She suddenly looked very fragile; a girl in expensive clothes slowly getting just as scruffy as the rest of them.

"Easy bruv," said Tyrone. "She was just saying we don't know for sure whether this is it or not. I think Georgie's right though, we've waited long enough. If anyone had seen the fireworks they would have been here by now." He looked kindly at Sarah, towering over her with his lanky frame. "We have to assume no one else is coming and we have to make a plan."

"What sort of plan?" asked William, one meaty hand rubbing the back of his neck.

Tyrone looked over at Georgie encouragingly.

"We need a long-term plan and a short-term plan," she began. "We need to decide how we are going to survive. I don't want to upset anyone, but if no one is coming to rescue us we have to organise ourselves. We have to find food and shelter - a permanent place to live that's comfortable and dry and warm; we have to collect food and stuff so we don't have to keep foraging every day. I think keeping warm will be the most important thing."

"We're almost out of boxes to burn," added Tyrone.

"Exactly," said Georgie, pulling her mousy hair back in a scrunchy as she got into her stride, "I don't know about the rest of you but I'm not very warm *now* and it's only about six-thirty. When it gets to four in the morning and we don't have a fire it's going to get pretty cold. We have to get organised."

"I haven't been properly warm since the heating and gas stopped working," said Sarah, her delicate hands still fiddling with the rocket stick.

"Me either," admitted Farran, his irritability fading slightly. "So what d'we do?"

"We need to find some shelter first. Any ideas?" Georgie looked around the group.

"Sarah an' me have bin stayin' in a nice swanky hotel,"

said Donnie. "I'm sure there's one a those around here some-
wheres. There'll be plenty o' beds but ah have t'say ah've found
the room service is pretty poor these days."

This sparked interest from the group, several little conver-
sations flaring, until Tyrone spoke up again. "A hotel is a good
idea but what was it actually like? I'm guessing it was still cold,
right?" Donnie nodded. "One of those nice big hotels, with
central heating in every room, but there's no central heating
anymore. We'd be out of the wind, but not much warmer."

"True enough," admitted Donnie.

"We could light a campfire in every room," William
chipped in, with a slightly worrying grin on his freckled face,
"There's no one to tell us not to."

"Yeah but there ain't no fire brigade neither, genius," spat
Farran.

"What we need is somewhere old-fashioned, modern
technology isn't going to do much for us anymore," said
Georgie.

Silence fell over the group. Georgie felt bad about hitting
everyone with these home truths but she knew it had to be
done. They couldn't just stick their heads in the sand. She
shivered again; the cold seemed to be creeping up from the
ground now and into her bones.

Joanna broke the silence, "What 'bout the Houses of
Parliament?"

"Great," said Farran, "the weirdo finally speaks and comes
up with some big draughty old hall-"

"Actually, that's not a bad idea," interrupted Tyrone. "I've
been in there once with my granddad. He used to lecture me
that I," here Tyrone put on a thick Jamaican accent, '*needed to
hunderstand the way ma own country was governed*'. Said it was
my '*responsibility*'. He was a bit of an activist. Anyway, that
place isn't just some big draughty hall, it's got lots of comfy
leather benches; alright they're not beds, but they'll do. And
the thing is riddled with fireplaces. Those old codgers were

about a million years old. You know what old people're like, they're cold even in the summer. We could light some fires, and safely too. Best of all, it's right bloody there."

They all turned to follow Tyrone's outstretched finger. On the other side of Parliament Square they could just make out the tower of Big Ben and the jagged outline of the Houses of Parliament, silhouetted against the stars. It looked imposing and not at all welcoming.

"How the hell're we supposed to get in there?" said Farran. "I mean it's got to have security, gates an' that. I've seen it on TV, the place is usually crawlin' wiv uniforms."

"You got a better idea?" Tyrone stared at Farran calmly but it was clear to everyone, even Farran, that this was not a question that he should actually try to answer.

"Ah'm up for it. Goawd's sake, I'm Scottish, the chance to mount an assault on Parliament is like a dream come true." Donnie jumped up and dusted himself down. "What are we waitin' fur? Mah bum's gone numb already, I'll be lucky if ah get away wi'out piles as it is. Come on!" And with that he dashed off into the night, a scream of "*Freeedoooommmm!*" drifting back to the campfire.

The group picked up their meagre belongings and started off across the grass. They had only gone a few steps before Joanna suddenly let out a screech and ran off after Donnie. The rest of the survivors, almost unconsciously, started to increase their pace.

Tyrone led the way, followed closely by Farran, with Georgie and William bringing up the rear. Farran sped up so that he just nudged ahead of Tyrone. Tyrone looked over at the much shorter Bangladeshi boy and responded by walking faster too, easily regaining the lead.

Farran increased his speed again, so that now he looked like a power walker, his bum wiggling ridiculously. Both boys refused to run though, as a matter of pride.

Tyrone once more lengthened his rangy strides and kept

ahead. Meanwhile, Georgie, William and Sarah did their best to keep up, following just a little way behind.

Farran suddenly broke into a trot. On seeing that the rules were no longer being observed Tyrone exploded into a run. The look on Farran's face as he was overtaken made Tyrone laugh so hard he almost tripped.

"Oi!" shouted Farran and belted after him.

The others joined in the race. Backpacks bounced against backs, hands clasping hats to heads. Soon everyone was tearing across the grass, monochrome in the moonlight, a sense of purpose gripping them, an excitement that needed to be translated into movement.

They ran faster, rushing headlong across the road that bordered the square. William let out a whoop; this was a game he knew how to play. The others whooped in reply. Faster, fearlessly they ran. They didn't even stop when they reached the 'No Entry' signs and the fence, their momentum just carried them up and over, like an army storming the gates. Some scrabbled up themselves, some gave others a bunk up. It was messy - clothes got snagged and torn, but the taboo they were breaking was infectious, and like a fever it left them hot and sweaty and slightly delirious.

The group broke like a wave against the glass revolving door, but they would not be stopped. William kicked the glass, it didn't crack but the panel turned slightly; without any electricity to lock the gears of the mechanism it was only the sheer weight of the gate that kept them out. William threw his bulk against the panel, Tyrone, Donnie, Joanna added theirs. The gate squeaked and began to move, slowly at first. And then, all at once, it gave way and they went spinning inside, skidding in a heap along the polished floors of the reception.

They lay there panting as their laughter echoed off the stern walls of the hall.

* * * * *

An hour later the group were lounging in a mishmash of chairs, leather couches, and deep quilted armchairs, all arranged in a semi-circle around a crackling fire. It had not taken them much searching by torchlight to find an inviting-looking drawing room complete with polished desks and green desk lamps. The oak-panelled walls were covered with huge paintings of important-looking old men that none of them recognised. The group then tucked themselves up under rugs and tweed jackets until they thawed out. The scent of mahogany now filling the room was warm and welcoming. Donnie threw another antique desk-leg onto the fire.

"Well that's the fire sorted, what about some proper food?" he asked, adjusting the silver wig he was now wearing.

He'd had the bright idea of trying to cook something on the fire, but all they could find were some packets of crisps and chocolate. In the end he had put some bourbon biscuits on a silver serving tray in an attempt to give them something hot to eat, but the sweet filling had just oozed out and burnt on to the tray. When they had eventually been chipped off they had been bitter, mostly charcoal and totally inedible.

"There isn't much around. Just packets of nuts and sweets from the bar. I need a proper meal," complained Sarah. "I looked in one of the fridges - it smelled horrendous. Some of the sandwiches had mould on and I wouldn't want to eat the ones that hadn't because goodness knows how long they've been there, and we could all end up with food poisoning."

Georgie noticed that William looked slightly concerned and was pushing something under the couch with the back of his foot. She thought for a moment, "That's a good point, actually. I don't know about the rest of you but so far I've just been living off things I could scrounge out of fridges. It's only been a week since the electricity went off and it's been so cold that I guess it was ok, but pretty soon it won't be. I mean we certainly can't eat fresh meat anymore; if it's not bad now it soon will be. What will we do in a couple of weeks' time when all the bread has gone mouldy as too? Or a month's time when all the fruit has gone off?"

"We'll starve," wailed Sarah.

"No we won't," said Tyrone. "We can still eat tins of food, you can get almost anything in a can. Dried stuff like rice and pasta keeps forever too. We'll be fine. George, you're just scaring everyone."

"I ain't scared," said Farran, who had returned to his usual sullenness after the race.

"OK. George, you're scaring everyone *except* Farran."

Georgie looked around the room. It was true, a quiet despair had settled on them all.

"Look, I didn't mean to scare you guys, it's just like I said before - we need a plan. We need to think this through, ask a lot of questions. Where's the best place to get food now that everything is different? We don't want to forage every day. What about water? There's still some water in the taps here but that won't last us above a day. Where's the best place to be for everything we need?"

"We should stay here, we're right by the river - we can drink that," said William.

Farran looked at the chubby, ginger boy, "You can drink it if you like, man, but that water's pure tramp-piss. I ain't touchin' it."

"And," continued Georgie. "When we've done all that, found food and water and shelter and warmth, we have to decide on the long-term plan, like I was saying before. What to do next? Do we stay put? What happens if we do? Should we make another signal like the fireworks? I mean it's not like we're on a desert island but a signal fire or *some* sort of signal might be a good idea. Or do we go out and try to search for other survivors ourselves? Or do we split into groups, some stay and some go? I mean, what do we do?"

Questions. Each question seemed to cool the air above the children's heads and out of the cold, many choices crystal-lised, no two the same. Choices fell on top of each other and piled up a little deeper. Each of the survivors isolated in their own private drift of concerns and worries. Real freedom can be terrifying; too many choices and no choice at all can feel very similar. True freedom means there is no one else to make your choice, no one else to tell you what to do, no one else to blame. And choice weighed heavy on their shoulders.

"Look," said Donnie. "What are ya all so miserable about? Let's not worry about the future, that'll take care of itsel', let's look at right now. Ah don't think yer realise what's happened. Yer all worried about what's the right thing to do. But the word for crisis in Chinese also means opportunity…or spring roll…or somethin'. What I mean is, we can go anywhere. A-N-Y-W-H-E-R-E." He paused to let this sink in. "You name it, we can live there. C'mon, name somewhere, where would you most want to live?"

There was silence again - almost silence - but very faintly, just beneath the quiet, insipid noise of despair, began an almost inaudible hum, the hum of brains whirring, the rumble of ideas.

"This isn't a time for games, this is serious," said Georgie.

The hum faltered and almost died.

Tyrone looked at those faces poised on the brink. "No, wait a minute, he's got a point."

"What? Tyrone?"

Tyrone looked at her briefly. "Come on. Err…William, what about you?"

"What about me?"

"Where would you most like to live?"

"I dunno, lemme think…London Dungeon?"

Georgie moaned, exasperated.

Tyrone ignored her. "OK. Weird answer but it's a start."

"Aye," broke in Donnie, encouraged, "he's got the right idea though. Tyrone, yourself?"

"Ummm…White Hart Lane."

"Bit cold."

"We could have tents on the pitch."

"Cool. Joanna?"

"Cartoon Network."

"Uhm, that's a TV channel. Not sure you're understandin' the game here, but thanks for playin'. Never mind. Sarah?"

"A big posh house in Knightsbridge."

"No," said Donnie, suddenly serious. "Nowhere where there might be…where there might have been people."

They all shifted uncomfortably – none of them had discussed what they had been through in the last few weeks, when they'd been alone.

"C'mon then, Sarah."

"God. OK then. A shoe shop."

"Och, think bigger."

"A Prada shop."

"Bigger," commanded Donnie.

"A shopping mall," she replied slightly panicked.

"Bigger!!" shouted Donnie.

"Er, umm…Harrods."

"Better," he smiled briefly, she smiled back, then he shouted even louder, "BUT BIGGER!!"

"Er, ah," she fumbled for a moment then blurted out, "Buckingham Palace!"

"Now yer bloody talkin'," he sat back well pleased and Sarah sighed with relief.

The room exploded into a flurry of speculation and one-upmanship, each trying to come up with something more shocking or outlandish than the last.

While the others were occupied Georgie leaned over to Tyrone and hissed, "How could you? We were just getting somewhere. I thought you were on my side."

"Of course I'm on your side," he whispered back. "But you saw their faces. All that was happening was that you were panicking them. Yeah you were right, but man, they couldn't hack it. I don't know what they'll decide on, but look at them, they're laughing. It's not just practical things that're important."

Georgie returned her attention to the others.

"London Zoo."

"Aye, you can sleep in a monkey cage."

"A bank?"

"Too dull."

"MI5."

"Cool, but too hard."

"Madame Tussauds?"

"Too creepy."

"We could undress the waxworks."

"Definitely too creepy."

"What about the Louvre?"

"That ain't even in this country, you muppet," spat Farran.

"What about the Natural History Museum?" said Georgie at last.

"Booorrriiing," shouted William, "I hate history."

"It's not *that* kind of history," said Sarah, turning to him, "it's more nature and biology – dinosaur fossils, things like that."

"We might see some of your relatives," said Tyrone, with a pleasant smile.

"But they live in Leicester," said William, confused.

"So we're agreed then," said Georgie, cutting in quickly, "we get ourselves over to the Natural History Museum and set ourselves up there.

William still looked unconvinced.

"Come on," said Georgie, "it looks like a palace. It's near Knightsbridge. No one has ever lived in it, so there can't be anyone there and they used to host footie matches in it."

"Really, is that true?" asked William, almost convinced.

"Yes, everything but the last bit. It's a museum. How are they going to have football matches?" Then she added with a smile, "You *muppet*." Everyone creased up with laughter, including William.

When the noise subsided she added, "Plus it's near the park and shops for supplies and stuff. It's probably got its own generator, we might have some electricity, lights, even music. I can think of worse places."

"I've been there," added Joanna, "I love it. We did lots of worksheets and I nicked a pencil from the gift shop."

"Sounds good. Ah'm in," said Donnie.

"Me too," agreed Sarah.

Tyrone called for silence. "OK. Let's have a show of hands."

The vote was unanimously in favour.

"Alright," said William, "but it better not be boring."

CHAPTER 7.

The following morning Sarah found some edible, but very stale biscuits in a tiny kitchen that must have been used by the cleaners or caretakers. There was also some instant coffee, although no electricity to boil the kettle. Now the group sat round in a circle on desk chairs and heaps of files, drinking cold coffee and eating what had to pass for their breakfast. If they'd had a pathetic bonfire and been soaked through to the skin with rain, it would have been exactly like camping.

William grimaced, "This is gross."

"*William*," warned Georgie, with an apologetic glance at Sarah.

"No, it's ok," said Sarah, "He's right, it *is* pretty gross."

"Ah've had worse," Donnie said, giving her a friendly nudge in the ribs, "One of the times when mah uncle had forgotten to buy any milk ah had to have beer on mah cornflakes."

"Lidl's cornflakes are cheaper than Tesco's cornflakes by twenty-nine pee," said Joanna brightly, looking around at the group.

There was a moment's silence.

"So where's this natural history place?" said William through a mouthful of chocolate digestive.

"It's out South Ken way," replied Georgie.

Sarah nodded, "That's right. There are simply loads of them around there. The Victoria and Albert Museum; the Geology Museum; and the Science Museum is basically next door."

"There's no way we're all gonna fit in the Rover though," said Farran, rising.

"We need something else," added Sarah, "something more practical with plenty of space."

"Somethin' with a sun-roof, sat-nav, one year's free insurance and available right now fer a single low, low price!" said Donnie.

Sarah glared at him.

"There was a minivan parked on the corner opposite," said Tyrone.

"Do you think you can work your magic on it?" Georgie asked Farran. He looked at her as though she'd asked him if he could count to five. "O-kayyy, sorry," she said, "so that's that sorted. Let's get a move-on, then."

* * * * *

Sarah found a small A-to-Z in the glove compartment of the minivan; there was no inbuilt GPS like her father's car. She wondered whether it would have worked now anyway. Donnie had been given a couple of lessons by his uncle and wanted a turn at driving, so Tyrone, who plotted out the route, sat in the passenger seat next to him to give directions. At first they swerved everywhere, the minivan accelerating randomly and shooting down the streets, but in the end Farran had bellowed at him and Donnie had taken it a little more carefully. Farran frightened her, she'd never heard anyone talk like that in her life. Not even on EastEnders. Grandfather swore – Amanda was always making a big deal of how shocked she was by it – but not like him, not with that...venom.

Sarah tried to relax. She leaned her forehead against the dusty window of the van, feeling the gentle vibration of the engine and watching the streets slide by outside. Often cars had been abandoned in the middle of the road so that they had to double back and find new routes. Black bags of uncollected rubbish spilled their rotting contents over steps and front gardens; many of the houses had their curtains still drawn, as though they were hiding a secret, and she felt a wave of nausea at the thought of what lay within.

The course they took led them back through the area she'd been walking through with Donnie. The place was as deserted as ever, only the bare trees swaying in the wind and the occasional crow flapping into the grey sky. The streets passed by and Sarah could see that they were approaching the underpass, but as they flashed by she was almost certain that the policeman's body had disappeared. Sarah gasped, but no one seemed to have heard her. They had been moving fast – perhaps she had been mistaken. She decided it was better to forget about the whole thing and not mention it to anybody.

*   *   *   *   *

When they drew up outside the Natural History Museum they could see what Georgie had meant. It *was* an incredible building. Square towers topped huge walls, decorated by a vast arched entrance and more windows than they could count. Something between a castle and a cathedral - a complex puzzle of a thousand different bricks - the museum was at once delicate and powerful.

The crowds were missing though. No tourists, no shouting children, no mothers struggling up the steps with pushchairs, no kids with dripping ice creams. Today the grand building was deserted.

Donnie drew up and parked right in front of the gates, grinning to himself when he noticed the double yellow line.

As they filed into the museum compound some of the

group seemed to be hanging back. Georgie noticed this and, feeling strangely nervous herself, decided to take the lead, trotting up the steps and through the large door.

The first thing she saw was the skeleton – a dinosaur stretching its huge neck out towards her, regarding Georgie with dark, hollow eyes. Far above it rose the curved ceiling, echoed by the arched entranceways lining either side of the gallery. Georgie walked forward slowly, her footsteps ringing clear on the smooth, polished floor. The stonework and pillars seemed to spread as though they had sprouted from the marble floor, their tessellating patterns blending with carved vines and crouching monkeys as they reached the ceiling.

It was all familiar to her, but somehow it was the smell of the place – like floor polish and dust – which brought the memories back most vividly. She could see herself there, looking up at her mum as she wiped her face with a tissue after she'd finished a lolly; holding both of her parents' hands as they led her through the exhibitions when she was little.

There were no bodies here but she hadn't been prepared for the ghosts. Something felt tight and painful in her throat-

"Well, here we are," she said.

The others, gathering around her, paused for a moment, overawed. Museums were like libraries: quiet, ordered – places for good behaviour. She spotted a map on a sort of podium and the rest of them followed in a group around her. There was no electricity to illuminate it, but the pale winter sun shone brightly enough for them to be able to make out the plan. The entire museum was set out for them in three-dimensions, its different sections colour-coded and divided into zones covering things like *Ecology* or *Planet Earth*.

Georgie was the first to speak, "I think it might be an idea to work out this place one section at a time. Perhaps we could take the *Blue Zone* first, split up and get a sense of the lie-of-the-land."

As she finished, she realised she'd made it sound more

like a question than a decisive plan of action, but there was a general murmur of consent, and Tyrone was already looking around and trying to orientate himself.

"If yer don't mind," said Donnie, "I think ah might go to one of the upper floors – get a diff'rent view so to speak. Maybe have a look-see and a nose-poke in the 'behind-the-scenes' area as well."

"Typical," commented Sarah.

"Yeah, no problem," replied Georgie, "could be useful, I suppose."

There was a wide set of marble steps directly in front of them, but Donnie galloped off to the right – a strange, scruffy figure in a tuxedo disappearing through one of the great archways and off down a separate gallery. The rest of the group started to walk slowly to the left and in just a few moments had reached another of the arches. The navy carpet of the *Blue Zone* stretched ahead of them, branching-off at intervals, and the entryway was covered with images of animals, fish, human skeletons and roaring dinosaurs.

The group followed the long passage, pausing briefly when they came to the first turning. Sarah, Joanna and Tyrone began to file right but Georgie paused, and jerking her head towards the corridor's end said to Farran,

"C'mon. We need to get to the end of this section."

"Where're you draggin' me off to now?" he asked.

"To my favourite place in the museum."

* * * * *

Ahead was another entrance, smaller than the one they'd used earlier, but big enough to let in plenty of light. To the side, a silent escalator disappeared into a giant model of the globe before stretching towards the upper tier. When Donnie climbed onto it he felt a strange jolting sensation, his legs remembering movement.

Shafts of sunlight pushed through the windows on the top floor, solid with swirls of dust. Glass-topped tables displaying gemstones and geological samples stood in neat rows, but it was the little plinth which caught his eye, cradling a lone piece of moon rock. Something from another world. The pinnacle of human exploration.

The case shattered more easily than he had expected, and reaching carefully inside, Donnie was soon holding the little fragment between his fingers. He blew the light coating of glass dust from its pitted surface, *one small theft for man* he said to himself and placed it carefully into the inside pocket of his dinner jacket.

He followed the course of the room, idly trying the doors he came to and finding them locked. Donnie now ignored the large displays of gemstones – although he did stop to admire the scale model of a volcano which had once produced a miniature eruption, pouring neon-lit lava over a succession of helpless villages. He took a moment to flick over several of the tiny plastic farmers and screaming villagers, and stick a few sheep head-first into the Perspex magma. "I am your God and you have displeased me!" he boomed, grinning.

Finally he discovered a door which had been left unlocked. Nudging it open with his foot, Donnie found a small office inside. Along one wall he saw half a dozen CCTV monitors, all of them blank and dead. The desk was almost covered by a scattering of loose sheets, files and biros, and a polystyrene cup sat in the corner, chunky green mould having bubbled up over the top and down its side. He stabbed at a few random buttons and then searched the room, opening locker doors and riffling through the bits and pieces which had been left behind. Finally, picking up a discarded jacket he spotted a large bunch of keys.

"Jackpot," said Donnie.

* * * * *

William had held back as the others proceeded down the corridor, his eye caught by the entrance to the *Human Biology* gallery. He was unimpressed by the idea of a group scouting mission, so he let the others move on and slipped through the entranceway. This section was smaller, a maze of narrow passageways with low ceilings. Everything was set at the perfect height for little children and when up and running, lights and sound took the visitors on a journey through the human body.

William wandered amongst a display on nerve conduction, past the five senses with their models of oversized eyeballs and diagrams of soundwaves, until he came to the section on human reproduction. There were a dozen small diagrams, all of which, on first sight, looked like a tangle of spaghetti-like tubes and multicoloured sausages. William came to a stop before the models of the naked people and his jaw hung open.

* * * * *

Farran and Georgie walked quickly down the hall. There was something about the feel of carpet beneath their feet and the space in front of them which made them want to break into a run. Without thinking, Georgie was guiding Farran by the elbow. The pair passed by a gallery which was still offering a special exhibition of 'Christmas in the Wild' photography, and continued on before taking a sharp right and finding themselves at the entrance to a grand display hall.

The space inside was vast, but far from empty. From floor to arched ceiling hung life-size models of sea mammals: at least twenty different species of dolphin, the same number again of porpoises, and dwarfing them all, the gigantic form of a whale. To Georgie, it seemed as though someone had suddenly clicked their fingers at the sea and made the water magically disappear, leaving the creatures caught in mid-air. When she was little, she had the fantasy that they were all swimming together through the flood towards Noah's Ark – although they would be the last creatures to need it, of course – and the memory came back sharply as she stood in the hall once again, holding her dad's hand and feeling very small and very safe.

"Not bad," conceded Farran.

"It's great, isn't it?" replied Georgie. "The blue whale's my favourite. Look at it – a tongue the size of a car, some blood vessels so big a kid could crawl down them," she paused, "The biggest animal in the world. I've always wanted to see one in the wild."

They stood for a moment, looking at the model. Even such a vast space couldn't diminish the size of the whale, its massive form all the more stunning now that it was exposed from nose to tail in mid-flight.

"That mouth would be a great place to set up a sleeping spot," Georgie commented.

"If you could get up there," said Farran grudgingly, "but I dunno why you'd bother."

Georgie did her best to ignore his sour look. "This place is full of good spots for setting-up camp. I really think it could be fun."

"Dunno where that lardarse William would pick," said Farran, raising an eyebrow.

"It's Joanna I worry about," replied Georgie.

"It's lucky we've got you, Whale Girl, to keep us in order then, innit?"

That almost sounded friendly, thought Georgie, maybe this Farran guy wasn't such a tit after all.

*   *   *   *   *

William had already tried getting as close as he could – his pudgy nose almost touching the anatomical displays. It was fascinating.

Disgusting.

Horrible.

…but fascinating.

Now he took several steps back and this time tried bending forward and looking upwards through his legs so that he could see it all again from upside-down.

"Gross," William whispered happily, as he went to find a chair to stand on.

* * * * *

Farran and Georgie continued to wander, they went through an exhibition entitled 'The March of Progress' - they had come in through the exit so as they went on the machinery they walked past regressed from rockets to cars, to steam engines, to horse and carts, to stone tools as though time were running backwards.

"I've been thinking…"

"So what's new?"

Georgie ignored him. "Don't you think we should have seen more bodies on the streets?"

Farran stopped abruptly. "I don't wanna talk about that."

"No, I know, I don't either. It's just, well, mine, they got sick at home…"

"George."

"…but everybody can't have."

He shouted now, "I said I ain't gonna talk about it." And he stormed off muttering to himself, "Damn, girl just talks and talks. I mean…" But that was all Georgie heard.

"So where *is* everybody?" Georgie called after him.

* * * * *

In each of the glass cabinets, frozen in still-life, they could see countless specimens of stuffed animals – exotic birds perched on trees as if about to take flight; an antelope standing calmly next to a mixed group of lions, tigers and cheetahs.

"It's a bit like a zoo, really," said Sarah, "only more…" she looked for the word.

"Dead?" suggested Joanna, helpfully.

"Um," frowned Sarah, "I suppose so, yes."

Joanna stopped at one of the larger creatures. She looked at the pretty girl with the nice clothes and tugged at her sleeve, "What's that, then?" she asked, pointing.

Sarah peeled herself away and peered at the card underneath. "It says it's a wildcat. Apparently they're almost extinct."

"Nothing to do with them all being bunged full of sawdust and stuck in museums, then?" commented Tyrone.

Sarah stuck her tongue out at him in what she thought was quite a superior way.

"No. It says it's due to deforestation and hunting by man."

"'S'not a problem now though, is it?" said Joanna.

"No," replied Sarah, as Tyrone looked on, "no, it's not."

* * * * *

Georgie and Farran had followed a different route back and collected William, who they found looking down his trousers with a worried expression on his face. After that they met up with Sarah, Joanna and Tyrone.

"What did you two find?" asked Tyrone.

"Just some stupid room full of fish," replied Farran.

Oh, thought Georgie, I guess he *is* a tit.

Together, the group followed the course of the 'Dinosaur

Trail', passing skeletons and drawings of the Cretaceous Era; footprints in plaster and models of nests, complete with broken eggs and sharp-toothed raptor hatchlings.

Finally they reached the most impressive part of the display – a life-size recreation of a tyrannosaurus eating its prey, a triceratops. On normal days the model would have been turning to roar at the crowd, or slashing its claws and tearing at the other dinosaur as it writhed in agony.

Today, everything was still and silent; the bright lights off and the effects speakers dead.

"Show's over," commented Farran.

The group leaned over the guardrail to get a better view.

"I think Fido likes you, Sarah," said Tyrone.

"It's looking at her," agreed William.

"Nah, it's cross-eyed," said Georgie grinning, "it's eyeing-up Farran."

Farran gave her a filthy look.

"Bloody hell," said William, learning further in, "is that its…"

"No William, that's a power cable hanging down," put in Sarah, quickly.

"I think I might have a closer look," said Georgie.

There was a deep trench all around the little island on which the models were set – to keep people like her off, thought Georgie with a little smile as she clambered over the bar and jumped down. The bottle caps and gum wrappers amongst the fake moss and plastic ferns, even the old crisp packet caught beneath the T-Rex's claw, only reminded her with a subtle thrill that this part was normally forbidden to the public. It was like deliberately kicking your ball where it says 'Keep Off The Grass' and then running to get it.

Now she was here, Georgie was tempted to go a step further. She reached up and gave the dinosaur a smack on the snout. As solid as it looked, the tyrannosaurus shook slightly, the machinery inside rattling like a metal skeleton. The scaly rubber skin covering the model made it surprisingly easy for Georgie to grip as she climbed and in only a few moments she was sitting astride the thing like a horse.

"Giddyup!" she yelled, kicking its flanks with her heels.

"You're the expert, Sarah," said Tyrone, "how's she doing?"

Sarah giggled, "Not bad at all."

Georgie wondered how easy it would be for her to stand up and balance on the dinosaur's back. As she glanced down at the others she suddenly noticed that Joanna had moved away and was now looking off to the right, fear in her face.

The window in the door was reinforced with wire mesh, but amidst the shadows of the dark corridor beyond they could make out a figure walking towards them. It got nearer and nearer with every step, and in the swinging beam of its torch they could see the outline of the cap and security badge that it wore.

"Buggerin' ell," breathed William.

There was something about the figure which seemed mis-shapen somehow; the shoulders were too big, the arms too long. The beam of the torch swung back and forth more quickly than it should have. It shuffled towards them, nearing the little window, a shadow Georgie didn't want revealed. Then it was right at the door, the group frozen in fear, when the figure raised its head – and they saw Donnie's grinning face, topped by a cap that was too big for him.

There was the sound of a lock turning and the next thing he was standing before them.

"You absolute *idiot*!" blurted Sarah.

"We thought it was…" began Georgie.

Donnie hadn't stopped smiling. "Sorry about that. Look at these," he said, jangling his large bunch of keys, "Ah found 'em in the security guards' room. Now ah've swiped 'em, every inch of the place is ours."

"And the uniform?" asked Tyrone, raising an eyebrow.

"Jus' wanted to look the part," Donnie replied, with a wink and a tip of his cap.

"Then next time dress as a knob," growled Georgie.

Donnie turned to her with a look of respect. "Nice one. A'll get onto that immediately."

"What'd you find?" asked Tyrone, trying to hide a smile.

"Well ah think there's at least as much behind the scenes as there is open to the public," he replied, "some of it's jus' offices, but there're millions of storage rooms. Some have cardboard boxes full of different kinds of beetle and dusty ol' bones, and ah even found a room with shelves covered in big jars o' lizards and snakes in formaldehyde."

"Might not be that much use to us though," said Tyrone.

"I'm hungry," said Joanna thoughtfully, "and I wanna cup of tea."

"That's a point, actually," agreed Georgie, "We need something a bit more than pickled reptiles if we're going to keep going."

"Yeah, we need basic supplies," put in William.

"That's the idea, innit?" said Farran.

The fact that none of them had eaten more than stale biscuits that day was something that couldn't be ignored any longer.

"High Street Ken is round the corner – it's full of camping stores," suggested Sarah.

"Well, then," concluded Tyrone, "if everyone's agreed we can just pile back into the van."

"Yeah," Georgie smiled, "let's go shopping."

CHAPTER 8.

When Georgie woke she was warm, and for one beautiful moment she didn't remember where she was. Moving slightly, the bed gave an unfamiliar canvas creak. She felt the strange silkiness of her duvet, then became aware that something small and probably plastic had embedded itself in her cheek. She pulled it off, rubbing at the numb dimple it left behind. Finally she peeled open one eye, only to find herself staring up into the snarling face of a polar bear.

Now she remembered.

Letting out a sigh she pulled on the plastic toggle of her sleeping bag's hood and hid the world again.

She lay there in her cocoon enjoying the warmth and scraping experimentally with her tongue at the furry gunge that had collected on the roof of her mouth. *Just ten more minutes, Mum*, she thought and then was shocked when a single sorrowful gasp escaped from her throat. *No jokes, no jokes, got to think about something else. Can't give in to that. Uhhmm? God I'm hungry, wonder what we have for breakfast?*

Last night they'd chosen the most promising out of the half-dozen, top-of-the-range camping supply shops, reversing the van into the plate glass window until the entire thing collapsed over the pavement in a tide of sparkling shards. Everyone felt that same exhilarating sense of forbidden trespass, and the fact that the place sold coats and anoraks for £500 only made it the more delicious to be able to scoop up armfuls of whatever they wanted and walk away with it all for free.

Some of the group opted for snug one-man tents, whilst others, more ambitious, went straight for the biggest ones they could find. A couple of good camping stoves were added to the haul, as most of the group were missing tea and at the very least, hot food. Packets of freeze-dried meals seemed like the right kit for mountain climbers and extreme conditions, but unfortunately the 'Roast Turkey Dinner' and 'Strawberry Trifle' looked about as appealing as re-hydrated vomit with extra chunks.

Georgie opened her hood again. The room was huge and dark but here and there haloes of metallic white light illuminated the gloom, revealing the unmistakable humps of the others tucked up in their camp beds. *They've left the torches on all night. Oh well, we'll just have to get more batteries.* One of the beds was empty though. *What time was it? Nine. Who the hell would be up at nine?* Then Farran came creeping in from the hall; he had a long bin bag under his arm and he looked freezing.

"Morning," she whispered.

Farran turned round looking strangely guilty. "Awright," he said, quickly stuffing the bag under his own bed before getting in with his clothes on.

"Where you been?"

"Just out an' about, scoping the place."

"Oh yeah, whereabouts? See anything good?"

"What is this, man, the third degree?" said Farran, his tone rapidly rising.

A voice piped up from one of the tangled lumps. "D'you two lovebirds mind keepin' it down? Some of us ah tryin' t' snooze here." The boy's sleep-ruffled head appeared from under the covers.

"Sorry, Donnie, didn't mean to wake you, we were just–Donnie, are you sleeping with a koala?"

"Not in the biblical sense, no."

"I mean, is that a real stuffed koala in bed with you?"

"Maybe…"

"Why Donnie?"

"OK, you caught me. I can't sleep wi'out a pillow. An' this was the only soft thing I could find in the night," Donnie added sheepishly. "Actually it's still a bit firm for my likin', but it sort of works."

"OK, moving on," said Georgie. "What do we have for breakfast?"

"Plus, someone told me they were minty," continued Donnie. "You know, because they eat eucalyptus leaves all day. They're supposed to smell… menthol…"

"Back to breakfast–"

"It doesn't, by the way. It smells like old musty socks."

"And still you slept with it," said Georgie.

"Aye. So, breakfast?"

"I think we've still got some of that freeze-dried crap from the campin' shop," said Farran, "but I don't really fancy beef stroganoff, or whatever it was, for breakfast, I could barely get it down my neck last night."

"There was puddin' flavours," came a sleepy voice from the corner.

"Morning Joanna. Yeah, that sounds good to me."

They lit the camping stoves - with considerably more ease and fewer burnt fingers than the previous night - and then sat about wrapped up, eating freeze-dried, vitamin-enriched, banoffee-flavoured glue from out of the packet. So indescribably foul was the meal that they all agreed that the focus for the day ought to be finding a reliable supply of food and stockpiling it.

They decided to split up into three groups: Georgie and

Farran would take the minivan south for a general search; Tyrone, Donnie and Sarah would try to find another car and head west to what Sarah described as 'one of those out of town monstrosities'; while William, to his dismay, was paired with Joanna to look for a local supply of food and water.

* * * * *

An hour and a half later, William and Joanna had got no further than the front gates of their own museum. William inspected the contents of his kit bag one by one, like a child re-examining the goodies from his stocking on Christmas morning. Joanna leant untidily against the railings, whipping the zipper of her parka up and down and waiting patiently for him to finish. When she got bored of that she decided to explore the parka, her fingers eventually finding something crusted, melted and long-forgotten in the corner of one of the pockets. Could be a throat lozenge. Could be an old scab. Could be a fossilised raisin. She popped it in her mouth and chewed experimentally.

At last William heaved the bag onto his back, spat casually, and then set off down the road without so much as a backward glance at the girl.

Joanna followed, crunching thoughtfully.

They got all of ten yards before…"Where the hell are we supposed to find food round here? All the others got to do fun stuff, why did I have to get stuck with the freak?"

They continued to shamble down the middle of the road. William looked at Joanna as though he actually expected an answer.

Joanna shrugged her shoulders and looked apologetic.

* * * * *

Meanwhile Georgie and Farran were zipping down the broad roads of Southwest London. Georgie felt she had pretty much got the hang of the whole driving thing now and so long as she didn't change down from third and didn't have to stop for any obstacles, she was confident of not stalling. She'd decided that a fast and constant speed was the key, even if that made searching a little harder.

Before setting off, Farran had flicked quickly through the minivan's CDs and, finding nothing he liked, had slumped back grumpily into his seat. Georgie had taken over and found some classical stuff; she was no expert, but she recognized Mozart's *Magic Flute*, which her dad used to listen to and, much to the disgust of Farran, had put that on. Loud.

So they drove, ear-splitting opera blaring from the open vehicle, announcing their presence to no one but the pigeons. Or so they thought, for a desolate London looked on, grey and still, as the car spread the beautiful music through its ravaged streets. Arias and arpeggios, cadences and crescendos hummed against the stone and glass facades, making the windows dance in their frames. The high trills of the flute reverberated against rooftops and clattered off kerbstones, bringing life and beauty to the city. Then, as quickly as the car passed, the sound faded and the buildings settled back to their stony slumber once more. In her bubble of music and movement the beginnings of a smile began to tug at the sides of Georgie's mouth.

Farran leant over and flicked the little black knob on the dashboard. Instantly, the city was plunged into a deafening silence again.

"Oi!" squealed Georgie in disbelief. "I was listening to that."

"Too loud," replied Farran without expression and turned away, apparently intent on studying the streets. Georgie stared at the back of his head. She wasn't sure, but she thought she could detect the faintest smirk on his reflection in the wing mirror.

"Watch out!" Farran shouted suddenly.

Georgie turned back to the road just in time to swerve the car around an upturned wheelbarrow with a TV in it. Georgie puffed out her cheeks, *that was close!* She glanced over at Farran but he'd gone back to watching the shops fly past his window.

She returned her attention to the road and they continued on in disgruntled silence.

* * * * *

William absentmindedly picked up a pebble and sent it arcing on a trajectory that ended in a car window. So despondent was he about being paired up with this strange smelly girl, that he didn't even bother to turn his head and appreciate the riot of falling glass that ensued. She wasn't even fit *and* he still hadn't forgiven her for kneeing him in the nuts either. He reached under the right side of his shirt – always left untucked for this very reason - and scratched his belly in frustration.

"I don't see what bleedin' fun going an' looking for food is."

"Could go in there," suggested Joanna, pointing up the steps towards the Victoria and Albert Museum.

So much fussing and grumbling had been done by William that, in the time it had taken Tyrone and the others to find another car, break into it, start it and drive off, he and Joanna had covered approximately a hundred yards.

"What is it?"

"Museum."

"A museum? We already live in a museum, what the hell do I want to go into another one for? This is supposed to be fun and it's turning out worse than Mr Cheadle's trip to Wookie Hole."

"Sgotswordsinit," blurted Joanna.

William wasn't at all sure he liked the sound of that, he wasn't even sure it was English, so he gave her the look his dad gave foreigners when they came from the campsite to use the farm's toilet.

Joanna tried again. "'S'got swords in it."

A light came on in William's eyes - a light refracted from the somewhat underused screen in his brain that was currently showing a series of gladiator epics, all starring him.

"Old ones. Big ones," she encouraged.

She needn't have bothered, she'd had him at *swords*.

* * * * *

The car park was almost empty except for the plastic bags skittering past them on the wind or the occasional rogue shopping trolley. When they reached the doors to the super-market, Sarah, Donnie and Tyrone were surprised to find that they were open, the aisles stocked with an endless array of colourful packets, boxes, tins and bottles.

Despite the breeze, however, they were soon hit by a thick and fearsome stink. The chiller nearest the door was lined with cartons swollen close to bursting, milk which had exploded out of others forming a thick crust of green and yellow cheese over the shelves below. Avoiding the dairy section they went to the other side of the giant building, past the little tobac-conist's section – where Tyrone helped himself to a couple of cartons of cigarettes – and the stands of newspapers, empty but for a few lone magazines. Beyond this though, they were sent gagging and stumbling backwards by a cloud of flies and a far richer stench which Donnie, his stomach churning cold with a memory he didn't want, recognised as rotting meat.

* * * * *

Georgie couldn't stand it any longer.

"So what did you used to get up to before? You know, in your spare time and that?" Georgie knew that Farran didn't do polite conversation, or any conversation really for that matter, but the atmosphere in the car was beginning to drive her nuts, so she had to try something.

"Not a lot."

"You must have done something."

"I didn' have a lot of *spare time*."

"How come? No offence, but you don't exactly strike me as the homework type."

"I had to do a load of stuff for my mum 'n dad an' that."

"What sort of stuff?"

"You know, bills, letters, that sort of stuff."

"Bills? You mean your parents' bills? You used to pay the house bills?" Farran shrugged. "Cool. My folks would never trust me to do that. I had to argue with them for months just to get a clothing allowance so I could buy my own clothes."

"It's not like I wanted to do it," he snapped. There was a long pause during which Farran began to pick distractedly at the quick of his thumbnail. "My folks don't... *didn't* speak much English, so I had to do all that sort of thing."

Georgie nodded but didn't reply. She wasn't sure *how* to reply, so she started again. "So you lived with you parents?" She grimaced inwardly at her own lameness but continued, "Of course you did. Did you get on with them? Did you argue with them? I used to have huge stand-up rows with my dad. Normally over nothing in particular, but still - he'd be shouting, I'd be shouting-"

"Are you out of your mind? I never shouted at my dad." He gave a short humourless laugh. "He'd have wooped my arse. My dad's strict, man. He gave me a good crack if I gave him a dirty look." He sucked his teeth. "Shout at my dad. You're havin' a laugh, man."

The tyres made a low grumbling sound as they rumbled

over an uneven patch of tarmac.

"What about your mum?" she exhaled.

"What about 'er?"

"Did you have arguments with your mum?"

"Yeah sure…I had arguments wiv her, when she would get on my case. But that's jus' my mum. What's *she* gunna do?"

"Didn't she ever tell your dad, when you wouldn't do what you were told?"

His face dropped. "Yeah sometimes. If I'd been gettin' shit from my teachers at school an' that, and my mum had been whinging to my dad as well, then he would tell me he was gunna send me back to Bangladesh. Before all of this…stuff happened, I was on my last warnin' for bunkin' off Arabic school."

"Send you back to Bangladesh? You mean going back to Bangladesh was like a threat?"

"Yeah. Man, that place is a shit-hole. No way am I gonna get sent to live in that smelly, backward place. Still, if I'd got sent there and not here?…Maybe they're still alive there? Maybe this only happened in England. That'd be typical that would."

"I'm pretty sure that this has happened everywhere." Georgie swallowed. "The radio stations all went quiet one by one, even the foreign ones on my granddad's shortwave. Sometimes, when the weather was right, you could hear stations as far away as America on the Roberts radio. They all just kind of blinked out of existence at the same time. The last one I picked up was from Spain - Barcelona I think - I'm not sure, I don't really speak Spanish, but anyway I'm pretty sure this has happened everywhere - even Bangladesh." She smiled as if this would be some consolation to Farran, and oddly enough it was.

He gave a brief snort, "True. True."

They lapsed into silence again, but somehow it was a shared silence now, not a lonely one. Outside the car a slushy rain had begun to fall and Farran reached over to turn the windscreen wipers on before settling back to scanning the streets. A few minutes passed like this, with nothing but the patter of the rain and the rhythmic squeak of the wipers, then, much to Georgie's surprise, Farran broke the quiet. He spoke in a low tone, not looking at her as he did so.

"At first, when they died, I jus' sat around our flat, waitin' 'til I got sick, waitin' for me to start coughin' like they did, but nothin' happened. I sat on our couch, like actually sitting there thinking about coughin', an' one time I felt this tickle, an' I kind of...kind of forced it. I coughed a bit but then it stopped. That was it, it didn't...shit, I was so angry, like I'd been left out. In the end I went an' sat in my folks' room at the bottom of the bed - I faced the other way, towards the chest of drawers, an' I took deep breaths. I thought it would be like when I had chickenpox and my folks made my brothers stay in the sittin' room wiv me for a whole week... The chest of drawers was covered with my parents' stuff - scarves, some make up an' stuff in a green basket, picture of my auntie, an' my dad's good gold watch. All these bits an' pieces. But nothin', not even a sniffle. I left all that stuff there."

He paused before continuing in the same monotone, but now he seemed to be speaking more directly to Georgie than before. "Our Imam said once that you have to bury people quick. I don't know 'xactly how, never been to a funeral. I think you're s'posed to wash 'em, wrap 'em in the kafan and put them lyin' on their right side facin' Mecca. It...it's very important..." Here his words just petered out.

Georgie looked at him as much as her driving would allow. "I felt the same when my family got ill. I'm not sure why we didn't get sick, but I don't think we will either, I think..."

"Stop the car!" shouted Farran.

"What?"

"Stop the car now!"

Georgie slammed her foot on the brake and the huge,

top-heavy van heaved to a standstill, throwing both of them forward. Before Georgie had even had time to recover, Farran had kicked open the passenger door and was up and out on the street. She leant towards the still open door, straining against her seatbelt, scanning the road for what had made him shout so urgently. She fumbled with the clasp and tumbled out of the car after him.

When she caught up with him he was standing, hands thrust into his jacket pockets, two hundred meters up the road in the direction that they had come, focused intently on something.

"What is it?" gasped Georgie. "Did you see something, someone, a sign of life?"

"I saw a sign alright."

She followed his gaze but it took a few moments to catch his meaning. Then she understood. She read the letters *H M V*.

"You have got to be kidding me."

* * * * *

Joanna was used to wandering about on her own. She wasn't an orphan, she wasn't beaten or locked in a cupboard for being bad. She'd *had* a mother, it's just that her mother'd had a tough time remembering that she had Joanna.

Mrs McGillis hadn't intended to get pregnant the first time round with Joanna's older sister, Kelly. She'd had plans. So when, three years later, while watching the National Lottery Extra she realised that her period was at least a week overdue for a second time, she held a moment's silence for the untimely death of her dreams before she got up, made another cup of tea and had a hobnob. It was this attitude of resignation that Joanna's mother transmitted to her unborn child in the womb.

There was one thing that Joanna loved – well two, if you included next door's pitbull, who she would sit and talk to for hours until Mrs Ping would ask her politely if she shouldn't be getting along home now – and that was her older sister Kelly. As well as a passing resemblance to Rex (no one in the McGillis household was blessed with a superabundance of good looks) Kelly also shared its snappy temperament. However, Kelly at 17 inhabited a world of bands, boys and illicit booze that seemed impossibly glamorous to Joanna. Kelly's fiery temper and indifference only made Joanna worship her more.

Their mother had a long-term job cleaning an office building at night and slept through the day, and as a consequence the duty of looking after Joanna fell to Kelly. Kelly was not by nature a bad person but she was stuffed full of hormones, a sense of injustice, and a vague flabby self-hatred that meant that she constantly lost the battle between her resentment and her better angels.

Once, when they were ten and thirteen, Kelly had done Joanna up in her clothes and makeup as if she'd been a very large doll. Joanna'd ended up looking somewhere between a child beauty pageant contestant and a hooker, but she'd been on cloud nine. The next day, when Kelly went to pick Joanna up from the play park, Joanna had introduced her as her mum. Kelly was mortified and went ballistic, effing and blinding the whole way home.

Joanna never did it again. At least not in earshot.

Most evenings Kelly would wait until their mother had grumbled her way out of the flat before plopping a bowl of Shreddies in front of her sister and heading out into the streets of Pimlico to find a misguided sense of belonging in alchopops and groping.

Joanna would then stay up watching endless home improvement and cookery programmes on the Lifestyle Channel until she fell asleep on the couch. When her sister clunked noisily back through the front door, many hours later but long before their mother returned, Joanna would wait for the sound of snoring, then creep through the dark to her sister's bed. If she were lucky, Kelly, softened by alcohol and regret, would groggily lift up the covers. Joanna would tentatively nestle into her sister's back. She'd feel the sweet fug of alcohol that hung about Kelly's body embrace her and drift happily off to sleep.

Left as she was to her own devices, Joanna's internal world grew into a pleasant place peopled by television presenters, cartoon characters, politicians, neighbours from the estate, and none any more or less real than any of the others. Had she been brought up in a household surrounded by novels and tomes of philosophy she would have been quite interesting, but she hadn't and she wasn't. As it was though she tended to play a kind of Russian roulette with the television channels, watching whatever came on, so there were pockets of knowledge locked away inside her head that neither her teachers nor her family would ever have guessed at.

Rex knew, but Rex kept it to himself.

Joanna had learnt from one of these random documentaries that there were some very beautiful things in the Victoria and Albert Museum. Very beautiful and very desirable.

* * * * *

Tyrone, Donnie and Sarah had plunged into the endless aisles of the supermarket. Tyrone, fresh cigarette on the go, had wandered off on his own, but Donnie had remained with Sarah. He claimed that he was only hanging around to make sure she was ok, but Sarah began to doubt this when he insisted that she push him around in one of the larger trolleys.

Although Sarah did her best to stick to the list she had made and make sure they got all the essentials, Donnie continually reached out and grabbed whatever took his fancy, from blocks of jelly to a dozen disposable cameras. Finally becoming exasperated as she returned Superman bubble bath to the shelf, she glanced into the trolley and looked at Donnie with a deep frown.

"Is it really necessary to have a foot-high pile of chocolate bars?"

"O' course. Chocolate is one of the essential food-groups along with squirty cream and processed cheese slices," replied Donnie, "I mean, look at these bite-size balls – crunchy on the inside, chocolatey goodness on the outside…"

"And what are you going to do with those?"

"Fill a paddlin' pool with 'em and then swim around with my mouth open."

Sarah sent Donnie off to get his own trolley.

* * * * *

It was the most beautiful thing William had ever seen. The label read – Katana, Shinto era (1597-1780), made in Osaka, worn by high ranking samurai and taking many months to create by expert craftsmen - all William cared about was that it looked like it would have your arm in a second. The sword was about a foot and a half long, extending in an elegant curve that was so perfect he had to spend a couple of minutes just following the spine of the scabbard back and forth. It was black, and polished to the point that it didn't so much reflect William's wide-eyed amazement as trap it somewhere deep beneath its lacquered surface. He gripped the ridged handle with a sweaty hand and pulled it from the scabbard, making a satisfying shhhnick. The metal of the blade had a fine grain that light travelled up and down, animating it like waves. He let out a breath - now he felt invincible.

When William and Joanna had entered the V&A, they'd discovered that the large front doors had already been forced open with what William had deduced was a crowbar. There were three clues: the gauges in the door, the wood around the lock furred up into long splinters and, of course, most decisively, there was the crowbar on the mat. They'd decided that it must have been the work of looters from when all of the chaos was happening, brief as it had been, before it all went quiet. But still, they'd felt a little uneasy as they stalked through the museum's echoing halls and corridors. William's disquiet hadn't been helped by the continued mournful bang of those doors. They thudded again now. Maybe he could get the girl to stick a bin against them or something. *That was a point, actually, where was she? He had better find her.*

He caressed his prize once more before laying it gently in his carry-all, lodging it securely between a bullet-proof vest and a large box of Sugar Puffs – the packet had partially split, spilling little yellow beads into the carry-all and spreading a sweet musty smell throughout. William hadn't noticed this of course, but if he had it wouldn't have bothered him, he would have considered it to be a bit like potpourri.

Content that the sword was safe he trundled off to find the girl - while somewhere in Southern Japan, by a quiet hillside temple reserved for the country's greatest artisans, a swordsmith was spinning in his grave.

William finally caught up with Joanna in the main hall, standing with her parka zipped up to her neck and acting decidedly shifty.

"Where you been?" asked William in his usual bullish tone.

"Nowhere," replied Joanna, discretely brushing a small piece of display cabinet glass from her sleeve.

* * * * *

Donnie and Tyrone met in the middle of the cereal aisle. Looking into Tyrone's trolley, Donnie saw tea bags, sugar, UHT milk, then picked up a large plastic bottle.

"What's this stuff, then?"

"Washing liquid," replied Tyrone, with just a hint of tetchiness.

"What d'ye want something like that for, y'great streak o' bouncy spring-fresh nonsense?" asked Donnie incredulously.

"Well, what're you gonna do when you clothes start to get filthy?" replied Tyrone, eyebrows raised.

"I don't know. Smell?"

Tyrone had no reply to that. Instead he had a look inside Donnie's trolley, far fuller than his own. The thing was filled with every sort of pop, fizzy drink and cheap own-brand cola.

"*You* must be kiddin'," he said, wrinkling up his nose, "you can't want all that crap - the stuff'll rot your teeth in seconds."

"Sod that," replied Donnie with his best cavalier air, "I'll gargle with it. Who's gonna say ah can't?"

"No one," conceded Tyrone with a casual shrug, "but in the absence of dentists, when you get a cavity we'll have to pull your rotten teeth out with a claw hammer."

Donnie thought for a moment, and then replaced all of the drinks with the sugar-free kind.

* * * * *

Georgie slumped into the shop's shutters and turned her collar up against the weather; it was still sleeting, but she refused to go inside and help Farran. Taking what you needed to survive was one thing - that was common sense - but taking games and DVDs that you didn't really need was just stealing. They'd had an argument about it, just for a change. Farran said that he could never have afforded any of these things before, not without a 'five finger discount' anyway, and that now there was nothing to stop him. No fuzz, no filth, and it was about time he got his. Everybody else had what they wanted, why not him? Georgie'd felt that he was looking at her significantly when he said this but she couldn't for the life of her think what it was supposed to mean.

She looked over the road to where someone had graffitied on one of the shop fronts; in hurried looking blasts of purple aerosol paint was what Georgie thought she recognised as a verse from the bible – '*Death rides triumphantly on his pale horse through our streets and breaks into every house almost where any inhabitants are to be found*'. She'd seen some of that type of thing all over London on her travels but it never ceased to amaze her that when the city had been going to hell in a handbag (an expression her mother always liked), someone had decided they'd nothing better to do than scribble on walls. There'd been one drawing she'd liked though. In Mile End, before she'd met Farran for the first time, she'd come across a dead body lying against a wall. Someone had drawn a family of rats on the wall so that they looked like they were actually standing on the body. The family of rats were celebrating, some were throwing tickertape or drinking champagne, some were wearing party hats and others workmen's hats and uniforms. Down one of the slumped arms the rats had even started to build a little rat-sized castle. It shouldn't have, but at the time it had made Georgie laugh like a drain; she'd still been laughing as she was crossing the road when Farran came speeding towards her.

To the left of the scrawled verse in front of her now, was something else; the sleet was coming down heavier though and it wasn't so easy to see. Small and in orange paint, sprayed on with a stencil – the words *Leviathan: com check* in a circle. She squinted at it. It seemed out of place, too formal, and at the same time vaguely familiar. Had she seen it somewhere before? There was a splodge of the same paint on the lamp-post in front of the wall. Georgie's eyes followed the dark tube of metal. It wasn't a lamppost after all, but one of those multi-camera observation posts that they seemed to have on all the big high streets these days. She stared up at the sinister dark lenses. A soggy flake drifted out of the sky and landed in her eye, briefly streaking the world with lines and sparkly edges - and that's when it happened.

The camera moved.

CHAPTER 9.

The crashing sounds had been going on for nearly five minutes before Sarah, her shopping finally complete, went to investigate the commotion. Her trolley was unusual in that, instead of the standard, single wonky wheel, hers possessed two; the one on the left twisted to the right, the one on the right twisted to the left and as a result, for the first time in supermarket history, the two cancelled each other out and she was able to move in an almost straight line.

Her pleasure at this good fortune was short-lived however, when she discovered the cause of the commotion.

Tyrone was charging down the aisle pushing a shopping trolley in which Donnie sat, still in his dishevelled dinner jacket. The end of the aisle was blocked by an enormous pyramid of tins, and as soon as Tyrone judged that they'd gained enough momentum he let go, the thing shooting away before it finally hit its target, sending canned goods cascading into the air and onto Donnie and the floor all around.

"Nice to see you're taking our plight seriously," she scolded.

Donnie climbed, a little unsteadily, from the trolley, "It's jus' a bit o' fun, hen."

"But look at those cans," Sarah continued, "they'll all be dented – unusable."

"Good," said Tyrone, "I hate baked beans."

"So what did you collect then?" Donnie asked, and without waiting for an answer had a poke around Sarah's full trolley, finding carrots and potatoes; rice, tins of vegetables, pens, batteries, plasters and paracetamol and lots and lots of pasta.

Holding up a tube of skin cream he said, "I can't believe the pointless stuff that girls get."

Sarah glanced at Donnie's trolley and noted the water pistols and Jaffa Cakes. There were times when Sarah just knew she was in the right, and this was so definitely one of them. She didn't feel the need to reply to such a comment. Instead she changed the subject.

"We need to get a move on," she said, addressing both boys.

"No problem," replied Tyrone, "look – no queues!"

Sarah, now feeling the pleasant swell of righteousness, ignored this too.

"First, the pair of you need to get some things yourselves. We're not leaving this place until you each have a full load of supplies." And with that she turned and started to push her trolley away.

"Where are you goin'?" asked Donnie.

"Nowhere. Just to pick up some items." She continued on her way.

"What sort o' 'items'?"

"Just items," she snapped.

Donnie waited until Sarah had reached the end of the aisle before bellowing after her, "Tampons are on aisle four by the way!"

Sarah turned the corner without looking back.

Tyrone's face lit up with an idea, "Hey, Donnie, have you ever heard of something called a 'Trolley dash'?"

"Nice one - Tyrone, I like yer style, sir."

* * * * *

Georgie dragged Farran bodily out of the shop, DVDs spiralling from his arms as they ran. She stood him right in the same spot and told him breathlessly to watch the camera.

Nothing happened.

"What the hell am I supposed to be lookin' at, woman?"

"It moved! The camera moved! There must be electricity here, or something."

"Well if there is then its doin' a bloody god job of pretending there ain't. Do you see any lights on?"

"No but it…it moved. No it didn't *just* move, it moved one way and then the other and then it stopped. It, it was like it was looking at me."

"We'll it ain't now, it's lookin' straight down the road the other way and it sure as gravy ain't movin'."

"But it did move." The exasperation was building in her voice. "I was looking at the writing on the wall, then I looked up at the pole and this big snowflake got in my eye and then-"

"Ahh," interrupted Farran, "so this big snowflake fell in your eye, blindin' you…"

"Yes, well no…"

"…and when you was blinded, that's when you saw it move."

"No, I…that's not what I said."

"OK," said Farran wandering off. "I'm just gonna get back to my shoppin' now." And he left Georgie to flounder in her anger.

* * * * *

Sarah wasn't sure that it was all useful, but at least both boys now had full trolleys. Pushing her own she led the way through the empty supermarket, the other two behind her in single file – *just like ducklings*, she thought with a smile.

One duckling had a cigarette in its mouth and the other was admiring the half-dozen bottles of assorted whiskies it had chosen.

Donnie was thoroughly enjoying the whole thing. He'd loved his uncle – admired the man. He couldn't walk into a pub in their little town without a warm welcome and a pat on the back. He could knock pool balls around and play dominos like no one else, name every Falkirk player since 1973, wasn't much bother when he came home pished and had introduced Donnie to some of the most colourful language in western Scotland. But Donnie had never relied on him. He'd perfected his diet of cheese on toast and microwave meals, made his own entertainment, kept his own hours and treated school like a fairly optional activity. The only difference now – for the most part – was that his freedom was even greater than it had been before. All in all, Donnie felt pretty relaxed.

For just a second, as they passed the thick smell of rotting meat on their way out, he felt troubled and quickened his pace, but once outside his buoyant mood soon returned and he happily entered a heated argument with Tyrone over who was going to drive them back to the museum.

* * * * *

When Georgie and Farran turned into Museum Road, Tyrone's party were already unloading the back of a delivery van. Georgie pulled up alongside, noticing that the front of the van was dented and the left headlight hung from a wire like a popped eye.

Tyrone raised a hand to welcome her and caught her gaze. "Donnie was driving," he said by way of explanation.

Georgie nodded.

"You'll notice this isn't the car we left in, that one didn't even make it out the car park."

"Successful trip though?" she asked.

"Yeah, yeah, great. How'd you guys do?"

Georgie thought for a moment, Farran had almost convinced her that she'd been imagining things; she wasn't going to mention the camera to anyone else – not if they were just going to think she was nuts. In the end she just gave a rueful smile.

Farran leant across her and shoved his head out of the driver's window, crushing her back into the seat. "It was awesome, wait till you see what I got."

Georgie parked and the two of them strolled back to the van where they were met by an indignant looking Sarah.

"Well I hope you had more luck reigning-in Farran than I did with these boys," she said, ignoring Farran altogether. "You would not believe the trouble I had getting them to behave. They wanted to steal all kinds of useless things. I mean, we have to take the necessities in order to survive until order is restored but we don't have to behave like common criminals. This one here," she pointed at Donnie accusingly, "wanted to pinch a lot of frivolous sports equipment. I mean, can you imagine? It was all I could do to get them to the supermarket. Sadly we couldn't find an M&S, but I think we have all of the basics that we need really?"

Georgie wasn't quite sure how that was a question or how she should respond so she just said "Yes," rather weakly.

"So what did you pick up, Fran?" chipped in Donnie, eyeing the cardboard box in Farran's arms.

"I got some…did you just call me *Fran*?"

"Yeah, thought it was a nice wee nickname, been givin' it some thought. You know Farran - Fran."

"Well don't."

"OK. So what did you get, Fran?"

Farran glowered.

Donnie smiled back sweetly.

So Farran just sighed and continued, "Well, we was gonna get some food an' stuff an' then I thought 'screw it'." With that he tipped out the contents of his box, spilling a huge collection of the latest DVDs and computer games onto the pavement.

"Sweet!" The two boys began rifling through the pile.

Sarah gave Georgie a withering look, "I'm not angry, just disappointed."

"What?... I'm...it wasn't my...I told him not to," she blustered. Georgie felt as if she'd broken some sacred girl code that she didn't even realise had existed. *This is why all of my friends are boys*, she thought to herself. She looked up and to her relief spotted Joanna and William coming towards them. "Look, the others are here."

"I hope you did better than Georgina, Joanna," Sarah called out in a friendly sing-song voice. Georgie could feel herself blushing.

The other girl said nothing and no expression could be seen as her parka was zipped up all the way to her nose, but she did give a manic little wave before her arms returned to their usual position clamped across her chest.

"You guys are gonna love this..." And with that William reached behind his head and in one smooth, impressive swipe, unsheathed his sword and held it glittering in the late afternoon sun.

"I don't believe it, you stole a sword. Tell me you got some supplies as well. You spent four hours stealing a sword?"

"No," said William, confused and defensive, "I stole the sword in about an hour but it took me the rest of the time to work out how to pull it out in that cool way."

Donnie sniggered. Sarah shot him a teacher's glare then went back to addressing William.

"We were supposed to be borrowing essential supplies to help us survive. We are not supposed to run around *thieving* whatever we like. You are going to be in so much trouble when the adults get back. Hold on. Is that an antique sword? Did you steal that from the V&A? Oh my God, it's probably one of the nation's priceless treasures."

"Well now it's *my* priceless treasure." Although William sounded a lot less confident than he had meant to; she may have been skinny and blond but she had a way of talking that confused the hell out of him. That and she always thought she was right.

"Am I the only one who has a sense of right and wrong? A sense of propriety? Georgina goes off with Farran to steal video games…" - Georgie tried to object but Sarah was building up a head of steam, pink rising to her porcelain cheeks - "It's all I can do to stop these two stealing everything in sight and now William has gone and stolen a priceless artefact. Joanna and I are the only two with any sense of decency."

Joanna said nothing, but shifted her weight uncomfortably from foot to foot.

"Hmm? Aren't we, Joanna?"

Still the girl said nothing, but very slowly she unzipped her parka to reveal two red cheeks, a regretful mouth and finally an enormous and intricately wrought gold necklace.

Sarah was speechless.

"Cleopatra," Joanna squeaked by way of explanation.

Sarah let out an exasperated shriek and stomped off into the museum.

There then came a long pause, as the others wrestled, ultimately unsuccessfully, with a strong desire to dissolve into laughter.

They were still giggling uncontrollably when they unloaded the last of the supplies into the main hall, almost an hour later.

* * * * *

The group realised that they had only just begun to tap the almost limitless potential of the great, unprotected city around them. That night their imaginations sparked into life and none of them slept. Instead the museum reverberated with the excited sounds of ideas, garbled and intoxicating. After their weeks of solitary and unmentionable sorrow there began a week of joyous exploration. Little by little the idea of rescue was forgotten, each of the survivors indulging their wildest materialistic fantasies; for the city was theirs now and so was everything in it.

On the first day:

Tyrone, inspired by Farran's acquisition, went back to HMV and picked up a complete collection of Bruce Lee films.

Farran found himself a scooter and set about getting it running.

Donnie went back to the V&A with William where they found themselves two sets of medieval armour, and spent the rest of the day testing it by battering each other around the head and chest with broom handles.

Sarah refused to get involved in this frankly childish and illegal behaviour and spent the day reading riding magazines instead.

Georgie went down to Harrods food hall and gathered together the most expensive items she could find, which in the evening, through some alchemy not entirely understood even by her, she managed to turn into a meal that tasted almost exactly like a beef and tarmac pot noodle.

Joanna had gone to Harrods with Georgie and returned with a lamp, a child's paddling pool, coasters, and several duvets.

On the second day:

Not to be outdone by Tyrone, Farran returned to HMV and collected every action film he could find.

Impressed by the strength of the armour, Donnie and William graduated to real swords. In the heat of battle a cabinet of priceless Greek vases was accidentally obliterated as William toppled over in mid-swing.

Sarah decided that if everyone else was going to get what *they* wanted then she would go shopping too. At the crack of dawn she was up, washed and on her way to Harvey Nics. Late afternoon, she pushed back through the door looking tired but happy, staggering under the weight of half a dozen bags. She proceeded to unpack an incredible number of the most expensive items, each carefully folded, tucked into the appropriate designer-label bag and even wrapped in tissue paper. She had of course made up a hand-written receipt for all of her purchases - just in case anyone ever asked her to pay.

Joanna went out and returned with SodaStream refills, some silk cushions, a picture of a horse and more duvets.

On the third day:

Tyrone got hold of all of the chick-flicks he could find - and gave them to Farran.

Having found the destruction to be more fun than fighting, Donnie and William donned their armour again and amused themselves by pushing each other through countless display cases. This was only interrupted by the time Donnie nicked his arm, at which point William giggled so hard that a little bit of wee leaked out into his metal codpiece.

Sarah, disgusted by their wanton vandalism, went back to Harvey Nics.

Joanna went out and returned with denture cream, a rug, a battery-powered ashtray, a foot spa, self-warming slippers - and duvets.

On the fourth day:

Farran raided the store for every film that had the possibility of a glimpse of boobs, even the *poncey* foreign ones.

Georgie realised that Sarah might actually have a point about the whole clothes thing.

William went out early in the morning with an arsenal of hammers, chisels and saws, returning in the evening with a rucksack full of twenty-pound notes and looking very pleased with himself. Tyrone asked William how he'd transported it, to which William responded that he'd used a scooter. When Tyrone asked him where he'd bought the scooter, William replied that he'd just taken it like everything else. Tyrone patted William's shoulder and walked away shaking his head.

Joanna went out and returned with a wireless doorbell, a letter rack, a welcome mat, a dehumidifier and more duvets.

On the fifth day:

Tyrone went back to HMV and took the lot. Even the Disney films. He ran up and down the aisles of the store scooping up all of the DVDs as he ran. He then went into the stockroom and cleared that out too.

Farran and William spent the majority of the day collecting all of the maths textbooks they could find, and the remainder of it burning them.

Donnie came and asked Georgie if she needed anything washing as, after receiving several complaints, he was going to give it a try. Much to his surprise she declined his offer. Two hours later he returned with red hands and dripping hair to see Georgie unpacking a huge quantity of brand new underwear. With a smile Donnie realised that he would never need to wash anything again. Ever.

Joanna went out and came back with a keyboard hoover, an egg timer in the shape of Snoopy, a multi-dicer, a small non-steam mirror, a ukulele, worming pills for a cat. And more duvets.

On the sixth day:

Tyrone and Farran realised they really needed a DVD player. And possibly a source of electricity.

Joanna arranged her booty and sat back well pleased with herself, although Sarah said that what she had created looked like a surrealist's dream of a particularly homey brothel. Georgie claimed that she could understand almost everything except the worming pills and the denture cream. Joanna said that at some point they might get a cat, and that if they did she would definitely look after it; and as for the cream, well, she just wanted to see what it tasted like.

On the seventh day:

They rested.

CHAPTER 10.

It felt strange to be smelling 'school' again. Slightly stale biscuits and pine disinfectant – that's what it seemed like to Georgie. This one wasn't even that similar to her own comprehensive – too modern and too clean – but the memories came flooding back anyway. A Geography lesson on a really beautiful, sunny afternoon, the scent of freshly-cut grass drifting in from somewhere. A flash picture of a giggling class flinging half-dissected bits of earthworm around the room at each other. The scrawls and doodles on her Maths textbook. The smell of Tipp-Ex. The sound of dozens and dozens of shouting voices.

She looked at Tyrone, marching ahead. He seemed to know where he was going.

Stupid. Of course he did, this had been his school.

"Everything here looks pretty new. Must've been a nice place."

"Think so?" Tyrone replied, looking back briefly.

"I take it you weren't a big fan of school."

"More like school wasn't a big fan of me."

Fair enough, thought Georgie. She supposed most people felt like that. In fact, it was kind of hard to imagine Tyrone at school. Georgie watched as he paused for a moment. It just didn't seem to...suit him.

They were in a corridor full of rooms for French classes, the walls covered in posters the students had made, displaying pretend French menus and pictures labelled 'Croissant' which looked more like gently coiled turds.

"Hey, Tyrone?"

"Yup?"

"Do you actually *know* this place has a portable generator, or is that just a guess?"

"Don't worry, George, I'm sure. Sometimes I'd sneak into the caretaker's place in the cellar during break-time. There were two or three of the things – although one of them was always in separate pieces being oiled or something."

"What were you doing in there," Georgie grinned, "having a sneaky smoke?"

"Just getting out of the way, avoiding the hassle."

Georgie watched him walking, the top of his head nearly brushing against the neon strip-lights on the ceiling. It was hard to imagine Tyrone ever getting any 'hassle'.

Those concerns were things of the past. School was just something else that had somehow faded, something which had gone from being the biggest part of the week to being an irrelevance in their new lives. They were aliens in this place of narrow, pastel-coloured walls, assemblies and 60 minute lunch breaks. Georgie began to smile again at the relics of eager GCSE Art projects when she stopped dead.

There was a boy standing at the end of the corridor.

The kid just held there, frozen, staring at them. He was about twenty paces away, but she could see that he was skinny, his head - with its matted red hair - looking too big for his scrawny neck. He had an odd expression on his face – sort of twisted, like he was in pain – and it took a moment before Georgie realised it was a look of horror.

In that instant the boy was off and round the corner, his bare feet squeaking on the lino floor. Tyrone was after him almost at once - no fear, no hesitation – and Georgie felt a sort of fierce gratitude that they were together.

Tyrone had always been one of the best runners in his year, but this kid was really moving: he flew around yet another corner, thin arms flailing, and scampered down a staircase towards the ground floor. Tyrone followed, taking the stairs two at a time, almost tumbling and tripping in his haste, but when he reached the lower level the boy had already vanished.

The hallway was long and windowless and Tyrone paused and listened for a moment, trying to still his own noisy breathing.

There it was.

The slap of the boy's feet on the smooth floor echoed in the distance and Tyrone was moving again. His eyes began to acclimatise and he got a better sense of the space ahead.

He spun round a corner just a second behind, the figure of the boy closer now - baggy clothes almost falling off him, his limbs loose and jerky.

A fire exit stood at the end of the corridor, the boy crashed through it, tumbling out into the playground beyond with Tyrone just a second behind him. He was visibly slowing now, his steps looking ragged and painful, and Tyrone was only a metre away when they finally came to a dead-end, nothing left but the concrete frame of an old bike-shed blocking their path.

Tyrone could see the boy's fear as he frantically looked for a way over, his nails scrabbling at the rough surface as he tried to gain purchase. He turned, his panicked eyes fixed on Tyrone's every movement. Tyrone stepped forward and the boy's face just... broke.

That was how it looked to Tyrone. That hunted, desperate look, with all of its wild energy, suddenly collapsed. The boy's eyes seemed to lose focus, his face becoming limp, as though he'd been switched off. Slowly he slumped to the ground, shrinking back into the darkened corner.

Tyrone tried to look less tall, to make his smile extra friendly, to duck his head down a little so he seemed less threatening.

Just like before. Just like he used to do.

"It's alright," he whispered, "I'm not going to hurt you." Carefully, almost crouched down, Tyrone shuffled a little nearer.

One of the boy's eyes was bloodshot and crusty. His breath was sour and a thick odour like rotting vegetables hung about him.

"I'm sorry," he whispered.

"Sorry?" Tyrone tried to keep his voice as calm and gentle as possible, "It's OK – you ran, no harm done."

"I didn't want to. I'm sorry about them all."

"Who?"

The boy seemed to shrink, hugging his arms around himself, "Everyone. I killed everyone."

"You didn't… it wasn't you. They just got sick."

The boy frowned in concentration as though seeing something. "They coughed it out of me in a big stream. It just went everywhere."

Tyrone had assumed he was much younger since he was so thin, but he could see now the boy was closer to his own age. His clothes were dirty and far too thin for this freezing weather, he clutched an old backpack in front of himself as though it were a shield. What the hell had he been through?

"It was a disease; just one of those things."

Suddenly the boy turned to him, looking Tyrone in the eye for the first time, and asked abruptly, "Am I dead?"

"What? No… no, we're OK."

Tyrone felt Georgie walk up and crouch quietly just behind him. He was worried for a moment that he would take off again, but the boy seemed to be far away.

"This place is full of ghosts," the boy murmured, "I see them sometimes - out of the corner of my eye. White and shimmery-shiny. They hide round corners. They want to drag me back down to Hell."

Tyrone reached for the boy's arm and saw that it was

scored by four or five long, festering scratches, writing beneath them. He'd probably done it to himself, but for the briefest of moments Tyrone found himself wondering...

Georgie stirred behind him. "How long have you been living in the school?" she asked gently. But the boy didn't seem to know she was there.

"It started watching me. The city. All the time. Even when I was sleeping. Always looking at me and spying."

Tyrone suddenly felt sad – sad and embarrassed. Embarrassed for the boy, embarrassed to be there, standing over him as he sat on the floor of the playground looking so repulsive and so frightened. Where would he have been – or Georgie or any of the others for that matter – if they had been on their own all this time? How much harder would they have found this new world if the nights and the mealtimes and the decisions had all been faced alone?

He smiled at the boy. "Just wait here for a minute, OK? It's going to be alright."

Tyrone took Georgie's arm and walked with her until they were around the corner and out of earshot.

She spoke before he did, "Has he been here all this time? We just assumed..."

"I know," he replied in a half-whisper, "There's no way we could've known. Look, we have to help. We can't leave him knocking around this school on his own."

"I know," said Georgie, "I wonder..."

But she was interrupted by a thump and the sound of scraping. The two of them looked at one another and driven by the same unspoken fear raced back towards the bike-shed.

His backpack, battered and dirty, lay abandoned on the ground.

But the boy had disappeared.

CHAPTER 11.

Georgie and Tyrone's encounter with the red-haired boy disturbed the group. Old questions resurfaced: were they alone? Should they be looking for more survivors? William said bluntly that one crazy kid who ran off wasn't a reason to get excited. But he had disappeared, not run away. It was hard to explain to the others. There was something in the way he'd vanished that made Georgie uneasy. It was so sudden. And the writing on his arm had been facing outward, the wrong way. He couldn't have written it himself, could he?

There was something in what he'd said that made her uneasy too. *The ghosts. The city watching.* She knew that feeling. She'd felt it that day she was alone and the camera moved. Had it though? Or was that what happened when you spent too much time on your own thinking? You started to feel the city's ghosts watching you. God knows there ought to be enough of them. Then she remembered the boy's eyes; looking into them had been like looking down from a cliff-edge. It made her dizzy and she had to step away. The others were a little surprised when it was Georgie who suggested they leave food and a note for the red-haired boy and then stop looking.

After that the group gradually drifted back to their regular routine. They would generally lie about in their hammocks, camp beds and nests, until one by one they woke up and joined the usual morning conversation. Cocooned in the warmth of their covers they would chat about anything and everything until their bellies convinced them that they would have to get up.

* * * * *

That terrible and destructive day, that day that was to be the beginning of the end of so many things, had started out like any other, any other since the end of the world anyway. On that particular morning the urging rumble of stomachs had begun much earlier than normal, as someone had raised the topic of what food they missed most. William had talked about his mum's corned beef pie; salty and gooey and served with ladles of sticky baked beans. Sarah had reminisced about a very posh French meal that her father and stepmum had taken her to in Kensington. After a great deal of *umming* and *ahhing* - through which he would not be rushed as this was a sacred and serious matter - Donnie had been stuck between the skin of fish fingers drenched in malt vinegar (just the skins mind, he had been quite fierce about that) and a trusty Big Mac. Joanna had piped up with a very definitive *Wagon Wheels* and then settled back happily to listen to the others.

Farran extolled the virtues of PFC chicken and the feasts they had there every Eid. Tyrone argued that nothing beat his gran's spag bol. *Still*, thought Georgie, *nice to see them agree on something for a change.* Then she had tried to get people excited about the idea of dim sum but no one had even heard of it, so she was left to her own saliva-steeped memories. She thought of her family's favourite restaurant in Soho where trolley after trolley carried steaming bamboo baskets of little Chinese delicacies. Her favourite pork dumplings that she would dip in a little bowl of gingery vinegar until the juicy meat filling had absorbed the-

"Biscuits!" said a heavy voice from far away.

"What?" demanded Georgie, trying to hold on to her carefully crafted vision. But it was no good, it was gone and all that food would just get cold and go to waste somewhere in her imagination.

"What?" she said again, annoyed.

"Biscuits," repeated William. "When we were on the school trip, we were somewhere near Monument or something; our teacher went in this posh bakers while we all had to wait outside in the cold; anyway, when he came out he had these great little biscuit things in lots of different colours – green and red and, and yellow and a kind of purpley colour or a sort of blue…"

"We get it, man," interrupted Farran, "there were lots of colours."

"Well these biscuits - biscuity things – 'cos they weren't like normal biscuits…well they were the best biscuit…y things I ever had." He looked around the room with a happy, expectant face, a little like a toddler who has used his potty and is showing his mum how clever he's been.

The room descended into a confused hush. Tyrone wanted to say something so that William wouldn't feel offended but no - no, he had absolutely no idea where William was going with this or what it was he wanted them to say now.

William's face clouded. "God you guys are thick sometimes. We could go and get some."

There were a few noises of vague agreement, with lots of *great ideas* and *of courses* and the like, then it died down again.

William spoke slowly this time, humouring the dummies, "All of your things, yeah, we can't have, but mine, yeah, we could go and get. My biscuits may be out there!"

"You want us tey go half-way across London for some biscuits?" asked Donnie.

William's eyes widened encouragingly, with an equally encouraging grin stretching his wide, freckled face.

"Oh," said Donnie, "Okay."

And that was that.

They decided to load up the minivan, siphon off some petrol from the tank of the next nearest car - they had worked their way up about five hundred meters of parked cars already – and then set off to find William's mythical comestibles. As Donnie pointed out with a happy laugh, what else did they have to do?

* * * * *

It had been an unusually dry February; the whole month they had gone to bed with crisp clear skies, stars shining through the museum's skylights, and woken to bright mornings, the sun just starting to burn the hoar frost from the glass. Today was different though, today the sky glowered grey and brooding and a strong wind from the southeast chopped the river into angry swells. The survivors were finding it difficult to stay upright as they staggered along the Thames Footpath. They had ditched the car down by Blackfriars because of an overturned bus and headed out on foot, a decision that they were all now beginning to regret. All except Donnie that is, who, seemingly impervious to the cold, had unzipped his jacket and was seeing how far into the wind he could lean before falling flat on his face. Unusually, William had taken the lead and kept looking up the narrow side streets with an air of authority, secretly hoping that he would remember which of them led to the bakery.

At last they came to a point where the footpath was interrupted and they had to ascend a little flight of stone steps to street level. Here the waterfront buildings parted to reveal an imposing vista; a series of wide, shiny black terraces, at the summit of which a distant, impressively white building sat like an enormous heap of rock-hard meringue.

"It's near that," shouted William, straining to make himself heard over the gale.

"You might have mentioned that earlier," complained Sarah. "I'm practically frozen to the core. I mean it's fairly memorable as landmarks go, it *is* Saint Paul's Cathedral."

"Well, I've remembered now, haven't I?"

They staggered up the steps - pushed and prodded all the way by the wind at their backs - until they entered the sanctuary of Paternoster Square, whereupon the wind suddenly died away, leaving their ears ringing and their cheeks boiling. The group found themselves enclosed by arcades of tranquil white stone at the centre of which stood the bronze statue of a shepherd, crook in hand, calmly leading his flock. The ground floors of the buildings were devoted to shops and above them empty offices could be seen through tall tinted windows. Two alleys gave access to the square – the arched passageway they had just entered and a second, narrower lane on the opposite side. To the left of this an office block rose twenty stories, the flags that topped it whipping about wildly in the blustery weather.

Down at ground level their footsteps echoed in the oasis of hush.

"That's it, that's the one," shouted William

In front of the dishevelled group was the most impressive bakery any of them had ever seen. A large sign reading 'Farriner's' in ornate writing jutted out from the wall, and beneath it was a shop front crammed full of glistening confectionary.

They ran up to the glass only to see that the rows of sticky buns, chocolate-studded twists and colourful fruit pastries now sported thick beards of mould. Here and there hints of their former deliciousness poked through, tantalising the group, but the fur covered almost everything. In places the goodies had started to dissolve and drip from their glass platters; the mould, blue-green, had dripped with them, creating sickly - and entirely inedible - puddles of decay. Their disappointment was palpable.

Tyrone, always supportive, looked at the others. "Well, what were you expecting? We knew all the fresh stuff would be bad but biscuits are different, they last for ages. Go on, mate."

With that, William gave the front door a well-practised kick, and it burst open.

The inside of the shop was fuggy and foul-smelling and completely devoid of anything worth eating - not a cake, not a macaroon, not a Danish pastry. Losing interest, most of the group gradually drifted off to explore the rest of the square, but William stayed behind, doggedly searching for his biscuits. He ransacked the front of the shop, rummaging along the shelves and delving into boxes tucked beneath the counter, until at last, all possibilities exhausted, he headed to the kitchen.

The kitchen was even darker than the front. William had to explore the kitchen almost by touch alone – his hands brushed over the reassuringly smooth curves of jars, poked soft sacks of flour, and then touched the coldness of metal. Chubby fingers examined the object's surface until they came to what felt like a plastic knob. He turned it and heard the unmistakeable hiss of gas escaping. *They must have a working oven!* Reaching into his bulging pockets, he eventually found his favourite lighter – the one with a Hawaiian dancer whose coconut bikini disappeared when you turned it upside down. He clicked it and, *whoomp*, a ball of blue flame flashed into life, almost taking off his eyebrows before dying down to a gentle height.

Right, William thought, *if I can't find any biscuits I'll just have to make my own*. And by the light of the hob's flame he set about assembling what he imagined were the ingredients of a biscuit.

Roughly an hour and a half later he staggered back into the square to be met by Donnie laughing and pointing out that he looked like he'd just had a fight with a mixing bowl. This was a particularly apt description as William *had* just had a fight with a mixing bowl. It was difficult to say who had won - admittedly the bowl now lay in three jagged pieces against the kitchen wall - but during the struggle it had outwitted the boy and, in a last-ditch attempt to teach the ill-tempered cook a lesson, had succeeded in disgorging its entire contents all over his face and shoulders. William now looked like a cross between a ghost and a swamp creature - thick clumps of eggy mixture stuck to his curly ginger hair, flour was plastered across his ruddy face and what Donnie hoped was a chocolate chip, clung tenaciously to one of William's singed eyebrows. William didn't care because clasped in a pair of oven gloves of dubious hygiene, was a tray of smouldering biscuits.

The group sat themselves down at a collection of metal tables and chairs and tucked into the fruits of William's hard-fought labours. The biscuits, though a little burnt on the top and a little raw in the middle, were by general consensus delicious. Huddled up against the winter chill they munched away happily and listened to the gale raging outside the square.

"It's not bad this," said Tyrone.

"Aye," said Donnie, "You'll mek someone a good little wife one day, William."

"Shut up." But William was too pleased with himself to be convincingly annoyed.

They went back to eating.

After a moment, Georgie took a thoughtful breath and, while examining her biscuit, asked, "Do any of you guys ever wonder why we're alive?"

"Buggerin' 'ell," huffed William, "I knew it was too good to be true. Sitting here eating a nice biccie and you have to go and get all thinky."

"I believe that God put us here," said Sarah.

"Random. All of it's random," countered Tyrone.

"Ah think we're the universe tryin' tah work itsel' out," said Donnie.

"Isn't that from Star Trek?" asked Tyrone.

"Babylon Five," confirmed Donnie.

"My nan said it was the stork what brung us," added Joanna.

Sarah rolled her eyes and groaned.

"Oh, that kind of 'why are we alive'. Georgie, Ah'm surprised at you," said Donnie. "Well, when a mummy an' a daddy love each other very much they have a special kind of cuddle…"

"No, no, oh for God's sake," shouted Georgie exasperated, "I mean why are *we* alive when no one else is."

"Oh," said Donnie "that's a bit gloomy for teatime." And they all sunk into a heavy silence.

After a moment Georgie started again, "It's just that me and Farran…" Everyone groaned together now. "Me and Farran," she persisted, "were chatting – and we were thinking, why us? Has no one ever thought it's a bit weird that we're all exactly the same age? More or less anyway."

"That *is* weird," said Donnie, thoughtfully, "you and Farran were chattin'? Is there something you want to tell us? Should we be expecting wedding bells? Or the repopulation of the human race?"

"Maybe we've all got the same whatsits… genes or somethin'," said William.

"That's funny," said Tyrone "'cos actually I was just think ing we could be brothers."

Everyone laughed.

"Yeah, yeah, very funny," grumbled William.

"Seriously though?" said Georgie.

"Who cares? Maybe we got superpowers. Maybe it's 'cos we all eat our five a day. Whatever, what does it matter now?" replied Farran.

"Jeez, I just thought it was worth asking." *Screw it, she'd embarrass him.* "You seemed interested enough the other day." And she took a bite out of her third biscuit.

Farran reddened slightly and looked away.

"Hey?" asked Tyrone suddenly in an excited tone, "Did that place still have electricity?"

"No, gas cooker with bottles," replied William spraying crumbs liberally as he spoke. "Why?"

"Well, how come you left the lights on?"

"I didn't, I cooked in the dark."

"Oh, that explains it," mumbled Georgie, spitting a quarter ounce weight out of her mouth and into her hand.

"No, you left some lights on," Tyrone persisted.

William looked behind him, and sure enough, there did seem to be lights on in the bakery. Maybe they were on the fritz though because the bulbs seemed to flicker; or maybe more like candles or firelight. Yes, that was it, it was more like the warm flickering of firelight.

"Bloody hell," yelled Tyrone, "the place is on fire!"

As the group looked, bright flames danced rapidly across the shelves at the back of the shop, spreading out from the kitchen as thick smoke seeped out from under the front door and slithered into the street.

There was a moment's hesitation among the group before they burst into panicked indecision.

Tyrone let out an ear-splitting whistle. "Right!" he shouted, standing to his full height and impressively calm, "this is serious, we have to get organised and get this under control. We need a source of water, we need buckets, tubs - cups if you have to - anything that we can use to put this fire out. Split up - search the shops and houses. Go, go, go!"

They ran off at top speed in all directions, combing the area for anything they could use, but the neighbourhood was almost all offices, pickings were thin and every building had to be broken into separately. It was a good twenty minutes before they returned to the bakery with a motley collection of waste paper baskets and washing up bowls. Tyrone had broken into a small café to find a tap and they began filling their containers one by one, scurrying back and forth to the fire.

The tap was slow and they got in one another's way as they tried to squeeze past each other. When they did get to the fire the small amount of water they threw just seemed to evaporate into nothing.

Back and forth they ran, increasingly frantic.

Dashing from the fire Tyrone collided with Farran who was carrying a precarious basin of water, the contents spilling pointlessly onto the ground.

"Your plan is shit, it ain't workin' at all," yelled Farran, squaring up to the taller boy.

"I haven't got time for this, Farran."

"We need another tap or somthin'."

"We all need to stay here and work together." He tried to move past but Farran moved with him. Tyrone really didn't want this.

"Who the hell put you in charge anyway?"

Tyrone shouted over his head, "George, George, we need to organise a human chain. Get the buckets moving." Up at the café, Georgie nodded and started marshalling everyone into a line.

"Don't ignore me, right? That ain't gunna cut it, man - that tap'll just run out."

Tyrone again tried to get past him, concentrating on the task in hand. Finally, without thinking, he pushed Farran to one side. Farran stumbled backwards, tripped and landed on his backside in an undignified sprawl. Realising what he'd done, Tyrone turned back to apologise but Farran glared daggers at him from the ground.

"Sorry, man, but you were in my way. We need to…Farran, *Farran!*"

Farran had picked himself up and run off towards the

narrow lane that led from the square.

Tyrone's regret quickly turned to anger – "Farran! Where the hell are you going, we need everyone here, *now!*"

But he had disappeared around the corner.

* * * * *

Bucket after bucket they poured on the flames, passing the heavy containers down the line and the empties back up again until their shoulders ached - but still the fire grew. Now it billowed out of the bakery door and Tyrone at the end of the human chain was drenched in sweat from the heat radiating out into the afternoon air.

With a final, wheezing splutter, the tap coughed out its last trickle of water and died.

At that moment, Farran reappeared dragging four huge CO_2 fire extinguishers behind him. He let three of them drop with a clang at Tyrone's feet, forcing him to jump backwards, then rushed towards the fire, lugging the fourth. Bent low under the intensity of the fire, he pulled the pin out and unleashed a huge cloud of white gas at the base of the blaze. He squeezed the trigger until the canister ran dry and then returned for a second and a third, each time inching his way forward as the flames retreated under the onslaught.

By the fourth canister Farran was right up to the door of the bakery, firing into the heart of the blaze. He turned round to the others, jubilant.

"You see," he bellowed, all the time his eyes on Tyrone, "a little more you listen, a little longer you live! Come on, we've got it licked now."

He was raising his arms in a triumphant salute when the upstairs windows of the bakery exploded outwards, covering him in a spray of glass.

Farran was sent reeling back towards the group, shedding debris as he went.

Donnie caught his arm, steadying him. "Are y'alright, pal?"

"I, I think so." Farran was shaking, flecks of glass studded the right side of his face.

They all gawped at the building. Great tongues of flame now licked out of the top casements and crept up the front of the bakery, higher and higher towards the roof. In no time at all the tips of the flames had reached above the shelter of the square, and then something terrifying happened: the raging wind above caught them up and sent them dancing across the rooftops of the next three houses. In a flash the fire caught hold of these too. A chain reaction began that set the blaze moving inexorably beyond the confines of the bakery and around the whole stretch of shops north of the square.

"We have to try again," shouted Tyrone. "We can't stop now."

Joanna looked round, it was only then that she noticed smoke pouring from one of the buildings behind them. How did that happen? No buildings on fire either side, just this one, smouldering alone. Then the fire burst forth, young and ferocious as the windows shattered onto the cobbles. None of the others had noticed, too focused on the problem directly in front of them.

Tyrone began to run with their last buckets of water, manic - cajoling the others, insulting them, whatever it took. It was already too hot again to get near enough to the bakery door – the water just made an ineffectual splash on the ground.

"It's burnin' behind us too," called Joanna, breaking the spell.

For the first time since the fire began, Georgie took a moment to look about her. To her horror, not only were the shops behind them aflame but the west side of the square was burning now.

Smoke was starting to fill the air, stinging their eyes and

filling their mouths with a dry chemical taste that caught at the back of their throats. Some of the buildings to the west were already looking ready to collapse. This was getting out of control.

"Guys, GUYS, this is no good. There's nothing we can do, we're just putting ourselves in danger. We need to get out of here now before the whole place goes up."

"Shit, Will, what the hell did you do?" yelled Farran, rounding on the bewildered boy.

"Me? What are you talking about?"

Farran pushed his soot-smeared face right up against William's. "You, you tubby bitch. You almost got me killed." He thrust his glass-studded cheek towards him as proof. "You drag us here to make some stupid cookies an' end up burnin' the whole place down. How the hell are we supposed to put all this out?"

"I didn't do this."

"Yeah you did, you ginger fool. You went and left the oven on or somethin', didn't ya?"

"No," squealed William, his face draining to a sickly white so that his freckles stood out like raisins in custard. "I, I didn't do this."

"Man, I ought to beat you." Farran raised his fist threateningly. William tried to back away, but Farran stayed uncomfortably close.

"I didn't do it. I didn't do it," he bleated, having to shout to make himself heard above the roar of the fire.

"Alright Farran, that's enough." Tyrone stepped towards the pair.

"Mind your own damned business." Farran was now so close that his chest was puffed up right against William's.

William tried to peer round his persecutor in an appeal for help. "Tyrone, it wasn't me. I didn't do it. I turned everything off when I finished. It, it was dark in the kitchen when I left. How could it be dark if I hadn't turned everything off?

I didn't do it."

Farran felt Tyrone's firm hand on his shoulder. "That's enough, now is *not* the time."

Farran batted the hand away, pushed William back by his face, and then rounded on Tyrone, the full force of his anger, frustration and fear suddenly focused in a new direction.

"Get your black hand off me. Don't you ever touch me!"

Thrown by Farran's violence, Tyrone stepped back with appeasing words, "Alright mate, we haven't got time for this, we need to put this fire out." But his words seemed to have the opposite effect.

"Don't *mate* me, I ain't your mate an' I ain't your pal. Don't you ever put your hand on me…"

"I'm not even touching you–"

"…Don't touch me an' don't talk to me. I'm sick of people tellin' me what to do. You wanna get into to this? You wanna get into this, I'll shiv you, man."

"You'll *shiv* me? Where the hell d'you think we are, man? You're ridiculous." Tyrone spat the last with complete contempt and turned back towards the others.

This was too much for Farran. He grabbed the other boy's shoulder, spinning him round off balance, and hit him hard in the mouth. But he didn't stop there.

Farran was no stranger to grubby street brawls, gang fights on the estates of Mile End, even muggings; he'd learnt the hard way that if you started a fight in real life you hit first and you kept on hitting.

He grabbed hold of Tyrone's jacket with his left hand, keeping him off balance, and flailed a vicious salvo of blows. He punched Tyrone's chest, his stomach, his neck. Hitting till his knuckles hurt. Tired at last, he lost his grip and Tyrone was able to totter back, sinking to his knees.

Farran stood panting.

The others stared in shocked disbelief.

The fire blazed.

Donnie ran over to the dazed Tyrone. "What the hell's the matter with you, Farran?"

Georgie followed swiftly after, "Are you some kind of animal? All he's done is try and help us." She knelt down next to Tyrone and tried to wipe the blood off his face.

Farran glowered at the others; he tried to say something but couldn't. All of their faces were set hard against him. He spat onto the ground and then ran through the arched passage and out of Paternoster Square.

For a moment they listened to the sound of the burning all around them. From somewhere, deep in one of the buildings, came a muffled blast. A wave of smoke crashed outwards, half blinding them.

"It's spreading. Let's get out of here!" shouted Georgie.

They peered through the haze, looked about them at the wild, uncontrollable thing that had been unleashed and they didn't need any more convincing. They ran like hell.

* * * * *

In the confusion, no one had noticed that Tyrone had stayed behind; Donnie's supporting hand had drifted away in the rush to escape and now he was alone.

There has to be something I can do. He touched his bruised neck gingerly – Farran could wait. If they didn't stop the fire here who knew how far it would spread? *I have to try something, we've lost too much already.* He shuddered, thinking how quickly that little fire had grown in just the space of a few minutes. Scratching at his chin, he racked his brains for some way to put it out. He stood, a centre of silent concentration amid a circle of destruction.

Tyrone span.

"Hello, is anyone there?"

It was hard to be sure over the bellowing of the fire, but he thought he had heard a movement in the narrow lane. Maybe someone had come back looking for him.

"Farran? Is that you?"

Nothing but the sound of burning.

He tried to peer through the thickening gloom. The buildings on the north side of the square were now completely ablaze, the last shop on the row spewing smoke, the lane beside it just a lighter patch in the swirls of black and grey.

A great cracking sound came from Tyrone's right, he looked around him - there were now walls of flame on three sides. This was impossible, he could never put it out now. The smoke started to overwhelm him, he began to cough uncontrollably and suddenly felt very frightened and very vulnerable.

What the hell was I thinking? I have to get to the others. We'll have to find some way to put it out, he thought, and was turning to find the rest of the group when again a movement caught his eye, again from the smoke-filled lane.

"Hello? Who *is* that? Farran stop mucking about, we need to get the hell out of here…Farran?"

Something shifted, a shadow darkened, somewhere deep in the drifts an indistinct shape seemed to congeal and then it was gone again. A ghost in the smoke.

But it had definitely been there.

Tyrone edged towards it, pushing forwards against the wall of heat, sweat pearled on his brow. It was almost too hot to bear now. How could anything living be moving about in there? He was forced to retreat, arms raised to shield his face.

There it was again. Not a trick of the light; a human form, a human movement - an arm perhaps, perhaps a head – a man's, but huge, deformed somehow.

Gone.

Tyrone tried again to move forward, blinking the soot from his eyes. What *was* it?

He heard a clink, like the clinking of glass, from deep within the turmoil of smoke.

He saw the dark blur of an arm in motion.

Something flew out of the haze, small and solid - in the confusion he couldn't be sure what. It soared over his head. Tyrone just had time to glance back at the alley before he felt a searing heat char his back as the building behind him exploded.

*   *   *   *   *

At last Georgie slowed to a jog. The others were just ahead, panting. They were safe. Wait, this wasn't all of them – Donnie, Sarah, William, Joanna. What happened to-

"Guys, where are the others? Where are Tyrone and Farran?"

"What do you mean?" said Sarah. "Tyrone was right behind us." She slumped heavily onto the kerb, relieved to be out of sight of the fire.

"And ah'm sure Fran was only a couple a yards in front."

"Well they're not now. William, did you see them leave?"

William just shook his head very slowly, avoiding her eye.

"William, answer me."

"No," he replied in a strange, strangled voice. Georgie could see that he was close to tears.

"Joanna?"

"Thought they was with us."

*   *   *   *   *

Tyrone pushed himself up onto his forearms. A long graze ran along his jaw and his back hurt like hell - but he was alive. He tried to get to his knees but the skin on his back felt frighteningly stiff and the pain made him light-headed.

With a great effort he managed to sit. Tyrone looked at the strange world around him - the entire square was blazing; the tops of enormous flames jutted above the roofs of the buildings, curling up to form a terrifying crown and almost completely obscuring the sky.

Crawling beneath the smoke, he searched desperately for a way out. The arched passage the others had taken was now burning too, but he thought he might get through. It was his only option. He prepared to run.

Suddenly a pair of powerful hands slipped around his mouth from behind and he was jerked off his feet. *What was happening?* He was being dragged backwards. He tried to twist round to see what was going on. *Was someone trying to help him? Why were they being so rough?* He couldn't turn far enough to see. Frantically he tried to free his head. The hand over his mouth, rubbery and smelly, flexed briefly and then the thumb and forefinger clamped over his nose. He couldn't breathe. In a panic he realised they weren't trying to help him at all, they were trying to kill him.

Gasping desperately through the gloved hand, his lungs pulled vainly against themselves. Tyrone clawed at the arm, but he was already weak. He reached out a hand, grasping for the statue at his side. The bronze shepherd looked down at him impassively. Tyrone's feet scrabbled on the cobbles. If he could only reach it...

As the world started to fade away at the edges of his vision, the last thing Tyrone was aware of was another almighty explosion somewhere nearby, but a strange calm had overcome him and it didn't really seem to matter anymore.

His body relaxed, and then, nothingness.

CHAPTER 12.

On Ludgate Hill Road, Georgie heard the explosion. She stood next to St Paul's looking into Paternoster Square, daunted by what she saw: above the western side of the quadrangle a mushroom cloud now bubbled and churned, and the covered passage looked like the mouth of an inferno. She couldn't believe that anyone could still be alive in there, but she had to be sure.

Looking around, Georgie spied some bags that they'd dropped as they'd fled. Running over to one of Sarah's she pulled out a pashmina then soaked it in a puddle. She took a deep breath, wrapped the wet material around her, careful to cover her hair, and ran headlong into the fire.

The fire was actually just a thin curtain of flame across the mouth of the alley. Beyond it the centre of the square, though thick with smoke and hot as hell, was still clear. She scanned the oven-like space for any signs of the other two. Nothing. The eastern and northern sides of the square were solid walls of fire. The western arcade was beginning to burn in earnest now too, and the furthest end was obscured by one of the buildings that had collapsed completely.

Steam rose from the damp pashmina and Georgie began to cough as the smoke rasped at her lungs. She was starting to think it was hopeless when, through a drift in the smog, she spied a crumpled form.

Vaulting over the rubble she made it to the body.

"Farran, Farran wake up!" Crouching, she propped him up against her leg. The boy opened his eyes groggily, finally fixing them on Georgie's face.

"Farran, where's Tyrone? What happened?" The boy continued to stare at her, blood trickled down his face from a cut in his hairline. A horrible thought began to grow in her and she took her hands away. In a frightened voice she asked, "Farran, what did you do?"

Farran's reply was quiet and hoarse, Georgie had to put her ear next to his mouth just to hear.

"I came back for him," he whispered

Again Farran's eyes seemed to dull and they began to close. Georgie shook him hard. "Farran, did you hurt him? Where is he?"

His eyes snapped open and he looked around, frightened, as though only now realising where he was, but his voice remained distant. "He was here. I saw 'im through the smoke. There was a struggle, then there was a loud noise, I think the buildin' collapsed, then…"

His head lolled on his shoulders. Georgie slapped him. The heavy lids opened again. "Stay awake. Where is Tyrone? Is he…was he crushed by the building?"

"No, he was standin' by the shepherd. It couldn't 'ave. The ghost had him…shouldn't have struggled…" With that he slipped away into unconsciousness.

Georgie looked over to the statue which gleamed fiercely in the light of the fire. There was nobody there; apart from Farran and the impassive shepherd, she was alone.

"TYRONE!" she screamed, but her voice turned to ashes on the hot wind.

What Farran had said made no sense, but Tyrone wasn't here; that much she was sure of. Perhaps he'd found some other way to get to safety. She had to believe that.

Grabbing Farran under the arms she began to haul him towards the passage. She struggled with the dead weight, his legs dragging along the rough ground.

The curtain of flame flickered hungrily. She took the pash-mina from about her and laid it across Farran's prone body like a shroud. It was nearly dry but she hoped it would afford him some protection. The fire was terrifyingly close now, she felt it all about her. She was bathed in it. It licked and pawed painfully at her hair and clothes. She steeled herself and then dragged Farran backwards as quickly as she could, the pair of them disappearing into the inferno.

CHAPTER 13.

Georgie had cleaned up Farran's face as best she could, pulling out the pieces of glass and bandaging his face with torn strips of clothing. She doused herself and Farran with water. Her hair was singed and part of the leg of Farran's trousers smouldered in a patch of melted fabric.

Throughout the whole process neither had said a word. The others found them propped up against a phone box looking blackened and despondent. They greeted them with shouts, glad to see that Farran was alive. Georgie though, was devastated to find that Tyrone wasn't with them.

The atmosphere suddenly became awkward when the group drew close. No one quite knew how to behave towards Farran. After a moment Sarah asked, "Where's Tyrone? Is he getting supplies or something?"

Georgie said nothing but tears drew white lines down her dirty cheeks. The others recoiled as though she had told them everything.

The pestering wind tugged at their clothing.

At last Donnie spoke, "Did ya see him? Did ya see him die?"

Georgie couldn't answer.

"He's not dead. He's missin'," said Farran in a cracked voice.

Georgie turned to stare at him.

Donnie looked from one to the other, trying to work out

what had happened and what this strange tension between them was.

Farran continued, "I came back for 'im. He was in the square when I got back; I called, but he didn't hear me. Then there was this explosion... threw me to the ground, him as well. I was pretty well out of it from then on...I don't really remember what happened next...I remember seein' him move...he was still alive...then I think I blacked out...there was another explosion..."

"You seemed to remember more than that before," spat Georgie through gritted teeth.

Farran looked blankly at her, so confused that Georgie began to doubt herself.

"So you didn't actually see him die?" asked Sarah

"No," admitted Georgie. "I couldn't see him anywhere in the square when I came back, only Farran."

"So he coulda got out," suggested Donnie.

Georgie shrugged.

"He was alive last time I saw 'im, that's all I know," said Farran.

"Maybe he's on his way back to the museum already. He'll probably be waiting for us when we get back," said William smiling.

"Well, ah don't think it's a good idea to hang around here much longer. D'you think ya can stand, Fran?" Donnie looked east towards where he should have seen the bulk of St Paul's, but only the dome now showed above a pall of smoke. "It seems to be spreadin' toward us."

"If we head up the road a bit and then keep heading west we should eventually get back to where we parked the car." Georgie heaved herself up onto her feet.

"If y' say so. This is your town," said Donnie, extending a hand to Farran and hauling him upright.

"What are we going to do about the fire?" called out Sarah, following the others.

"Yeah, what we gonna do 'bout the fire?" echoed Joanna.

William shrugged, "Leave it alone; it'll probably just burn itself out. We shouldn't have tried to put it out in the first place. We should go back home, get ourselves some food, meet up with Tyrone, but let's just go - I'm starving."

"I think William's right," said Georgie

"Do ya?"

"Yeah, whatever happened to him he got out of the square. We'll never find him now. Our only option is to go back," she said angrily.

They carried on up the road, shuffling as quickly as they were able.

"We turn right here…" Georgie stopped, Ave Maria Lane was full of thick black smoke. "Let's try the next one."

They continued up Ludgate Hill, a little faster now. Reaching Old Bailey Street they were shocked to see that this too was full of rolling black clouds.

It had spread so far.

Georgie and the others broke into a trot.

"How's it moving so fast?" There was real fear in her voice now.

"It must have been spreading outside the square the whole time we were fighting the fire, only we didn't notice," said Sarah.

"How far's it gone?" shouted Donnie from the back.

When they got to Farringdon Road they were relieved to see that it was clear and turned into it without slowing.

"I was beginning to get worried," sighed Sarah.

"Still, let's not hang about," called Georgie, returning to a light jog.

"Farran's no' so good, Georgie-girl, we need to slow down a bit."

"I'm OK, I can keep up."

Georgie hadn't even looked back.

Suddenly the group stopped dead in the street; each of

them felt that something was wrong. The hair prickled at the nape of their necks. Then the strange high-pitched sound became audible – a sing-song moaning that filled the air, growing so loud it set their teeth on edge and made their chests vibrate.

"What the hell?" mouthed Farran.

They stood rooted to the spot, searching for the cause of the sound. It was now so loud that all they could hear was a bristling hum; a tightness in their lungs, an itching in the bones of their ears.

Time seemed to move very slowly. A huge shadow travelled over them as though a cloud had passed across the setting sun. Then they saw it.

With a screaming of metal and concrete, a burning office block reared up over the tops of the buildings. Like a toppled domino the pillar of fire fell, crushing the smaller buildings beneath it and obliterating them completely. Down it went, beginning to split apart under its own weight, smashing to the pavement three hundred yards in front of them with the force of an earthquake and sending the group flying. Tonnes of fiery debris spewed forth, shooting across the road and into the buildings on the opposite side.

Great clouds of dust and ash expanded rapidly out from the crash covering everything. On the ground all they could do was cover their mouths and noses whilst the buildings exploded into torrents of flame.

The heat was overwhelming. They turned back the way they had come in time to see more buildings burst into flame, blocking their escape.

Before they know it they are running, they forget everything - they just run. They head into the tangle of dark passageways, courtyards and underpasses, the maze of tiny backstreets that make up the bowels of London. Away from the fire, they run.

There now begins a race that will be burnt into their memories: the smell of cinders hot in their nostrils; the feel of sweaty fear evaporating on their skin as soon as it is made; the sounds of destruction.

They run.

It seems that everywhere behind them is aflame. All of London. Like an army it fans out, marching inexorably after them. They bolt, panicked like forest animals, a fear that comes from somewhere deep within, primordial. Always at their backs is the roaring, sighing, crackling, exploding fire. They do not need to turn to check its progress, they can feel the heat, a constant presence – if they slow it grows and they know they must run faster.

They run onwards, onwards.

Blindly down alleys, up broad streets, always westwards with the wind. They turn into an alley but the fire is here before them. Have they taken a wrong turn? No. The fire leapfrogs now, spread by floating wisps of papery fire on the wind. Embers crackle into the sky and then rain down again, flakes of fire stinging their faces and singeing their clothes. It is a contagious thing, spreading incandescent, consuming everything it touches. They must head to the water, south to the Thames and safety.

They run for the river.

Every man for himself. Hearts beating in chests, lungs gasping in the smoke-fouled air.

They become separated.

For a time Farran runs alone. He turns a corner and is arrested by a terrible sight. He pauses despite himself.

An ancient church is on fire in front of him; flame pyramids out of the roof towards the stars. He is humbled by its power. He wonders at the majestic stained glass image of the Last Judgement, illuminated by the fire within. A ladder leads from Hell to Heaven, people scrabble up desperately from the pit, old trample on the young to save themselves, frantic violence, they clutch at salvation, civilisation overturned. The lead in the window begins to weep. Sagging inward, the scene animates, the reality of the image distorting as the solid stuff that holds it together disintegrates – glass shards that form faces, arms, hands, flow apart. At last it loses all cohesion, falling, dripping inwards to be replaced by that awesome truth behind the image; fire - simple and pure.

It is the most beautiful thing he has ever seen. And the most terrible.

He runs again.

All at once they are together again, running as a pack along the riverside. Feet clatter the pavement.

They stop to catch their breath and look back.

For a moment it seems that the Thames itself is burning. That the fire is so intense it has spread to the elements and now air and water burn too. But it is only the city's reflection in the river - a ribbon of orange and gold and white that snakes like a tendril of fire into what remains of the darkness, heralding what is to come.

Soot falls about the group like grey snow, with the same muffling effect. They look upriver, desperate for salvation.

"The tower," one of them cries, "head for the BT tower."

Dwarfing the buildings around it a pillar encrusted with satellite dishes stretches high into the sky, an isolated column that might provide a sanctuary even from the burning city.

They set off again, jagging right, away from the river, fearing that they are heading back into the mouth of the fire.

Suddenly there is an eerie silence. The wind drops, then for a moment, dies altogether.

The respite is brief. The wind begins to pick up again, blowing stronger and stronger but now towards the fire itself. It devours all the oxygen available, air rushes in to fill the vacuum, only serving to inflame it further.

The speed of the wind grows and grows, stirred up by the rising firestorm, until the children have to battle just to stay upright, the fire threatening to suck them into its terrible maw. The flotsam of London's empty streets whips past them, drawn inexorably in to feed the beast.

They fumble desperately at car handles until one yields. They pile in, safe for a moment. Farran works to start the car, all the time aware of the danger that fills the rearview mirror. The others watch him anxiously, urging him on. The wires spark together again and again but nothing happens. Then all at once the engine bursts into life and they speed off, the BT Tower guiding them like the North Star.

CHAPTER 14.

From the street the group stared up in hope at the huge sceptre jutting over six hundred feet into the blackened sky; a mosaic of green glass and grey concrete, the BT Tower swayed almost imperceptibly in the fearsome winds of the firestorm. Near its top an ugly collar of barnacle-like dishes and antennae replaced the windows and above that were balanced the three concentric rings of its viewing platforms.

"We need to get up top, we'll be safe there," shouted Georgie.

But entry to the tower was more difficult than they had imagined. Unable to find any way in other than the main revolving door, they were forced, exhausted and shaking, to smash their way through each successive pane of toughened glass in turn. They were rewarded for their perseverance though for, to their amazement, they discovered that the tower had electricity – another hangover from the building's place in national security.

They padded through the space-age lobby and took the lift up to the revolving restaurant on the tower's thirty-fourth floor, anxious to see the full extent of the fire. What they now saw so terrified them that they abandoned the shelter of the restaurant for the viewing platform above it. They feared what might happen if they left the fire unwatched, preferring the terrible reality to their imaginations and feeling that some-how they gained some small intangible amount of control.

Though in truth they knew that all they could do was pray.

The freezers were still on in the building so they were treated to the first proper food they had had in ages. There was enough in the kitchens to last them for a couple of weeks if necessary. They grabbed food and using tablecloths as blankets began their vigil in the cold night air.

* * * * *

The group looked out over the city from their eyrie. It seemed as though the whole of London was on fire. It moved westward now, so fast that pigeons were unable to outrun it; Icarus-like, their feathers bursting into flames, they dropped out of the hateful sky. It was like a biblical vision of Hell, as though their refuge was one of the towers of that citadel of damned souls; as though they were watching an infernal kingdom coming to life in those early days after the Devil's fall from Heaven, when he first set about to make his city, having only fire to build with. The streets were like veins of fire; the shapes of buildings were picked out in fire; pointed spires of fire rolled in billows, fluid, moving, alive. Clouds swirled black, grey, and purple, drifting across the skyline. One massive vault of flame spanned the city, one single inferno a mile long and growing unhindered.

"Wow, William. That's impressive," whispered Donnie in awestruck tones.

"I told you, it wasn't me."

"S'true," came a quiet voice from the gantry. They all turned to look at Joanna, her face suffused with a red glow from the burning city below. "Least, I don't see 'ow it could've been."

"What do you mean, JoJo?" asked Georgie.

The girl swallowed, "We was all fightin' the fire - in the

bakery, right? We was all together the whole time. But while you guys was runnin' about I looked behind us an' that clothes shop was on fire an' all. That's how come it spread so fast."

The group looked on, uncomprehending.

"It was all the way over the other side of the square. It coulda never caught from the bakery. It musta caught light separate."

"Are you saying that somebody set fire to the building, to the square, deliberately?" asked Sarah

Joanna shrugged. Their faces were gripped by fear and confusion.

"D'ya know, Joanna, that's the most I think I've ever heard y' say," said Donnie thoughtfully.

"Hang on, if we were all together and someone started the fire deliberately, then who?" asked William.

"That's the question, innit?" said Farran darkly.

* * * * *

The survivors now lived a strange existence - days and nights under the shadow of the fire. They spent their time curled up against the cold, buffeted by the relentless southwest wind, watching the progress of the fire and afraid it would consume everything in its unchecked hunger. Black clouds hung over the whole of London. Nature seemed to be reversed: the days were dark as night and when the sun did manage to break through it shone blood red and so faint you could look directly at it; at night the clouds were lit from within by a strange orange glow so that it was never really dark. Instead they lived in a perpetual half-light, the howl of the fire a constant background din.

"It reminds me of somethin' ma uncle made me learn," Donnie's voice came from a corner of the dusk-shrouded balcony. "He wasn't very big on readin' but he felt that wee kiddies ought to memorise stuff - said it would give me character, an' if he thought it would scare the crap outta me, so much the better." He began to recite-

"A dungeon horrible, on all sides round
As one great furnace flamed, yet from those flames
No light, but rather darkness visible
Served only to discover sights of woe."

"Gosh, well I'm ready to slit my wrists now. Thanks, Donnie," said Sarah.

"Is that from The Bible?" asked Farran, impressed.

"No, Milton, Paradise Lost."

In a quiet voice Farran replied, "It's awesome, man."

"Your uncle didn't like you much, did he?" observed William simply.

"No, not a lot. Still, thought ah would just share that with ya. You know, a trouble shared is a trouble doubled an' all that."

"Yeah, cheers."

* * * * *

Super-heated winds from the fire ignited anything flammable far ahead of the actual flames. The stench of ash and burning drifted up from below. Above, on the platform, lightless days and nights limped by.

* * * * *

It was sometime on the third or fourth day of the fire - Sarah couldn't be sure. It was so hard to tell when one day ended and the next began and she had lost her watch during their mad dash. It had been a beautiful blue one with a real diamond set in the centre – her father had given it to her last Christmas. She rubbed the white patch on her wrist now as she watched Donnie, who sat crosslegged against the railings, a look of pleased concentration spread across his elfin face. In his lap was a box of Jaffa Cakes, and he held one reverently in the palm of his hand. He proceeded, with meticulous care, to nibble away the thick chocolaty rim, leaving a ragged-edged circle. He then prized the remaining cake layer away from the rest of the biscuit and ate that. This done, he briefly inspected what remained for crumbs before bringing it up to his mouth, at which point he inserted his tongue between the thin chocolate shell and the fruity centre, lifting off the chocolate and leaving a perfectly clean bright orange disc. He popped it in his mouth, and began the process all over again. It was not until halfway through his third helping that he noticed Sarah watching him.

"What? D'you want a bit?" he said, sticking his tongue out. "You can have the orangey bit of this one if you like. I'm very good at sharing."

"Doesn't anything bother you?" asked Sarah.

"Eh?"

"Never mind." And Sarah went back to watching London burn.

* * * * *

The ferocity of the fire had abated, but still it spread, slowly consuming the abandoned city. Buildings below them flew apart or simply crumpled, giving way to gravity and slumping to the ground, their supports burnt away. From the comparative safety of their tower, they watched on, helpless. Georgie imagined Tyrone out there in that horrible chaos alone and she prayed that he was alright.

* * * * *

Farran looked at his Casio; it was gone midnight but sleep wouldn't come. How many days had they sat vigil now? Six? Seven? He looked over at Georgie, who sat heavy-eyed, her head lolling forward, her grubby hair blowing in whipping tangles over her face, though by now she was too exhausted to bother to smooth it back anymore. Reluctantly his eyes left her and he began to pick thoughtfully at the dirt under his nails. Georgie had said nothing to the others but he knew she suspected that something had happened between him and Tyrone; that he was somehow responsible for Tyrone's disappearance. She spoke to him differently now and he had caught her looking at him when she thought he wasn't paying attention.

Shifting slightly towards her, "I didn't do anything," he said in a low voice, looking about him to ensure the others couldn't hear. They all seemed to be asleep.

Georgie raised her head fractionally, so he knew she was listening, but she didn't reply.

A boom and crackle reached their ears from somewhere in the distance.

He continued, "I know I lost my temper-"

Georgie snorted, "That's a bloody understatement."

"I'm tryin' to explain, right." He took a breath, calming himself. "Like I say, I know I lost my temper but I came back, not to try an' do anythin' bad like you think. I came back to look for all of you; I didn't know how hard I hit Tyrone, I didn't know if he would, y'know, need help carryin' out or whatever." He paused expectantly.

"How come you were talking about a struggle, then? What about that?"

"What struggle? When?"

"When we were in the square, before I dragged you out."

"I don't know what you're on about…"

"Don't lie to me," she hissed, flicking her bloodshot eyes up to his face.

"I don't remember no struggle."

He didn't. He was aware of jumbled images. The Devil dragging someone into the flames. The shepherd. A white figure. Hands outstretched. No, he was getting confused. That was the church window. That was later.

"After the explosion it's all pretty fuzzy, but I didn't go back there like that. I was sorry, not pissed. All I know is last thing I saw he was up an' about, then I wake up outside and he's not there an' you are. That's it, man."

"The way you spoke to him…"

"I lose it sometimes. I didn't mean it – I don't even remember what I said. I just saw red."

"Saw black."

"Oh…I didn't mean that. I don't…that ain't me."

Georgie grunted in a non-committal way and let her head bow again. This wasn't going the way he had hoped it would, but he wasn't about to beg.

"I'm tellin' you, he's gunna be waitin' for us at the museum wiv' a big grin on his face."

"I hope so," she said without looking up. "I hope so."

Farran returned to picking at his thumb. When he looked back, Georgie's hair was trailing behind her over the railing, revealing her pale, tired face, thrown into relief by the dark circles under her eyes and matching soot smudges under her nostrils. She hadn't moved but now that the wind had changed he could see how exhausted she really was. They all were. Then something clicked: she hadn't moved but her hair wasn't covering her face anymore. Farran rushed to his feet and looked out over London. He turned excitedly to the others.

"Guys, the wind's changed!"

"What now?" said Georgie, sounding tired and anxious.

Sarah pulled herself to her feet and joined Farran. "No, no, it could be a good thing. The wind was blowing from the southeast before, yes?"

"If you say so," said William.

"Well, now it's blowing from the northwest," she continued, "From the opposite direction. At the very least it's going to blow the fire away from our museum now and at best, if the wind holds, it might blow the fire back on itself to where it's already been."

"There won't be anythin' f'rit to burn no more," added Farran.

Now all of them were up on their feet. For the next few hours they stood in silent concentration, watching the progress of the fire. Sure enough, the wind gradually turned the tide of the fire and for the first time in days they began to hope.

Towards dawn the forward progress of the fire had halted altogether and it began to creep southeast.

"It must be burning by the river now. Right where we were running on the first day of the fire," observed Georgie. It seemed like a lifetime ago.

Anxiously they watched, unable to tear themselves away.

By midday it began to seem as though the intensity of the fire had lessened, but they couldn't be sure.

By the middle of the afternoon Georgie was confident, "It's dying, it's dying," she shouted. "It can't cross the river. The wind's blown it right up against the water and it can't go any further so it's burning itself out."

With nightfall came the long-dreamt-of rain; just a smattering at first and then in glorious showers that soaked them through to the skin and washed the soot from their faces. A great steaming sigh of relief drifted up from the ravaged city below, mingling with their own. A last they felt secure enough to turn their backs on the fire and seek the shelter of the tower's top floor restaurant.

The fire was out.

That night, tucked up under tablecloth blankets, they slept free from the nagging wind and fear, a grateful sleep of total exhaustion.

CHAPTER 15.

A pale winter sun sparkled above them in a frigid sky. At ground level the group were met by a world transformed; a wasteland stretching as far as the eye could see, right to the hills that form the basin in which London sits, from Tower Bridge to Gray's Inn Road.

The group picked their way slowly through this alien landscape. Georgie had never before seen such a flat, bleak expanse: dust and ash covered everything, metal had melted into the dirt and molten glass had solidified to form a brittle crust that crunched dangerously, giving unsure footing. The ground was a mingling of elements, unnatural and ugly. Lampposts drooped at crazy Daliesque angles, the lights and cameras that had topped them hanging like heavy fruit, cracked and lumpish. Twisted metal remained here and there like grasping fingers reaching up from beneath the debris – the blackened skeletons of buildings, naked and mournful in the morning light. They stood embarrassed, iron bones revealed, the stone and concrete charred from their bodies.

It was a monochrome landscape of silhouettes and shadows.

At one point they came across a place where the fire had only recently died and had left an entire structure glowing like a shining coal, a great building of burnished brass. The hot ground around it steamed from the newly fallen rain.

They shuffled on through the deep ash until they reached an area where large rectangles were picked out by the ruins of foundations like an ancient burial site. Here the ground echoed with a metallic clang. Georgie noticed that the soles of her trainers were melting.

"The ground's still hot here," she called, "everybody be careful."

"I dinnae think it's just from the fire," Donnie called back, a look of excitement lighting his face. "I think we're walkin' on top of a load of cellars. Under the ground the fire's still burnin'."

"How comes there's no smoke, then? And how can it burn when it hasn't got any air?" asked William, indignant.

"You don' always need lots of air for a fire. All sealed up, these cellars could smoulder for weeks an' weeks jus' waiting for oxygen so they can reignite. I read about this town once; this place in America that was built on top of a coal seam - it was a mining town – and one day the coal underground caught fire and they couldnae put it out, it just kept burnin' under the town. The fire started in like nineteen-sixty-some-thin' and it's still burnin' - or at least it was last I heard. They had to abandon the whole town cos o' the fumes driftin' up from the pits. It's a ghost town now. Jus' imagine all those homes sittin' empty on top of ah permanent fire, like it was built on Hell or somethin'."

"Cool," said William, obviously impressed.

"Ya like that do ya, Billy Boy? If I'd ah known you were so ghoulish I'd ah told ya lots of ma stories ages ago."

"Well, if we're standing on top of a fire shouldn't we get off it?" asked Sarah.

As though in answer, there was a rusty creak from the floor, a metallic ice-crack, and then the ground beneath Donnie gave way, his legs disappearing into the nothingness. A sudden up-rush of flame burst from the hole, briefly engulfing his lower body, and then just as suddenly disappeared. Donnie screamed, the legs of his trousers now aflame somewhere in the dark below him. His elbows wedged in the dust, it was all he could do to stop himself slipping away.

As William stepped towards Donnie the ground in front of him gave an alarming groan and he jumped backwards. But Farran was already in motion – he threw himself down on the ground and, spreading his weight out, scrambled towards his panicked friend.

Donnie clawed at the dirt in front of him, trying to stop himself slipping down into the burning darkness.

When Farran reached him he stretched over Donnie's back and grabbed the waist of his jeans, from there he could see over the jagged lip of the opening, down into the fissure – a long way below a lake of fire seethed and boiled. Heaving till his forearms ached, he slowly hauled Donnie up out of the hole and dragged him back to solid ground.

The moment they were safe he covered Donnie's legs in dirt, patting out the flames. The two boys lay in the sooty earth, Farran panting and Donnie groaning with pain.

The others ran over. Sarah gently rolled up Donnie's trouser legs to inspect his burns.

"How bad is it?" sniffed Donnie.

"It's not as bad as I thought it was going to be," she replied looking at the two angry and inflamed patches of skin on the back of his pale calf, "but we need to get cold water on it to stop it getting worse. Can you stand?"

"Yes, but it bloody-well hurts." Gingerly he got to his feet, rolling up his trousers so that the material didn't rub against his burns. He craned his neck over the hole, the others looking with him.

"That could've bin a hell of a lot worse though. Thank you, Farran." He stretched out a hand.

"You had me worried there, mate," he said, beaming at the little Scot as he took his hand.

"Me too. In fact come here, give me a hug." Reluctantly Farran submitted to the hug, awkward at first, then the smile returned to his face and he clapped the other boy on the back.

"I'm just glad you're alright." Then gently but firmly he pushed Donnie away from him again.

"Alright, I'll let you break the hug this time. You're a good man."

"OK, enough bonding, boys, let's get you some water, Donnie," said Sarah. She tucked herself under one shoulder and, Joanna taking the other side, they led him over to the low remains of a wall.

Georgie and Farran were left alone as Farran brushed himself down.

"That was very brave of you." She smiled at him, a confused, appraising smile, but a smile nonetheless.

"What else was I gonna do?"

"Hmm," said Georgie and wandered off to join the others fussing around Donnie.

For the first time in days Farran felt like the tension between them was thawing.

* * * * *

The journey through the devastation of the fire was long and arduous; Donnie's injuries meant he had to hobble along at a slow pace and they were forced to pick their way carefully through the wreckage. Even the streets at the edges of the fire, where the destruction wasn't so complete, were blocked by fallen masonry and charred timbers and they repeatedly had to double-back on themselves to find a safe way through.

When they reached the end of the destruction they looked back to take in the full extent of the fire, an area which sat brown, ragged and ugly, like a bite in a discarded apple. A great swathe of London from Saint Paul's to King's Cross was completely destroyed. But outside of the burnt region it was as if nothing had ever happened.

When the group eventually arrived back home – for they all called the museum home now, as though their separation from it and their fear for its destruction had made it dearer to them – they ran inside, shouting for Tyrone. They rushed through every room in the museum, searching for some sign that he had been there, calling his name again and again, but they were met only by the echoes of their own voices and by their disappointment. The museum was dark, cold and empty. This was not the homecoming they had hoped for. Tyrone was nowhere to be found.

Eventually they congregated one by one in the whale room. Each new arrival would shake their head and then join the others sitting in silence. None of them knew quite what to do or how to feel; they had not seen him die, and yet he was gone. Should they mourn or should they hope? They all felt isolated by their grief, together in one room but alone.

"We should never have left. I…we should have kept looking," said Georgie.

"We couldn't."

"The crazy thing is," said Donnie, easing his legs up onto his camp bed, "that Tyrone always seemed so grown up, we could do with havin' him here to tell us what t'do, y'know, hold us together." He gave a short humourless laugh.

Joanna began to cry.

Georgie knew that Donnie was right but she couldn't help but feel a little jealous - she liked to think that she held the group together more than Tyrone. She felt her face flush, embarrassed that she had let such a thought enter her head. She looked quickly about the room, anxious that someone might have heard her thoughts. Her eyes began to fill, then she noticed that Sarah was standing by Tyrone's bed going through his clothes. "What are you doing?"

"I'm tidying his things so that when he comes back everything is nice and neat for him."

Georgie sniffed back her tears and went over to Sarah.

They stood there without saying a word to one another and they began to fold his clothes.

CHAPTER 16.

Dark. Dark, red-threaded blackness.

Pain. Don't know where. Everywhere. Nowhere.

Eyes open. Blinding-bright.

Close eyes. Dark again. Swimming spots in the dark.

Noise. Echo-loud, like moth wings in ears. Voices? A machine's ping.

Pain. A hot sharp stab inside, in side, my side. No. My arm.

Open eyes. Bright. A globe. An oval in the white globe. Closer. Behind the oval, eyes. A black face in the eyes. Reflection?

Close eyes.

Noise. A name. Leviathan?

Close eyes. Close noise. Close pain.

Darkness. Nothing.

CHAPTER 17.

Georgie wandered through the streets on her own. It was a chill, grey afternoon, a continuous drizzle floating softly about her; not enough to call rain, just enough to get her wet - typical London weather. But Georgie was glad of the clean smell that had finally returned after the fire. Clouds of smoke still hung low over the smouldering wasteland that had been the Square Mile, but it no longer contaminated the rest of town.

It seemed like she was on her own more and more these days; Farran had become increasingly moody since the fire. Half the time he was sullen and secretive, disappearing off to who knows where, and when he *was* around he would suddenly snap for no reason, then apologise without anyone even telling him to. It was like living with Jekyll and Hyde – never knowing who he might be at any given moment.

As for the rest of them, they just carried on as if nothing had happened, as if Tyrone hadn't…disappeared. All they wanted to do was sleep all the time or invent some silly childish game - planning to steal paintings or play bumper-cars with real lorries. She wanted none of it. No one wanted to talk about Georgie's idea for a signal, or come up with a long-term plan, it was almost impossible just to get the others to fetch supplies and cook a proper meal. Donnie had now even resorted to an all-crisp diet, his one concession being Jaffa Cakes - which according to him he only ate to avoid getting scurvy.

More and more Georgie had retreated into reading books. As she'd finished her current supply she'd decided to use it as an excuse to get out and head to the bookshops on Charing Cross Road. She'd ended up having to leave her moped at Hyde Park Corner – having found herself wheeling it around the abandoned traffic as much as riding it - so the whole expedition had taken most of the day.

Walking back up Oxford Street she looked in the windows of the big department stores; once animated, the elaborate scenes from fairy tales were now frozen – Sleeping Beauty waiting, a prince forever poised inches away from awakening her; a witch crouched on the point of being kicked into an oven by Hansel; and a life-size girl about to be pounced on by a huge wolf. There was something about the wolf that made Georgie uneasy; it was supposed to be 'jolly', but in the shadows of the shop the dust and cobwebs that clung to its dark fur gave the thing a sinister appearance.

The displays were still there from Christmas and festooned with glitter and sale signs even though it was March. She realised that they always would be. The dark was gathering, so she pulled her hoody up around her ears and decided to head straight for home.

As Georgie turned to go she noticed that the window had graffiti covering it. Someone had scrawled the words '*solitary, poor, nasty, brutish, and short – Lev xiii*'. That was either a quote from somewhere or the worst names for dwarves ever. Whichever, it gave her the creeps. Next to it was something smaller, and she realised with a start that it was the same stencilled word she'd seen before: *Leviathan*. It was strange though, she was sure she hadn't noticed this earlier. Maybe it was just one of those things – once you see one, you see them everywhere.

Georgie suddenly had the horrible feeling that she was being watched. Looking up she saw that, on the other side of the glass and only inches away, a face was leering down at her.

She screamed and jumped back. But the face didn't move, it just stared at the same spot.

She edged forward again.

A mannequin. A sodding store mannequin! The hunter from the scene had obviously toppled over at some point and now rested forlorn against the glass, his hat and wig pushed off to reveal the dummy beneath. *OK, no more Stephen King for you, Georgie. Not if you're going to get this jumpy.*

She hauled her rucksack back onto her shoulder but something made her look up, a movement in the distance where the street was swallowed up by the swirl of evening mist.

"Hello? Guys?"

A pack of dogs barked somewhere far away.

"Farran is that you?"

She blinked into the rain, straining to see better. A light appeared - a smudge far off in the haze.

Was that a torch?

"Hello??" she called again.

And then it winked out of existence.

Had someone switched off the torch when they heard her calling?

The light came again and closer, but there were two points of brightness in the mist now.

Again they flicked off as suddenly as they'd appeared.

Her hand tightened on her shoulder strap.

The lights flared once more, closer still, then off. There was no pause this time before they returned even closer. She realised with a sharp breath that it was the street lights. The dead street lights.

Both lamps either side of the road flashed on then off, only to be replaced by the next set closer to her, as though the lights were jumping from bulb to bulb, as though they were searching for her. Quicker and quicker the light came now, the line rushing up towards her.

She made to run but fascination or fear held her in place.

The light was at the end of the block.

It was coming for her.

Now half a block.

Her heart thumped.

Now light blazed all about her, blindingly bright and terrifying.

Then just as suddenly, it was gone and she was in darkness once more.

There was a sense of anti-climax.

Nothing had happened.

She waited. Tense. Alert.

Afterimages danced in Georgie's vision and her heartbeat continued to pound in the drizzling gloom.

What the hell was that?

In a moment the light engulfed her again, the lamps so bright the bulbs fizzed in their housings. The shop windows burst into life: Christmas music blaring out fast and distorted, glitter balls spinning flashes all about her, the dummies moving manically in their set routines. The wolf jumped on Red Riding Hood, she screamed, it reset. Again and again it happened... jump, scream, reset, jump, scream, reset, jump scream-

The streetlamps exploded in showers of sparks and everything went still.

This time Georgie didn't wait, she dropped her bag and ran.

* * * * *

Every morning when Farran got up to pray, alone, before the others were awake, he would first check the sky and rub his fingers together through the damp air, as if he could touch the imperceptible change that meant that spring was coming and he would have to leave. It was not that he hid his praying from the others - if they had asked he would have told them where he went - but it was still so new to him that he was simply shy of it.

This morning as he lay his mat down on the marble of the entryway he noticed that the sun was a little warmer, strong enough to release the scents that had lain dormant inside everything - stone and tree and grass -and raise them up invisibly towards him. Spring was here. The harsh edge had disappeared from the air and he knew that the ground, even under the shade of the tower blocks of East London, would have thawed.

Having rolled up the 13th Century rug he'd taken from the V&A, and wrapped it up in its black bin bag, he went back into the main hall. He crept amongst the sleeping forms of his comrades saying his own silent goodbyes and collecting all of the things he thought he would need for his journey. When he reached Donnie he stopped and ruffled his hair. Donnie mumbled something about 'koalas' but otherwise didn't stir. Then Farran slipped out of the main doors again, feeling like a thief who had stolen something he couldn't define but knew was precious, and walked guiltily to his moped.

He was strapping his pack to the back of the bike when he turned suddenly, hearing a noise.

"Going without saying goodbye?"

Georgie stood with her hoody wrapped around her and her tousled hair still radiating the heat of sleep.

Farran stammered, "I, I would 'ave but no one was awake yet. I'll be back soon anyway. There's just somethin'…"

Georgie stopped him with a smile. "I know. I know there's been something bothering you. Just come back to us when you've sorted it out."

"I will."

"And take *care*, there's something…Last night I…" She remembered Farran's reaction to the CCTV camera. "Forget it. Just take care is all."

"Yes, Mum." A rare smile appeared on the boy's face and

then was gone again, so quickly that Georgie wasn't sure if it had been there at all.

"Don't turn your engine on until you get to the bottom of the road. I'll explain to the others when they wake up or you'll never get away."

Then Georgie turned her back on the boy and ran inside without another word.

* * * * *

Light danced on the Thames, gold on milky green, flashing so bright at times that Georgie had to squint her eyes almost closed to keep looking. Ever-moving reflections drew patterns across her pensive face; the light was hypnotic, allowing her to drift off into her thoughts. She thought about the way the city had 'come alive' and wondered yet again if she shouldn't risk telling the others. It was probably just a blip in the electrical grid, the final spasm of a dying creature, London's death rattle before giving up the ghost.

She thought about Farran and his journey; she wondered how long he would be gone, and whether he would be alright out there alone. Should she have tried to tell *him* at least, to warn him? There had been so much loss; Tyrone, now Farran, her parents. Her parents – she couldn't get her head round that still, it felt like it had happened to someone else, like a very sad story that someone had told her; she felt sorry for the girl in the story but she didn't know how to feel enough to make it real.

She found herself thinking about her dad, an image came to her clear and strong. Her dad in the kitchen, someone had asked for a glass of tap water. She saw him through the crack in the door; as he filled the glass he would tap it and a little smile would creep onto his face, a private joke – *tap* water – not for anyone else, just himself. A private joke that he thought no one else saw. But she'd seen it. Strange, why had that come to her now? It was such an inconsequential memory. Somehow it comforted her, though why, she couldn't say.

Just then a shape broke the surface of the river, a stream-lined arch, black against the bright water. It curved through the air shedding droplets that glowed like baubles before shattering into a thousand filaments and rejoining the body of the water. A dolphin. A solitary dolphin that danced with the dancing light, each great leap seeming to knit water and air together, mingling them until they were indistinguishable. A dolphin in the Thames. Georgie had never heard of such a thing, let alone seen it. It felt like a silent song of forgiveness, nature returning to the once polluted landscape of London. She felt her heart lift.

"It's beautiful," said a voice beside her.

She turned. Sarah was there, her hair a little wild in the breeze but otherwise as neat as ever. *How does she do that?* she wondered, but all she said was, "Hi, Sarah. How'd you find me down here?"

She hadn't expected it but now that she was here, Georgie was glad of the company.

"By accident. I sometimes come down to the river too. I love the water." She took a deep, savouring breath. "I used to sail with my father before..."

The dolphin had headed up river, and was now just a dark speck appearing briefly then disappearing again, flickering into the distance.

"You can sail? I didn't know that."

"Yes, my father took me sailing every time I was home from boarding school for the holidays; since I was as young as I can remember. We had a little yacht but my stepmother hated sailing, she would get seasick, so it was just my father and I. I loved it."

"Do you think you could teach me?"

"I should think so, yes. If we had a little boat…"

"We must be able to find one somewhere along the river."

"Then yes. I don't see why not. I would be happy to." She smiled down at Georgie.

"Could you teach me to sail something big?"

"Well, let's start small at first, but the principles are the same really, no matter what size. Why?"

"No reason. Let's start small," she said. There was a glint in Georgie's eye that excited Sarah, but also made her a little anxious.

CHAPTER 18.

Tyrone realised he was somewhere. Not where exactly, just that he actually *was* – as though he'd been dead and then just snapped into existence again, the way it seems after a very long, deep sleep.

Now he felt sick. Really sick. His head pounded and the world smeared by in a sickly blur every time he turned. He wasn't sure if the rest of his body was there any more, but bright strips of light were passing above him in a smooth succession and he realised that he was moving.

His mouth was so dry his tongue had stuck to his cheek and the edges of it felt sore and bitten. Something was clipped to one of his fingers but he couldn't get it off. If he could feel that, he must still have fingers at least. He tried twitching them. They hurt.

The lights still moved overhead and he was on something soft; some sort of smooth, plastic mattress against his burnt back. He tried to move his arms, but they wouldn't budge and he could feel - with a quick, clawing panic - that he was strapped down.

CHAPTER 19.

The great pillared houses around Regent's Park were never supposed to be warm and cosy; occupied or not, they always stood like royal sentinels, marking the edge of London's grand and imposing heart. Each row was repainted the same colour every few years, as regularly as clockwork, and their cream exteriors seemed to glow against the grey day. Sarah had to tear her eyes away from them.

"When yer round here it's like tha fire nevah happened," said Donnie. "Hey, ah was talkin' to yer, zombie gal," poking her arm as many times as he could until she, inevitably, slapped his hand away.

"Who are you calling zombie, *Donald*?" she replied, relishing the way he winced when she used his full name, "And if anyone round here deserves that title it's the pair of you," she finished, with her best schoolteacher glare.

"What d'you mean?" asked William.

"Don't pout, Willy," another satisfying wince, "Have you seen the state of you two? The pair of you look like you haven't washed for a month."

"That's not true actually," retorted William, a smug look on his grimy face, "we filled that paddling pool up with hot water only yesterday."

"Yeah," put in Donnie, "and we tipped an entire bottle o' bubble bath inteh the thing too, and then swam around in it like soapy ducklings."

"That's right," added William, laughing, "and Donnie made himself white hair and a beard out of the foam,"

"Sshhh," Donnie gave William a despairing look, "don't tell her that – she'll think we were havin' a bath together."

"But it was more like a swimming pool," protested William.

"That's no' the point..." began Donnie, but he was interrupted by Sarah.

"If you two want to play submarines together that's none of my business. But if you two just had a bath," continued Sarah, "then why is it that you're both so dirty?"

"Ah. The potato incident," said Donnie.

"Yes, the potato incident," agreed William solemnly.

"I'm not even going to ask," said Sarah.

They carried on past the park for a few moments before Sarah said, "So how do you intend to break into the zoo?"

"We *don't* intend to break in," replied Donnie, with mock weariness, "*Breakin' in* implies theft, and *theft* is only possible when someone *owns* somethin' and, as I keep tellin' yer, no one owns *anythin'* anymore. Except me, an' am willin' to share it all with the rest of yer."

"You're most gracious, King Donnie of Britain."

"King Donnie of *Scotland*."

"So how are we getting in?"

"It *is* a problem, hen, the front gates are pretty hefty."

"Hang on, look at the brochure," said William, jabbing a grubby finger at the leaflet he held. "On the map, the edge of the zoo goes right up to the park here. Looks like a picnic area or something," pointing ahead, "just on the other side of those railings, and they're dead low."

"Y'know, William, sometimes yeh're not as stupid as yeh look," said Donnie.

"Thanks," replied William, grinning happily.

* * * * *

The ground beyond the railings was more like sand; parched and yellow. The bushes, with their long, sharp leaves, didn't seem to match the green park behind them and as William kicked at the patches of brown grass his boot turned over sticky bones, half buried amongst its spikey blades.

"Got a lot ah messy picnickers in London," said Donnie.

"Yes, it's disgusting," said Sarah, "Just a moment, I don't…"

Her sentence was cut short by a sudden, fierce growl from behind the bushes. The three of them stood frozen, watching as a shaggy head appeared – mouth lolling open to reveal rows of yellow teeth and a fat, livid tongue – then as another form limped after it, nostrils working as it sniffed the air.

Sarah had forgotten to breathe; William felt the weight of his kit bag, wondering how quickly he could get to it, and then Donnie shouted,

"Leg it!" and in a second they were sprinting towards the next set of railings without looking back.

Donnie had taken his jacket off as they ran and, flinging it over the spikes, boosted first Sarah and then William over before William grabbed his hand and dragged him desperately up and over. He tumbled onto the ground next to Sarah, hardly noticing his burns stinging, but when he looked, he realised that the patch of ground was clear and the snarling creatures he had expected were nowhere to be seen.

After a few moments he looked up at the other two, "What the hell was that?"

"Dogs," William replied, "Must've been looking for left-overs."

"That wasnae the picnic area, ya dunce," said Donnie, laughing from fear and relief.

"Give me that map," said Sarah, still breathing hard, "*African hunting dogs.*"

"Sorry."

"They looked like hyenas," said Donnie.

"Nastier," Sarah said, exhaling slowly, "I saw a programme about them on television once."

"Then why didn't they chase us?"

William and Sarah had no reply.

* * * * *

They got to their feet and began to walk, despite their encounter, trying to get their bearings in the zoo. They were all more robust these days - tougher. Sarah had seen it in the group; sometimes she wasn't sure what was stranger – the things that happened: the fire; the emptiness; the way everything was theirs; the way they went where they wanted – or the fact that, in the end, they all seemed to get on with things without just grinding to a halt at the weirdness of it all. Teachers were gone, days of the week and locks meant nothing; nobody cooked their supper or did the washing, but still each of them slept and ate and walked around. It was like being in a dream that became the truth, where the rules had changed but you still had to brush your hair or go to the toilet. She would try to get a grip on how things were, but Sarah could *feel* the way the thoughts were confused in her head, as though she didn't recognise her own voice anymore.

Now she was in London Zoo; without a ticket, without sign of another soul.

The area they were walking through must have been set aside for administrative buildings – sheds, offices, perhaps the veterinary surgery – but even as they were crossing the bridge over the canal, things were unnaturally still.

According to the map the first enclosure they came to was for giraffes, but when they neared the paddock the stench hit them - earthy dung and that same, sickly-sweet rotten smell - and they realised what had happened. Why should animals be any different? They needed food too, and trapped in their cages and pens without anyone to care for them many had died from starvation. Every tree and bush had been picked bare of leaves. One prone giraffe raised its head weakly but the two others they could see were still – their bodies bloated and their sticky fur picked over by clouds of black flies.

Sarah felt a lump catching in her throat and her vision begin to cloud with tears. Even William seemed stunned.

"That's why those dogs didnae chase us," murmured Donnie, "they were too weak."

"It's too cold for them," said Sarah, her voice croaky, "London's too cold without food. They need to be kept warm, they need to be looked after."

Donnie put a hand on her shoulder, but William didn't even comment on it.

Without any real plan, they walked on, ignoring the shuttered café, until they came to a set of enclosures filled with scattered straw and a clutter of ropes and hanging tyres. Even now they could see the greasy, smeared fingerprints from children on the huge glass window, but there was no sign of movement within the shadowy space beyond and it seemed empty until William spotted a dark shape slumped in the opposite corner.

The gorilla must have been dead for weeks. The skin on its face had dried like leather, the lips and gums pulled back around the teeth into a sad grin, the powerful body now lax and slumped, arms spread outwards. Sarah had never let herself look closely at any of the corpses they had come across, but the gorilla, almost human, filled her with sadness - like a hard stab in the centre of her chest - when other things had only shocked or sickened.

William's map showed that the aquarium and reptile house were only a minute away, but it was clear to all three of them that without electricity to keep the tropical tanks and the snakes and lizards warm, there would be nothing in those dark buildings that they would want to see.

This wasn't why they'd come, it was supposed to be fun.

They walked on to the centre of the zoo, not far from the main entrance. From here they could take in the strange skyline of the place; the gigantic, angular aviaries – great swoops of wire and scaffolding like ships' sails; the artificial mountaintop, a brown papier-mâché model complete with neat caves and little steps; the concrete elephant house with its square turrets of green copper.

And as Donnie, Sarah and William looked around and wandered a little further, they found that they were wrong, that there was still life here.

In the aviary, they could make out the shapes of birds flitting from perch to perch. The strange squawks and eerie cries of more exotic birds echoed towards them from the distance as the animals became aware that humans walked amongst them again. Sarah reasoned that the birds were smaller and had probably found enough in their large enclosures to keep them fed. But as they walked on, the group found to their delight that other animals had also clung to life.

In the area for apes and monkeys they saw the little gibbons and lemurs leaping their way through the shaking branches, chewing on green leaves from the thick canopy. Flamingos and pelicans still waded through the zoo's ornamental pond and a growing hum of snuffles, snorts and crunches suggested that other creatures had also found enough to keep them from starvation.

Sarah was the first to speak, "We shouldn't leave them like this. There's no need – not now."

"So what d'you reckon we should do?" asked William.

"Set them loose," replied Sarah, decisively.

Donnie looked at her with a grin, "Ah never thought ah'd hear yer talkin' like that."

Sarah shrugged, "Some things are just right."

"Open up the cages and let everythin' go, let things run wild," agreed Donnie, "Ah don't see why they shouldn't be free too."

"Alright," said William, nodding, "sounds like fun."

* * * * *

There was a lot of ground to cover, but luckily William found a sort of golf cart painted in safari colours.

Driving straight between the aquarium and the reptile house the first thing they came to was an impressive, new-looking exhibit. Large placards proclaimed it as the home of a 'Komodo Dragon', a recent arrival from Indonesia. Sarah raised a hand to signal that the other two should wait, and read the short description.

"Does the beastie have a name?" called Donnie.

"I doubt it would come if we called it," replied Sarah. "It says here that they grow up to three metres, eat dogs, pigs and water buffalo and have toxic spit. Oh, and they eat people sometimes."

"And we're settin' it loose?" asked Donnie.

"Yeah," said William, "we should skewer the bastard while it's trapped."

"Look," replied Sarah, addressing both of the boys, "we'll only let it get into the park. There's railings all around that. If we open up some sort of gap into it from the zoo, it – and everything else – will just clear off into Regent's Park and have the whole place to run about in."

"Like a safari park with ducks in," suggested William.

"Exactly."

"I pity the ducks," said Donnie.

They walked inside to where a shaded gallery with benches

faced the leafy enclosure, separated by at least twenty metres of some of the thickest plate glass they'd ever seen.

Nothing stirred within.

The three of them came closer, leaning forward and craning their necks to try and see round corners and under bushes in an attempt to spot its sole inhabitant, but the place seemed empty.

Impatient and more than a little disappointed, Donnie began hollering and slapping against the glass with his palms until, finally defeated, he leant his forehead up against the window.

He had barely paused when, in a blur, a mass of dark green flesh shot out from a bush and slammed up against the glass. Donnie tumbled backwards with a yell. Thick claws squealed across the glass leaving long scratches, there was a spray of saliva and hot breath and in another moment the huge creature had whipped round, moving back into the undergrowth so quickly that in a second there was nothing to be seen but the last few centimetres of its tail sliding away.

Donnie heaved himself upright, panting, and watched as the last of the leaves swayed and shook.

"Where the bloody hell did that come from?" he gasped, looking wide-eyed at the other two. Then he smiled, "Close call. Looks like thah place isn't empty after all."

"Seems pretty full," agreed William.

"So are my trousers if ah'm honest."

"I can see why they call it a dragon," said Sarah.

"Yeah," said William, "it looks like a lizard, only it's the size of one of my uncle's heifers."

"Reminds me of some of the dinosaur models in the museum," added Donnie, "like somethin' that shouldn' be around anymore."

"Looking at it, it's hard to believe the thing's actually real," agreed Sarah.

"So how are we goin' ta get it outta there?"

"*If* we should get it out of there," said William.

"Ah think ah know a safe way of doin' it," said Donnie, thoughtfully.

"But what about the enormous padlock on the door?" asked Sarah.

William slid the huge green kit-bag off his back and onto the floor,

"Might be able to help with that."

He reached in, arm disappearing up to the shoulder, and rooted around with the sounds of clinking and crashing, before withdrawing a long pair of bolt-cutters a moment later like a magician at the end of his act.

"That thing's got everything," said Donnie, genuinely impressed, "it's like Mary Poppins' bag."

"I guess so," said William, "if Mary Poppins carried a crossbow and a set of nunchuks."

* * * * *

The plan reminded Sarah of a Wild West rodeo for some reason. She and Donnie were to get into the buggy and make themselves scarce after the lock had been dealt with. When the coast was clear, William was to tie one end of a rope to the heavy door, climb up onto the beams above and when he was well out of reach, yank the rope, heave the door open and let the Komodo dragon run free. Then it could get out through the large hole they'd cut in the fencing near the park. That was the plan, anyway.

Donnie and William set to work, taking it in turns to use the large bolt cutters to gouge chunks out of the padlock. Donnie was a little surprised at how hard he was finding it. After only a few seconds of effort his head spun and his burn throbbed painfully. He was boiling hot, and despite the weather beads of sweat were soon running down his forehead.

Luckily William seemed prepared to take on most of the work, grunting and swearing under his breath whilst he attacked the padlock, and after another ten minutes of hard work, they were ready.

* * * * *

William didn't have second thoughts exactly, but crouching precariously on a beam with one end of the rope it did, for just a moment, strike him that releasing a wild predator just a few metres beneath his feet was an odd thing to do. How did Donnie talk him into these things?

But when he tugged on the rope and opened the heavy door, once again the Komodo seemed to have vanished.

For ten long minutes he remained crouched, cramp steadily gnawing its way into both of his legs and then, as though it had been there all along, he saw with a start that the beast was now directly below him. The lizard stopped, its long, forked tongue whipping out, and then tipped its thick snout slowly upwards. William held his breath and hugged the beam. For several seconds it seemed to sniff and taste the air and then with the same surprising speed it began to run, lumbering forward on its muscular legs until it turned the corner and disappeared from view.

William was stuck; there was no way he could risk jumping down and making a run for it. Perhaps it was only around the next corner, waiting to pounce on its long-awaited meal. He even worried as the drips of sweat fell from the end of his nose and hit the floor, in case the sound and the scent of fresh William-meat should call the dragon back to this spot.

It was a relief therefore, when he heard the approaching hum of an electric motor and a few seconds later the golf buggy swung steadily around the corner. Both of them were waving.

"It worked!" shouted Donnie.

"It worked?"

Sarah nodded, "Yep! We shut ourselves inside one of the cafes."

"Place stunk, but it seemed a safe spot t' hide," cut in Donnie.

"And we watched the Komodo from there," continued Sarah, "It crossed the bridge over the canal, went straight through the hole and just disappeared into the park."

"So what now?" asked William.

"We finish the job," replied Sarah.

* * * * *

The birds from the gigantic aviary seemed shy, but first singly, then in twos and threes – peacocks, vultures and other fluffy, waddling birds scurrying away on foot – they began to peep hesitantly from the open doors, until eventually whole flocks of everything from toucans to pelicans were flying off and over the trees into the park.

The emaciated giraffe, some camels and even a herd of scrawny zebra also took little encouragement before they too bolted from their pens and galloped off southwards into the waiting park. They watched in deep satisfaction as, unnaturally thin and mangy as they were, lions and tigers found a new lease of life in the face of freedom and padded off, drawn by the smell of thick, damp grass and of a breeze which had blown free from bars or cages.

The hippos slipped contentedly into the canal which ran by the park, looking thoroughly bizarre amongst the narrow-boats and terraced houses as they twitched their ears and squirted the grimy water through their nostrils. At least twenty penguins, surprisingly adaptable, waddled in the same direction, hopping one after another over the side and then swimming en masse in the direction of Camden Town.

A ragged cloud of bats swooped hurriedly away in search of darkness. With a satisfied grunt a warthog settled itself in the muddy puddle left in front of some goal posts. Later, the trio stood happily as a newly-freed antelope skipped joyfully into the green bounds of the park. Then watched rather less happily as a lion sprang out of nowhere and began to eat it.

One by one and two by two, whether from jungle, savannah or Arctic, Regent's Park of the Royal Parks of London was slowly becoming the world's newest and strangest ecosystem.

* * * * *

"Looks like we need to head towards the centre of the zoo again," said William.

"Right. And then move on to here and then here," agreed Sarah, tracing a rough route on the map with her finger.

"What's this thing?" asked Donnie, poking at the map.

"It says 'Baby Changing Facility'," replied Sarah.

"Fantastic!" said Donnie, "D'you think people change babies often? Maybe they go in there and say 'Hello. Can I swap this for one with more hair?' or, ''scuse me, would you accept my toddler in part-exchange for a couple of flamingos?' Ah never dreamed the zoo offered such amazin' services."

"If all that were the case, Donnie, someone would have changed you years ago for something more useful – like a microwave or a pot plant."

They turned their attention to the leaflet once again.

"Look," said William, "here on the map right next to the llamas, there's the children's zoo."

"It's the guinea pigs, isn' it?" said Donnie, "Come on, you can tell me. You just want to stroke and love the iddle fwuffy guinea pigs. It's OK, pal, there's no need to be embarrassed."

William searched for a satisfactory riposte.

"Bugger off."

Donnie clasped his chest and began to make agonized faces as though he'd just been mortally wounded. Sarah took the map from a scowling William.

"He's right. It's only round the corner; we may as well see what's there. Donnie, get up off the floor and stop playing silly buggers."

With Sarah leading the way they were there in only a couple of minutes. The place was more like a small farmyard than a zoo and designed mostly for young children, but the little white gate which led into the mini farmyard had rusted on its hinges and took a couple of hefty kicks before it would open. There were whitewashed fences and brightly painted little houses for the sheep and goats, but the paddock itself was concrete. The hay scattered around it had been left out for some time and since nobody had been mucking out the stalls either, the rich, dungy farm smell was even stronger than usual. The three of them wandered over to the pens and stables, peering tentatively into the gloom to see which of its inhabitants had survived. Finally they paused by the pungent sty of an unfeasibly large and surprisingly noisy pig.

"They havnae done so badly, eh?"

"Yes," replied Sarah, "I'm impressed with how many of them have survived. I guess they had plenty of hay left for them – maybe a particularly dedicated keeper."

"She's pregnant," said William, indicating the enormous pig with a jerk of his head, "prob'ly about three months, so she's pretty close, aren't you girl? She's a bit thin for a landrace but she'll pick up. The sheep aren't in bad condition either, apart from a bit of scab."

Donnie and Sarah were open-mouthed.

"I don't believe it," Donnie said.

"Nah, look – you can see the raw patches on their skin where the fleece has been rubbed off."

"No, he means that we're astounded by your knowledge," explained Sarah.

There was a slight glow to William's freckled cheeks. "Nah, anyone would know that. There's tonnes more I don't know about."

"Well ah reckon this place is a goldmine," Donnie announced.

"A bit small," replied William with a shrug, "but I guess you're right."

"Seriously. This children's zoo is the best find yet. I haven't had fresh meat for weeks."

"True," agreed William, giving a scrawny goat an appraising look.

"What!" Sarah cut in, "are you *serious*? No way. Just…no way," she finished decisively.

"Have yeh ever fed the animals at a pettin' zoo?" asked Donnie, "Well now it's their turn teh feed us."

"That's sick!" exclaimed Sarah, "*You're* sick. How can you say something like that?"

"I don't want to eat out of cans forever," said William.

"How long do y'think that sort of thing's gonna last anyway?" added Donnie, "Besides, it's nature's way."

"Survival of the fittest," agreed William.

"It's all that circle of life type o' thing," Donnie reasoned, "You're in a zoo, with wild animals, and it's all, y'know – wild stuff."

"*You* may be wild, I'm trying to stay civilised," replied Sarah haughtily.

"Wimpy vegetarian tree-hugger."

"I'm not a vegetarian," Sarah snapped back at William.

"So I take it ya don't want t'embrace yer innah beast?"

"It'd be horrible."

"C'mon now; it all depends on whether yeh see the kebab as half full or half empty. Personally, ah'm a half-full kinda guy. With chilli sauce."

Sarah was not about to be convinced at that moment, so they decided to open up all of the gates so that the animals could run free – or fatten up, depending on your point of view – with the agreement that the whole group would discuss the issue at a later date.

* * * * *

A cold breeze rippled across the long, dark grass of the park, but now the place was dotted with grazing herds of zebra, llamas, camels. The giraffe stretched to pick the first of the new green shoots from the highest twigs of a tree, whilst elsewhere bright cockatoos and toucans perched on branches and tapirs snuffled amongst the fallen leaves.

The park's railings hadn't kept everything in, however. Outside the zoo, as they walked back the way they had come, the group spotted a lemur clinging to a bright red post box, peering into it as if looking for hidden nuts or grubs. Just as they had got over the surprise of spotting an anteater scuttle out of sight beneath a car, they turned a corner only to see dozens of monkeys scrambling amongst the houses and using drainpipes and scaffolding as a makeshift jungle. One pair sat upon a windowsill grooming each other whilst another hung by one hand from a street lamp, watching them pass by with wide brown eyes.

"Probably not the kind of residents this neighbourhood's used to," said Sarah, smiling.

"Well, ah guess we have t' share the city now," replied Donnie, philosophically.

"That's true. Hang on," said Sarah, stopping to look

Donnie up and down, "why do you look pregnant?"

"I don't," Donnie answered, defensively.

"Yes you do. What's that zipped up inside your Jacket? Donnie – is that a koala under there?"

CHAPTER 20.

Georgie walked through the corridors of the Thames Barrier Control Centre. She hadn't been here since her geography field trip, what, some three years ago?

There was the same damp smell and there were the same old posters bolted to the concrete walls; smiling, happy-faced workers in yellow hats and orange vests hard at work and, superimposed over them, facts about the Thames: descriptions of what this particular bit of the barrier did, how this great feat of human engineering had tamed nature and now kept London safe from flooding.

Georgie didn't know what had made her come here; she'd been drawn almost against her will. It was isolated - stuck out in the middle of the river in East London. Perhaps that's why she'd come; perhaps someone had survived, cut off from the rest of the city.

How had she got here? She couldn't exactly remember, which was odd. Maybe she'd sailed here with Sarah. Yes, that must have been it. But then where was Sarah?

She continued down the passageway, the latticed metal clanking unpleasantly under her as she walked. She followed a system of thick ducts to the left and then up a staircase.

At the end was a large metal door with a porthole window and a circular locking system like you'd see on a battleship or a submarine. A little uneasily she walked towards it. An aquatic light shifted and slid behind the glass; some of it spilled onto the walls about her. There was something in the shape of those walls, their grimy clutter and the way they pulsed silence back at her, that made her think of the tube tunnels.

But she would never go back into the tunnels. Full of loneliness and something else, something she never wanted to think about. She couldn't be there.

But now she looked, there was a ticket office and a row of turnstiles in front of her, barring her way. *Odd*, she thought.

She couldn't help herself, she placed her tube pass on the reader and the gate sprung open.

She couldn't turn back. She had to know what was beyond that door.

There was a movement from behind the glass, a shape blocked the light and then was gone.

She took a breath. "Hello, is anyone there?"

She continued cautiously towards the door and pressed her face up against the window, trying to look through. Beyond was a control room full of monitors and panels of important-looking flashing lights - so many lights - like the cockpit of an aeroplane. The room seemed empty of people, but with all of the units and control desks and pipes jutting out into the space it was impossible to be sure. She turned the round handle and with a hiss of seals breaking the door eased open.

Inside there was a painfully loud hum of machinery. Somehow everything must still be working.

She heard a clang from somewhere in the shadowed corner of the room. She pressed onwards, craning her neck to see past the banks of unmanned controls that blocked her view.

Stepping round the central unit she saw no one, but there, on the iron floor, sat a child's toy. A wind-up merry-go-round that was buzzing and tinkling as it whizzed round. It was exactly like one she'd had as a baby but it looked as though it had been in a fire. The plastic was charred and smoke still rose from it.

After a few moments the whirring slowed as it wound down and came to a stop. At the same time the overwhelming hum of the machines stopped too and Georgie was left with just the beating of her heart and her own ragged breath.

She bent down to touch the merry-go-round but drew her hand away quickly – it was still hot enough to burn.

A shadow moved in front of the light again, drawing her attention up from the floor.

Tyrone was standing in the middle of the control room, the lights blinking urgently around him.

He was hideously burned; the skin on his face had melted, dripped in rivulets down his features, and then congealed like candlewax.

"You left me, Georgie," his voice came as a low rasp.

"I, I, we looked, we couldn't find you…"

"You left me and never looked back." Again he rasped and a pink tongue came out to try to moisten his dry lips. "You left us all."

"All? I…what are you talking about?"

"I'm not alone, Georgie." He swallowed dryly and he breathed with that same wheezing rasp that seemed so horribly familiar to her. "Look behind you," he said at last.

Georgie spun around and saw that there were more people clustered silently behind her.

"Who are you? How did you get here?"

The people – young, old, men, women, children - just stood there looking at her, passive and terrifying.

"Who are you? Talk to me? Why won't you talk to me?"

The crowd slowly parted, and from amongst them appeared a familiar face. A woman's face, middle-aged with mousy brown hair.

"Mum? What? I don't understand." She could feel the sweat trickling down her back now. "Mum, what are you doing here? Where have you been? How did you survive?"

A sad, pitying look came into the woman's eyes, "I'm sorry, sweetheart, I didn't."

Georgie woke up, the sweat still pouring down her back. She was bolt upright on her camp bed in the dark. From about her in the museum drifted the soft shuffles and breathing of her sleeping friends.

Gradually her heart rate began to slow. She grabbed a jumper from beside her bed and put it on; the sweat was beginning to dry and had made her suddenly very cold.

She needed some air, needed to blow away the remaining shreds of the nightmare that still clung to her. Pulling herself out of bed she slipped her feet into her shoes, already wearing her jeans from yesterday, and padded out of the room to the stairs.

On top of the museum, Georgie stared out over the rooftops of London. A light rain pattered about her. It always seemed to be raining at the moment - a constant drizzle. The moon shone through a thin blanket of cloud giving it a ghostly halo; below it, picked out in the cold silver of moonlight and lying as peaceful and unprotected as a sleeper, stretched London.

What the hell was that dream about? On second thoughts she wasn't sure she wanted to know. She just wouldn't think about it again; she'd look at the beauty of the city and not think about it. She was good at that.

Sometimes she worried that she'd shut down too well, sometimes she worried that she couldn't feel anything now, the way she just got on with it. She'd read a book on genocide in Rwanda once – well part of one, she had found it too upsetting, too confusing. People in that country had just adapted and got on with life. They didn't go around weeping in the streets and tearing their clothes all day, they got up and opened their shops and went to work and lived. Life was just too big a habit to break, you couldn't just stop, even if you wanted to, even if you thought it was right to want to stop everything. Those people in Rwanda weren't monsters they were just…people.

Georgie had started reading the book again recently. She'd come across it by accident in the museum's small library. She'd been reading in there one day – something completely different - and then found it and just carried on. The only way she could explain it was that she was trying to *feel*, trying to understand. She'd been reading Austen, or maybe Eliot - that was it - but it just didn't mean anything to her – like it was science fiction, written by an alien species. Then after that book she'd picked up one of William's horrors and she hadn't been able to stop, she hated them but she just read one and then another.

That's what had brought on the dream. All those horror books. *If you live on a diet of junk food you're going to get a bellyache,* she told herself.

The drizzle continued to tap at her skin, but she was glad of its cold.

She turned back to London. She noticed the way the river punctured it; a shining slither of a blade that penetrated right through the city from one side to the other.

It was an intrusion of nature that struck to the heart of the city. It was untameable nature, a domesticated wolf that man had welcomed in but was still wild, still unpredictable. She wondered how often it had turned and bitten an unsuspecting hand. How many people had drowned in it? How many times had it risen up before man had shackled it with things like the barrier? How many buildings had it swept aside in a raging flood?

What must it have been like for those early settlers? For the Romans when they first invaded, creeping along the

Thames, knowing that they were surrounded by wilderness. How must England have appeared to them, having left everything civilised behind them to find nothing but animals and savages? What was the difference between then and now? Except that *they* knew the dangers of nature, the indifference of it, unlike those who came later and built blinkers of civilisation, blindfolds of concrete and glass.

She looked at London and she pitied it. Without man to shore it up and tend to it what chance did it have? In the end what protection was there against a river or nature or a disease?

From somewhere down in those distant moonlit streets a newly-formed pack of dogs howled.

Above, a shower of sparks tore across the sky; a multi-million dollar satellite falling to earth as shooting stars.

CHAPTER 21.

Wham

The alarm clock flew through the air, hit a stack of shelves and shattered into a dozen pieces.

Crash

A large china coffee mug received a similar fate.

Whump

A carton of milk exploded in a satisfying splatter over a three-metre radius.

"Looks good," said William, nodding his head appreciatively and removing the safety glasses.

"Try a different bat?" suggested Georgie.

"Nah," replied William, "We'll definitely add baseball to the list. Good chucking, Georgie."

"*Pitching*," Georgie corrected.

William stood with a clipboard. He hadn't actually bothered to write anything on it, but he liked holding it anyway.

"Y'sure you don't want a go, Donnie?" Georgie asked.

Donnie looked up from where he was sitting on the floor, "No thanks, hen – mebbe later."

"You alright?" Georgie asked, concerned, "You've been spookily quiet all day."

"Ah'm ok."

Donnie gave one of his best grins, but as soon as Georgie turned away his head drooped again. He'd never had flu this bad. He felt like an egg could fry on his face he was so hot, and even weirder, it wasn't as easy to breathe as usual – as if the air was thinner or something. The burn on his leg hurt like crazy. It had been getting a little worse every day but now his whole leg throbbed and felt swollen, like a sausage about to burst.

What was the point of making a fuss though? Back straight, chest out. Where had Uncle Robert got crusty phrases like that from anyway? It didn't matter, had a point, buck up, the Olympics had been his idea after all. So, trying to hide his limp, he hobbled after the other two as they strode up another of the impossibly long aisles which made up this warehouse of toys.

That morning, Donnie'd felt too tired to go exploring, but when Sarah returned and let slip that the shopping complex included a toy store the size of a small village and, further-more, that William had stayed behind to explore it, he'd found a new burst of energy.

At first there was no sign of William among the rows of prams, the stacks of Monopoly boxes, acres of soft toys and endless selections of dolls, guns and action figures. It was nearly five minutes before Donnie tripped over the first box.

Others like it - ripped open and empty - were scattered over the floor. He followed them like a trail of breadcrumbs towards where the debris grew thickest until, finally, he found William sitting crosslegged in the middle of the biggest Lego town he'd ever seen.

In fact it wasn't a town; it was more of a metropolis. The multi-coloured houses and shops stretched most of the way down the aisle; he had put together at least thirty or forty cars, trucks and helicopters so far and, not content with the one fire station, William had painstakingly constructed a full set of emergency services for every street corner. He hadn't wasted a brick.

At that moment he was providing both the *vroom, vroom*

sound and the wails of high-pitched sirens for a newly-completed ambulance when he noticed Donnie standing there. With almost record speed his round face turned a deep shade of red.

"I was bored," he stammered, "was jus' trying to think of summat to do. Found this rubbish so I could, er, smash it up when I'd finished building it."

"No, pal," said Donnie, casting his glance over the expanse of William's creation, "that's a masterpiece – a work o' art."

"Really?"

"That, sir, is a transcendent expression of the human spirit."

William frowned with suspicion, "Does that mean it's poofy?"

Donnie sighed a little and shook his head.

"You've certainly been mekin' the most o' this place."

William perked up, "It's great, isn't it? You should see the kiddies' racing cars they've got. It's a bit of a squeeze but they can bomb up and down these aisles."

"Oh, really, racing cars, you say?" said Donnie, raising a mischievous eyebrow.

The 'electric car Grand Prix' led in a natural progression to 'mini-motorbike jousting'. The basic equipment for this included one sawn-off broom handle; one dustbin lid; one adult-sized crash helmet; a set of plastic chest armour taken from a dressing-up kit with soft toys Gaffa-taped to it, and bikes so small that William's knees were up next to his ears when he tried to ride one.

Later they found some laser tag sets where hits actually gave you a small electric shock. William was convinced he could connect these up to a bigger twelve-volt car battery – but even he admitted that it might not be a good idea.

After that things had devolved into the sheer destructiveness of trying to find the best way of smashing things up.

* * * * *

For someone so dedicated to messing about, Donnie took this sort of task surprisingly seriously. But today Georgie noticed something more manic about him; he was certainly enjoying himself, but sometimes, when she was on the sidelines of everything and just watching, it seemed as though it was becoming hard work for him, as if Donnie was using an unusual amount of concentration just to maintain his enthusiasm.

Sometimes he held back when others were rushing off to find something and when he thought no one was looking, Georgie spotted him wiping his forehead on his sleeve or breathing heavily, eyes closed, as though in pain. She wasn't sure why she didn't say anything.

The fire had attacked more than just the city's buildings. They all had a dark corner in their minds – a place where doubts and chaos lived; the fire had revealed all those things, throwing light on disasters and losses which they had tried to leave hidden in the shadows. Perhaps Georgie was more like the others than she'd thought; none of them wanted to look there again. As long as they kept moving, their minds didn't catch up with them and they felt more like kings than refugees.

It was William who found the trampolines, but Georgie who came up with the idea of setting them all out in a row and then using a set of canoe paddles to batter each other with whilst they were up on them.

Once the stage had been set, Donnie insisted on going up first.

"You're climbing like an old woman!" scoffed William.

"Leave him alone," snapped Georgie.

Donnie seemed to wince more at Georgie's protectiveness than William's jeers.

"It's wobbly up here, Will, get stuffed."

Donnie got unsteadily to his feet and tried a few tentative steps.

"It looks like you're walking on the moon or something," laughed William.

"You alright?" called Georgie.

"Course ah am," Donnie replied, "watch."

He bounced, getting a couple of feet of air, to a round of applause from Georgie and William. He jumped again and again, encouraged by the others' whoops of excitement. He made an extra big effort for the next one and then, as he came to land, his legs completely gave way like a newborn foal's. With a sickening 'thud' he crashed into the side of the trampoline, his head cracking into the nearest shelves before he tumbled over the edge and hit the floor below.

Georgie knew something was seriously wrong. Even William didn't laugh. The pair were moving as soon as he fell, William grabbing him under the arms, dragging him out from under the trampoline and into the centre of the aisle. All the while Donnie didn't say a word; his eyes were half closed and though his lips moved only his breathing could be heard, coming in dry, painful rasps.

"Did he knock himself out?" asked William.

But straight away Georgie noticed his leg, where a dark patch had spread across his jeans. They rolled up a coat and slid it beneath his head, though Donnie didn't seem aware of what was going on, and then using William's pocket knife Georgie crouched down next to him and cut through the material.

She jerked away instinctively and toppled backwards as soon as she saw what was there.

A sickly yellow blister had covered almost the entire side of Donnie's leg; swelling more and more, filling with fluid and infection as the days passed, the fall had finally burst it. Now his leg was a mess of split skin revealing raw and weeping flesh beneath. The edges were a strange greeny-grey and a smell like damp and bad meat curled its way down Georgie's throat.

Tentatively she reached out and felt his brow. It was hot. She didn't know why, but she lay down to listen to his heart, though all that she could tell was that it seemed to be beating as though he were in a race.

"What is it?" William asked, whispering.

"I don't know. He's ill," Georgie replied without taking her eyes off Donnie.

"But why? What's wrong with him? What is it?" William repeated, almost pleading in the way he looked at Georgie.

"It's his burn, I think. It's not right. C'mon, help; we have to get him back home."

* * * * *

Sarah had taken charge the moment she'd seen Georgie and William carrying Donnie through the front door of the museum. Now he lay on the bed, shivering. His face was flushed and glistening with sweat; every time they tried to cover him with blankets he kicked them off, struggling as though he were burning up. He mumbled but didn't speak; his breathing became quicker and quicker and soon the others heard only his shallow panting. Sarah tried to make him drink, but when she tipped the cup at his lips, Donnie just coughed, spluttering the water down his chin before sinking back heavily without seeming to notice that anyone else was there.

Georgie, Joanna and William stood near, looking anxiously on as Sarah took his temperature.

"'as he got a fever?" asked Joanna, whispering.

"Looks like 40 degrees. It's one of those glass thermometers, it's hard to tell."

"Is that bad?"

"Normal is 37," Sarah replied, frowning at the tiny numbers.

"That's Celsius though," said Georgie, "I only know the other one. What's it supposed to be in that?"

"98.6."

"Are you sure?"

"I think so."

"*Think* so?"

Sarah whirled round to face her, "Look, I'm not a bloody doctor, OK? I'm doing my best."

Georgie felt guilty at once, "I know, I know. I'm sorry – really. How can we help?"

Next to her, Joanna nodded.

Sarah turned back to Donnie but spoke a little more calmly now.

"He's got an infection. The burn has gone bad. We need to get books on first aid, anatomy – medical textbooks, that kind of thing."

"OK, don't worry. We'll get anything that looks good. C'mon, William."

They came back from the library with piles of books, but the difficulty was finding the most useful. Georgie picked up one with the title *Clinical Predication Rules in Cases of Endocarditis* and another called *The Epidemiology of Hemophilus Influenzae*; it was like reading a Latin dictionary – nothing inside made sense, the chemical notations and the descriptions only made her panic. It was like having a school exam in a subject you'd never even studied. In the end between them they managed to narrow it down to six or seven books, which looked like they might really help, and each began to pore through them, desperately trying to sift through the acres of words until they found something that would tell them what to do.

Finally, Georgie waved the book she was holding and spoke to the others, "Hey – Donnie's really hot, and he's breathing funny and he has an infection."

"Yeah, we know that," said William gruffly.

"No, I mean according to this medical dictionary that sounds like 'sepsis'."

"I've heard of septicaemia," said Sarah, "is it like that?"

"I think so," replied Georgie, scanning the pages again.

"Here, let me look," said Sarah, reaching out.

A minute or two passed in anxious silence.

"What's it say?" urged Joanna, "What we s'posed to do?"

"Antibiotics," Sarah replied, looking up just a fraction.

"What sort?" asked Georgie.

"Ami…amic…" Sarah began, her voice cracking, "Oh, I don't know. I can't pronounce them."

"You don't have to," Georgie said, putting an arm round her, "we'll take the book."

* * * * *

Even now there was something clean and clinical about the chemist's. White walls, neat shelves of vitamins, rows of nappies and cough syrup. Despite the dust there was the familiar smell of toothpaste and lozenges. Past the counter at the back of the shop lay the storeroom, the place where hundreds of identical bottles and packets of pills were lined up, a coded monotony of medicine.

"Right," said Georgie, looking along the stacks, "start searching for antibiotics."

William took a squat, dark bottle from a shelf and squinted

at the label, "How do we know which is which?"

"Book, remember?" Joanna said.

"But there're loads listed in it, which do we choose?"

"Just take them all," Georgie replied, "if it's an antibiotic throw it in the bag. We're wasting time."

With Joanna and William calling out the names and Georgie checking them off against the list it took the three of them over twenty minutes to get what they needed. Adding some fresh dressings, antiseptic cream and a dozen boxes of random painkillers they climbed through the shattered window of the shop and ran back in the direction of the museum.

* * * * *

The damp night had already set in. Now the fluorescent glare from the camping lanterns felt cold and eerie as they sat around Donnie's bed, isolated by the miserable pool of light in the echoing hall.

Sarah sobbed in frustration, flinging the plastic bottle onto the ground. "The capsules are no good." She ran her fingers through her hair. It looked like she hadn't washed it in days.

"He ain't swallowin''em," added Joanna, "can't we make 'im swallow 'em?"

"It's not only that," Sarah said, "I think it's gone too far - the infection. Those pills are too weak and the books say his body can't use the antibiotics that way once he gets really ill."

"So what the hell do we do now?" said William, "This whole thing's bloody stupid," and with that he stomped off, disappearing somewhere through one of the distant exits. Georgie had half a mind to ask him what right he of all people had to feel stressed, but there didn't seem any point.

Donnie's gasps were coming in quick, sharp wheezes, like

a person choking.

Sarah gnawed at her lip, working painful decisions round in her mind. At last she spoke, "I think we have to use a syringe – inject antibiotics into him."

"Do we have any syringes?" asked Georgie.

Sarah didn't answer, her eyes focused elsewhere.

"*Sarah,*" Georgie repeated gently, "syringes?"

"Oh," said Sarah, blinking and turning to Georgie as though she'd been dreaming, "We've got lots of first aid kits. There should be some in one of those."

When Georgie and Joanna returned with a selection of needles, Sarah was poring over a list of antibiotics, sat on the floor amongst wet cloths and crumpled antiseptic wipes. She looked up.

"Georgie, I don't know which one - I don't know which of these is right. I don't want to kill him, but I just don't know."

"Pick one. That's all we can do – not just you, *we.*"

Sarah nodded, looking at Donnie, "OK. OK, I'm alright."

"Good," said Georgie, "Hand me the book will you, I need to have a look at that page." She ran her finger down the list, finally pausing, "I think we've got some of that one."

Rummaging through the bag they'd brought back she read the label on a tiny glass bottle and then checked it back against the list. After that she cross-referenced with another section of the medical dictionary so that she had a rough idea of how much of it they'd need for a dose.

"This is it."

"What do we do?" asked Sarah, looking nervously at Georgie.

Joanna spoke, "I've seen it in films. You stick the needle in that bottle and then squirt some of the stuff out in the air."

Georgie smiled at the other two, hoping they'd feel better, "Well, it looks like William's run off to hide in a corner and cry, so I guess it's up to us girls to sort things out. Here," she said, taking the syringe from Sarah, "let me at least fill it up."

Sarah tied something round the top of his arm, like they'd done to her when she'd had blood taken at the hospital. There was no reaction from Donnie at all now. Sarah knelt down next to him, gently taking hold of his wrist. She was breathing deeply, her chest heaving, but she didn't seem to be moving. She held up her hands, her thin fingers trembling,

"I'm shaking too much, Georgie. I can't do it."

"It's OK," said Georgie, kneeling beside her and taking the syringe, "I'll do it."

She felt more than saw Sarah rise and move out of the way, since she was now unable to take her eyes from Donnie's arm. She looked at the blue veins, running plump and vulnerable just beneath his white skin. Georgie could feel the cold pinpricks of sweat break out over her face and the back of her neck. Her head swam and her stomach churned. The tip of the needle looked viciously sharp; seeing it being done was one thing – actually pushing it into someone else's flesh was something else.

The first time she tried, the vein just seemed to squish out of the way of the needle. She held Donnie's wrist more firmly, his skin clammy beneath hers, but this time the needle went too deep, missing altogether and stabbing down into his arm. Trickles of blood began to pump out and run down his elbow and onto the sheets and Georgie had to start all over again, bandaging it up and trying on the other arm.

Each time, the sensation of stabbing Donnie with the needle made her feel sick, but on the third attempt she finally hit the vessel. Georgie didn't dare empty the syringe too quickly; sickening images of the vein swelling up and bursting kept entering her head, but in the end she managed to get all of the clear liquid out. The job was done. Now there was nothing left to do but wait.

* * * * *

Although she knew it was stupid, Sarah expected something to happen immediately. Five minutes turned to ten, then ten to thirty. The group wondered whether it was a good sign that nothing seemed to have changed.

The night drew slowly on. They sat in silence, but Sarah didn't know how long Donnie's breathing had been different before she finally noticed it. There was a sort of stillness, and when she went over to have a closer look she found that Donnie had opened his eyes. For the first time that day they seemed focused, as though he were finally in the same room as them.

"Where am ah?" he asked, hoarsely.

"You're in bed. Back in the museum," replied Sarah, stroking the damp hair out of his eyes.

Donnie tried to raise his head a little, "Hang on, ah'm in mah pyjamas now," he frowned, "Someone changed me out of mah clothes. Does that mean yeh stole a quick peek at mah winkie, y' wee hussy?"

"No," said Sarah, smiling, "Actually we got William to see to things."

"That's even worse," sighed Donnie, closing his eyes.

He let his head sink back onto the pillow. Sarah pulled the sheet up under his chin.

"Go back to sleep, you need your rest."

Donnie didn't open his eyes and in a few moments it was clear that he was unconscious again. Peaceful for the first time in hours his face looked different, child-like somehow. The restless, joking Donnie wasn't there and it made Sarah ache with a new, sharper pain than she had expected.

The evening darkened towards night. Donnie no longer struggled restlessly, but he was now a sickly, clammy white and his breathing had faded to a weak sigh, floating like an ebbing tide in the shadowed corner of the room.

William skulked back into the room and crawled sullenly into his sleeping bag. Sarah and Georgie looked through some of the medical textbooks and discussed treatments. Neither really seemed to concentrate and their conversation meandered in circles and vague repetitions, whilst Joanna heated a tin of beans none of them got around to eating.

Talk amongst the group became infrequent until they all fell silent, lost in their own thoughts and feeling the painful passing of time each in their own way.

Sometime in the middle of the night, when the others were asleep, Donnie stopped breathing once and for all.

CHAPTER 22.

London was under attack. Like an army laying siege, winter had pounded away at the city and softened her up for the onslaught of spring – and nature had finally succeeded where countless other armies had failed. Without man to support and sustain it, the city had little defence against the ravages of the changing seasons, and nature had already begun to reclaim the landscape as its own.

Moisture had crept unseen into London's buildings, under roof tiles and behind flashing. Once inside it had begun to seep into wood, entering through the tender flesh around nails and saw cuts. With the damp had come a greenish mould, beneath which insidious tendrils secreted enzymes that would slowly rot the wood. Bolts and screws had begun to leech a brownish stain into the material surrounding them: the beginnings of rust. Nature was feasting on London's corpse.

Once smooth paint began to flake like dry skin, and mortar to crumble and powder. Frost forced open dangerous cracks all over the city. With no one to tend to heating, pipes had frozen and burst and then the warmer spring weather had brought a thaw that sent cascades of water flooding down walls into the streets, until the reservoirs ran dry and the ground soaked it all away.

In the otherwise barren expanse of the fire, rivers once trapped underground now stormed through the dust. The

Fleet River and the Walbrook that had given their names to the streets that had imprisoned them, shook off their shackles of stone and clay, and now ran riotously along long-forgotten paths to the Thames.

Finally, the wind and squadrons of birds had dropped seeds all over the city - in drainpipes and gutters, sills and patios, shoots clung to clumps of detritus and un-swept leaves. In every road and lane, thoroughfare and alley - anywhere there was dampness and the barest nourishment, anywhere it could get a foothold - nature had invaded, and now the whole city was overrun with the rustle of new growth. The pollution had gone and, spurred on by clean air and soil, the streets burst into life with a vengeance. Roots and vines held the city in a stranglehold and roofs that had collapsed under the weight of late winter snow now sprouted pale bushes like the white flags of surrender.

* * * * *

Farran was amazed by the speed with which nature had begun to take over, at the transformation that had taken place in the time he had been away. The grasses that ran down the middle of Kensington High Street were already tall enough to brush against his knees as he waded through. The damp breeze that tousled his shaggy hair brought an unfamiliar smell of earth and leaves that clung thickly to the inside of his nose. He wore a brown salwar kameez and a pair of mud-caked walking boots. Across his shoulder was slung a satchel, out of the corner of which poked a tattered prayer mat. In his hand he carried a makeshift walking stick that was almost as tall as he was, its end scratched and chewed and the area where his hand met the wood worn smooth. At first it had been cumbersome but now the staff felt like a part of his body; it had already saved his life twice and he would sooner part with his shoes than that stick.

Farran drank down another lungful of air happily - this was not a London he knew. A little disorientated he paused and scratched at the newly sprouted beard on the underside of his chin. There was a different atmosphere in the city's streets: a new sound, or absence of sound; he wasn't sure which. He listened hard for the change. It was the harshness that had gone - the emptiness that used to echo from the walls had been absorbed by the vegetation, sucked up in the stomata of the leaves and breathed out again in companionable whispers. Absence had been replaced by a presence and Farran knew that the change was not just in the landscape around him.

He looked about: indoors and outdoors had begun to blend - ivy emerged from some of the windows now and dripped down exterior walls. Facades had cracked off buildings to reveal their insides; rooms perfectly preserved, furniture still cluttered with crockery.

A clatter broke the peace and made Farran turn.

There before him stood a giraffe. It was craning its neck to reach a patch of tufted grass that sprouted from a sodden carpet in a first floor living room. What the hell had been going on while he'd been away?

Taking a step forward he sent a discarded bottle spinning. The creature turned lazily to look at him with its wet eyes, but not considering him a threat, went back to chewing. *First Regent's Park, now this*, he thought.

Earlier in the day he had hiked down from Camden, along the wide street that ran past the park, and that had just been bizarre. It was like something off the National Geographic Channel - but seeing a giraffe on the high street, happy as you like, was something else.

The beauty of the park had been overwhelming, a herd of zebra grazed twitchily by the bandstand, some sort of small white-faced monkeys had set up home in the children's play area and they chattered amongst themselves as he approached. He had decided to name them Abdi Monkeys after his old best friend - because everything that wasn't welded down, they tried to run off with.

He'd rested his head against the railings and watched the park for a good hour. It was a kind of paradise, everything so calm and peaceful. Eventually the temptation had been too strong and he began to climb. At the top of the railings he'd paused, it seemed safe - the lions were still sunning themselves lazily by a chestnut tree on the other side of what had once been a football pitch and now looked more like the savannah. Reassured, he hooked his leg over. Just then there was a flash of green movement among the bushes, something large and serpent-like lunged at his leg, crashed into the fence and sent him tumbling backwards onto the pavement. Farran got up, looking for his attacker, but there was nothing except a rustle of leaves and an ominous low hissing that disappeared into the distance. He decided that he would just stay on his side of the fence from now on.

While he'd been away he'd needed to be on his own, but he'd seen things, things that he couldn't be sure he'd seen, times when London hadn't felt as friendly as now, times when he'd felt the city alert to his presence, as though he were a tick on the back of a great beast that was searching for the cause of the irritation. Sometimes he'd felt the city twitch, the buildings bristling like hairs, nothing he could put his finger on, just the uncertain feeling of another presence out there. At the prospect of seeing the others again he quickened his steps. He wondered what stupidity they'd been up to since he had last seen them.

As he walked up towards the junction with Museum Street, he began to see signs of the others as the unkempt city gave way to a more deliberate chaos. All of the cars that he passed now had their bonnets up and their petrol caps open; in many, the windows had been smashed out and glass crunched under his boots like gravel. Here and there random objects littered the road, dropped like the toys of a spoilt child: swords; a large cracked lamp; a pair of scooters tangled together. He spotted a painting of a beautiful woman sitting with children in a gold frame which lay propped at an angle against a car, a jagged prong of bumper spearing the mother's chest. Elsewhere, a sack of money lay open and crumpled on the ground. It must once must have contained hundreds of thousands of pounds, but now the wind had dispersed most of the contents so that the area around it looked like someone had plucked a red chicken, leaving feathery notes sticking to everything.

He smiled to himself, he knew he was getting warmer. Still, there was no actual sight or sound of his friends. *Even they can't still be asleep,* he thought.

When he reached the museum he was met by a filthy smell. Heaped up against the railings was a huge pile of rubbish that spilled down the entire length of the museum. Cans, bottles, rotten ready meal packets, half empty tuna fish tins all humming with flies, sent up such a stink that Farran almost gagged. *What'd been going on?*

Just then he heard someone on the steps above him. Sarah came into view eating something from a tin with no label. She finished the last mouthful before tossing the tin carelessly over the railing, and as she did so she caught sight of Farran. She looked at him blankly for a moment before turning and walking away.

He meant to call after her but something in that look caught the sound in his throat, as though he were afraid of waking her. The excitement that had briefly bubbled up inside him suddenly cooled.

Sarah's face had been dirty and her blond hair had clung in coppery tendrils to her head. Not like the Sarah he knew at all. She'd looked more like a wraith than a person. This wasn't the welcome he had expected. *What the hell had been going on?*

Anxiously he clambered over the pile of rubbish, through the gate and into the gardens in front of the museum. This too was changed beyond recognition; hardly an inch of grass could be seen now, and it looked more like a scrapyard. Only one square patch was clear. In its centre was a rectangular mound of gravel, kept in shape by garden fencing and levelled off to form a flat platform for a strange collection of objects. Farran lent over to inspect them - a crossbow and bolt, a saucer with a soggy-looking Jaffa Cake, a pair of small solid gold statues, an old rusty lighter, and a bright children's windmill that whirred quietly to itself - all formed part of a neatly arranged shape that culminated in a framed photograph of James Bond. Farran wrinkled his brow in confusion.

"We didn't have a photo of him."

Farran turned around. Sarah was staring past him at the mound.

She continued in a flat, toneless voice, "We didn't have one so William put that photo there instead. It's what he would have wanted. We all put out what we loved most." In her hand she held a packet of biscuits and as she finished speaking she bent down, scooped up the Jaffa Cake from the saucer, and flung it onto the rubbish pile before replacing it with a fresh one. She turned and walked slowly back up the steps without another word.

Confused, Farran followed after her. He could see the full extent of the changes in her; her shirt hung loosely from her shoulders and where it lay against her skin - as she plodded, hunched, across the portico - he could see the awkward shapes of her protruding ribs and backbone. Her once immaculate clothes were now wrinkled and stained and they gave off a sour smell.

The central hall had the same sour smell but stronger, mustier. Particles swam in the shafts of sunshine as though the light made the stench visible. The inside of the museum had fared no better than the outside: refuse and dirty dishes were jumbled up with packing boxes, toys, CDs. There was a vast assortment of random objects, as though a charity shop had been hit by a tidal wave which had then broken against the walls of the museum, leaving a high tide of junk heaped on every possible surface.

Sarah and Farran picked their way along a narrow path between the banks of flotsam towards the Whale Room and their old sleeping quarters. Looking about him he saw that the room had been divided into distinct areas; one corner covered in paintings, another section with weapons, one topped by fairy lights. But the place had grown shabby.

Farran smiled to himself when he saw that an area under a dolphin had been kept empty except for two waiting camp beds.

He continued to turn his head, inspecting the room. There, curled up reading, was the familiar shape of Georgie. Sarah wandered off wordlessly and climbed onto her bed. Farran watched her go and then turned back to Georgie. As he approached she looked up from her book. For a moment she stared at Farran as though from some faraway place, then she threw down her novel and sprang to her feet -

"Farran!" she screamed, and running over, flung her arms around the boy. She was so glad to see him that she forgot to be surprised when he hugged her back.

"Alright," he said breathlessly.

She pushed herself back from him but kept a hold of his shoulders. "Let me get a proper look at you. You look older. Love the beard, and the glass scars have healed nicely. I'm so glad you're safe. The others will be so pleased to see you." And she hugged him again.

Over her shoulder, Farran's eyes came to rest once more on the two camp beds by the giraffe. "Any news on Tyrone?"

He felt Georgie's body go limp. "No," she pulled away

from him and sat down on the platform with a thump. "Oh, Farran," she cried, "it's been just awful." She burst into tears, hiding her face in her hands.

Sliding his bags to the floor he went and sat beside her. He rested a hand briefly on her shoulder before allowing it to plop back into his lap.

"What's happened? This place is like a bombsite. Where is everyone? Where's William and Joanna and Donnie?"

Georgie looked up into his face, "He died. Donnie died," and she pushed her face into his arm. He could feel the sadness being transmitted through his arm with the Morse code of her sobs.

He sat there for a moment, stunned. Then in a quiet voice he asked how, and Georgie told him everything - about the illness, and Donnie's death, how they had done everything they could but still couldn't save him. How eventually, after four days, they'd buried him and built the shrine. How it had affected them all, but none more than Sarah who now did little more than sleep, hardly bothering to eat or speak.

Farran was surprised by the way in which Georgie spoke about Sarah, as though she wasn't in the room, and a lack of sympathy that he didn't recognise; but glancing up a little guiltily he noticed that Sarah hadn't even moved and soon he too began to think of her as absent.

"It was awful when Tyrone disappeared, but we just acted as though one day he could come walking back in. We didn't want to think about the truth. But when Donnie died it was too much, it was as though all of those people we loved…as though it had all happened again. There was just no getting away from it."

Georgie talked and Farran listened. She felt as though she hadn't spoken to anyone for weeks and now it all came out in a torrent. When Georgie had told him everything they sat together for a while, in a kind of comfortable awkwardness, the quiet occasionally punctuated by Georgie's dying sniffles.

It reminded Georgie of when they'd driven together in silence and she was struck that there was a difference between not talking and not needing to talk.

At last she looked at Farran from behind her crumpled tissue, "How did your...stuff go?"

"OK," and then a little more definitely, "Yeah, OK. As well as could be expected." He smiled at her, a thin sad smile that let her know that that was all he could say. In his head though, Farran ran through all the horrible things he had seen and done since they'd last been together, and wished he could say more.

Sitting opposite him and studying his face, Georgie could almost see the sentences forming, and she in turn wished she could decipher the fine twitches in the muscles of his face and read his mind, but she understood enough.

As though as a consolation to them both he added, "I did a lot of thinkin'."

Georgie nodded.

He focused his eyes now on the collection of empty bottles he'd been pretending to look at. "I like what you've done with the place."

"What?" Georgie looked about the room as though for the first time and blushed, suddenly ashamed at what had become of their home. "We, er...because there was no more water in the taps we had to drink the bottled stuff. It's been a real pain carting enough in every day."

"No doubt, man. Shall we go find Will and Joanna?"

"I'm not really sure where they are, but they're bound to be about here some place."

They were both sitting crosslegged in the dinosaur exhibition, listening to some droning music from a stereo hooked up to a car battery. Stretched out between their hands was a tangle of string.

When they heard the others enter they both jumped to their feet. William gave Farran a huge clap on the shoulder and Joanna gave him a happy little pinched smiled and waved manically.

"Thank God you're back, I've been stuck here with just girls to talk to," said William, and then went pink as he continued to try to peel the remnants of the cats cradle string from his fingers.

"Thanks, William," exclaimed Georgie with mock hurt.

"What?" asked William, genuinely clueless.

Farran looked from one to the other, "It's good to be back."

*   *   *   *   *

Later on that night, when the others were asleep, Farran went out alone to Donnie's grave. He opened his book and prayed, and then he unclasped a heavy gold watch from his wrist and placed it gently onto the pile of offerings.

*   *   *   *   *

The next morning Farran got up before the others, found himself a clean spot in the museum and rolled out his prayer mat. He had a lot to pray about. Last night he'd realised just how bad things had been for the others since Donnie's death. That meal was obviously the first time they'd eaten together in a long while. Georgie'd gone to a lot of trouble to make it a nice occasion but there was none of the energy or the joy that there had been before. For a while he was hurt, feeling that the others weren't as pleased to see him as he'd hoped, worrying that the incident in the fire still wasn't forgotten, but gradually it dawned on him that when Donnie had died something had died in the group too. The meal wasn't fancy because they hadn't bothered to stockpile any food; they ate crisps and things scrabbled together and served straight out of the tin. And there wasn't any joy, because they didn't have any of that in the larder either.

He noticed Sarah most at first; she had to be guided in by Joanna to join the others and then she sat on a box, absent-mindedly pushing corned beef about a piece of cardboard she was using as a plate. Georgie quickly lost patience encouraging her to eat, but Joanna, sitting close by, would give her a gentle nudge from time to time, spurring Sarah into putting a forkful of food into her mouth.

Farran began to think about the memorial outside, and the offerings they'd all put on top and that's when he decided what he had to do. He hurried out to put together a few essential bits and pieces, then he went back for Georgie...

Snuggled under his Man Utd duvet, William had been woken by Farran dragging a large sack full of stuff in one hand, and what looked like the inside of a bin in the other. Through drooping eyes he saw Farran go over and shake Georgie awake, then sit down and begin talking to her very earnestly. Georgie looked confused but William couldn't hear from where he was, so he wasn't sure if that was because she was sleepy or because of what Farran was saying. His eyes closed. When he forced them open again after a few minutes, they were still sat on the bed - only Georgie now looked sad and Farran seemed to be telling her off and pointing to the sack at his feet. That's odd, thought William, as he drifted into a dream in which the others' voices dissolved into the wailing of cats.

His eyes flicked open again some time later, to see Georgie and Farran striding off together purposefully. "Too early," he muttered, then looked briefly at his watch which, reading

11:30, confirmed this. He decided to head back to his dream, he could still feel the banger in his hand and smell the cordite. *Here kitty kitty*, he thought to himself as he drifted back to sleep with a contented smile on his face.

Bang, bang, bang, bang, bang.

"I'm sorry, don't eat me, don't eat me," shouted William out loud, finding himself on his feet in his jim-jams and with no idea where he was or why he had been shouting.

Farran and Georgie stood in the middle of the bedroom, while Farran banged his stick against the metal bin.

"Alright, guys, it's time to wake up."

Like a group of under-achieving zombies the others shuffled out of bed and formed a semi-circle around Farran and Georgie.

"What's going on?" mumbled Sarah resentfully.

"It's time we got ourselves organised." Farran took a breath "Will, what did you do yesterday?"

William looked a bit confused, "You know, the usual."

"Yeah but what was that?"

"What do you mean? The usual stuff."

"But like *what*?"

William's eyes narrowed, "What did Georgie tell you?"

"Georgie told me everythin', man, so come on, what did you do?"

"Stuff."

Slowly now, like an irritable teacher pretending to be patient, "I know, but *what*?..."

"OK, OK," blurted William angrily. "I kicked some display cabinets in and Jo and I did some knitting. OK? Happy now?"

"That's my point, we need…really, *knitting*? Huh." He paused, then shook the surprising image out of his head.

"Anyway, the point is you did nothin' useful. None of you did. Not that I was any better before I went away."

William, still confused and now defensive shouted back, "Yeah but at least we used to have fun before Donnie kicked the bucket."

"William!" shrieked Georgie and all eyes turned briefly to Sarah, but she just stood staring at her feet, as impassive as before.

"We got distracted," continued Georgie, taking over from Farran. "We used to have plans, we didn't quite have one we all agreed on, like whether to try and find help or stay in one place, but we had a purpose. And then we just started mucking around all the time and then…you know, stuff happened and we stopped doing even that."

With a screech, Farran pulled the bin in front of him and then began untying the green sack he was holding. "The grave outside, yeah? It got me thinkin'. All them things you put on it…When I was at school, right, before, I had nothin'. Now…" He opened the sack and took out item after item: a beautiful pair of ice-white trainers, a stack of DVDs and games, a wad of money from the pile outside, a brand new mobile phone still in its box. He dropped them all ceremoniously into the bin, holding each one aloft first so that everyone could see it. He took a can of lighter fluid out of his pocket and emptied it on top. He struck a match, then, pausing once more, let it drop.

The bin ignited in a miniature mushroom cloud of acrid black smoke that sent them all running. Farran swore loudly and a few minutes of mild panic followed while water was found to douse the fire. When it was under control, Farran continued. He felt he'd lost a little of his authority and the rest of his speech had to take place at the other end of the room because of the smell, but, still, it had woken everyone up a bit.

"My point," he said, "is that all that stuff that I always

dreamed about havin', I can have. But that it don't mean nothin' anymore, not in this world. I can have better trainers than Abdi ever did…"

"Who's Abdi?" whispered William but Georgie shushed him.

"…but Abdi ain't around to know that I got those trainers. An' as for all of you? Well you can have 'em too, all you got to do is go an' pick up a pair that's lyin' about. So where does that leave us?"

"I don't know," grumbled William beginning to get impatient. "'Cos I don't even like those trainers."

Georgie saw the blood rush to Farran's face and he stood up fast but before she'd even reached out to calm him down, he had puffed out his cheeks and sat back down again.

A little amazed, she tried to continue. "The point is, doofus, that we're all rich, we can all have whatever we want. So, in a way, none of us is rich. What does any of this stuff mean now?"

"I don't get it," said William, partly because this was true and partly because he resented the disruption of his daily ritual of doing bugger all and was concerned that it was starting to sound alarmingly like these two busybodies wanted to take that away from him permanently.

"We can have whatever we want," said Georgie, "It's like we won the lottery, but what next?"

"We sit on our arses," replied William. "Why the hell am I having to say this? What's wrong with you, Farran? You used to be fun."

Georgie sighed. "We've had our fun. We've done stupid things; we've emptied the zoo, we've ransacked galleries and taken priceless works of art. It was childish."

Suddenly Sarah yelled, "Those things weren't childish, they were all Donnie's ideas and they were they best things we've done. Don't you call him childish." Her face was red, she was panting and glaring at Georgie.

Joanna put a gentle hand on Sarah's shoulder.

"I'm sorry, I'm sorry…" But Georgie didn't know what else to say; instead she reached down for a box at her feet and up-ended it. Onto the floor tumbled a collection of books, ampoules of liquid and packets of medical equipment.

"You realise that we're relying on the work and knowledge of our parents, as soon as that's lost we can't get it back. As soon as their technology breaks down we can't replace it. We all assume that what people have created is permanent, even now, because it's powerful and everywhere and all we've ever known, but it's as fragile as we are. In the back of our minds we keep thinking that this is just temporary, we've stopped talking about it but somewhere we all think that this is just a kind of holiday, that some day we'll be rescued and have to go back to our lives – but what if it's not? What if this is it from now on for the rest of our lives? What if we really are all that's left of humanity, of, of *civilisation*?"

"What's your problem?" William was now genuinely angry. "Why are you always doing this, George? There's a whole city full of stuff outside. We're never going to get through it, not in our whole lives."

"*We* might be alright, but what about anyone else, people in the future. Pretty soon the human race – us - we're going to end up being cavemen. I mean, a few months ago the skies were full of planes and you could get to anywhere in the world in a day, now who here can fly a plane? Fix a car? Make a new tyre once all our bikes have flats? Pretty soon in a day we won't even be able to get to the other side of London."

"But why we gonna need to? Ain't we alright 'ere?" asked Joanna.

"Let me put it another way," Georgie's eyes filled with tears and her voice cracked, "Who here knows how to fix a person? When Donnie got sick we were powerless. We should have known more. If we'd have known more maybe…" Georgie stood there, fists clenched, trying to fight back the tears that were now trickling down her cheeks and looking from person to person. "We need to learn everything we can as soon as we can. We need to collect knowledge. You see all of that," she jabbed her finger at the pile of stuff by her feet, "That's all of the stuff that we needed to save Donnie. I've been reading books, I know that's the stuff. I don't know how to use it yet but I'm bloody well going to learn."

"But there must be adults…" said Sarah, automatically, as though it were a tick from her old self.

"What we don't know no one's going to teach us. We need to take responsibility – this is *our* London. *We* are in charge."

Farran spoke up, his voice measured now, "We don't have to make our parents' mistakes. We can have anythin' we want. The whole world is out there – what're we gonna do with it? So far we've just made a friggin' mess – look at this place. Everythin' is ours for the takin'. What do we do now?"

"We have to make a list of what we need to learn," continued George.

"Oh God. I knew it couldn't last, you're going to make me go to school an' do geography, aren't you?" whined William, though he sounded a little less angry now.

"No," said Farran. "We need to learn practical things – medicine, mechanics – how to fix cars, make energy, run engines 'n fridges, how to grow our own food. We've got to start eatin' properly. Everyone can learn what they want to, what they're good at. But we are gonna work – an' hard."

CHAPTER 23.

Over the next few weeks they set about getting things organised. Georgie gradually felt life flowing back into her and, impressed by the change in Farran, she began to look at herself too. It was the organising, the preparation that revived her and made her feel as though she were in control of her own destiny once more.

She was careful not to overwhelm people. When she could feel herself becoming frustrated with the others' efforts and the speed at which they worked, she would hear Tyrone's voice in her head telling her that it wasn't all about the work, to ease up. At these moments she'd miss him terribly. She tried to think of ways to make people have fun but she knew that she wasn't very good at it. And then she'd miss Donnie too. Donnie who couldn't help but have fun and make others laugh - whether they wanted to or not. It was Donnie that had kept them all going in the darkest days, she knew that now. In the end she consoled herself that people weren't really ready for fun yet and that if she could just get them moving maybe the rest would come in time.

So she did what she could. She and Sarah picked up their sailing lessons, enjoying the chance to escape from the others in secret, and as well as organising practical things she set about making the museum a home again. They began by carting away the festering rubbish, creating a dump close enough that they'd actually bother to use it but far enough away that they wouldn't suffer from the smell or from rats. Then they transformed the main hall into a living space – cabinets full of fossils became the supports for marble work surfaces; fairy lights were strung up in great strands across the spines of the dinosaurs; along one entire wall shelves were stocked with every foodstuff imaginable. They hauled in cookers and connected them up to big gas cylinders and finally, at Farran's insistence, they dragged in a huge oak table for meal times. And they all ate – together.

Once they'd dealt with comfort, they turned to the more practical things. It turned out that despite his whinging, William, with his farm upbringing, was a font of practical knowledge. He knew what vegetables to plant and when; he knew how to look after livestock; he knew something about maintaining engines from helping his dad to keep their old tractor running.

This revelation had come about one day when William found Farran and Joanna caked in grease and bent over an old two-stroke engine. Georgie'd been sitting crosslegged next to them, a large book on basic mechanics in hand, barking advice. She was so dirty that she looked like she had been dipped in molasses and she was fighting with pages that stuck together and became more unreadable the more she thumbed through them.

The three of them had just reached the point where all of them, even Joanna, had descended into screaming abuse, when William had wandered over, tightened the gaskets, connected the battery to the starter and fired it up.

What began as an accidental discovery grew to be relied upon. At first Georgie had felt like she would have to beat the information out of him he was so reticent, but this wasn't stubbornness on William's part, he just couldn't believe that the others didn't know these basic things. He'd never been the person others came to for answers and at first it threw him, but gradually he began to like it, and eventually, despite himself, he found that not only was he willingly helping the others' plans but was coming up with ideas of his own. This was uncharted territory for William.

With his help the group began to put things in place so that they could be self-sufficient. They built water butts outside; set-up a library; hooked-up a generator for power; installed Portaloos and spent a long, messy afternoon cutting each other's hair.

Then they turned their minds to food. They rounded up what was left of the animals from the petting zoo, though sadly they'd been released into Regent's Park with the others and the predators had seen to the majority of them. So the group found a children's guide to London and went in search of the city farms. As with the zoo, many of the animals were dead or dying, but in Hackney Farm a well-meaning volunteer had opened the animals' cages as a final act of kindness and they were now roaming the surrounding area, a little thin, but alive.

One by one, with great effort, they caught them and loaded the pigs, goats and chickens into the back of a taxi. This operation had taken over a week, not just because the animals had been so hard to catch, but because the roads were now so pitted, cracked and overgrown that driving down them was a slow and dangerous process. Throughout it all Sarah worked ceaselessly, with a quiet fervour that was a little disturbing to the others and that left her silent and exhausted every night.

They moved the animals into rough-built enclosures in Hyde Park. Then the really hard work began. Under William's direction they began planting. Georgie had naively assumed that this would just mean sprinkling some seeds in the park and making sure that they got watered every now and again. William, however, would allow no shortcuts - possibly because in his role as foreman he did very little of the actual work.

First they staked out an area near the lake about the size of a football pitch, then they had to remove the grass and topsoil, and then condition the soil. Now to those uninitiated in farming (which was all of them) this sounded like a good idea, but when they discovered that this meant long back-breaking days removing every stone, can and plastic bag from the soil, it drew complaints from everyone. Finally though, they had cleared their patch and stood stiff-backed, admiring the large black mark they had created in the otherwise verdant park.

"Thank God we don't have to do that again," said Georgie, examining her mud-caked clothes. She looked back up the slope to where William sat in his deckchair supervising. "We don't do we, William? That's it, isn't it? *Isn't* it?"

"Yes. That's it, all done - we can start sowing now. At least corn anyway."

"What?" said Sarah.

"Well, that will do as a patch for the corn. I thought you were enjoying the exercise."

Sarah said nothing.

"It'll do for the corn," William quailed a little under the weight of Sarah's gaze, "but you'll need to do the same again for the other veg."

"*Other* veg?" she asked in a low growl.

"Yes. That was just the start."

Sarah began to stomp up the hill towards him.

William began to panic, "Of course you could get a tractor to do the next one…"

That was it, after all the work she had put in to get this hateful job finished and they could've used a tractor! She ran full tilt at William, who scrabbled to get to his feet but couldn't seem to leaver himself out of the rickety seat.

By the time Sarah hit him with the full force of her skinny body he was only just tottering onto his heels.

He was snapped back into the deckchair, which folded up around them both, and their joint momentum sent them tumbling down the far slope of the embankment and out of sight.

By the time the others had scrambled up after their fallen comrades the two of them were lying sprawled at the bottom of the hill. They formed one tangled mess of limbs and deck-chair, like a horrible collision between stripy turtles. William was on his back, purple-faced and screaming at people to get the crazy witch off him, Sarah was similarly unable to move but, to everyone's surprise, she was howling with laughter.

* * * * *

Sarah gunned the engine on the Ferrari but the wheels continued to spin uselessly. She leaned out of the window. "Come on, slaves, push or there will be no gruel for you tonight."

Farran and Georgie looked up from their positions at the back of the car. They pushed with all their might, but it still wouldn't budge.

Using the Ferrari to drag the makeshift plough had been Sarah's idea. She'd suggested that if they were going to do it they should do it in style and had gone on to reason that the sports car's wide wheels would give it a better purchase on the muddy fields. But she had been wrong. The car's low profile just meant that it got stuck on every uneven bit of ground and Georgie and Farran had spent most of the day knee-deep in churned-up park rather than having the cushy time Sarah had promised. The two of them had only persevered because it had been so great to hear an idea come out of Sarah's mouth - or anything in fact. Her mood had been brighter recently and they would have done almost anything to keep her happy. But their patience was now running out.

Farran shifted his weight on the edge of the car bringing the rear axle lower. The wheels bit into solid ground, and the Ferrari lurched forward, leaving the two of them floundering face-first in the mud.

Sarah looked back out of the window again, "Come on, you two, no lying about on the job!"

Farran wiped a gobbet of soil from his forehead. "I think I liked her better when she was depressed."

"Don't worry," said Georgie mildly, "She can't possibly keep it up, she'll be whining again in no time."

Farran settled where he was on the ground and watched as the car skidded along for all of twenty yards before grinding to an inevitable halt again.

"OK, game over," yelled Georgie above the roar of the engine. "This isn't working."

Sarah cut the motor, hopped out and trotted back to the others. "But it was going so well," she said with a smile.

"You wanna try pushin' instead?" asked Farran.

"Aaah, Fawwan, did 'ou get all mucky?" and she pinched his cheek.

Farran looked over at Georgie with the pleading eyes of a dog being mauled by its owner's child.

Georgie raised her eyebrows. "Perhaps she *can* keep it up."

"Who can?"

"Nobody," said Farran

"You'd better get hold of William," said Georgie. "It's obvious we don't have the first clue about what we're doing."

Farran pulled the walkie-talkie out of his back pocket but Sarah grabbed it from him.

"Actually, I'll do it. I haven't had a go on one of these yet… Hello good buddy this is Ice-Queen, come back."

William's confused voice came on the line, "Sarah, is that you?"

"Sure is. What's your twenty? Over."

"Eh? Sarah, are you feeling alright?"

Sarah laughed, "Don't you watch films? What's your twenty - where…are … you? Over."

"Oh, OK. I'm…" William's voice died away in a fuzz of static.

Sarah looked at the others. "I think I've lost the signal. What happens if I twiddle this?"

As she twisted the frequency button the handset gave out an almighty screech...

"...*search... Infected continues. Current...Sector G3. Over.*"

It was an efficient voice, a strange voice - an adult voice.

The group stared dumbfounded at the walkie-talkie in Sarah's hands.

A second voice came on the line, perhaps a woman's, "*Proceed...Leviathan*" it said, "...*-emain covert...Over.*"

The three looked at each other in alarm. "Quick, quick, say something before they hang up."

Sarah brought the handset up to her mouth, blustering, "Uhm...Hello? Hello? Can you hear me? We are survivors, there are five of us...children. Can you help us?"

The second voice cut in, "*Shut...transmission...squaaark-*" and the walkie-talkie went dead.

Sarah clicked frantically at the transmit button on her handset. "Hello, hello? We are in the Natural History Museum, come and rescue us. There are five survivors. Hello? Hello?" She looked up at Georgie, "Nothing."

"What d'you think?" asked Farran.

Sarah looked at them both with wild hope in her eyes. "Maybe there are people still alive on the continent. They said 'infected', maybe they're just waiting until there's no more danger of disease before they come and get us?"

"They seemed like they were in a proper hurry to get off," said Farran.

"And," said Georgie, and an edge of worry crept into her voice that even she didn't fully understand, "these walkie-talkies only have a range of a couple of miles or so. That means that whoever was sending that transmission must be somewhere *in* London."

Farran's face clouded. "Well, whoever they were, they know where *we* are now."

CHAPTER 24.

Tyrone realised he was wearing a backless hospital gown. He realised someone had dressed him in it and it made him ashamed and it made him angry. He screwed his eyes up tight, tried to breathe, long and deep; then he listened.

He could hear the repeating squeak of the bed's wheels and below that, the distant rumble of machinery. There was a sharp scent of hospitals, but mostly he could smell the stale soot of the fire, the blood clotted in his own nostrils and could taste the irony residue on the roof of his mouth.

Who are you?

He couldn't be sure if he was talking out loud or only in his head.

What do you want from me?

Whoever was pushing him was behind him and he could see nothing.

P...please? Please answer me.

A set of double doors loomed ahead and then crashed open as the bed charged through them. A second set followed quickly and then they came to a halt in a small, bright room. Now that they had stopped moving a horrible feeling of exposure wriggled over his body.

There was the clank of metal and then the bed was tipped until Tyrone found he was lying almost vertically. Hazy figures stepped out from somewhere, blocking his view, and Tyrone caught a smell of stale sweat which didn't seem to fit.

A leather strap was fastened about his forehead, pinning him so that he was now completely immobile. He could sense the white figures moving somewhere to his side, then he felt a sharp sting in his arm and saw that a tube now led up to a clear bag of liquid above him.

Everything became confused.

Or maybe more real.

Tyrone didn't know, because his ears were ringing and sights were drowning in front of his eyes. He saw white shapes with claws like knives. He felt pain - agonising, cutting pain – and the hot, sickly feel of his own blood dribbling away. There was the smell of rubber making him want to gag. He thought he saw the face of the red-headed boy from the school, his eyes blank like fish eyes and his white gown soaked with blood.

He had to warn the others. Warn them of the danger. Of the monsters. Warn them that the ghosts were real. He could feel his arms tingling and growing colder, sense a fading somewhere inside and a new certainty that this was the end. He had to get away.

Had to warn...

CHAPTER 25.

Over the next weeks and months the changes grew in them; the grumbling subsided, and, as plants began to grow and the animals grew fat and healthy once more, the group began to feel a sense of pride and direction. At first a tension remained - each day Sarah would listen on the frequency that she'd found, waiting for contact, but no more was heard, and no one came. Eventually the tension and fear just got ploughed into the soil along with the seeds. Routine and the unending stillness of their world seemed to make the idea of 'others' ridiculous. A peace settled on them.

Each day they got a little stronger and their attachment to their land got stronger too. By the end of August the black, unyielding earth had become neat rows of sprouting growth. Orange football nets drooped from posts above the vegetable patch, and CDs on string span in the breeze sending multic-oloured flashes of light across the park, protecting their little harvest.

Georgie stood on the platform of the Royal Albert Memorial in the yellowing of a late summer evening and sur-veyed their work. It was after sunset but light lingered in the sky like the dying warmth in the stone beneath her feet. She pushed her tousled hair back with hands on which the nails were now stubby, with soil crammed beneath them. Hands on which newly hardened calluses formed a Braille pattern that read 'work'. She breathed out a happy sigh which almost sounded like 'mine'.

Down in the field below, Sarah put aside her trowel and eased the crick out of her back; to stretch her legs she decided to wander over towards the chicken run. She stopped at the fence and watched Joanna with the chickens, throwing out handfuls of popping corn. She had named them all, and although Sarah was too far away from the girl to hear what she said, she could tell that Joanna was talking to each individually as she fed them. She had taken them on as her special responsibility, tucking them up into their shed at night and nursing them when they were sick. Right then she was bent over a russet-coloured hen which seemed completely unperturbed by the girl's stroking and fussing. This was Joanna's little kingdom, it was nice for her.

"How's Justin doing?" called Sarah, deliberately pointing at the wrong chicken.

Joanna turned. "That ain't Justin, that's Ashton. Justin's the one with the limp," she said simply. They watched as the chicken hopped up onto the fence. "But you knew that, he's the one you found by Harrods."

Sarah felt herself blush as though she'd been caught doing something childish and sneaky. She felt a momentary flush of anger - she had only been trying to be nice after all, give Joanna a chance to show off a bit. The old her would have clenched around that resentment, nurturing it like an oyster with a bit of grit, but somehow now the feeling just travelled down through her and was earthed into the soil.

She smiled and gave a little snort of acknowledgement.

Joanna plonked herself down on the bench next to Sarah and plunged her right hand into one of the deep pockets of the parka. She seemed determined to wear the old coat despite it being far too warm, which had the unfortunate effect of making the girl smell slightly of sweat. Out of the offending coat Joanna pulled a crumpled bag of pistachio nuts. She put one of the nuts in her mouth, cracked the shell with her teeth and then stored the shell up between her gum and her cheek while she ate the nut.

Sarah tried to make conversation, "It's warm-" Joanna spat the two halves of the shell in a powerful and unselfconscious gob. Sarah tried to continue unfazed "-this evening. Isn't it?"

Joanna nodded and put another pistachio in her face, repeating the process.

"D'you know, I was well scared of the chickens when we first got 'em," mumbled Joanna, the words having to negotiate their way around crumbs of pistachio nut. "I fought chickens 'ad teeth, I was 'fraid they'd bite me." She instantly flashed a look up at Sarah as though she had said too much, she had that expression she wore sometimes, like a dog expecting to be kicked.

Sarah didn't say anything but she didn't mock either.

Joanna continued. "My mum wouldn't let my sister 'ave a pet. She wanted a budgie or summink – *ptweee* - I was glad. Geezer in one of the flats downstairs - looked like a paedo – 'ad a cockatoo, right nasty bastard it was – *ptweee* - go for ya as soon as look at ya. I guess I thought they was all gonna be like that - *ptweee* - but I reckon it's 'ow you treat 'em. If you treat 'em nice then *they're* nice back."

"I think you're right. These lot seem to love you."

Joanna's face lit up with a little smile, "Yeah, they do." She put another pistachio in her mouth as though pushing that delicious but dangerous thought back inside her mouth along with the nut. She noticed Sarah looking at the bag. "Want one? Pistachio nuts, found 'em in this posh shop on the 'igh street. They're sorta salty an' sweet at the same time."

She thrust the bag at Sarah, who smiled politely and took one.

"Take a few."

Sarah took a few. She hesitated momentarily, thinking of the dubious hygiene of Joanna's hands. She didn't want to get sick like...

She shoved a nut in her mouth.

Joanna watched her intently. "You got to crack 'em then spit the shell. You can't eat that bit."

Sarah did as she was told. Cracked the shell and took it out of her mouth so she could eat the nut.

"You 'ave to spit it. It's half the fun," encouraged Joanna. Sarah half-heartedly spat - the shell landed with a pitiful splat on her own shoe, leaving a trail of spittle down her chin.

"Don't you know 'ow to spit?" chuckled Joanna.

"I guess not." A slightly peevish note had entered Sarah's voice.

"You gotta really gob it, else you get it all over. Look..." And she gave an almighty flob that sent a projectile of spit and shell a good six feet.

"Wow!" exclaimed Sarah, impressed and disgusted in more or less equal measure.

"You try."

Sarah demurred for a minute or two, but Joanna's insistence and enthusiasm won out. She tried again, this time with force, and was surprised and delighted - and surprised to *be* delighted - when her oyster of spit landed just short of Joanna's own effort.

"Right, now you 'ave to work on your aim..."

Walking by the chicken run William was intrigued by a strange noise coming from the fence. Moving closer he was met by a hail of pistachios being spat at him by the two girls, followed by cackles of laughter. He jumped back, narrowly avoiding an indiscriminate scattergun effect as the girls stuffed their mouths full of nuts and spat them as long and as hard as they could.

"That is *disgusting*," shouted William indignantly, but this only seemed to make the girls cackle louder. He turned on his heel and marched back towards the vegetable patch, thoroughly jealous.

William picked up Sarah's fallen trowel. Walking past Farran to the top of the hill he grumbled, "I think I liked it better when she was miserable."

"That's what I said," Farran called after him. "Don't worry, Georgie promised me she can't keep it up."

From her vantage point Georgie watched the little scene. She saw William exchanging looks and comments with Farran and then return to digging. Down below her, the heads of her companions bobbed up and down amongst the vegetables as they worked, careless laughter and snatches of conversation drifting up to her.

But those echoing sounds didn't stop there, they drifted past her, reaching another set of ears. Somewhere behind her something lurked, unseen…

It watched from the deep shadows thrown by the buildings. It skulked at the edges of the streets, like a nasty memory at the edge of remembering, afraid to cross the wide-open space of the road that separated it from the safe shrouding darkness beneath the trees.

It paced the hinterland back and forth, back and forth, all the time watching the backs of the children, dividing its attention between the sentry up high and the group in the field bellow. It was a feral thing, running on instinct; it loped frustrated, torn between its desire to reach the unsuspecting people and its need to remain hidden.

A beetle of tiredness ran up its spine making it twitch and shiver. The damp of the evening began to settle on the blackness of its sinewy back, making the scars there stand out warm against the growing cold.

Desperation overcame fear and it bounded out across the road. It had made its decision.

Silently, swiftly it padded up the steps of the memorial, darting its head now and again to make sure it remained unseen but always remaining focused on the back of the girl above it.

Closer and closer until it was just a breath away from the girl…

Hearing a sudden noise behind her Georgie turned. She let out a brief gasp.

"Tyrone?"

The boy fell half-naked in a crumpled heap at her feet. She dropped to her knees and cradled his head. Her friend looked up at her from vein-cracked eyes, he spoke one sentence and then he collapsed into unconsciousness—

"They're coming!"

CHAPTER 26.

The rest of the group had come running towards the monument - William and Farran still brushing the soil from their hands; Sarah, face pale and eyes red, wet with tears, Joanna holding tightly on to one of her sleeves.

"Is that Tyrone?" gasped William, astonished.

"I thought he was...Where's he been?"

Farran looked up at Georgie, "He looks bad. What happened to him?"

But she had no answers.

Tyrone's face was drawn, hair matted with grease and filth, his clothes shredded. As he panted for air Georgie could feel his bones against her, thin and fragile. There was a smell about him; disinfectant and something rotten and horribly sweet – a thick smell of illness and neglect. She looked at the cuts and oozing scabs which encrusted his grubby face and neck and was ashamed by the nausea she felt.

He was still twisting feebly and Georgie had to turn his face towards her, "What did you say?" she asked with growing fear, "*Who's* coming, Tyrone?"

But it was no good, there was no response.

Georgie tried to think, feeling that the others needed an explanation - but she had no idea what to say. She looked up from them and out across the expanse of park. A light evening wind was shaking the leaves on the distant trees, their shadows creating a lengthening shade along the borders of the park. Georgie allowed her gaze to drift towards the few iron railings which still stood around the place; she saw the patches of rich earth they'd cultivated, the quiet grey of the tall buildings beyond – then her eye caught something out of place.

A white form was wading its way slowly through the waist-high grass.

Georgie turned to the others, "Hey guys – guys look! What the hell is that?"

The rest of them turned, following the direction of her trembling finger.

The thing almost moved like a man, ploughing towards them, but it was featureless, baggy – a creature half-formed. As she squinted through the fading sunset Georgie caught sight of another one to the right, emerging slowly from the tree line, moving silently as apparitions. Then she saw another and another, until scanning round she found that they were everywhere about them now, a ragged circle pressing slowly inwards from every direction.

Sarah and the others were frozen, staring in horror as the strange figures shuffled closer.

Georgie frowned, trying to reach sense through the fog of shock.

Closer.

What were they?

There was something terrifying about them, a menace in their silence. These things moved with dogged purpose, plodding rhythmically as the circle tightened around the edge of the hill. The sense of unreality, of merely observing changed rapidly to fear. Georgie's stomach clenched, her breath choking like a hunted animal as it tries to bolt.

But she didn't bolt. Somehow, she stood her ground whilst the others drew towards her in a loose knot at the top of the monument. They stopped, unable to move further, their hands reaching out as they felt for one another.

The faceless creatures came on, closing the gaps, fixed on the children.

Georgie edged a little way around the stone step of the monument, trying to get as much of a view as she could. By the time she reached the other side she found that the figures were even nearer, one coming closer than the others until it was climbing the steps.

The thing rushed forward suddenly and Georgie, high granite steps behind her, stumbled and collapsed clumsily onto her backside. Reaching down it grabbed a handful of her hair and began to pull Georgie towards itself. Instinctively, she grabbed hold of its hand, but her fingers slipped against a greasy surface and as the figure twisted and pulled she found herself struggling to keep her balance.

In panic, Georgie lashed out, striking something hard with her right hand. It wasn't much of a blow, but to her surprise the creature jerked quickly backwards and stumbled. In that second its hand was wrenched away from her head, still clutching a thick strand of her hair, and despite the pain Georgie seized her chance and rolled away, scrambling and clattering back up the steps towards the others.

As if in a dream she looked about her. All around, forms were moving in towards the others. Chaos had erupted. Sarah and Farran were lobbing lumps of rock for all they were worth, William swung a heavy shovel to try and keep them at bay, whilst Joanna was nowhere to be seen, as though she'd mysteriously disappeared into thin air.

Tyrone was suddenly staggering to his feet beside her, a look of terror on his battered face. He turned, filled with urgency, and screamed simply-

"It's Leviathan - run!"

Something snapped in Georgie – there was suddenly a fear so strong that it seemed to slice through the immobility, a rush of adrenaline making legs which had felt dead and wobbly, desperate to move.

The others looked over.

"There!" Georgie pointed to the widest gap in the circle of figures around them, "Head there. Run through, go!"

And as if released, Farran, William and Sarah led the way with crazy half-balanced strides down the steps and the grassy slope, always one step away from going head-over-heels but picking up speed in a flailing whirl of arms.

Farran was the first to burst through, sparing a glance over his shoulder to see William just half a step behind. The two of them raced off towards the nearby stretch of trees where Joanna had appeared, waving them on. Sarah and Tyrone were barely a step behind after that, their long legs eating up the space as they shot through.

Now as Georgie rushed headlong she saw that the figures were closing what remained of the gap, stretching out their arms even as they moved to close the circle off for good. She ducked her head down, charging like a bull with a shriek half meant to terrify the creatures and half meant to drown her own fears.

Her eyes were almost closed, but she felt something grasp her sweater – then the hold rip free as she hurtled through, her shoulders smashing something heavy out of the way with a blow that almost sent her off balance.

Georgie didn't look back, but she heard the sounds of pursuit and redoubled her pace as she made for the forested grove ahead.

She turned to Tyrone, loping painfully beside her, "What the hell are those things?"

"Leviathan," he wheezed not slowing for a moment.

"Are they human?"

Tyrone didn't answer.

CHAPTER 27.

Weeks before.

Tyrone didn't know how many of them there were but he knew now that they were human. They all wore white plastic suits, faces hard to see in the depths of their masks, and he couldn't distinguish them from one another but they were flesh and blood.

He was prodded and examined; they took his temperature and his blood pressure. They took him to the room with blue walls and they jabbed him again and again and drained blood from him until Tyrone thought he was going to pass out. But nobody said a word to him or even made eye contact; it was as though he wasn't even there, just a piece of meat to be processed.

Someone was holding his arm; he was surprised by how heavy it felt. They were lifting it so they could feel for his pulse, moving him like he was a lifeless puppet.

Tyrone wanted to move, to feel sure again that his body worked. But it was like he had to remember how, to try and work out what it was he should do, which thoughts sent the impulse shooting to his limbs.

He tried and his arm twitched, flapping heavily like a dying fish. As his hand flicked upwards it clipped the edge of the nearest person's hood, catching at the overhanging flap and pulling it away slightly.

He could hear the man's scream, muffled by the plastic; gloved hands scrabbling, terrified, tugging the suit back into place as he stumbled backwards as though he'd been scalded.

Tyrone sensed commotion erupt around him.

Then came the needle again and again blackness.

*   *   *   *   *

Just as cities grow upwards, so too they have their roots; pipes to feed it gas and water, wires to bring it power, tunnels flowing with trains full of people.

And whilst London had blossomed, busy and bustling above, there had always been a different, secret world hiding in the dark beneath. Disused tube stations, forgotten service tunnels, graveyard catacombs and ancient sewers. These were just the first, decaying and silent layers.

But cut deeper through the strata of the ancient city and it was clear that newer growth had spread; tendrils of steel and concrete - pulsing with the buzz of electricity and the hum of florescent lights - had bored a city beneath the city.

With civilisation came secrets. Throughout the country the government had hidden fragments of its fear and its power away from prying eyes - their acres of files; their research centres; shelters and nuclear weapons. Fearing a war which never came, installations with miles of corridors, space for hundreds of personnel and impregnable communication arrays had been built beneath green fields and rolling hills in the countryside. Before anyone even realised that they were there they had been packed away and sealed off.

The Government made sure it was safe in the cities too. There were rumours of bunkers beneath offices, tunnels from Parliament to Downing Street and highways made for evacuation from Buckingham Palace to distant airfields. Years before, one reporter claimed he had taken his bike through a hatch in Trafalgar Square and spent the night cycling through a maze of empty tunnels, but nobody had believed him.

But there was truth to some of the stories.

Almost two decades ago it had been built. Leviathan. There was so much compartmentalised information, so many departments, dead ends and buried files that it wasn't clear who had ordered it. Perhaps nobody had really and the entire project was just a bizarre bureaucratic accident.

* * * * *

With a lurch he felt himself and the bed turn, the ceiling spinning. One by one the straps which held him down were unbuckled, though his limbs still felt numb and impossibly heavy. Someone lifted his wilting body up by the armpits, dragged him through a doorway and dumped him painfully down, the burns on his back suddenly throbbing.

Tyrone heard the door slam and tried desperately to focus on where he was. The floor was covered with cold white tiles and he dragged himself over their smooth surface and onto an army camp bed against the far wall. His head swam and he felt like he was going to throw up, but at least he was sitting upright now.

The bed had no sheets or pillow. In the corner he saw a small sink and next to it a plastic bucket instead of a toilet. The only window was a tiny one in the top of the door, but it was covered with wire and made from frosted glass.

* * * * *

Leviathan's workers seemed like normal inhabitants of London. They had homes and pets and barbecues and wore suits to work. They had shopped in supermarkets at the weekends and argued with their husbands and wives about mortgages. They weren't monsters.

Or they hadn't been.

They would tell people they worked for the Department of Regional Networks. Nobody knew what that meant – but then it didn't really mean anything. If someone at a party ever asked what the job involved, they only had to talk for a couple of minutes about 'local budget accountability' or the 'sub-management of contracted spending agreements' before the other person became so bored they stopped caring.

They hated Mondays like everyone else and looked forward to the weekends. They braved the rush-hour traffic with the other commuters. But when they got to work the smart clothes came off and they put on white lab coats and plastic biohazard suits.

* * * * *

Tyrone was alone in his room. He didn't know how long he'd been lying in the stuffy cell, there was no way to tell. All he knew was that the flurry of activity had suddenly ceased. It felt like days since anyone had been in. No one had brought him water or food, no shadows had passed by the frosted window of his door. He began to worry that they'd forgotten him completely.

He'd been over every inch of the cell; the walls were cold and hard and they gave a depressingly solid thud when he sounded them with his knuckles. There were no grates and no vents - the only way in or out was through the rounded metal door.

He sat back down on the bare bed and thought of his friends, hoping they were safe, that they'd escaped from the fire. He wondered if they were worried about him, if they even knew what had happened to him - if they knew they were not alone.

More time passed. Finally Tyrone heard the echo of quick footsteps coming up the corridor. They stopped outside the room. Tyrone shouted, he yelled for food, but no reply came. Another set of footsteps followed down the corridor. There were loud voices raised, then what sounded like a scuffle. Tyrone heard the familiar hiss that meant his door would release, but it only opened a fraction before it was slammed shut.

The voices were raised in anger again. There was a single loud shout, followed seconds later by the tramp of many pairs of feet. Someone knocked the light outside his room and the shadows flew around the walls. Something slammed heavily against the door of his cell and then there was silence.

Hungry as he was Tyrone was too afraid to call out now. He waited in the quiet and the swinging shadows. All he knew was that he had to find some way to get free, he had to find some way to warn the others.

* * * * *

Above ground, the place was as dull as any other ministry building. The revolving glass doors led through to a clean, simple lobby in which two receptionists sat. If anyone came to the building by accident they were politely but firmly re-directed to another department.

When they arrived, the men and women would nod to each other or comment on the weather before making their way to the lift at the back of the lobby. There were no stairs here, no offices somewhere out back – only the one, ordinary-looking lift.

No unauthorised person ever made it as far as this lift, but if they had, they would have seen to their surprise that there was only one button, and if they had known where this button sent them they would have been even more surprised.

Through the earth under London, past the pipes and telephone cables; through soil and clay, past the bones of ancient plague victims and forgotten flint tools. Slicing through solid rock the shaft went a thousand feet below the surface of London.

From there, four sub-levels branched out in long corridors, labs, storerooms and living quarters. A small town had grown under the great city like the root system of a tree.

There was space for hundreds down there.

In theory.

* * * * *

Tyrone was back in the blue room. He tried to turn his head but could barely move it. He heard the door open and caught movement at the corner of his eye as two people entered the room. Both of them were in baggy biohazard suits, white and shapeless. Inhuman. Patches of steam bloomed then receded on their small plastic faceplates, and at a distance it was impossible to tell what they looked like or even what sex they were. They stopped, staring at him like blank-faced statues until Tyrone shrivelled like a specimen under a hot light.

After a minute they moved closer to the bed, bending stiffly at the waist to stare down at him. Tyrone was able to get a better look at them, the lights inside their hoods casting a harsh glow upon their faces. One of them - a woman – was strangely tall and had bony, horse-like features. She looked like she might be in her late forties, but it was hard to tell since her hair had been dyed a dense black and lay scraped-back from her forehead in strands like dry nylon. Her skin too looked unnatural, hanging from her neck and chin in waxy folds as though her sallow face were slowly melting.

The man who stood next to her was much shorter, but he had a quiet, cold power and reminded Tyrone of an irritable headmaster. He had thin, greasy hair which was wiped over his balding head in a stringy comb-over. His scalp was red and patchy, and as he leant over, Tyrone could see that it was topped with a layer of crusty yellow flakes, some of which had collected at the bottom of the mask.

"Welcome," said the woman. She used the word without any warmth, "I am Dr. Hubbard and this is Dr. Lightbourne. You are?"

"Tyrone."

"Tyrone. Tyrone," she rolled the name around as though tasting it.

"Tell me, Tyrone. Is there any history of heart disease in your family?"

"What?"

"What about cancer? Any lung disease?"

"I...," began Tyrone.

"Are you taking any type of medication?" asked Hubbard.

"No," said the man called Dr. Lightbourne, "probably not. Not so easy to pop round to your GP or the chemist anymore, is it, young man?"

Dr. Hubbard didn't wait for Tyrone to reply, "Do you know why you're alive, Tyrone?" she asked, looking at him intently. Even the whites of her eyes were yellow, as though she had somehow gone stale.

"Did it cross your mind that you've been really rather lucky in that regard?"

Tyrone was confused. "I don't..." he began.

"A massive plague wipes out almost every living human

and you've never wondered why you're running around fresh and free?" It wasn't just a question. She sounded so bitter, so angry.

"Who are you? Why am I here?" asked Tyrone, but they ignored him.

Dr. Lightbourne leant forward and pulled up the sleeve of Tyrone's gown. He examined his arm carefully and turned to his colleague, "It's there."

"Good," replied Hubbard, "we'll begin full spectrum testing and biopsies this afternoon. Prep for lumbar puncture."

She turned back to Tyrone, "Well, young man, let's hope you're as much help to us as we'd like you to be."

* * * * *

Leviathan's personnel had survived because that was exactly what the place had been designed for. The plague broke out and they retreated inside. They closed and sealed the doors and whether from panic or a single-minded sense of duty, cut themselves off forever from mortgages and families.

But the plague had hit suddenly – a whirlwind of panic and chaos. Nobody had ever planned for the confusion of disinformation; the evasion of the politicians; the clashes between civil-servants and the military, between the scientists and the managers. Only some made it to Leviathan – a crazy mix of surgeons and policy-makers and half-retired army officers. Going to the surface without protection meant certain death. Most of what they needed they didn't have, and what they did possess didn't seem to help a bit.

They muddled through, arguing, discussing, failing and slowly, in-between the lab work and the writing of reports, all of those trapped in the base had begun to realise that everyone outside their little project had died.

* * * * *

The next few days were a blur of pain and sickness.

They took more blood and even removed tiny plugs of flesh from his body. They put something like a cotton bud in his mouth and rubbed it around the inside of his cheeks. One time they painted his spine with something which was cold and smelled of alcohol and then, without warning or the soothing, professional words he expected from hospitals, something was pushed through his skin and deep into his back with a flame of searing pain that almost made him vomit and blackout - so deep he could hear the bone crack as it made way for the needle.

Then the questions began. He couldn't remember what they were, only that they asked him again and again and they never seemed satisfied with what he told them.

They'd put a needle in his arm; he'd feel the icy sensation of something being pumped into his blood and then after that only flashes of memory he didn't know if he could believe.

* * * * *

In the Arctic Circle, when winter really sets in, the darkness can last for months. The stresses are unbelievable; people get depressed, they drink, they fight, some commit suicide. They slowly go crazy. Then the summer returns and they're rewarded by long months of bright summer sun.

Everyone in Leviathan had spent the past long months trapped underground. But here there was no end, no fresh change of season and no hope. Just the stale air trapped between the sterile corridors.

The unceasing glare of the fluorescent lights was almost as bad as constant darkness. There was no dawn, no warm blush of sunset. Twenty-four hours a day the same sickly blue light shone. When they woke up, when they ate in the canteen – everywhere they walked or worked it was impossible to escape its constant, merciless hum. Just like with guilt, there was nowhere to hide.

Their milky, bloodshot eyes were ringed by dark shadows. They grew pale – skin waxy and so translucent that you could see the fine thread of blue veins beneath its surface, parchment-thin as though the smallest movement would split the flesh along their cheeks. Soon they hardly recognised themselves in the mirror anymore.

* * * * *

One day he was wheeled back to the room, but this time only Dr. Hubbard and Dr. Lightbourne were there. The room felt quiet without the usual clinical bustle, and Tyrone's unease grew at this odd change.

"Hello Tyrone," said Dr. Lightbourne, jovially, his voice strangely muffled behind the mask, "thank you for your help the last few weeks. Hope it hasn't all been too uncomfortable for you."

The man gave a flat, professional smile.

Tyrone looked back in disbelief as he continued.

"As you probably know, we've run a fair few tests to try and get a bit of a clearer picture," Lightbourne tapped a thick file of papers. Tyrone saw that the binder was covered in scrawls and stains, odd against the man's formal façade. "It's been tremendously helpful."

Tyrone looked from the man to the woman in front of him, expecting something more, but they just seemed to be watching him.

"What do you mean?" he croaked, throat dry. Tyrone realised he hadn't spoken proper words for a long time. "What's all this about? I don't want to be here."

As he said it he felt stupid, like a whining child. Then, just as quickly, he wondered why these people had the right to give a damn what he sounded like.

The woman, Dr. Hubbard, leaned towards him now, her bony features a relief of glare and shadow behind the mask.

"This isn't just about you. It isn't about what you want or what you need. Right now you don't know what is best for you. It's far more likely we do, don't you think, Tyrone, so why don't you let us get on with our job?"

There was something about the two, something out of place - an intensity behind their words, subtly and chillingly wrong, like a film going slightly out of sync.

Dr. Lightbourne carried on as before, "Your blood told us a lot. It told us why you're alive."

Even as he said it, Tyrone could feel his arm, bruised from all the needles, and the sickening ache in his bandaged spine.

"You were lucky. Blessed. You have cause to be grateful, Tyrone," added Hubbard.

Tyrone tried his best to meet their gazes, "What happened?"

The question didn't quite fit - he knew that – but it was the best his mind was able to scrape together.

Dr. Lightbourne tapped the file he held with a pen, "The thing is, old chap," he said, ignoring the question, "although you've been a useful resource, we really need more than one harvest subject to be sure we've got it cracked." He leaned in closer, patting Tyrone's knee like a friendly uncle, "But you look tired, my boy. We'll pop you back for a little rest and the three of us will chat more later, eh?"

* * * * *

As the months after the plague had gone by, the people in the base had begun to feel despair creep in. They had performed their jobs, done what they were trained to do and, at first, that had kept them going. But the apparatus which had held them together soon became their undoing. Its rigidity warped and broke them instead of strengthening them.

Nobody else seemed to be out there. The machinery of government was silent. They used every form of communication they could think of; but the internet had become a silent void, every radio frequency a hum of empty static. They were forced to rely on their own generators and food supplies. The city's CCTV network, that web of cameras which had followed Londoners every minute of their lives, was all they had left. But power was failing, cameras blinking on and off in a random pattern across the city, leaving them groping like blind men, searching for any signs of life. Finding nothing.

They were alone. Buried alive. Trapped only with each other and their fears and suspicions.

* * * * *

With difficulty, Tyrone turned his head, feeling the stiff bones crunch in his neck. Doorways broke the interminable sweep of grey walls at regular intervals. He caught a glimpse of a desk with a computer and a phone; in another room, rows of pristine white benches with an array of glass containers and microscopes. A few were filled with what looked like glass-fronted fridges, others piled to the ceiling with cardboard boxes.

What he saw next was only a flash, but it was too shocking to miss. The sickness lingered in his belly and the image still glared brightly - he had not been mistaken.

Laid out on steel tables were children, silent and still.

Even in the dim light he couldn't mistake the skin mottled with the pale blue sheen of death. In that flash he had seen the ruthless surgical excavation: the red chasm splitting their torso from the neck downwards, the white stubs of sawn-up ribs, the livid pink flesh like butchers' meat. He thought with a groggy horror, though he could never be sure, that one of those children was the red-haired boy that had disappeared from the school.

The people here were looking for answers. And in their search for them, nothing else mattered.

* * * * *

"Now, Tyrone, you're only the beginning – there are more of you. Both of us know this. We need to speak to your friends and you're going to tell us where to find them."

Dr. Lightbourne leaned forward this time, "This is science, Tyrone, you don't want to stand in the way of science do you, my lad?" his balding head was cocked to one side, as though waiting for an answer. "Think of it as all being in the spirit of co-operation."

"If it's all about co-operation," said Tyrone, "then why do you keep locking me in that cell?" He didn't dare mention that he'd seen what they did in the spirit of cooperation.

"I'll admit we haven't much to offer in the way of hospitality," said Lightbourne, with a little smirk, "but it's hardly a cell, my dear chap."

Dr. Hubbard stood suddenly, "Forget it, Harold. I'm not bothering with any more of this. We haven't the time and frankly I haven't the patience."

Lightbourne merely arched an eyebrow, as though all of it made little difference to him.

Rising to her full height she stepped over to Tyrone and

grabbed him roughly by the jaw, twisting his head so that their eyes met. "You've had your chance and I'm not babying you anymore."

She gave his head a shake. Her gloved fingers dug hard into his jaw and Tyrone felt the humiliation of tears beginning to well up in his eyes.

"You're going to tell us the location of the others. You're going to point right to it on a map and draw us the bloody route if you have to. Is that understood?"

Tyrone's heart beat so hard he could hardly breathe, his throat felt as if it was closing up. He squeezed his eyes to clear them and looked back into that waxy face. Without even thinking about it, he'd made a decision.

"Kiss. My. Arse."

Her face darkened. Tyrone thought he heard a sharp intake of breath from Dr. Lightbourne in the background.

Hubbard turned, walking silently across the room and over to a tray of stainless steel instruments. In a moment she returned, holding something which looked like a heavy set of clamps attached to a rod.

"Do you know what this is, Tyrone?"

Her eyes didn't leave his for a moment as she turned the bright object over in the light.

"It's called a rib spreader," she leaned in a little closer until he could see her cruel mouth above the mask's respirator, "once we've used a chisel to crack the chest open, this thing pushes the ribs aside, usually snapping each and every one of them. This is just one of my toys, Tyrone; I've got drills and scalpels and even pliers. And if you won't tell me voluntarily, I'll just have to get it out of you some other way."

Tyrone still didn't speak. He hoped it was bravery, but inside he knew he was partly too damn scared to say anything.

"I suggest that you give my colleague's words serious consideration, young man," put in Dr. Lightbourne.

"There's just me," said Tyrone. "There aren't any others."

"Liar!" snapped Hubbard.

"No, honestly. That's all there's ever been – just me."

The two doctors looked at one another, Lightbourne raising his shoulders in an almost imperceptible shrug. Dr. Hubbard went once more to the tray across the room, returning with a small syringe which already seemed to be full. The needle was in his arm before Tyrone could brace himself; he felt ice seeping through his veins and had time for one final thought – *escape…*

CHAPTER 28.

The group crashed through the door of the museum like the devil was at their heels.

"What the hell were they?"

"Were they people? I think they were people."

"They were adults."

"What?! No."

"Did we lose them?"

They rushed to the windows but saw nothing. They couldn't be sure though, those things could be out there watching and waiting.

"What did they want?"

"They just came from nowhere."

"Damn that was scary."

"Where did they come from?"

"They just kept coming, slow and quiet."

"Are we safe?"

"They couldn't move too fast - we outran them. I think we're safe in here."

Suddenly Tyrone, who had been panting on the ground saying nothing, scrambled up. He flung himself at the door and began slamming the bolts in place with his thin, trembling hands. There was something contagious in his actions. Without another word the others ran to help him, locking the entrances, moving in a fever as they hammered the windows shut.

Dragging sleeping bags and blankets, the six of them huddled together in the smallest room they could find, waiting in anxiety, crammed together and watching the door as though it might crash open at any moment.

That evening the darkness settled like a curse. No streetlights, no help to call on – only shadows, the silent silhouettes of empty vehicles and the barking of lonely dogs in the distance. The magnificent building of the Natural History Museum subtly changed. It had been a palace – ornate, vast, limitless - now it felt full of holes. Its cavernous halls made them feel exposed; creeping sensations at their backs, hearts jumping with every icy echo.

The silence in the room was painful; tension hummed but a dull exhaustion fought with it, pressing down upon them all. They'd lost track of the time, isolated in a fuzz of darkness and fear, then Tyrone spoke-

"I didn't know how many of them there were. They all wore those white plastic suits…"

* * * * *

When Georgie awoke, she only knew it was morning by looking at her watch. They'd deliberately chosen a storeroom without windows and they'd pushed filing cabinets right up against the door. She was surprised to see that Farran had slept – he was still rubbing sleep from his eyes as he crouched over the camping stove, trying to warm himself as he watched a pan of coffee start to boil.

Sarah lay slumped under a bright orange blanket and sometime during the night Joanna had huddled in next to her and now lay asleep on Sarah's lap. It was difficult to tell if William had slept. His eyes looked red and sore, but there was something about the way he was glaring at the door, the muscles in his jaw pulsing like a heartbeat, which made her think he'd been on guard all night.

Tyrone's story seemed so shocking, so strange; if she hadn't seen the white suits for herself, seen the terrible state that he was in, Georgie didn't think she would have believed him. It changed everything.

Leviathan. The word had been bothering her. Where did she know it from? *Leviathan.* Then it hit her – the walls! The graffiti. Every time something had happened - the camera moving, the lights on Oxford Street – she'd seen that word stencilled onto the walls. They'd been there all along, just like Tyrone had said.

She didn't know how long Tyrone had been looking at her before she noticed him. His eyes were dark-rimmed, his head very still. But the hollow look she had seen yesterday was gone; there was something behind those dark eyes - prowling, demanding. After only a second she had to break his gaze, then she walked quietly from the room.

Something he had said stuck with her more than anything – *I escaped in the end…but I think they wanted me to…*

She'd checked from the windows again, but even so, Georgie felt the knot of anxiety as she slid back the bolts and wrenched the big door open. The air surprised her - cool and smelling faintly of damp blossom – as though in some way she expected that summer had been cancelled. Emboldened, she took a pace out onto the flight of stone steps, but now she was looking out instead of in, seeing London as the object, the unknown quantity.

Was it a playground or a jungle? She saw the cracked windows of distant buildings and wondered what might be behind them. A paper bag rustled bumpily along the road in front of her and for just the fraction of a second she felt an instinctive clench in her belly, an animal suspicion of the movement.

She knew the others were all behind her in the museum somewhere; but for the first time, that knowledge of the group didn't give her the comfort she was used to.

Yesterday had done something to them. Knocked the spirit out of them. It wasn't just that they'd been attacked, it was *who* they'd been attacked by; it was what Tyrone had finally been able to tell them and everything that it meant.

Independence had cost them through these past months. It had cost time and labour, and it had cost them Donnie. It had cost them their parents and everyone they had ever loved or relied on. But it had also cost them something else; a version of themselves, an old self which had had to die too. Things they'd believed about themselves, things they'd believed about the paths which lay before them in their lives and everything they'd believed about the way they thought the world worked. They'd abandoned all of that – like shedding a skin. They'd made these sacrifices and lost their childhoods because that's what circumstances had demanded of them.

And now it seemed that, like a lurking cancer, this remnant of the old world - the adults' world – had been waiting all along. Adults had been there all the time, during everything they'd struggled through. The group had missed the old world, had held a vision of grown-ups which represented for them the order they craved and which they had then to rebuild, no matter how many mistakes they made along the way and no matter how much they still had to learn. They had sacrificed what they had been before on the altar of this belief.

Then the old world had returned – the *adults* returned – not as they had remembered but as something sick and frightening. If even half of what Tyrone had said was true, none of them were safe. It felt like a betrayal of their memory - as though things hadn't fallen apart after everyone died but had all been corrupt and rotten before.

After the air outside, Georgie now noticed how rank the atmosphere had become in the tiny room, thick with the stale smells of morning - unwashed bodies, stale food and bad breath. It was stifling, but nobody seemed to be stirring, each of them silent, slumped against the wall and wrapped up in coats and blankets like invalids.

This wasn't right. It wasn't the way. Now that they understood what had happened to Tyrone it was clear – these people were cautious, scared even, but they were determined. It might take them a while to regroup but they *would* come again.

* * * * *

"I say we leg it, get out of here and find somewhere good to hide."

"And where do we go, William? Do we just keep running? Living off of tins of food we scrounge and sleeping under bridges forever? We're here, we have a place to live already."

"But we can't fight 'em, can we?" asked Joanna.

"Why not?" demanded Georgie.

"But they're *adults*," said Sarah.

"And there's lots of 'em," added Farran, although he seemed more to be thinking it through than making an objection.

"This isn't right," objected Sarah. "This just isn't right. Why are we acting like this? How do we know they're not trying to help us?"

"Are you bloody mad?" William turned on her, "Are you cracked or somethin'? Where have you been? You can see what they did to Tyrone. You heard what he said."

"Our stuff's here. Why run?" Georgie said, turning to Farran for support. "Why *not* fight? Why *not* defend this place?"

"It's too big, there's no way we can keep them out all

by ourselves," Sarah was sitting up straight now, her fists clenched, grasping the hem of her blanket.

"The fact that it's so big could work in our favour." Georgie was animated now, turning to each of them, gesturing as she spoke, "This place is like a bloody maze – seriously, do any of us even know how many rooms there are here? Have you got any idea how many fire-escapes and attics and basement tunnels this place has got?"

"So we stay here?" asked William.

She noticed that now, though he was scrutinising her every word, the line of tension had begun to disappear from his jaw. Georgie nodded, "We stay here and we defend it. We fight."

"Fight," said William with a nod, a smile beginning to tickle the corners of his mouth.

"We can make this place secure. Get weapons, fight 'em off." Farran was warming to the idea, clearly on board.

"But how? We're not an army," protested Sarah.

Tyrone spoke for the first time, "*They're* not an army," he said, and his voice sounded clearer than it had since he returned, stronger.

"What do you mean?" asked William.

"Things weren't...*right* with them. It's hard to explain," Tyrone faltered, "they're cracked. I don't know what they were supposed to be but something didn't work. I heard fights. I got the feeling that they're just as lost as we are. They're making it up as they go along. This woman Hubbard is in charge and she's a nasty old bitch but she's not a soldier or anything."

"So we fight to protect ourselves," said Farran.

"It's not like we have to kill them or anything," added Georgie, "just make them realise it's not worth their while. That we can protect ourselves."

"We fight," said Tyrone, "we have no choice, and anyway, I owe them. We do what we can."

"Like what?" asked Joanna, more inquisitive than anything.

"Look," said Georgie, her voice rising with excitement, "Remember all those things our parents always told us not to do because they were too dangerous? Like messing with fireworks or playing with broken glass?"

"Or firin' catapults?" said Joanna.

"Yes," nodded Georgie.

"Throwing bricks," put in Farran.

"Exactly."

"Shooting cats up the bumhole."

"Er, not really. But I guess you're on the right track, William."

"So we grab a bunch of stuff," said William, "and we fix this place up and we make it tight as a mermaid's..."

"Something like that, yes," agreed Georgie.

* * * * *

One of them was always up on the roof, taking it in turns to stand sentry duty and scan the horizon and the streets below with a pair of binoculars and a walkie-talkie.

Down below, William and Tyrone seemed to have worked out a system between them, running back and forth tirelessly with armfuls of baseball bats or swords stolen from the Victoria and Albert Museum. They collected bags of supplies and tools and took air rifles from army surplus shops. Later, they ripped the back seats out of the Land Rover and drove off again. When they returned it was clear why they had wanted the extra room. The boot was stacked with fireworks, the remaining stock from newsagents and even toyshops throughout the neighbourhood, scooped up in armfuls and stacked in the back of the car. Together, the group left caches of weapons everywhere about the building, stacked bundles of arrows on the upper floors, and barricaded every way in they could find.

Eventually, Tyrone skulked off to get on with what he mysteriously referred to as 'special traps', so Georgie and Sarah were left to make a tour of the museum and try to spot any potential weak points. Having completed their inspection of the second floor they were walking down the staircase to the main hall when Farran and Joanna walked in.

"How's it going guys?"

"Alright," said Farran, "We put planks across all the windows. We even managed to nail some sheets of corrugated iron over the windows on the ground floor. Every level's been sorted." He indicated outside with a nod of his head, "The broken glass in the trash out back was handy. We stuck it on the ledges an' that. If the cement has time to dry it'll be good. That stuff rips yer hands up bad if you're tryin' to break into someone's gaff."

"I won't even ask how you know that," said Georgie.

"Fair enough. We also got extra chains for the doors and scavenged some scaffolding poles to prop some of them closed."

"And we trailed some spikey wire everywhere," put in Joanna.

"Barbed wire," Farran clarified with a look at Georgie, "Couldn't use too much 'cos even with gloves and that it's tough to drag about."

William crashed his way carelessly through the front doors lugging, as ever, his large canvas bag behind him.

"Everyone good?" he asked, matter-of-factly.

Farran shrugged, as though the question was pointless, but Joanna smiled at him sweetly.

"So," said Georgie, suddenly feeling like some sort of middle-management plonker on a team-building exercise, "anyone have any plans? Any more ideas we can initiate?"

Georgie cringed inside. *Any more ideas we can initiate?* What the hell was she on about? Why not just start a Power-

Point presentation and hand round coffee and biscuits. Were any of them buying this?

"We've got an arsenal of weapons now," offered Sarah.

"And this too," said William.

"What's that?"

"It's a super-soaker," replied William with the air of explaining something painfully obvious.

"For water?" Sarah asked, her brows knitting.

"Not this time, no."

"So what are you going to put in a giant water-pistol if not water?"

William smiled, his eyes wide with creative wonder, "Sewage."

"As in...y'know...pooh and wee? *Toilet* stuff?" asked Sarah, incredulous.

"Yup," answered William proudly, "got it fresh from the Portaloo outside. I mean, who wants *this* stuff fired at them?"

"These people are murderers. Killers," said Tyrone, "They're going to charge in here and you think that thing is going to stop them?" he shook his head. "We need some more batteries. I'll see you later."

* * * * *

Georgie gathered the scattered medical supplies into one room, William double-checked the local camping shops, Joanna stockpiled food – they all worked. The fear hadn't dissipated, but the rhythm they'd developed over those months, the easy division of labour the group had managed in the fields, seemed to keep them focused.

Just after lunchtime, as Georgie and Sarah were on the top floor, ferrying armfuls of bricks up to the roof, the lights overhead flickered and went black for just a second. The girls looked at one another. *The generator. Someone was trying to cut the power.* The two of them dropped what they were doing and ran down to the ground floor.

There, in an odd moment of relief, they saw William trotting out of the Mammal Room whilst stuffing a set of jump leads into his pocket and whistling. He noticed them and paused.

"Alright? How's the work going?"

Georgie let out a breath, visibly relaxing.

"We thought they were attacking. The lights went out."

"Oh that," nodded William, casually, "don't worry about it."

"Was that you?" Sarah asked, eyes still wide with anxiety.

"Yeah, Tyrone had an idea for something using the electricity and asked me to sort it."

"Something for this place? Y'know," Georgie said, looking about, "something to help?"

"That's the plan," William replied.

William had taken what looked like a plastic disc out of his pocket and was now turning it over and over in the palm of his hand.

"What's that?" asked Georgie

William looked down at the bright plastic, a strange expression on his face, like someone who'd just woken up.

"It's one of those infrared thingies. A motion-detector. Donnie and me found 'em in the toy shop."

Georgie realised that the look on William's face was one of sadness; an expression so rare for him that it had taken her a moment to recognise it.

"Oh yeah," she said, looking at the discarded 'Junior Spy Kit' boxes at his feet, "I remember you guys arguing about whether to bring any back."

"I was right though, wasn't I?" said William, without meeting her eyes. "I was right saying they'd be useful."

"Yeah," agreed Georgie, "they were a good find."

This sudden dip of William's gave her an uncomfortable feeling. Water was wet, ice was cold, the sun rose every day – and William was… William. He was good at hitting things with heavy sticks, and as long as he wasn't hungry things were pretty much OK. She was glad when Farran, Joanna and Tyrone appeared.

Each of them was sweaty and covered with grime.

"Hi guys," said Sarah, far more relaxed now that most of them were present.

"Hey," said Farran, although Tyrone only nodded by way of answer.

"Got it done," said William, addressing Tyrone now.

Tyrone nodded grimly, "Good."

Georgie noticed it again: the change that was clear even in his face. Tyrone had been quiet before, but there was always kindness there, bubbling beneath the sarcastic wit. Now she saw something which made her sad and frightened at the same time – something furious and lost.

"How're things going?" William asked them.

"Pretty good," Farran replied, "Me 'n Tyrone siphoned off more than enough petrol."

"How many water balloons did you fill?"

"Dunno. Twenty or so. They take ages. We weren't sure how to do it at first but we found a kind of pump thing in the kitchen; that way we can get 'em filled pretty fast without them bursting and coverin' the floor in petrol."

"What about if they get in – have we done enough?" asked Georgie.

"Made a start at least," said Farran.

"How about we tie a paint can to some string so that if someone opens the door it swings down and hits them in the face?" suggested William.

"Great," said Tyrone, in a voice filled with sarcasm, "That'll really help. Or maybe we could put glue on the walls so they get messy clothes or sandpaper on door handles so that their fingers get all scratchy. Do you really think a couple of paint cans are going to stop these monsters, William?"

"They will if I put six-inch nails through them."

Tyrone nodded thoughtfully, "Fair enough, then."

CHAPTER 29.

Farran found it just as easy to look through the scope as to use the binoculars. The sky was steadily darkening. The atmosphere had grown heavy, a faint breeze growing from the east, and he was sure a storm was coming.

He liked the feel of the air rifle pressing against his shoulder; it was like being able to see something in the distance and touch it at the same time. One little squeeze on the trigger and a lead pellet would hit whatever was under his crosshairs. He scanned the streets again, the black cross sweeping over the parked cars; a post box, standing like a red sentry on the corner; the patches of tall, wild grass which had begun to grow in every abandoned spot.

Farran paused, swept back. Was that a pigeon - another quick fluttering of wings? The view flew past as he searched the corner of a building. Lifting his head he surveyed the wider scene with his bare eyes; he still couldn't see anything, but it was as though he could *sense* that there was movement waiting somewhere, a disturbance about to appear again.

He let his eyes relax, just waiting.

There it was – a flash of movement in the same spot. A shape appeared, but this time it didn't move away. Then, moving slowly into the stillness of the streets, he caught two or three more white shapes beginning to creep from the shelter of the distant buildings. It was easy to point the scope this time and zero it in. He could see them clearly now, their

white bio-suits hiding their bodies, bunching up around their
breathing apparatus, making them look deformed, hunch-
backed. They walked with the same slow, relentless movement
that he remembered from the attack in the park. Worst of all
though was the silence: they moved without a sound, except
for the slight squeak of their suits and the faint hiss of their
breathing.

He picked up the walkie-talkie by his side.

"William? William, are you there?"

The handset crackled.

"You're s'posed to call me 'Nighthawk'."

"Screw that, just get up here."

"Why? What's happening?"

"They're here."

"Who?"

"Pizza Hut, who d'you think?"

"Bugger!"

"Exactly. Just tell the others and then get your backside
up here."

A minute later he heard clattering as William climbed up
through the skylight and, closely followed by Tyrone, made
his way across the flat part of the roof and over to where he
was lying.

"Where?" asked Tyrone. Even though he was moving with
an almost frightening energy and purpose, Farran could still
see the changes in the other boy – the gaunt cheeks, the ugly
bruises and scratches.

Farran pointed to the street below, "There. And over there
– see? They're everywhere now."

William had picked up another air rifle, "Yeah, I've got
'em. One just moving past that van."

"Have they seen you?" Tyrone asked him.

"Nah," Farran shook his head, "don't think so. I've kept my
'ead down."

Farran watched through his scope as the man, crouched

low, crept forward. A second later there was a loud 'crack' as William fired and an almost instant puff of dust appeared, the shot snapping into the brick wall behind the intruder.

"Bugger," William cursed.

The man was close when seen through the scope but oddly distant at the same time, as though Farran were watching a movie with the sound turned off.

William cocked the rifle and slipped in another pellet. He pulled the rifle into his cheek again, holding it perfectly still and taking advantage of the man's sudden stillness to aim with care.

This time the instant the gun cracked the man jerked and grabbed his neck like he'd been stung. Even at this distance Farran could make out the blood which trickled down his suit.

"Nice," he whispered.

"Cheers," replied William, matter-of-factly, "Ha! Look – the bastard's ducked down beneath the van."

"Can you get him from here?" asked Tyrone.

William gave a little shrug, "Sure. But hitting his ankle isn't going to do much."

Farran looked out across the street again. Two more had appeared, shuffling round a distant corner. Another materialised behind a truck, then another, appearing like wraiths.

"There are so many of them," whispered William.

Farran wished they'd moved the parked cars, but there just hadn't been time.

Although moving cautiously, the suits were making up the ground between them quickly. They had already passed the first line of cars and were advancing into the road.

Farran caught his breath; he could tell now that there weren't only men, but women amongst them too. It was just like Tyrone had described. Women with long greasy hair; wretched-looking men with hollow eyes and chins covered with stubble. There was nothing official or formal about them at all, but instead something subtly horrifying in their dissolution. Dirty, mad, desperate – bringing chaos and cruelty.

Tyrone's voice broke his thoughts, "The air rifles are too slow."

"You're right," Farran nodded.

"The bows then. Only a little faster, but much more damage," said William.

*   *   *   *   *

It really gave Georgie the creeps. OK, they were high up and could easily see to the other side of the street, but it felt like they were leaving themselves unguarded downstairs. Perhaps Sarah had been right all along. Maybe this place was just too hard to defend, too full of holes.

She, Sarah and Joanna were together on the top floor. As soon as they'd heard Farran's warning over the walkie-talkies they'd run straight up and begun to slide the rockets into the lengths of pipe and line up the next dozen. They had a box full of the things, in different sizes. Bright blue ones with designs of silver stars, black ones decorated with a red dragon, smaller ones with lightning bolts. She formed a chain with the other two, passing rockets along and stacking them up. One minute it was like getting ready for a party on Guy Fawkes Night – then the next, Georgie looked outside and caught the terrifying sight of figures in white plastic suits creeping slowly towards the museum.

*   *   *   *   *

William had got into a good rhythm with the bow, notching and firing off arrows in quick succession. Farran, still crouching, shuffled over to the large canvas bag and picked out another bow for himself. He grabbed an arrow and tried to get it in place, but the pointy end simply slipped down at an alarming angle and ended up pointing at his crotch. Robin Hood always made it look so easy. He tried again. The arrow stayed where it was supposed to, but he was holding it too firmly – the second he let go it shot off sideways, clanging into the wall an inch from William's ribs.

"Watchit!" William yelped.

"Sorry," mumbled Farran.

"Other direction," griped William.

William turned, drawing back the bowstring with deceptive ease. The attackers were close enough for him to aim straight at them this time. He released. The arrow streaked down into the street below and embedded itself in a suited figure's foot with an oddly muffled thud. The man paused mid-step and looked down at his front foot as though confused.

There was a shout of pain, but it was only when Farran saw the blood begin to gush out over the man's boot that it hit home that there were people under the suits and they would have to be hurt if the group wanted to stay safe.

Two others made a scuttling dash across the road and over to the central traffic island. Slight shifts at the periphery of his vision told Farran that others were doing the same. He watched as a jagged line of white figures began to run towards the gates when suddenly there was a screeching whoosh, a streak of sparks and an explosion of bright blue stars right in front of them. Dark smoke wafted off to the right with the wind, obscuring the two for a second, but it was soon clear that they had ducked back behind the railings of the traffic island. Before their colleagues could react there was another screeching whistle - then another and another - as right the way along the street bright spheres of gold, red and purple fire ignited with a mighty crack. The bombardment continued to shoot out from the museum. The air was split with a confusion of deafening sound whilst the foremost of the attackers were forced to dive for cover or scurry backwards as the fireworks flew down into the street and burst into a blazing succession of colours.

The thick, familiar smell of gunpowder rose to Farran, William and Tyrone, as they saw the smoke thicken and swirl, its blackness broken by flashes like a lurid battlefield. The barrage was impassable. The girls on the floor beneath loaded and fired, loaded and fired until their stack of fireworks was empty.

Finally there was silence. The smoke wafted upwards towards their noses, reminding them of dark autumn evenings and bonfires. At first it was hard to make out anything down below; everything seemed still. Then indistinct movement began here and there amidst the thinning smoke, and a second later suited figures burst from the clouds in a crouching run. In a matter of moments at least a dozen of them had reached the steps and entranceway of the museum itself.

William dropped his bow and turned to the others.

"I can't get a decent angle now. They're too close to the building."

"The bastards are right up to the door," said Tyrone, lying flat with his head peering down.

The three of them could see the rising panic in each other's eyes. The sound of banging against the thick front doors echoed upwards.

"We have to stop this," said Farran.

Tyrone picked up one of the bricks from the pile they'd prepared. "We have to break them up otherwise they'll get through in no time."

He turned at the sound of the others clambering through the skylight to join them.

"We've run out," said Georgie, panting for breath, "all the fireworks are used up."

"The bricks," said Farran, indicating the neat piles arranged over the flat roof space, "give us a hand."

Tyrone took aim and lobbed the brick he was holding towards the tightest knot of invaders then began to pass them back to Sarah and Farran. William grabbed one in each hand and unceremoniously tossed them over the edge.

The first one hit the floor with a hollow 'clunk' and smashed into a dozen red fragments. The noise as the suits beat against the door was deafening, but as more and more projectiles clattered down around them they began to pause, then seek cover in the face of this devastating hail. Some flattened themselves back against the wall of the museum, others bolted like sheep in a hailstorm and tried to crouch behind bins or even use each other as shields.

Joanna and Sarah worked like a machine – Sarah handing over bricks as quickly as she could and Joanna simply flinging whatever reached her hands just as quickly. Tyrone, though, was taking careful aim, adding the strength of his arm to the force of gravity as he sent bricks flying towards the crowd below. None of the white-suited figures could stand in one place for long enough to assault the door.

One man paused, perhaps attempting to rally his colleagues. He had no sooner raised his arm than a chunk the size of an egg smacked into the top of his skull followed by another which struck his collar bone, snapping it with a crack. Barely able to stand upright the man staggered sideways, one hand trying to cover his split hood whilst the other hung limply at his side.

They weren't going to be given a chance to regroup.

Tyrone threw the first of the petrol balloons. Bright blue, it looked strangely festive for a moment as it span and wobbled through the air. The usual 'splat' when it burst was covered almost immediately as a bright pool of fire ignited and spread out on the pavement. William now also had his Zippo lighter out, setting fire to the wicks they'd tied to the balloons and passing them to Tyrone. Wherever he saw a safe haven below or a gathering of government people he'd pitch one of the deadly bombs. The stink of petrol grew, liquid swathes of blue flame caught and rose into burning walls.

"Not too near the building!" warned Farran, the memory of the fire's terror still fresh in his mind. As Tyrone raised another lit balloon, Farran could see the reflected flames burning in his eyes and it was only then he noticed Tyrone's chilling grin.

Below, one group were trying to make some sort of shield out of a park bench, carrying it above their heads and scurrying along like a wooden tortoise. It was a bad move, both William and Tyrone now concentrating on the target so that the colourful balls arced out in quick succession, splashing fire into life around them with ever-greater accuracy until finally one struck home. One of the men began to scream as fire crept quickly up his suit; in a second he dropped to roll on the floor, the bench instantly lurching sideways and sending others sprawling.

"That's it – we're out," shouted William. "There's nothing left to chuck unless anyone's got a pair of hand grenades hidden down their pants."

"I'm sure Donnie would've had something to say about that," whispered Georgie.

"They don't look like they're givin' up," said Joanna.

Sarah looked at the white shapes below, there were so many more of them than she'd imagined. "I think we've made a terrible mistake."

"We had no choice," breathed Tyrone.

"Back downstairs," said Farran, "go - we can't let 'em get in."

* * * * *

Standing in the lobby, the group stood frozen in indecision. Beyond the barricaded windows they could hear people yelling back and forth to one another, the voice of a woman shouting orders.

Dark shapes flitted behind the gaps in the boards.

A thumping began at the entrance, so hard that the massive doors rattled on their hinges. Then it seemed to spread so that there was pounding all around them, so loud it was hard to think. A hand poked through the letterbox and began scrabbling, searching for a handle. The pounding continued at the barricades, at the doors, at the walls themselves.

The glass of the window to their left broke a second before the planks inside began to shudder. There was the brutal sound of hammers and crowbars, then individual planks began to work loose from the wall, shafts of light slashing through the gloom of the museum as they fell.

"Stop them!" yelled Farran. "Don't let the bastards through!"

Georgie looked about and spotted a discarded sheet of corrugated iron.

"Help me with this," she called to Tyrone and Farran, "they'll smash that stuff in no time."

Together they dragged it up to the rapidly disintegrating barrier, shifting it up and into place across the gap. The blows still came, crashing the three of them back before they thrust forward again with their makeshift shield. The attacks were doubled and they could now feel the power of bodies shoving forward, adult hands trying to heave them back.

They couldn't hold it. There were just so many of them.

"What now?" gasped Georgie, the fear in her voice audible even above the sounds of splintering wood and ringing metal.

"Leg it," groaned Farran, "I'll hold this, you two get up those stairs and I'll catch up the minute I see ya round the corner."

* * * * *

William, Sarah and Joanna were already on the ground floor and running when they heard the door splinter. Without looking back the three of them sprinted down the corridor, through the Mammal Room and past their old beds, only pausing when they reached the gift shop beyond.

Dropping his heavy canvas holdall William heaved down the chain-link shutters which separated the shop from the rest of the museum and began to fiddle with its lock. Only the rear exit remained now, leading out from the shop and deeper into the museum's displays.

"What do we do?" Sarah said, voice rising, "William, what do we do?"

William reached into his bag and handed her a spiked, medieval mace. It thudded to the floor even as she tried to hold it with both hands.

"What am I supposed to do with this?"

William shrugged, "Hit 'em."

The metal shutters had been enough to keep wandering visitors from entering the shop after closing time, but they looked horribly flimsy now. Through its wide links they could see the white figures enter the corridor and begin to march swiftly towards them.

"They're comin'," whispered Joanna.

"It'll hold 'em," said William, his confidence surprising the other two.

A sallow, horse-faced woman seemed to be commanding the intruders, urging the gaggle forwards with a young man out at the front. Even though his eyes were dark-rimmed and hollow and his face a mess of curly stubble, Sarah thought he'd probably been handsome once. But as he marched up to the shutters his gaze swept across the three of them without any sign that he saw them as anything other than prey.

Sarah felt like her insides had jammed as she watched them advance, heart and stomach now a single lump. She was walking backwards without realising it, her hands raised as though she could make him change his mind.

The others behind him waited for his signal, looking half-expectant and half-nervous. Bracing his legs to rip the flimsy partition away, the man reached out and grabbed it with both hands.

His head jerked back with a painful grimace, his spine arching in a sharp spasm. Sparks began to smoke and sizzle where his hands now gripped the metal. A sharp, fizzing hum rose in the air as Sarah realised that the man was being wracked by an electric shock and she now saw the jump leads clipped to the bottom rungs, the red and black wires trailed over to the array of car batteries.

For a few moments the man's body shook and spasmed, the smell of burnt meat and plastic choking the air. Sarah felt dizzy almost immediately, the view swimming before her eyes as the blood thundered in her ears. Only William and Joanna could see the other figures freeze and start to retreat.

Sarah flopped over and sat down heavily. Little dots of perspiration stood out on her waxy face and her eyes were red and watery. It was horrible, just too horrible.

A little smoke still wafted across the room and Joanna zipped her parka up over her nose. William opened his mouth, about to speak, then suddenly stopped.

A high, repetitive beeping sound was coming from somewhere in the distance.

"Alarm clock?" asked Joanna, her head cocked to one side.

"No," William was alert, like a guarded animal, "it's one of the motion-detectors, they're trying to get round the back. Stay here."

And with that he was off, running out of the room and down the passage.

* * * * *

The sounds of smashing glass and splintering wood seemed to come from everywhere as Georgie and Tyrone pelted past the dinosaur skeletons towards the main staircase.

"Where did the others go?" shouted Tyrone above the noise.

"Dunno. They ran off to the left somewhere."

She turned to where a barrier of planks was beginning to split and fly away in chunks, but the shouts and crashes came from every side and she knew that if they paused for even a second they'd be trapped.

* * * * *

Sarah and Joanna watched William disappear round the corner, both hesitating for a moment. At the other side of the room, people in the corridor beyond the grille began to advance cautiously. Unable to take their eyes from them Joanna and Sarah walked slowly backwards, torn between that terrible view and the unknown dangers William was running towards. Soon their backs were pressed against the wall, but as though someone had been waiting, an arm smashed its way through the window behind them and grabbed Sarah by the hair, yanking her backwards so hard her skull smacked against the stone windowsill.

Sarah screamed and pulled at the hand, but the grip was firm and she was being swung around like a puppet. Joanna slapped and hit, but the huge hand just seemed to tighten its grip further, pulling Sarah backwards as though it meant to heave her straight through the window and out into the open.

The first cautious suit had tried the grille and found the power gone. Now they crowded against it, shaking and heaving at the flimsy barrier as they tried to get to the two girls beyond.

"Get out," gasped Sarah, both hands behind her head as she tried to pull her hair free, "Get out and find the others."

"No," said Joanna simply, not even pausing as she hammered at the intruder's arm with her small, grubby hands, "I'm stayin' with you."

There was the sound of snapping metal and a rattle as the grille lifted a few inches and stuck.

"Go!" yelled Sarah. She was panicked; there was no time. She felt the fear in her and it came out with the sound of anger, "Go now or you'll be caught as well. Get out I said!"

Joanna said nothing. She gave Sarah a quick, reproachful look and then turned, running out the way William had gone.

Again the arm pulled. Sarah could hardly resist the force now; her head flew back, a fuzz of gloom and bright dots clouding her vision as she heard the crack, then a searing pain as the splintered wood gouged a cut across her neck.

The arm pushed her forward again, preparing to repeat the blow. Her body sagged as she came away from the wall, a little freedom of movement, and somehow Sarah knew she had only that moment to react.

Grasping the gloved hand she pulled herself a little closer and sunk her teeth in until she tasted the iron tang of blood and felt smooth bone.

She heard the man's scream and swiped blindly at his head, her hands grasping the smooth plastic of his hood as she pulled the mask away.

The man screamed again, in fear this time, Sarah tumbling backwards still holding the mask.

She was on the floor, dizzy but free, and began an unsteady, meandering run through the far exit.

CHAPTER 30.

Crouched, William cautiously poked his head into the room. The man, who looked surprisingly like his wrinkly uncle Trevor – bulbous red nose and old-fashioned moustache visible even through the faceplate – was wriggling the top half of his body through the broken window, his suit caught in the trailing barbed-wire. William saw the fallen plank which had set off the motion-detector and at the same moment heard the last boards across the window begin to crack away.

This was no time for stealth.

He grabbed the plank, bounded to the window and whacked the man hard round the side of the head. Without pausing he was off and round the corner, disappearing into the corridor beyond before the man could manage to get the rest of his body into the room.

* * * * *

Joanna was lost. She'd been living here for months and now everything looked different. It's because she was scared, that's why. Left and right were getting mixed up, there was shouting and crashing all around, glass breaking and wood breaking. She wished she could find a friendly local policeman, or an escape ladder or a nice big weapon. Those people were everywhere down here and she was all alone.

* * * * *

One of the few real military types amongst them, the man had decided not to wait for the others. Carefully, he felt his pounding head, blood trickling down his hair and pooling at the base of his mask. They were meant to work as a unit but if he wasn't able to give that chubby ginger kid a good beating on his own he'd eat his own combat boots.

There were only a few rooms in the corridor; this door was as good a place to start as any. The man paused, looking up at the crudely written sign:

Beware of the Tiger!

He ripped it down from the door and screwed it into a ball. "Stupid kids think this is a bloody game," he snarled.

With a savage kick he smashed the door open, stepping into the room with both fists ready.

The trip wire went with impressive ease. If he'd had time to look up he would've spotted the five hundred pounds of stuffed Siberian tiger before it fell, crushing him instantly.

* * * * *

Just as Georgie and Tyrone were reaching the top of the first flight of stairs, they heard Farran galloping up after them and, barely a second later, shouts and the sound of crashing as the last of the barriers gave way and the invaders began to climb through.

"There's a load of weapons here," shouted Tyrone, retrieving a large holdall from where it had been stashed and positioning himself squarely to defend the head of the landing, "grab something and get ready."

He hefted a baseball bat with barbaric relish, anger animating his tired body. Farran had grabbed a golf club, and Georgie found herself holding an iron bar. Now armed, the three turned, standing shoulder to shoulder and bracing themselves. For a second they paused. With a thunder of footfalls the crowd of white-suited figures gathered at the bottom of the stairs. The collection of bespectacled scientists and haggard civil servants were angry, pumping with adrenaline and now deep in the primitive chaos of attack, but though they were greater in number, brawling didn't come naturally to them. They'd met resistance, seen blood and injuries. For a few seconds, chests heaving, the two sides locked gazes.

Then there was a shout from somewhere and the horde rushed up the stairs as one.

Georgie didn't hit very hard at first, swinging the bar more as a deterrent, swishing back and forth at the throng with eyes half closed. Then the man in front of her surged forward, his hand pushing against her chest and his face coming close enough for her to see his crusted, bloodshot eyes.

Outrage, fear. A bursting sensation in her gut and throat. She slapped at his face, kicking and swiping and yelling something which she could hardly hear. As the man faltered and she found space, the urge to fight back properly, with force, grabbed her. She lifted her arms and swung the iron bar right and left, beating downwards with the desire to smash the whole goddamn horde of them down the stairs and back out the door.

* * * * *

Even as she tumbled through into the room beyond, Sarah knew the man was right behind her. Her skull pounded but she heard his heavy footsteps.

Turning her head painfully she saw him now, no more than a step away. He hadn't bothered to replace his mask and she could see his eyes, burning with hate. Blood dripped from a jagged semi-circle on his hand and his breathing came in heavy, angry gasps.

She took a step backward but the man leapt; trying to move, Sarah tripped and tumbled to the floor.

There was no way she could get to her feet. She dragged herself backwards, her palms crunching over the broken glass which now littered the floor until she felt the wall behind her and could move no further. The man stopped at the same moment – there was no need to hurry now. She was cornered.

He straightened a little, arms held wide, and began to walk towards her.

"Here kitty, kitty…"

Sarah was unable to look away but her hands floundered about her almost unconsciously, reaching, searching for an exit she hadn't found before, some sort of magic door, anything. Her fingers found something and she yanked it towards her. She let herself steal the briefest of glances; her heart leapt – a weapon.

Then she saw the smirk crawling across the man's face and looked again. It was William's super-soaker.

"A water pistol?" The man snorted, grinning wider. He licked his bottom lip in a motion that made Sarah's flesh crawl. "Poor little princess, toys aren't going to help you now. The grownups are back and playtime's over. Hubbard wants you in one piece, but I'll just tell her you accidentally smashed your own head in."

He took a step closer and in an act of instinct, Sarah raised the muzzle and pulled the trigger.

A sudden torrent of lukewarm sewage exploded over the man with a splattering hiss. Sarah's finger held the trigger, her own surprise mirrored by the man's growing expression of shock until little more was left to be seen of him than a dripping brown mass. It only took a second before the rancid smell hit home Then the man was on all-fours, heaving and vomiting as if he was about to crack in half.

Sarah scrambled to her feet in fascinated horror, letting the empty water pistol clatter to the floor. She edged carefully around the puking man before running away, but the sounds of retching and high-pitched, pitiful wails reaching her ears told her he wasn't getting up anytime soon.

* * * * *

William had finally managed to join the others, wielding his sword with abandon, but the staircase was too wide. In their suits the adults' movements were sluggish and clumsy, and they seemed unable to push forward with enough ferocity to force them all back. But four of them could hardly cover the whole area.

Georgie found herself trying to beat back a man right in front of her, whilst at the same time people were trying to edge round her flank. No sooner had she managed to force the man back a step, catching him with a blow to the jaw that made him stagger, than she found a thin woman, grey-skinned and shrewish like an old librarian, trying to duck through under her arm. Georgie kicked out with her left leg, turning back the moment she felt her foot connect with the soft flesh of the woman's stomach.

To the side she could hear William and Farran's shouts and the hollow thud of the golf club, the panting breath and wild, terrifying yells of Tyrone as he thrashed and flailed with his baseball bat. Her own breathing was becoming ragged, throat burning, arms feeling heavier with every second. She forced a greater effort from herself, giving up any attempt at style as she let out a cry - half-rage half-fear - and brought her weapon down again and again. But although this frenzy battered the man in front of her down into a cowering ball, she had ignored her own defence. A sharp jabbing punch in the side left her so winded she felt herself gasping and swinging blindly from left to right just to give herself time to breathe.

Reinforcements, fresh and eager, seemed to be joining the back of the pressing crowd. This wasn't just about territory; if the group buckled they would be overwhelmed so suddenly and in such force that they would never escape.

From the corner of her eye she noticed that no one was next to her; Farran had been forced to retreat a step and, beyond him, William and even the ferocious Tyrone were beginning to inch back before the invaders' onslaught.

As Georgie began to feel a sharp, sapping cramp creeping up her thighs, she heard, from somewhere below, the loud, buzzing sound of an engine trying to start.

What now?

It came once more, twice, then the air was ripped by an insistent high-pitched roar. The mob had noticed it too. She saw their heads turn and then, before she knew why, an awkward ripple as the crowd shoved each other backwards.

She craned to see better just as Joanna appeared behind the crowd in a tremendous blossoming of engine noise. With Sarah leaning unsteadily on her shoulder she waved a bright yellow chainsaw before herself like a scythe, forcing the tide to part before her as she edged round and up the stairs.

The fumes from its diesel motor shimmered up and around her grubby face, now fixed in a grimace of effort and concentration. Joanna could barely lift the thing, but the more it lurched and swung the more desperate the invaders seemed to get out of its way. Some tripped over one another and toppled like drunks, others shoved and squirmed, but their eyes never left her.

Heaving herself and Sarah up step by step, she eventually reached the top of the stairway. Like a child taking extra care with scissors, Joanna pointed the roaring chainsaw out and towards the invaders but seemed unsure of what to do next.

Georgie looked down at the crowd below, sure that they had only seconds.

"What now?"

"We fight on," said Tyrone decisively.

"There's too many and we're exhausted," Georgie replied, "we can't just fight."

Joanna waved the growling chainsaw through the air, almost shaking it at the people below like a threat.

"Hang on," said William, an idea hitting him. He reached inside his old army surplus coat and pulled out a small orange can, "Lighter fluid."

Pulling the cap off with his teeth he pointed the nozzle at the top of the staircase and began to liberally squirt the area with the flammable liquid. Sensing something was wrong, a few of the people below made a move up the stairs, but a decisive sweep of the chainsaw left them pausing again. When the can had been emptied to the last drop William took out a lighter, set fire to a crusty tissue he found in his pocket and flung the burning paper onto the glistening step. Bright blue flames instantly sprung up across the staircase, heat and fumes so intense that he and the others had to step back.

They'd bought a few precious moments.

"What now?" yelled Farran, shielding his face from the billowing heat.

"The vault," Georgie answered.

"The *what*?" asked William, eyes still on the small inferno he'd brought to life.

"Georgie's right, they won't be able to get in there."

"If the back staircase is blocked," shouted Tyrone, "we're all screwed."

The flames were beginning to die.

"We'll have to risk it. Let's go."

CHAPTER 31.

Far to the west of London, above the hills that surround Thames Head, the sky darkens, silent and oppressive. Waiting. The clouds gather and heap, blocking out any hope of sunshine, until the day that the river winds through is as black as night.

A fine mist descends, smothering the landscape.

* * * * *

The atmosphere inside the vault was stuffy and unpleasant. Georgie didn't know how long they'd been sitting there, hunched between the curved metal walls that made up their hiding place.

"Anyone got any idea what time it is?"

"Don't know, my new watch must have smashed at some point," croaked Sarah, her hand moving unconsciously to the injuries on her throat.

"You need to put another bandage on your neck."

"Got some in this bag, I'll do it." Joanna shuffled to her knees and moved over to Sarah.

"Thanks."

"We've got through two and a bit candles," said William.

"I reckon it must be about three in the mornin', then," added Farran, raising his head from the bag he was using as a pillow.

Georgie looked around the small circular room. They nursed their wounds in silence. All were cut and bleeding; William cradled his right hand, knuckles red and shapeless; Farran had a swollen eye, the skin darkened to the same shade as the glass scars beneath it; and Georgie felt with a wince how her own ribs hurt when she breathed. But no one complained.

The group were huddled on the hard floor, tattered clothes pulled around them for comfort, except for Tyrone who was propped against the vault's doors. He'd been on guard for hours listening for any sign of the suits, but had gradually slumped until his ear rested heavily at the crack in the door. Above them all, in their glass housing, the precious stones twinkled in the candlelight.

"How long since you heard anything, Tyrone?"

"Not for ages now. Not since they did that one big sweep. To be honest, Georgie, I don't think they have a clue where we are. This room's pretty hard to spot from the outside. Long as we're quiet I don't think they'll find us."

"Even if they did, it'd take a batterin' ram to get those doors open," reassured Farran.

"But how long can we stay in here?" asked Sarah.

Farran grimaced, "We could take the back door…"

Georgie's eyes turned to the rear exit. About four foot high and really no more than a ventilation panel, it led to a tiny passageway between the walls and then on to an emergency stairwell beyond. They'd dragged a heavy cabinet in front and this now stood blocking it.

"But," continued Farran, "as soon as we're out of this room we're in the shit - every inch of the museum will be crawlin' with those suits by now."

They all felt the walls of the vault close in a little more.

"What the hell are we gonna do?" asked William of no one in particular.

A crackle broke the silence, there was a painful high-pitched whine of static and a disembodied voice filled the room.

"*TESTING, testing…*"

"What the 'ell's that?" Joanna yelped.

"*This is Dr Hubbard, acting director of the MOD civil contingency centre, Leviathan…*"

"The speakers. They must've got the PA system up and runnin'," said Farran.

"*We are the government…*"

"It's her from the base. She was in charge of the tests." Georgie saw that Tyrone was ashen and terrified.

"I think she's the one from the radio too," said Sarah.

"Are you sure?" asked Georgie.

"I think so. I recognise the voice."

"*We have you surrounded,*" the voice persisted, "*We know you're still in the building…*"

"D'you think they do, or are they just guessing?"

"Don't really matter, Georgie, they can't know exactly where we are or they'd've been in by now," said Farran.

"*Come out now and there will be no more trouble.*"

"What do we have in the way of supplies?" asked Georgie.

"A few cereal bars, some flares, couple of knives, some bats, a few other bits and pieces and a can of Coke," replied William.

"Everythin' else got left downstairs in the panic," said Farran, adding, "I just didn' think they'd get in so fast."

"None of us did," said Tyrone, his voice soft with regret.

"It'll be OK," said Georgie, "We'll just have to try and wait them out…"

*　*　*　*　*

A steady, hard downpour begins to fall on the already rainsoaked ground. The river's acned surface sparkles dully in what little light there is.

Constant, undramatic rain.

It rains without any let-up for hours.

The water table, already full from the unusually wet spring is high; soon, having nowhere to drain, the rain begins to run directly down the surface of hills and into the growing river. The embankments are gradually eroded, the tributaries of the Thames begin to fill, swelling at an alarming rate, desperate to be free, held back only by the river's locks, unmanned and vulnerable.

* * * * *

Dr Hubbard was sitting at a desk within the museum, the PA. system set up in front of her. She clicked it off and sucked at a tube within her hood, slaking her dry throat with water that tasted of plastic and iodine. All about her men and women in suits were hurrying past with boxes and monitors and cables.

Two of the men carrying a long wooden crate between them let it slip from their gloved hands. It crashed to the ground, cracking open and spilling its contents over the floor.

"Be careful, you idiots!" snapped Hubbard, "we're going to need those…no, no, don't bother with the crate, just start handing them out."

The two men nodded and began to pick up the rifles.

* * * * *

"Hey Tyrone," whispered Farran. "Tyrone, you awake?"

"I am now."

"I just wanted to…well, what wiv the attack and everythin' I never got a chance to say…well, you know I'm…back at the fire, all them weeks ago…"

"Don't worry about it, it's forgotten."

Farran smiled, "It's good to have you back, man." He thought for a moment, took a breath. "Listen, I'm not like that anymore, I've changed…"

"*We have tried appealing to your better nature…*"

"She's back. Regular as clockwork," groaned Tyrone.

"Every twen'y minutes."

"*…but you leave us no choice. We will give you one hour to come out of hiding…*"

"Bloody hell, I'd just finally got to sleep," complained Georgie, pulling herself upright.

"I once fell asleep with my headphones on," William's voice was as tired and croaky as everyone else's, "Led Zeppelin, full volume, all night - and I slept like a baby. But there's something about that voice…"

"*…we will take serious action. You cannot keep this up…*"

"I'm sorry, I tried to block the speaker wiv a coat but it don't make no difference," apologised Joanna.

The voice carried on chipping away in the background.

"I don't know how much more I can take," said Sarah, "I'm exhausted and hungry and this tiny little room is starting to drive me crazy." She got up, thrusting her arms through the sleeves of her jacket.

"Where you goin' Sarah? We can't go out, it's not safe."

"I need a pee and I do not intend doing it in here." She went over and began pushing ineffectually against the cabinet that covered the back vent.

Farran got reluctantly to his feet.

"I'm not sure that's a good idea," said Georgie

He shrugged apologetically. "William, give me a hand will you?"

"Well, are you going to help me or do you really want to see me squat like an animal?" said Sarah.

"William," repeated Farran, "c'mon, man."

"Don't rush me, I'm trying to decide. I've never seen a girl pee."

Farran screwed up his face in disgust and began to help Sarah push the cabinet.

Georgie stood to one side, "Guys, I'm really not sure that's a good idea."

"Get out of the way, Georgina."

"Look, wait a second, let's discuss this."

The ventilation panel was now exposed and Sarah had just begun to fiddle with the latch when the lights came on.

Everyone froze.

"Guys, the lights just came on."

"Thanks William, you will keep us posted won't you?" breathed Georgie. "What does it mean?"

"Not sure. I can't hear anything so far." Tyrone had his ear pressed hard against the crack again.

"I'll cover it back up again. I'm sorry, Georgie, I didn't think it would do any harm." Sarah rushed round to the other side of the cabinet and tried to push it back in place.

"No, no, it's alright. I don't think it 'as anythin' to do with that," said Farran.

"What d'you think they're up to, then?" Georgie asked anxiously.

"I dunno, somethin' that needs power, obviously. Maybe it's to help them search better."

"That means they don't know where we are, then," said Sarah.

"True," Georgie agreed. "Maybe it's not such a bad idea to leave that panel uncovered – just in case we need it."

"What do we do then, Georgie?" asked Joanna.

"What we've been doing: we listen and we wait."

Farran nodded, "All they have is that tannoy – long as we stick together and keep our cool, how bad can it get?"

The voice droned on.

* * * * *

There is danger from another direction. At the same time as the relentless rain swells the river west of London, in the east, far out to sea, a tempest rages. The sea beneath the storm has risen to form an enormous hump of water, drawn ever onwards. Already swells are reaching fifteen feet, whipped up by winds gusting ninety miles an hour. Steel-dark waves are topped by white frothing chargers, like the flecks of spittle that gather in the corners of a mad dog's muzzle. Onwards they fly, towards an undefended and unsuspecting coastline.

The huge mass of water from the deep ocean hits the shallows, sending a surge towards the bottleneck of the Strait of Dover. Beyond it, downstream from the city of London, lies the mouth of the Thames Estuary.

* * * * *

"Maybe we should listen to them." Sarah was anxiously looking at each of them in turn, pulling at the fingers of her hands and pacing.

"What the hell are you talking about? Did you not hear *any* of what I told you?" snapped Tyrone in disbelief.

"I know that they've been bad, but they *are* the government. They know what they're doing…"

Tyrone wanted to argue back but the anger in him made his throat close and his tongue seem to swell; all that came out was a strangled growl. He turned away in disgust.

Sarah tried again, her voice quieter and more desperate. As she spoke she looked for an ally but found none, "We could go back to normal, back to real life…" Her voice petered out, absorbed into the cold metal of the walls.

Georgie spoke - and it was only while speaking that she made up her mind, as if she were listening to someone else and was surprised to find she was in agreement, "What's so great about 'real life'? Stuck in an office doing a nine-to-five job that you can't stand for forty years and retiring just in time to snuff it. Give me the apocalypse every time. Each of us has achieved…we've done so much. Who are they to tell us what we can and can't do? Who says they got it right?"

Perhaps what Georgie said was true. Sarah's head swam. She felt like she was in a raging river that threatened to wash everything away, even her, *especially* her, and possibilities kept drifting past her, life-rafts that she could cling to. But which was the right choice? Was Georgie right? Or could she just give in, relax and let someone else take charge of her decisions for a while? She was so tired of keeping herself afloat. Perhaps they should run? Or then again, maybe they should stand and fight as Tyrone said? But what chance could they possibly have against adults?

Then to everyone's surprise Joanna spoke up, "People goin' - us bein' left - was the best thing that ever happened to me." She faltered and her eyes flicked over to Sarah. "Before, I never went out, I never did *nothin'*. But now we all 'ave fun together. I got the animals…I got you guys…I don't wanna go back…I don't need nuffin' else…"

The voice came over the tannoy again - one moment wheedling and caressing, the next stern. "*This is getting silly now, someone is going to get really hurt. It's not too late. It hasn't gone too far…yet. Come out and all will be forgiven. We just want to help you.*"

The voice echoed and was just dying away when it came back, hurt, indignant, "*It's very selfish of you; you are all safe, healthy. All we want to do is make people well again.*"

"Ha," snorted Tyrone.

Sarah darted her eyes over to him from some faraway

place. If any of the others had been looking they would have seen the threads of sweat beginning to form on her forehead, but they were all struggling with their own demons. Wrestling against the voice.

Again it came, soft and caring this time, all threat gone. "*We don't want to hurt you. We're worried about you. How long do you think you can carry on by yourselves? All alone? You've done so well so far, all of you.*"

It really sounded like she cared.

The voice continued, unrelenting, "*But you must be tired. Let us take care of you. We don't want anything to happen to you. We will make sure nothing bad happens to you, like it did to your poor friend Donnie. So sad. So young. Such a tragedy...*"

The voice carried on but that was it, that was all Sarah heard. She was right back in the cold pools of their torchlights as Donnie slipped away from her. All of a sudden she became acutely aware of her own breathing, it was no longer automatic for her, she had to think - breathe in, breathe out. She couldn't get enough air in her lungs. And then her heartbeat - it thumped in her ears. How could it just beat like that on its own? Why was it beating so fast? Was it meant to beat that fast? Maybe she was having a heart attack. No, she was too young. Wasn't she? Weren't you supposed to get a pain in your arm too? What if she *was* having a heart attack or something? What would they do? What could a bunch of kids do? She felt the sweat run cold down her back and the air was hard to pull in...

"Are you listening to this old bitch, Farran?" said Tyrone. "Like she knows us. Like she knew Donnie."

"Nah, she don't know us at all," agreed Farran.

"Hey, where's Sarah?"

"I don't know, maybe she's gone to pee." Georgie got up from the desk to look.

"S'alright. I'll go," said Joanna.

No one else had noticed the look on Sarah's face, seen the

terror. Seen the quiet way in which she had snuck away. Seen the guilty look on her face as she slipped through the vent and out of the room.

But Joanna had. And she knew where Sarah was heading.

* * * * *

Betrayed by the endless rain, the river can no longer contain itself. The Thames upstream of London bursts its banks. Overcoming its confinement, mud-corrupted water seeps out into the surrounding countryside, a dirty brown torrent three miles wide.

* * * * *

Sarah scraped the brick dust from her hair and hurried down the tiny passageway. Through the fire door she went, and out onto the mezzanine level above the main hall of the museum.

Down the stairwell, running now.

* * * * *

"Where the hell are Joanna and Sarah?" asked Tyrone.

"They must've gone to the toilet together. You know what girls are like."

"What, outside?"

"Well they could hardly do it in here could they?"

"They better be careful."

"I think Sarah was a bit ill or something. Jojo probably just went to look after her," said Georgie.

William chuckled at the thought of his friend's discomfort. "Yeah, Sarah was fidgeting like she was bursting."

CHAPTER 32.

Dr Hubbard examined the skinny girl with her unrelenting gaze. Sarah, standing on the threshold of the dinosaur room - now the government's base of operations - felt terrified, exposed. She didn't know what to do with her hands. She crossed and uncrossed her arms, then looked about her uncomfortably. She was sweating and there was an unpleasant churning in her stomach.

There must have been thirty of the government men and women in the room, all in the clumsy, white environmental suits. They were rushing about, engrossed in tasks, and paid her little attention. All, that is, except for the three men who had brought her in and who now stood a little way off, one on either side and one behind - and of course there was Hubbard. Sarah tried not to meet her gaze and continued to look around.

Monitors had been banked-up on every available surface. Dozens upon dozens of screens were stacked in precarious pyramids, messy tangles of wires led to a big console from which a fat blue cable snaked out of the room. Each of the screens flickered with grainy black and white images that rotated every few seconds - buildings, courtyards, roads. Then it clicked - she was looking at pictures of the museum and the surrounding area. They must have somehow connected up the electricity and hooked into the CCTV network, that must be why the power had come back on all over the building.

It looked like they had every camera in the area under their control.

Sarah turned her attention back to the intimidating figure of Dr Hubbard who still examined her from behind her face-plate, an internal light throwing jagged shadows onto her face.

"Well, at least one of you has finally come to your senses. Just as well, things were about to get a lot more serious." She moved towards the frightened girl. "Come in, come in, sit down." Hubbard beckoned Sarah in. "Have a seat; you must be tired, sit, sit."

Hubbard turned to a large, broad-shouldered man and barked at him to get a chair in a voice that made Sarah flinch, then her eyes were on Sarah once more. Her mouth turned upward in a smile that seemed to have just flicked on.

"Ms Hobbes isn't it? Ah, don't be surprised, we *are* the government after all; we know everything, that's our job."

Sarah shifted uncomfortably in her chair. Dr Hubbard beckoned to someone behind her and a middle-aged man with a comb-over came into view.

"A pleasure to meet you, young lady, I am Dr Lightbourne."

The man gave a moist smile that made Sarah's skin crawl. Bending at the waist he leant towards her and in a voice that was meant to be soothing said, "You must have a lot of questions."

Sarah wasn't sure where to begin. "Why are we alive?" she asked hesitantly.

Lightbourne straightened, "Did you ever receive a vaccination against tuberculosis? Every child in Britain is given it, usually at around thirteen or fourteen. You line up, you tease each other about how painful it's going to be, then the school nurse gives you your BCG."

"You had that jab, didn't you Sarah?" said Dr Hubbard, though she obviously wasn't really asking a question, "At some you point you lined up just like every other child but something was different about yours…"

"It's funny really, because under normal circumstances I suppose you could sue," said Dr. Lightbourne.

"Sue?" mumbled Sarah, words and confusion swirling thicker and faster in her head.

Lightbourne nodded, "You were given the wrong injection. A bad batch. A defective product."

"We've found that the disease is a form of tuberculosis – extremely virulent, extremely deadly," said Hubbard.

"Obviously," added Lightbourne with a smile.

"Obviously," agreed Hubbard. "And because of some mistake, some quirk of fate only God Himself could have foreseen, you received antibodies that protected you from this new form of tuberculosis."

This part – this part made some sense to Sarah. She could follow this strand at least.

"How?"

Hubbard's head turned towards her a little straighter, fixing her with those pale eyes as though they had reached the crux of the matter, "We think that some of the vaccination the company sent out to schools was an anomaly, unusual stuff that should never have left the factory. Not all of it was bad – just a few doses here and there."

"But it turns out that this mutated form you were given is exactly what saved your life. It ended up giving you immunity to a disease nobody even knew about."

"And now we want it," said Dr. Hubbard, her voice dropping, "we want that immunity. Now, why don't you be a good girl and tell us where your friends are hiding."

* * * * *

In the west, locks holding back the water's course are overwhelmed and soon begin to crumble, an insidious rot having set in without people there to tend and repair them. The river spreads out past these barriers; they are no more than an annoyance to be engulfed by the rapidly swelling tide.

* * * * *

"But you do promise? You promise you won't hurt them."

"My dear girl, what kind of people do you think we are?" Lighbourne's eyebrows were raised as though the Sarah's question were so ridiculous that he actually pitied her.

"But..but Tyrone said…"

"Tyrone was very badly burnt," interrupted Hubbard.

"Very badly. Delirious in fact," agreed Lightbourne.

"And we did our best to treat him. Of course we had to restrain him and we had to take precautions to protect ourselves…"

"From infection."

"…and we can see that the whole experience must have been very confusing…"

"Frightening even."

"…but we are not monsters. You can rest assured that thanks to your cooperation we can make sure that none of your friends will be harmed when we take them into protective care."

Other suits bustled in the background, comparing Sarah's information against blueprints and CCTV footage.

"But what about the facility?" asked Sarah. "He said you were underground."

"Yes?" Lightbourne blinked at her, the smile still fixed in place.

"Why didn't you come to rescue us sooner? Why did you wait underground?"

"Ah," sighed Lightbourne indulgently.

Hubbard stepped a little closer to Sarah. "We went there to wait out the infection, to stay buried like an acorn. Our function: wait for contamination to pass, re-establish order, support re-installation of civil sections and interim government."

Sarah thought that the last part sounded rehearsed, like a rhyme or a chant.

Hubbard began to pace as she spoke. "Our section, Leviathan, was intended for research and support. We were to wait until contacted by Base Alpha – the facility where cabinet ministers and heads of ministries were to be taken in the event of a disaster, a military base outside London. But the disease hit too fast, no contact came, no word. Our protocol was to await orders, but there were no orders; there was no one left to give them. Many of us felt that we needed to take charge."

Here Lightbourne nodded vigorously. Hubbard was talking more quickly, no longer paying any attention to Sarah.

"There was dissent. The head of our section, a Colonel Matthews, insisted that we wait for the government proper to make contact. He refused to see the truth that no one would ever come. He refused to see that all of the preparations had come to nothing, that all of the protocols were useless, that the plans were useless, the orders *meaningless*. He wanted us to wait, to, to rot down there. But I wouldn't let that happen."

Her eyes flicked back to Sarah as though suddenly remembering her audience.

She took a breath.

"So, we began to take steps. It still wasn't safe to go above ground –to feel sun and air on our skin again - not until all sources of possible infection had been removed. The bodies. It was a slow and laborious process, we could only work above ground in these clumsy suits. We began clearing, purging sector by sector. We re-established connection with the CCTV network as routine, only having enough power to activate and search one small grid at a time. But imagine our surprise when we saw a girl pop up on our screens, standing on a street corner as though nothing had happened."

A cutting bitterness had begun to enter her voice; the fixed smile becoming more of a grimace.

"We were stuck down in our hole while you were running about carefree like a pack of plague rats. So we initiated the burn; we couldn't have you acting as vectors for the disease. Except Dr Lightbourne here decided to bring one of you back alive. And lucky for us that he did, since you may hold the key to a cure. All of you have survived but you're still infected with TB s11."

"Dr Hubbard?" Lightbourne said.

But she ignored Lightbourne and carried on regardless, "You're all carriers of the strain, though you have no symptoms – oh yes, after the outbreak, it was in all likelihood you yourselves who gave it quietly and lovingly to every member of your family."

The smile on Hubbards face was genuine enough now.

Sarah's head spun. There was just so much to take in.

"I, I don't understand," said Sarah, "*you* started the fire?"

"Yes," snapped Dr Hubbard, "do try to keep up."

"But Donnie died because of that fire. You killed Donnie." Her tone was one of utter bewilderment.

"Try to see it from our point of view, you had be destroyed for the sake of the majority. But then, of course, Dr Lightbourne's preliminary tests on Tyrone suggested that we might be on to something, and everything changed."

"You killed Donnie," repeated Sarah, as though saying it out loud might help her to comprehend how these people, the government, the adults, had killed someone she loved.

"You don't understand do you, you're just a child."

Dr Hubbard stooped down so that their faces were level. Sarah could see through the Perspex panel in Hubbard's facemask, through to pale blue eyes sagging with the weight of condescension and exaggerated concern. She looked at those eyes for a moment, noting they were the same washed-out blue as photographs that have been stuck up in a shop window too long. There was no real emotion in them, just a pale, washed-out imitation.

From somewhere inside her a flash of anger surged and she felt the first murderous impulse of her life.

Before she knew it her hand had struck out with all the strength in her arm.

The ring on her finger snagged in the mask and Dr Hubbard reeled backwards, trying to disentangle it with panicked movements.

Once free, Hubbard ran to check her reflection in a display case, poking and examining the hole. She turned to the guard next to her and screamed, "Has it gone through? Has it gone through? Is it intact? Look, for God's sake, tell me."

"There's no sign that the suit's been breached, Ma'am."

Sarah could only stare in amazement. She watched Hubbard's back as the woman tried to regain her composure. Then Hubbard returned her attention to Sarah with a glare that turned her stomach to water.

Hubbard strode swiftly back to where Sarah was sitting, paused for a moment, then struck her so hard that Sarah and her chair went toppling to the floor.

Everything went black and all Sarah could hear was a whistling rush as though there were a tunnel running through her head.

Through the high-pitched wind she could just make out Hubbard -

"If the mask had torn, it would have been very much worse. Tie her up. If she's going to behave like an animal, then we will treat her like one."

Then Sarah sunk somewhere far away.

* * * * *

In the east, beneath the boiling of the waves – deep down in the depths of the sea – there lies a stillness, a silent calm. A place of safety where all of the beautiful things that live in the sea continue unharmed by the chaos above.

* * * * *

A song tingled on the tip of Sarah's brain, half-remembered, half-heard. A song that Joanna always played, something about a garden - an old song - an octopus's garden? She wished she could remember the words but she couldn't grasp them.

Sarah surfaced from unconsciousness. She was staring along the dirty parquet flooring of the museum.

Needs a good sweep.

Sensation slowly came back to her and with it the memory of her situation. She was on her side, her arms were stretched back behind her and they were numb. She tried to pull them back round but they wouldn't respond. She realised they were tied together with something. She tried once more to move her hands but the tape wouldn't budge. There was still a whistling in her head and the warm liquid that had seeped out of her left ear had dried to an irritating stickiness that prickled when she tried to get her jaw working.

Sarah had been quiet so long that the suits were just ignoring her, and had turned their attention to a set of schematics spread out over one of the display cases. They were discussing the best way to break into the vault and take the others.

This was her fault. The others would get captured by these murderers and it would be her fault. She couldn't let that happen. She twisted her arms back and forth trying to loosen the tape, pulling out the fine hairs on her arm. Still she couldn't get free. Tears of frustration began to trickle down her cheek to the floor.

She had to try again, to warn the others before it was too late. Her shoes squeaked against the floor. She tensed and looked up. Nobody had looked towards her, but she couldn't afford to attract their attention. She had to be quieter.

Again she began working at the tape around her arms.

"Sarah."

For a moment her heart jumped but it wasn't Hubbard, it was a familiar voice.

"Sarah? Over 'ere. No, behind you. It's me."

She tilted her head as far as she could, her cheek rubbing against the dusty floor, and there was the grubby face of Joanna. She was squatting, tucked between two cabinets at the back of the room.

"You alright?"

"I-I think so," she whispered, "my head hurts like hell and I can't free my hands, but otherwise I'm OK." Then added hastily, "They caught me when I left and tied me up."

"I know, I followed you."

Sarah felt a wave of queasiness worm through her. "You know? How long have you been here?"

"The 'ole time. Waited 'til now."

Sarah looked anxiously into the other girl's face but there was no judgment there, only concern. She felt a mixture of shame and relief and started to cry.

"S'okay Sarah, I'll get you outta there in a jif."

Sarah closed her eyes to try and stop the tears. When she opened them Joanna had gone.

"Joanna? Joanna? Where are you?" she whispered as loud as she dared but there was no reply.

Sarah frantically tried to turn her head further. She couldn't see her.

She's probably left me to it, she thought, *I don't blame her.*

Then something touched her hands.

"Got a flint out of a display. Had to find sommink to cut you free."

* * * * *

The towns of Oxford, Reading, Eton are drowned one by one as the flood flows unfettered onwards towards London.

* * * * *

Sarah was running as fast and as quietly as she was able, with Joanna just behind her; if they could only get to the mezzanine they might be able to slip unseen into one of the vents and from there onto the emergency stairs.

They raced through the main hall, past the dinosaurs still strung with fairy lights, past the kitchen and the table they had struggled to bring in.

The shouts still rang out behind them but they were a little further off now.

She looked back at Joanna.

They were going to make it; they were at the main staircase. They were going to make it and they'd warn the others and somehow they'd all get away from this terrible situation together.

Sarah had reached the first step.

Joanna smiled, giving Sarah the thumbs-up and then a funny thing happened: the front of Joanna's parka burst outwards with a spray of feathers. Sarah didn't hear anything. There was just a brief puff of red mist and then Joanna fell away behind her.

She skidded to a halt.

Joanna lay splayed out on the bottom steps; she hadn't put her hands out to break her fall and had come to a stop resting heavily on her face, her neck twisted at an odd angle.

She ran back down the steps crouched over her friend. "Joanna, are you OK? Joanna, get up, we have to go." Sarah looked up and saw that Hubbard and the others had reached the far end of the hall.

"Joanna, get up." She tugged at Joanna's hood, unable to take her eyes from the advancing suits. Then she noticed that something in Dr Hubbard's hand was smoking. Sarah looked down at Joanna with a new panic.

"Joanna. Joanna? No, no, no, no, no."

She hauled Joanna's body over, limp and heavy. Her eyes remained shut. Sarah eyes darted over her body. There didn't seem to be any signs of injury; no cuts, no scrapes, no blood, thank God, just the tear in the pink parka. She let her fingers explore the rough edges of down and fabric.

"Joanna, wake up. If you don't get your lazy arse up we are going to be in deep-" Sarah's fingers touched something wet. She turned her hand over and they were stained red.

In an instant she pulled the coat aside only to see purple defusing into the dirty blue of Joanna's shirt. At the centre of the stain was a burnt black hole.

She clasped her hand over the wound; she knew she had to stop the bleeding. It wasn't too big a hole just so long as she could stop the bleeding-

"Sarah?"

Sarah looked down into Joanna's pale face. "Oh thank God, for a minute there...Are you alright. Are you in much pain?"

"Chest feels sore and my arm feels 'eavy. I think they shot me." Her voice was quiet but strong.

Sarah laughed. "I think they did too. Look, we haven't got much time. I'm going to need you to put pressure on the wound while I rip up my shirt. We have to stop the bleeding so that we can get out of here."

"Okey dokey, Sarah, whatever you say."

"Right, hang on."

The government people seemed to have paused at the end of the hall. Sarah realised that Joanna had said something to her-

"What?"

"Don't tell the others…"

"I…"

"Don't tell 'em." Joanna pressed something into the palm of Sarah's free hand.

"Look, let's not worry about that now. We have to get you patched up and get out of here." She flicked an anxious glance upwards – the suits were advancing again and were already at the T-Rex.

"I could do with a cuppa, I'm so thirsty."

"Thirsty?" Sarah quickly looked back down at the hand covering the wound.

Blood bubbled up from between her fingers. Fear gripped her once more. Looking back into Joanna's eyes, she saw that the spark had left them and there was a new glassiness there that terrified her.

"Joanna I, I…"

Joanna read the look in Sarah's face in an instant. "Oh." Her voice was weaker now and her skin unnaturally white, almost translucent. Sarah felt Joanna's whole body deflate, resigned and defeated. Then, almost as swiftly there was another change - Joanna stiffened and tried to sit up and raise her head from Sarah's knee.

"Sarah, I don't wanna die. I'm frightened." A look of panic came into her eyes. "Sarah!"

Fear and need but there was nothing she could do.

Joanna began to claw at Sarah's jacket.

"Sarah, Sarah don't let me die…"

Sarah wanted so much to reassure Joanna, to calm her, but

what could she do?

It was too much, it was all too much.

Sarah closed her eyes as tight as she could.

"Sarah, please…"

And turned her head away.

"Sarah…"

She squeezed her eyes shut.

"Sarah please…" - fainter now.

"Sar-"

Sarah felt the hand fall away from her sleeve and Joanna was still at last.

In the extreme silence that followed, Sarah heard the rapid pounding of her own heart and then, after a few more moments, the slow creak of rubber boots.

She heard breathing and the mechanical hiss of filters, and knew that Dr Hubbard was standing there. They had her. But Sarah didn't care any longer, something had broken inside her.

* * * * *

Waves reach the coast with an inescapable force. The consequences of the stormtide are unstoppable; it rolls over the land, submerging pretty little seaside towns without even slowing. Surf lashes the white cliffs. Seawalls disappear; pebble-dashed cottages give way becoming nothing but jetsam, rolled along by the sheer volume of saltwater. Rusting piers and promontories are torn away like matchstick models, pleasure arcades and quaint pubs are washed away as though they never existed. Everything is change and destruction in the face of the flood.

CHAPTER 33.

"I'm telling you it was a gunshot," said William.

"D'you think that's it, do you think they've got guns now?" said Georgie.

"We're in deep shit if they 'ave," replied Farran.

"Where the hell are Sarah and Joanna? It's been ages."

"Maybe someone should go out and look for them."

"Maybe someone took a pot-shot at them and they had to hide somewhere, so they can't get back," said Georgie.

"Did they take a walkie-talkie?" asked Tyrone.

"I've tried 'em, no reply," Farran answered.

A creak came from the vent and they turned in time to see Sarah replacing the panel. She was panting heavily and there were rusty brown handprints smeared down the front of her shirt.

"Sarah! What happened?" asked Georgie.

"You alright?"

"Is that blood?"

"I'm OK, they caught me," said Sarah at last.

"They caught you?!" gasped William.

"How did you get away?" asked Georgie.

"I managed to slip out."

Georgie craned her neck, looking behind Sarah at the half-open door. "Where's Jojo? We thought she'd gone with you."

"They had us tied up and we tried to get away but Joanna... and in the confusion I just got away...they shot her."

"They what?!"

"Is she OK? Where is she?" asked Farran.

"They shot her," was all Sarah seemed able to say.

"They shot her, but where *is* she? Do they have her?"

"We have to go get her."

"How? There are so many of them."

"Maybe we should leave her with them, they have doctors at least."

"We need to get her now, screw the doctors."

"Grab somethin' you can use as a weapon."

Sarah watched her friends rushing about, grabbing supplies and riffling through bags until she couldn't take it any longer. "They shot her! She's dead!" she screamed.

They all stopped what they were doing.

"What do you mean, Sarah? Sarah what happened?" asked Georgie in a soft voice.

There were no tears or hysterics from Sarah, she was strangely calm now. "We were running away. Joanna got us free and we were running away and they shot her in the back and she died."

"Are you sure, are you sure she's actually dead?"

"Maybe she's just hurt?"

Sarah gave a pained smile, "Yes, I'm sure. I was with her when she died."

"Shit," Farran sat back heavily onto the table.

"Those bastards!" shouted Tyrone, smashing his fist into the wall.

"I can't believe it," breathed Georgie, "I just can't believe it." Then after a moment, "How did you manage to get away, they didn't hurt you did they?"

"No, I'm OK. They- it happened when we were running away. I kept going."

"Then you can't be sure she's dead. Maybe she's just hurt."

"I stopped, I...look I know she's dead." Then she added, "I'm sorry."

"I don't understand what happened. You were running away?"

"Yes."

"But you said you were tied up before. How did you get free?"

"Joanna cut us loose."

"How."

"She had a flint." She squeezed the cold stone in her pocket until it cut into her palm. "Anyway, what does it matter?" Sarah was growing increasingly exasperated.

"How did you get away after they shot Joanna?"

"I kept running."

"But you're sure she's dead."

"I stopped."

"I don't get it, wha-"

"For the love of God, she's dead OK, what does it matter!"

"Sorry it's just-"

"Georgie," said Farran.

"I'm sorry, I'm sorry, Sarah, I really am, I just...I want to understand is all." She stepped forward and hugged her friend, but Sarah remained rigid.

Eventually Sarah broke away, "They know where we are. We have to get out of here now, they'll be coming soon. We have to get out of here no matter what it takes. They don't give a damn about us. I've seen what they're capable of. Tyrone was right, they'll capture us if they can but they'd rather see us dead than let us get away."

"I can't believe this is happening. They're really going to kill us." William suddenly seemed terribly young and frightened. "I don't want to die," he added.

"Pull it together, bruv," ordered Farran, adding a little more softly, "we'll get out of this."

"Right, we head out the back door to the fire exit and get out of here," announced Georgie.

"It won't work," said Sarah.

"We have to risk making a run for it."

"It won't work," repeated Sarah

Tyrone nodded in agreement with Georgie, "We duck out the back way, slip into one of the offices. Try and get up onto the roof, make our way up the street and down to one of the university car parks, all pile in one of the cars and drive as fast and as far as we can."

Sarah – "It won't work."

"And go where?" asked William mournfully.

"Anywhere away from here," replied Georgie.

Tyrone growled, "Then one day I'll come back and kill those bastards."

"Sounds dodgy but what else is there? Let's do it," urged Farran, grabbing his backpack from the floor.

"It's no use," said Sarah.

"Look, we don't have time for this from you right now," snapped Georgie. She turned her back on Sarah and continued to move towards the door, ushering the others as she went

"Stop!" Sarah shouted. This time they did. "It's no use because we won't make it."

"We can…" Georgie began angrily.

"We won't make it," continued Sarah in a calm forceful voice, "because they have cameras everywhere. They have control over the CCTV network. That's how they found us in the first place, and that's why, if we go with your plan, we are all going to get caught in about five minutes. They'll see us in the car park, block off the exits and then they can take their time about getting us; we'll be trapped like rats."

"Damn," puffed Farran, "thank God you told us, we…it don't bear thinkin' about."

"You're sure they're even watching the university car park?"

"Yes," she replied quickly, "they're watching everywhere."

William went pale. "We're trapped, then. There's no way out."

"But how do they know where we are *inside* the museum and how do you know all this about the cameras?" Georgie stared levelly at Sarah.

"I saw it."

"*How* did you see it?"

Tyrone interrupted, paying no attention to the turn the conversation had taken between the two girls, "Another thing worries me now we've stopped to think this through – I know these bastards, they aren't gonna stop chasing us. Even if we do get to a car, they're gonna just keep following us, there are more of them and they've got better resources, they don't have to catch us right away. They'll just keep on following until we run out of petrol or we get tired and make a mistake."

"We're buggered, totally buggered."

"Will, do me a favour, just stop talkin' for a while," said Farran kindly.

Tyrone continued, "We have to disappear clean or…"

"Or?" William, hopeful.

"Or *we* have to kill *them*."

William sank down again, moaning, "Oh God, oh God."

"That's just friggin' stupid." Scorn dripped from Farran's voice, "That's the sort of dumb thing I would have said. We are *not* goin' to kill them."

"The idea was just to make them realise that we were more trouble than we were worth, that's all," said Georgie. "It didn't work but we can't kill people. Think what you're actually saying."

"Tyrone's right."

Farran was dumbfounded. "What? Sarah, what the hell, man?"

"This is serious. Like Tyrone says, no one is going to come and save us; no marine is going to land on shore just at the last moment; no nice soldiers; no angels; no one." Sarah looked at them all, "It's very basic: us or them; their will or ours. If we run we're going to die."

"But..." stammered Georgie.

"We kill them – unless anyone here wants to surrender, give in and accept what they do to us in the hope that some of us survive."

The room was silent.

"Fine, then we don't just run, we disappear," said Georgie, defiant.

"How the hell are we supposed to do that, eh? They've found this place now, apparently, and they're gonna come burstin' in here any minute," William whined, "and we've just been talking about how they have the whole place covered, and, and-"

"Is that what you want?" said Sarah to Georgie, "Do you really want to disappear?"

"Hell yeah, if we can, but how?" answered William for her.

"There must be a way for us to hide."

"There is - the tubes. If you want to hide, then we have to use the tube tunnels," replied Sarah.

* * * * *

"Sergeant Horner, take four men, go out, tear down the scaffolding and bring back the short poles. Mr Simon, take a few men and collect up all of the fire axes you can lay your hands on. One way or another we will smash our way in to those little brats." Then picking up the walkie-talkie she barked into it, "Leviathan Control, transfer power from all systems into the surveillance grid, I don't want any risk of losing them."

"But Dr Hubbard," came back a plaintive voice, "if we do that we'll lose control of the monitoring systems throughout the rest of the city, we may even lose control of basic systems within Leviathan itself..."

"I didn't ask for your opinion, just get it done."

"But…"

She slammed the handset down onto a display cabinet.

"Dr Lightbourne?" Hubbard had turned amid the flurry of activity to see the small man creeping off.

"I am going to fetch some fire extinguishers." A grin illuminated his pale skin beneath the mask. "If we can't smash through to them, we can burn the little blighters out."

And with that he scurried off.

"Good. Now, can someone get rid of this girl before she stinks the whole place up? Just dump it with the others."

* * * * *

A great tidal wave enters the Thames Estuary, a line of water twenty foot tall obliterating everything in its path. It rushes up towards the already rain-swollen river flowing from the west. The two floods form a pincer of fresh and saltwater, at the centre of which stands London.

A hundred miles inland the Thames Barrier crouches dark and unmanned. In an echoing room a single dust-covered warning light begins to flash in the tomb-like stillness.

* * * * *

"I, *we* are not taking the tubes, it's too dangerous," said Georgie. Terrible memories of that first, underground journey into London crowded her mind – the darkness, the deathlike stillness…

William looked at his friends. "Hang on a minute, now I may not be the brightest guy here…"

"True."

"…but I'm pretty sure Tyrone said the place they took him

was underground. What if they're in the tube tunnels, we'll be going right to them, we'll be totally buggered."

"We have to take the tubes." There was a strange expression on Sarah's face; determination, fear - and something else…

"And what do we do then?" Georgie paced anxiously, a look of intense concentration crumpling her brow. "*If* we can get to the tunnels and *if* there is no one there waiting for us? We need to disappear, but no food or water, in the cold underground-"

"We head to the ship," said Sarah

"All that way in the dark?"

"What ship?" asked Tyrone

"Sarah and I have been going out to this big old sailing ship by London Bridge - The Golden Hinde."

"Is that where you girls have been sneaking off to?"

"It was just a plan I was working on," said Georgie. "Look, we didn't say anything because we didn't want to upset people but I was thinking that we might eventually, one day, decide to leave and try to find other people, like maybe on the continent; France or Holland or somewhere. Anyway, I didn't want something that would run out of petrol and leave us stranded in the middle of the ocean so I found this sailing ship. It's old and creaky, but it works well enough. Sarah's been teaching me." Georgie cut herself short, "But it's not ready, *we're* not ready."

"The two of you have been taking this big ship out, all on your own?" said Tyrone.

"Yes, well, no," said Sarah.

"Right, that's clear then," said William.

"Well," fumbled Georgie, "we haven't exactly sailed it as such because it's docked; the two of us weren't strong enough to raise the barrier on our own. But Sarah's shown me how it all works in principal. But that's not the point…"

"I *have* taken her out in smaller boats. She's become a very competent sailor."

"Oh, well that's simply *smashing* then," shouted William. "We can all have gin and tonics on the deck, just before we bloody-well drown. If I–"

Something crashed against the door.

They all stared at it for a moment, terrified.

"They've found us."

The crash came again.

"Get that panel off, fast."

"The door isn't goin' to keep them out for long."

"That settles it; we make for the tunnels and head for the ship."

"Hang on a minute…" said Georgie.

"No time. That's the plan. If anyone gets split up from the others it doesn't matter, just head for the ship any way you can and we'll all meet there," said Farran.

"But what about the whole 'them maybe being underground' thing?" persisted Georgie.

"The tunnels are our only chance!" shouted Sarah.

"We have to get out of here now!"

"Leave the stuff."

"There isn't time."

"Damn it, Farran, get the bloody panel off."

"It's stuck, it won't open."

* * * * *

Bright silver, the seven cowls of the Thames Barrier glitter in what little light there is, standing silent sentry in the river, London's last defence against nature. The gates have been left partially closed, drawn up from their concrete sills in the river floor by dying hands. The crest of the tidal wave strikes the barrier; thick steel gates, weighing over three thousand tonnes, begin to buckle and give way.

* * * * *

There's a crash at the outer door. A cracking sound. Panic grips them all.

"The panel's jammed."

"We left it too late."

"They're coming through!"

* * * * *

The floodgates burst.

CHAPTER 34.

Dr Hubbard stood in the middle of the room, the door lying in pieces at her feet. The children were nowhere to be found.

Government men poured in and began tearing the small room apart, smashing-in the displays and prising off grates, more in frustration than anything.

"They're gone, ma'am. We were too late."

"Thank God I have you around, sergeant, to point out the bleeding obvious. Get on to the situation room and have them rotate through every camera within a ten-block radius. Get all of them on, I don't care if it means we have to cut power to every other system. And hand out the guns – I'd rather have them dead than let those diseased rats escape."

"Yes, ma'am." The sergeant hesitated a moment in confusion; he was used to his superior's terrifying temper by now - fearsome in the face of the smallest setback - and yet she seemed calm.

Hubbard appeared to pick up his thoughts in that unnerving way she had – "Don't worry, my dear Sergeant Horner, I have a feeling that I know exactly where they're heading."

*   *   *   *   *

The group huddled in the gloom of the stairwell, breathing hard.

"I think we lost them," whispered Tyrone.

"What now?" asked William.

Farran leant against the railing and looked at the frightened faces of his friends. "We stick to the plan. We take the subway to the tube and then we follow the underground as far as we can into the burnt area - it'll be the only place without CCTV. We head through it to the boat without bein' spotted."

Tyrone tiptoed up to the tinted window and pressed his face against it. There was still a worrying number of suits guarding the perimeter.

"We need to move fast if this is going to work. It's not going to take them long to figure out what happened and there are already enough of them out there to make this hard."

They moved quickly and silently through the dusty rooms of the research wing, making their way down and east, towards the ground floor. They hurried through room after room of desks scattered with abandoned work, heading for the furthest corner of the building.

Eventually they reached a locked door. They pushed against it and pried at it with anything they could lay their hands on, but it wouldn't budge.

"Let's get a fire axe and just hack the bugger down."

"Yeah and bring every one of those government bastards down on us in the space of five minutes," said Farran. "No, we've got to double back. Find another way down."

"There must be another option," said Georgie, "another way to escape."

"No, we stick to the plan. We have to head into the tube. It's the only way." Sarah looked at Georgie for a moment and then quickly turned away.

"But we need to get out right by the fence, as close to the subway as we can," replied Tyrone.

"What else can we do? We've got no choice," said Farran

* * * * *

As they made their way through the offices, Sarah's mind brought back cruel memories. She was in the hall again, kneeling beside Joanna's lifeless body.

Dr Hubbard loomed above her. "You must see, my dear girl, that things are quite hopeless for you and your friends. We have the numbers and the equipment and we are willing to use them. We will capture you and we will get our cure; I will have Lightbourne dissect all of you if I have to. You have no choice, you are powerless. You must accept that. The only thing you can do, the only one piece of...wiggle room that you have left, is to decide *how* it happens. We can take them in their little room - the location of which you have so kindly given us - and it will be bloody and violent and terrifying. But we don't want that, we don't want that at all. If you were to perhaps lead your little chums somewhere where we could scoop them up without any fuss, then we could be gentle – oh, we will still eviscerate every last one of them, have no illusions about that, but there is no need for them to suffer unduly. And maybe, just maybe, *you* could remain intact."

Hubbard leaned down close to Sarah so that the poisonous words dripping from her mouth slid seductively into Sarah's ear.

"Their fate is out of your hands, but *yours...*"

* * * * *

Georgie's hand hovered over the exit bar of the fire door. "We don't know if the alarm for this is working and we have no way of knowing who or what is waiting for us on the other side. You ready for this?"

The others nodded.

She pushed down and swung the door open.

Outside the morning was unusually dark. A strong wind was blowing, the air thick with the buzz of static. Black clouds rolled in the distance, heavy with rain.

Directly opposite them, across a concrete courtyard, were some ornamental shrubs. Beyond these was the covered walkway that ran along the length of the research building. Georgie pulled the door to.

"Get to the bushes and then we'll all make a break for the path together. Right, go!"

One by one they dashed into the undergrowth and crouched waiting, until only Farran and Georgie were left. Georgie ducked down and ran, Farran made to follow but caught sight of the ghostly white of a bio-hazard suit. He sprang back inside, and pulled the door closed except for a tiny crack and peered out. The others beckoned to him from the safety of the bushes. It was a risk now, but it was only going to get worse. He pushed through the door and ran headlong for cover.

Halfway across the courtyard the wind caught the open fire door and brought it slamming shut. The guard turned and stared directly at Farran. Farran stopped. He wanted to run to the others but that would be it, he'd give the game away. The guard was now running towards him as fast as his suit would allow. *Shit,* Farran thought to himself with a certain resignation, *this isn't gonna be easy.*

"Go, go," he hissed without turning, "he's only seen me, I'll lead him the other way, then meet you like we planned."

"No, Farran, no…"

But he dashed straight out across the lawn towards the ruined front entrance of the museum. The guard made after him, screaming for him to stop.

The others watched him run for a moment then made a break for the shadows under the arches of the research building. Once under the protection of the colonnade they were able to move more quickly. In a crouching jog they made it to the cover of the bins, pausing by the high wall which formed the eastern perimeter of the museum compound.

"Right," said Sarah, "we've almost made it. The entrance to the subway is just down there."

They slipped around the edge of the wall and down the stairs. At the bottom they were met by a concertina gate that shut off the entrance to the tunnel. It took all four of them to prise the rusted barriers far enough apart, the gate giving an agonisingly loud squeal.

Beyond, the tunnel was murky and uninviting, the light of day penetrating no more than a few feet.

"Are we sure this is the best way forward?" Georgie was remembering the horrors of the tunnels before she'd met the others, the way the mind could project into the blankness all of the fears that were coiled like snakes in the quiet corners of your brain.

"Bit late now," whispered Tyrone. "We gotta go. Ladies first," he added with a grin.

William and Tyrone pulled hard on the gate but still Georgie could only just scrape through. As soon as she was on the other side, the boys relaxed and the gate sprang back to a narrow slit. She was immediately hit by the irrational fear that they would leave her there, alone in the dark - that this was some elaborate practical joke.

"Come on. Who's next?"

"Just a minute." Tyrone seemed distracted, he stepped back from the gate.

Georgie's heart was pounding.

"What? What's going on out there?" From where she stood all Georgie could see were the figures of her three friends and the stairs behind them, all fractured into small, rust-rimmed diamonds.

Tyrone hissed at her to be quiet.

The others stood motionless and tense. Tyrone's head was

tilted upwards, fixed somewhere above the entrance. At the road perhaps.

Georgie pressed her face against the bars trying to find an angle that would allow her to see what he was seeing.

"Tyrone – someone - tell me what's happening." All she had to go on was Tyrone's expression and right now that was scaring the hell out of her.

"*Shut the hell up will you?*" There was real urgency and fear in his voice now. Had Farran's distraction not worked? Had he been caught? Had they been-

Suddenly Tyrone's face was at the gap. "They've spotted us."

"Hurry up and get through," she beckoned.

They scrabbled at the gate, trying to pull it wide again.

"No use, we're never gonna get through in time," he grunted.

"No, quick. Push yourselves through." She was afraid now - not for the others, but for herself.

Tyrone looked at her and then glanced back at the stairs.

"No, Tyrone. Tyrone, you guys can't leave me here."

"We have to or we're all gonna get caught. I'm sorry, George." Again he looked between her and the stairs, torn. His legs were telling him to run, only loyalty had kept him where he was this long.

"Meet at the boat like we said." And with that he made for the stairs.

Georgie's heart sank.

Sarah tugged at Tyrone's arm. "But we have to take the tunnel. We have to."

"No way, we have to go."

An angry shout came from somewhere above the subway entrance.

There was a moment of indecision and panic in Sarah, then just as they were breaking into a run, she dashed back and jammed herself into the gap in the gate. She pushed, turning her head this way and that, but the gap was too narrow.

Georgie pushed with all her might against the edges.

The doors gave a little, just enough, and Sarah's skinny form tumbled through. Her torch caught against the metal doors and bounced away towards the steps outside.

Sarah looked up at Georgie from the damp floor of the tunnel with oily scrapes on her cheeks. The boys had gone.

"Let's move."

* * * * *

Farran sprinted across the grass. Reaching the wall of the curved path he vaulted it and covered the distance to the other wall in a couple of strides before leaping over that too. The drop on the other side was much greater than he'd expected. He hit the ground hard, but rolled to absorb the impact and was back on his feet and running again in seconds.

Where the hell was he heading? He'd wanted to lead the guards away from the others - and judging by the number of shouts at his back, that part seemed to have been a success - but what now?

The perimeter fence was on his left; he could climb it, that he knew, but it would take time and by then the suits would be on him. To his right he was hemmed in by the wall of the museum. Dead ahead there was a small gap, barred by a low barrier, and beyond that, he remembered, were the museum gardens.

He glanced behind him; no choice, straight on it was.

But the gap was now plugged by a large government agent, waiting, legs and arms outspread to catch him - like some ridiculous game of British Bulldog. He hated that game. Farran ran straight at the man and, upon reaching the barrier, in one smooth movement, he stepped onto the barrier to bring him up to the man's height and headbutted him. The man dropped like a sack of spuds.

Despite the stars twinkling in front of his eyes, Farran kept going.

He just made it through to the garden, when he was met by another guard. No time for anything fancy. Farran barrelled straight into him, knocking him onto his back where he floundered on his heavy breathing apparatus like a fat turtle.

Farran couldn't help himself, he stopped dead in his tracks, nipped back and kicked the man in the ribs – *so much for non-violence.*

And then he was off again.

* * * * *

Georgie tried again to reach for the torch but it was just too far away.

"Leave it, they'll be here any minute, we need to leave," urged Sarah.

"I've almost got it."

"They could be here any second, Georgie. The only thing we have going for us is that they don't know where we're heading or how. Let's go."

"Sarah, we can't be in those tunnels without a torch, trust– what was that?"

"I don't know, but it didn't sound good."

"Damn it, OK let's go."

* * * * *

A booming peal of thunder rang out. Farran glanced up at the dark clouds above him. *Where's the lightning?* The thunder cracked again. This time he felt something whiz past his face.

They were shooting at him!

He looked about frantically - not searching for an exit this time, just somewhere to hide.

Ahead was Donnie's grave. It would have to do. Pumping his legs hard he arrived at the stone mound as shots continued to whistle about him. He leapt over it, landing badly on the other side and scouring his knees.

Panting, he peered over the edge. There was one suit far ahead of the others; in his gloved hand was a pistol and as he ran he fired off shaky shots in Farran's direction - it was only his hurry that had spoiled his aim. But seeing that he had stopped, the man took up a position on the edge of the low wall by the fence and began to line up his target.

Crouched behind the stones, Farran hunted urgently for an escape. He couldn't see any - moving at all from where he was would just get him shot.

A ricochet whinnied off the top of the tomb, sending something shiny and gold jumping into the air before it landed on the ground, shattered.

"You arsehole! That was my dad's watch," he yelled, forgetting himself and getting up.

He was answered by the crack of another shot which sent him diving for cover again.

But not before he saw William's offering.

* * * * *

Back at the museum's emergency exit, Tyrone stopped dead. "That's gunfire."

"Who're they shooting at?" said William, "Farran. Must

be. We have to go back, but what can we do if they've got guns now?"

Frightened, he looked at Tyrone.

There was the torment of different emotions on the other boy's face: Tyrone was frightened too, terrified in fact, but when he saw those suits he relived his powerlessness, his humiliation and he felt so angry he wanted to go straight out and kill them all.

The government men continued to close on them. There were just too many.

"These people have lost it, William. I mean, if I get a chance to go one-on-one with any of these guys, then there's going to be some serious payback but…they aren't screwing around. Live to fight another day."

* * * * *

Fumbling blindly, Farran reached over the burial mound and pulled the crossbow towards him. It was weather-beaten and battered - but it was loaded. He'd seen William use it and knew it was vicious; it wasn't William's favourite plaything for nothing.

He waited for a gap in the firing before popping up from behind the grave, taking hurried aim and squeezing the trigger. The crossbow went off with a resounding *thwap* that echoed in the stock.

Farran had aimed as best he could, lining the crosshair with the centre of the man's chest, but there was a difference between shooting at a target and shooting at a living person, even if they *were* trying to kill you. At the vital moment Farran had closed his eyes and hoped.

On opening his eyes he saw, with a perverse kind of relief, that he hadn't killed the man. The bolt had shot low and pierced the man's thigh. He was tottering around, swearing and clutching at the wound in his leg. In his distraction he staggered towards the edge of the path and slipped off, landing crotch first on the rim of the wall before sliding into the gully in a hedgehog-ball of pain.

"Damn," Farran laughed, "Donnie, you would have loved that, man."

He patted the grave affectionately before sprinting off towards the wall where the man had fallen.

Farran leaped the gully, landing on the fence beyond, scrabbling up and over then dropping easily down on the other side.

"Piece of piss, just like climbing the school fence. Now where did I leave my moped?"

CHAPTER 35.

"It's alright. I think we lost them," panted William, his face almost purple with exertion.

A shout came from one of the upper floors, a suited head poking out of a window. "I've located them on top of the research wing," the man spoke loudly into his radio. "The fat one and Tyrone."

"Oi!" shouted William, hurt.

"Not now," said Tyrone. "We need to go."

"But he called me fat…"

"I know, I heard."

"But I'm not fat, I'm…"

"Big-boned. I know."

"Exactly."

"Don't feel bad, he just doesn't know you like I do. Can we shitting-well go now?"

"But I'm *not* fat."

"We can stay here and you can tell him if you like - while he guts us and experiments on us - or we can get the hell out of here. Now which way onto the roof? You know this place better than me."

"Bugger. Yeah, OK, we head that way."

They ran over the research wing, scrabbling across the slippery tiles to the walkway that led along the edge of the museum buildings. The maze of flat lead roofs, fire exits, guttering and metal gangplanks stretched out into the distance, linking all the buildings in a patchwork for several blocks. Hugging the walkway they were able to make it to a rickety ladder that led up one side of the building and down onto a narrow ledge.

William, following as close as he could, watched as a piece of the crumbling stonework tumbled to the alley below. The gathering wind whipped about them dangerously.

"I don't like this, where are we going, Tyrone?"

"Car park, like we planned."

"Didn't we decide that was a bad idea?"

"We just have to hope the cameras are following the others."

"But…"

"Do you have any better ideas?"

William, standing on tiptoe, could see the white heads of at least four suits bobbing towards them over the rooftops.

"OK, but let's go faster."

* * * * *

Georgie slowed in the tunnel. "Sarah, what's going on?"

"What do you mean?" she whispered back.

Georgie stopped altogether. "I mean…Sarah, are we heading into a trap?"

"What are you talking about?"

"You know exactly what I'm talking about."

"*Shh*, keep your voice down."

Georgie ignored her, "I came down here because there didn't seem to be any alternative, it all happened so fast - but I'm not an idiot, Sarah. You've been acting weird ever since you 'escaped'."

"I wouldn't do anything to hurt any of you, you know that."

"Answer the question."

"Georgie, we really need to keep the noise down just in case." Sarah tried to keep the shaking out of her voice.

"In case what? Are they following us?"

"I don't know, they might be, they've followed us everywhere else."

For a moment the fear of the government agents overwhelmed everything else and they listened hard for any sign that they might have been heard, but there was nothing except their own breathing - quick and frightened.

At last Georgie whispered slowly, "Did you tell them we were coming down here?"

"No."

"Then what happened? What you said back at the vault didn't make sense."

"I…I…"

"*Sarah.*"

"Joanna rescued me," Sarah was glad that the dark hid her face. "Then when they killed her they caught me again." Sarah couldn't bring herself to tell Georgie the whole truth: that she'd planned to betray them, that she was sorry, that she'd still be a prisoner – they all would if not for Joanna - but most of all she couldn't bear to tell her friend that it was her fault that Joanna had died.

Tears trickled down her face unseen. She took a breath. "They wanted me to lead you all into a trap, and I nearly did…"

"Bloody hell, Sarah…"

"Wait, wait, let me explain. I nearly did - to save you. I know you guys; with the weapons we had in the vault you would never have given up without a fight and they'd have hurt you or even killed you trying to take that room. But if they'd taken you by surprise you might've been OK…"

"Great, thanks…"

"But, but I didn't do it. I saw what they're capable of - what they did to Joanna." She remembered Joanna's fear and she felt her own fear and anger burning inside. "When you suggested we hide I knew that down here was the only place we might have a chance. But we need to keep moving and we need to keep quiet, just in case."

"So they really don't know where we're heading?"

"No. The car park was the trap, just like I said. There's no way out of the car park."

* * * * *

William and Tyrone at last squatted at the top of several flights of black iron stairs. Sheltered in a nook of the building they scanned the area below. The car park was one large square; it ran away to deep shadow and a covered area at one end and tapered to a single narrow exit at the other, made all the smaller by a prefabricated guard house. It looked quiet enough, but how could they be sure that the government weren't watching from one of the darkened windows or down there already, waiting in those shadows…

"We're just gonna have to chance it, those government guys can't be far behind. What d'you think – slow and sneaky or make a dash for it?"

"Slow," puffed William, "I vote for slow."

From above them came the sound of a tile skittering free.

"Overruled." And with that, Tyrone began to fling himself down the stairs with William reluctantly running after as fast as his bulk would allow.

Unseen by the two boys, the car park's surveillance camera started a lazy arc over the courtyard below.

One flight, two flights, jump. Hitting the concrete at the bottom of the stairs they ran to the nearest car, William pulling a cricket bat from his kitbag as he ran. He was just about to swing it when Tyrone called for him to stop.

"No, not that one, too new. Alarmed."

William spied a beaten-up Ford Fiesta, and making for it in a couple of strides they'd soon smashed a window and clambered inside.

There was an awkward pause.

"Shouldn't one of us be doing something right about now?" hinted Tyrone, looking pointedly at the ignition in front of William.

William looked at him blankly. "Don't you know how to hotwire a car? I thought you would, 'cos y'know…"

Tyrone stared at him open mouthed.

"What? What'd I say?" pleaded William.

"When we get out of this you and I are going to have a long talk about stereotypes."

"What, like amps and speakers?"

"You're going to choose now to try and develop a sense of humour?"

"Can you or not?"

"Yes, because my uncle Phil taught me."

"See."

"My *white* uncle Phil. Who's an engineer- forget it. Hurry up, switch places."

Tyrone had the engine going in thirty seconds. They pulled out of the parking spot hurriedly and into the centre of the courtyard, aiming at the daylight past the narrow arch of the exit.

William craned his neck to look up at the rooftops in time to see four domed heads appear above the parapet. He was puzzled - they seemed to have stopped - then he noticed that one of the agents had raised a walkie-talkie.

The penny dropped and William turned urgently to Tyrone "It's a-"

A black four-wheel-drive suddenly appeared before them, blocking out the light as it screeched to a halt right in front of them.

Instantly the two boys had the car doors open, ready to run-

From out of the far shadows behind them roared two more identical jeeps cutting off the fire escape.

They sat back in their seats, momentarily defeated.

Tyrone felt sweat prickle his brow in fear. He looked out across the car park – the men already out of their cars in anticipation - then suddenly he released the handbrake.

"Screw this, and screw them. No way am I going back. William, buckle up!"

Tyrone had the engine revving again. He threw it into reverse, hardly noticing the sound of William's hands slapping the dashboard as he was thrown forward.

Tyrone brought the car to a stop just inches away from the 4x4s, sending the men scattering for safety.

"That ought to do as a run up."

He flung the gearstick back into first and floored it and then second gear and floored it again so that he'd picked up a head of speed in just a few short yards. He aimed the car at the front bumper of the much larger 4x4. If he could ram it out of the way just a little, there would still be room to get by.

Just before they hit, Tyrone tapped the brake and slammed the accelerator so the front of the Fiesta rose up the moment it collided with the shiny black bumper.

The Fiesta crashed to a teeth-clanging, bone-jarring and complete stop.

The jeep hadn't moved an inch.

"What the hell was that?" croaked William peeling the seatbelt strap away from his throat.

Tyrone tried to stop the rattling in his head. "I thought it would work kind of differently."

He glanced in the mirror, in the distance he could see the government agents doing their distinctive half-waddle half-run, growing larger by the second. Then he looked through his shattered windscreen at the driver of the 4x4, now just inches away. The man looked a little shaken but turned to glare down at the two boys. They were close enough to see him smile as he put his hand to the door handle.

"Oh bollocks," whispered William.

But the jeep's door didn't move. They saw the man's face drop from triumph to confusion and back up to anger. He tried again and again to open the door but the collision had bent it shut. Giving up, the man turned to make his way to the other side of the car but his suit made this all but impossible.

"I think we just got a break. Let's get out of here."

Tyrone pulled the wires dangling from the steering column apart and closed his eyes to say a little prayer as he sparked them together. The engine bubbled briefly, then choked and died.

The suits behind them were close now, almost filling the rearview mirror, too close for them to make a run for it. It was the car or nothing.

Tyrone took a breath and tried again, the car bubbled again but this time the engine turned over and took hold.

He put the car into reverse; for a terrifying moment the tangled bumpers held them, and then with a tear and a clang their bumper came away completely and they were moving.

A loud slap hit the rear windscreen. The government agents had reached them.

Tyrone started forward again, trying to ignore the shouts from behind.

One agent clawed at the rear of their car while another tried the door handles.

Agonisingly slowly, Tyrone scraped the car between the wall and the front of the 4x4 as the agents hammered on the glass.

A rear window cracked.

The back windshield fractured into a tracery of fine lines then smashed, sending tooth-sized nuggets of glass bouncing around the inside of the car.

A gloved arm entered through the hole.

"Bloody hell, man, get us out of here."

"I'm trying, I'm trying."

The hand reached through and caught hold of the back seat. The sickly smell of disinfectant now fought with the burnt rubber from their spinning tyres.

The wing mirror cracked off, falling through the open window onto William's lap.

And then they were through - the scream of metal on metal suddenly stopped and the car shot forwards.

Shattered glass sliced through the rubber of the agent's suit and he let go with a frightened yelp.

Tyrone slammed his foot on the accelerator and they lurched around the corner and away.

From somewhere behind them came the growl of a 4x4 starting up.

* * * * *

Hubbard stormed through the corridors of the museum. "What the hell do you mean they got away?!"

"Only temporarily, ma'am," bleated Mr Simon, struggling to keep up. "We are in pursuit of the two subjects, they won't get far."

Hubbard rounded on the man, "Two! What in God's name do you mean *two*?"

"Th...there were only two of the children at the car park, we-"

"Two – that little bitch tricked us."

"Ma'am, I..."

"Shut up, Mr Simon," she snatched her walkie-talkie from her belt, "Lightbourne come in, would you like to explain to me just WHAT is going on."

"We have reports of a vehicular pursuit of the two escapees from the car park and further riders are chasing down the other boy," came the crackled response.

"What happened, Lightbourne? You were supposed to have this under control."

"We spotted the Asian boy running west in front of the research wing, he got away but we're giving chase."

"He got away? You do realise that these are CHILDREN?"

"My dear, Dr Hubbard…"

"I don't want to hear it. What about the girls?"

"There are reports that they may've been in the east corner of the museum complex."

"Where's my bloody surveillance?" She smacked the wall in frustration, then raised the walkie-talkie once more. "This is what you're going to do, Lightbourne; you are going to take everyone not currently in pursuit back to Leviathan and you are going to get that CCTV network up and running…"

"But…"

"ALL OF IT. I don't care what you have to do - hook it up to car batteries, transfer *all* facility power, peddle on a bike, sit down there in the dark if you have to, but get the whole network up and running and find those bloody children. And Lightbourne, don't even think about failing me this time." She took a quick breath. "Mr Simon, you're with me – we'll sweep the grounds. I'm going to find those girls – and then I'm going to kill them."

* * * *

Again the jeep slammed into the side of the Fiesta, adding another ugly dent to the already buckled side of the small family car. Tyrone was just able to pull them away from the park railings.

"Don't let them force us into Hyde Park, if we get stuck in the mud we're finished," shouted William.

"We're not exactly doin' great now."

What remained of the front bumper scraped along the ground, sending an impressive shower of sparks up over the bonnet. Every obstacle on the pavement made the whole car rattle.

"I just can't lose them."

Tyrone kept the car on the narrow path of the pavements, the roads themselves too cracked and overgrown to drive down. The wider 4x4 couldn't fit on the pavement but it's height and powerful engine allowed it to contend with the difficult road. The thick saplings that sprouted out of the gutters provided some cover for the smaller car, the jeep only risking an occasional jab through the gaps.

"What the hell happened to all the abandoned cars?"

"We tidied," replied William apologetically. "Head towards Oxford Street - that's still a mess. It ought to slow them down."

Tyrone took the left turn fast, over-steering, only bringing the car back under control in time to avoid a bus stop. The 4x4 ploughed straight through it like a Saturday night drunk, sending graffitied glass and metal supports flying.

"Bloody hell, that's a tank not a car," shouted Tyrone.

"Bad fuel economy though," William shouted back over the roar of air through their smashed windshield.

"Somehow I don't think we can outlast them. They're going to cripple us any minute."

As if to prove his point the jeep rammed them hard again. There was a sound of shattering and something fell away from the rear of the car.

"I hope that wasn't anything important."

Tyrone struggled with the wheel, his hands clenched with effort.

"Oxford Street coming up, take a right."

The car crashed down from the pavement onto the road, a hubcap cracking off and disappearing under the wheels of the 4x4.

"There's not going to be any car left if we keep this up."

Tyrone turned right into Oxford Street and began to swerve the car through the slalom of abandoned taxis and buses that littered the once bustling street. The tips of the tall grasses whipped through the open windshield almost blinding both boys. The jeep kept pace easily, knocking stationary vehicles aside as it charged onwards.

"Nothing's slowing them down. We have to find a way to even things up or we're screwed."

"Head for Regent's Park."

"What?" Tyrone flashed a look at William. "But won't that be muddy as hell?"

"Yeah, but don't worry about that, you missed a lot while you were away. Trust me."

"Which way?"

"Hang on." Tyrone could see William out of the corner of his eye, rooting about in the glove compartment until he came up with something in his hand.

"You're kidding me. An A-Z?"

"Well, do you know the way?"

Tyrone slipped the car into the slim gap between two rows of what once must have been a traffic jam. The 4x4 was forced to veer off to the outside but Tyrone could see it through the gaps on his left, as dogged as ever.

"Take the second left," yelled William.

Tyrone squinted at the road ahead. "That's not the way."

"Who's got the map?"

"You."

"Well then?"

"Don't take that tone with me."

"Well listen then."

"I'm gonna pull-"

"Listen to me."

"-I will pull over, I will pull this car over, I swear it."

Just then the line of traffic ended and the jeep came into full view, drifting rapidly towards them.

"Turn now!" screamed William.

Tyrone yanked the wheel down and they turned hard left, straight across the path of the oncoming jeep. It clipped the back edge of the Fiesta and both vehicles went spinning through the corner of a shop front; plate glass and affordable clothing rained down everywhere, and then they were out through the other side, back on the street, the 4x4 right behind the Fiesta as though nothing had happened.

"Can you believe that?"

"I know, I wasn't sure it was the second left either." William checked the map again quickly. "OK, another left."

They swerved round the corner, the car heeling over dangerously as the two right wheels left the ground for an instant. Then the park appeared straight ahead.

"OK, Regent's Park, what now?" said Tyrone.

"Keep going."

"What?"

Floor it!"

"You serious?"

"DO IT!" screamed William.

Tyrone floored it.

The car hit the kerb, took off and smashed straight through the park fence.

It continued on for a few yards, cutting down great swathes of the long grass before grinding to a halt in the middle of what was once a playing field.

The top-heavy jeep hit the ground unevenly behind them, bounced once and crashed down on its side, coming to a stop not far behind.

CHAPTER 36.

Long smooth – short rough – long smooth – short rough – long smooth – short rough.

Their fingers felt out the rhythm of their walk. In the complete and utter absence of light, touch instead paced the terrain of the tunnel walls - the long smooth squares of the tiles punctuated by the rough of the grouting. Sometimes fingertips would stumble into a patch of wet and slime and the girls would flinch away - but only briefly - hands quickly seeking out the reassurance of contact, the comfort of information.

At first Georgie had counted out the undulation of the tiles like a prisoner ticking off days but she'd lost count in the thousands. Sometimes, as they paced like sleepwalkers, the two of them would stop and try to gauge where they were by the echoes of the dripping water - whether the blackness was squeezed into a tunnel or expanded outwards into a platform, darkness filling every crack and corner like smoke. When Georgie judged that they were at a platform she would pull out her Grandfather's lighter and check what station they'd reached. A short-lived halo of yellow light would reveal the girls' faces to one another - soot smeared, frightened, eyes wide-shining like dogs in the night. They were often as heartened by the close of the zippo as they were by the first staccato sparks that brought light.

They had entered a world defined only by slopes and

inclines, damp smells and clammy skin. It was a world that was familiar to Georgie - to her it was still that place of tomb-like loneliness she had entered so many months ago, and she thanked God that Sarah was with her this time.

There were crunches and shufflings away in the mildewed darkness from time to time. Then they would stop, terrified that the click they'd just heard was the sound of government boots on the uneven ground. But it never was and after a few minutes they would continue their journey.

Finally Georgie whispered, "I think we should take a rest now, we've been going for ages."

"Let's light one of the flares, we haven't heard anything, I think it'd be safe."

Georgie reached into her bag and fished out one of the three flares. She smacked the end of it and it fizzed into life, throwing monstrous shadows up the walls.

They were in a particularly narrow stretch of tunnel between two curves. There appeared to be a door recessed into the wall ahead, just before the track tapered around the corner, disappearing into darkness once more.

"We should be somewhere between Russell Square and King's Cross. If we head up when we hit the station it should bring us right into the middle of where the fire was."

"I hope the others got away alright."

"I'm sure they did. Those guys can handle themselves." But Georgie wasn't as sure as she hoped she sounded.

Suddenly the blaze and bang of a gun firing split open the darkness.

* * * * *

The moped ploughed into the soft dirt of the burnt wasteland sending a spray of dust fanning out behind, blinding the pursuers on their motorbikes. The scooter felt skittish under Farran's hands and when the rear wheel found nothing solid to bite into, the back began to fishtail wildly. He gripped the handlebars, fighting for control, but every little adjustment magnified into a violent swerve until the bike was bucking like a wild animal with a mind of its own and all he could do was hold on and hope for the best.

A hidden hump sent the bike skywards in an arc that brought his front wheel down hard into the dirt and sent Farran spiralling off the bike.

As he flew through the air he had just time to think one thing: *this is gonna hurt.*

And he wasn't wrong.

He hit the dirt flat, knocking the wind out of himself and continued at an alarming speed, digging out a furrow with his body until he thumped into the remains of a wall and the lights went out.

When he came to, Farran was staring straight up at the ominous storm clouds growing pregnant and angry in the skies above London. *Looks like rain*, he thought, *better bring the washing in.*

Then reports started to come into his brain from the rest of his body and he realised just how much pain he was in. He tentatively moved his limbs. Nothing seemed to be broken, but his back and legs were scuffed and bruised and it felt like someone had taken to him with a baseball bat.

"Shit," he said aloud, as his situation flooded back to him with the distasteful speed and clarity of a sick-burp.

He scrambled to his feet and regarded with wonder the mark he'd left in the ash. It looked like a crazy, elongated snow angel - a fallen snow angel.

He scanned the landscape for his pursuers but even in this flat wilderness he couldn't see anyone.

Where the hell were they?

He couldn't see them anywhere. Maybe he'd lost them.

He relaxed a little and was brushing himself down when a movement four hundred metres back made him look more closely.

He saw a disturbance on the horizon like a heat haze - a bubbling of the ground. Out of the ash rose ash-coloured figures, as though the dust itself were coming to life in the form of two golems. Farran froze. It was the two government men.

The riders had obviously been pitched off their bikes at the same time he had.

They were facing the other way and hadn't spotted him yet, but he didn't know what to do. He had to lose them. He couldn't risk meeting up with the others now, not without bringing them along and getting everyone caught. *What about?...* A memory flashed into his head and quickly transformed into a plan. *It might still be there if he could only find it.*

He could see, even at this distance, the two men checking themselves over, brushing themselves down as he'd done. He felt an odd moment of connection with them - they were human after all.

Could he do this? He'd promised himself he'd give up violence. But he had no choice; this was the only way. They didn't have to follow him and if they did it was their fault, not his. This was the only place without CCTV cameras. The only route he could take undetected, his only hope of escape.

Then one of the men turned.

Farran could feel something staring at him from under that dirt, under that suit, something malevolent and hateful.

That decided it.

He turned on his heels and ran.

* * * * *

"Hold your fire."

"I saw one."

"There was nothing there."

"I'm telling you I saw a light up ahead, and movement."

The government agents rounded the corner of the tube tunnel, the rubber of their suits whispering frantically as they ran.

The girls were nowhere to be seen, but lying in the middle of the tracks was a green canvas bag.

"I told you I saw one."

The large form of Dr Hubbard bent over and picked up the bag, tipping the contents onto the ground.

"Yes," came Hubbard's curt response, "We're close. But they know we're coming." Turning away she flicked on the powerful beam of her torch. "No need for subtlety now. Fire on sight."

Just beyond the next curve in the tracks, Sarah and Georgie were running for dear life.

"How did they find us?"

"They must've been tracking us for ages. Dammit, if that door had opened we might have had a chance. We've got no choice, we have to try and outrun them."

Behind they heard the deafening report of gunshots and looking back saw the strobing muzzle flashes away down the tunnel.

The flare fizzled out.

Not now!

Georgie flung it angrily to the floor.

"We have to keep running."

"But we can't see."

"Just run."

They clasped hands and sped headlong and blind into the darkness, tense, expecting any moment to slam into some hidden obstacle.

Georgie's foot hit a patch of uneven ground and she stumbled. Then her other foot hit something else, larger. This time she couldn't keep her balance and she fell. She tried to put her hands out before her but she couldn't see the ground and her palms hit the dirt sooner than she expected. The sockets of her shoulders jarred painfully.

She found herself splayed out on something soft. Patting around trying to get her bearings she noticed that the ground rose and fell randomly, hard in some places but elsewhere giving unexpectedly under her exploring hands.

"Georgie, are you all right? What's going on? Georgie we need to hurry, they're coming. Georgie?"

But Georgie didn't reply, a horrible thought had begun to form in her mind.

She scrabbled frantically for the lighter.

Clink, flick, spark.

The tunnel was heaped high with bodies.

There was no smell, other than the damp earthy odour of the tunnel, no gore. A thick layer of quicklime covered everything and glittered in the light of the flame.

The bodies were dry and still, resting in one great, ungainly pile. People of all ages and races; Londoners all lying together to the edges of Georgie's flickering light.

"They must have been dumping them down here from the very beginning," said Sarah. "Leviathan clearing the streets and houses and chucking them into the tubes. Like trash."

Georgie couldn't speak; on her knees in the half-light she was overwhelmed. This was the answer to the question she'd buried deep down. This was what was locked away in the tunnels. Death. Somehow she'd known it the very first time she'd come down here.

It should have been so sad and so horrifying. But she

didn't want to cry - oddly she felt nothing. The sensations were like bright, multi-coloured light all mixing together to create white, blankness. Her brain just wasn't equipped to process this kind of thing.

A cacophony of shouts and stamping boots brought her back to her senses. The government were just around the bend now, moments away.

"Run, run!" shouted Sarah, hauling Georgie to her feet.

Georgie and Sarah began frantically to pick their way among the bodies.

They could hear laboured breathing hissing out through the ventilators, almost upon them.

They scrambled onwards as fast as they could.

Perhaps they could make it out of sight.

Then the tunnel ahead began to blink with flashlights.

More men were coming from the front.

No, not after everything they'd been through.

But it was no use.

They were trapped.

* * * * *

Farran's lungs were burning now. Thank God he'd given up smoking otherwise he wouldn't even have made it this far.

Left or right? He just didn't know. The burnt landscape all looked the same: soft ashy ground and the stubs of buildings like a mouthful of rotten teeth, no landmarks.

He looked up at the sky, now so swamped with clouds that he couldn't even see the sun.

He stopped in confusion, aware that with every moment he wasted the men got closer.

Perhaps the twisted lamppost to his left looked familiar?

He glanced back - too late it would have to do.

He set off running again.

Just then there was a flash, followed almost instantly by a boom of thunder, and the heavens opened.

Fat droplets impacted on the loose surface of the ground creating a thousand dark dimples on the dust in the space of a few seconds. The rain plastered his hair to his head and cooled his hot limbs. It was only after a couple of paces that he realised that something was wrong.

The heavy rain was turning the ashy soil of the wasteland into sludge. Every step he was fighting against the suck of the mud, like running through quicksand.

In panic, he twisted his torso round towards the men, but his legs held fast. The men were closer - *frighteningly* close. He realised with horror that there was no escape. They were going to catch him.

CHAPTER 37.

Sergeant Horner had always been an ambitious man. He'd grown up in a small council house in Walthamstow and had been the only one of his three brothers and two sisters to go on to university - although back then it had been 'just a polytechnic' as his mother never ceased to remind him. He wasn't the world's most original thinker, but he'd worked hard on joining the police force and the fact that promotion had always eluded him was a source of constant disappointment. He'd tried being one of the lads, tried keeping his head down, tried taking on the work of others - but whatever it was that made someone stand out for promotion, he didn't have it. By the time he was forty he was still only a constable and had tried to be so many different people he'd forgotten who he was or why he was trying, and his family, thanks to the long hours and his constant restlessness, had largely forgotten who he was as well. So when he'd received an invitation to interview for a special unit of the CDC it had been with low expectations.

When the letter came to tell (the then) Constable Horner that his application had been accepted, he was so surprised and flattered that he hadn't stopped to think of any effects that the small print might have for him, his life and his family. By the time TB S11 hit he was almost a ghost to his 'loved ones' and vice versa; in fact, it was only several hours after the large steel doors of the underground complex had sealed shut that he remembered them at all. By which time of course it was too late.

Sergeant Horner looked groggily about the dark cab of the jeep he found himself in, but the condensation on his facemask made it difficult to see. He raised a gloved finger to the plastic but the condensation was on the inside. *How did he get here?* A heavy rain had begun to fall, spattering against the car and dripping through the smashed windows.

It was hard to think clearly. He raised himself up, resting on the divide between the two front seats. He thought his nose was bleeding but there was nothing he could do about that either. His superior, Inspector Finnegan, lay sprawled at the bottom of the car, either unconscious or dead, he wasn't sure.

It was so hot in the suit. Pushing the door above him open with some difficulty, Sergeant Horner pulled himself out of the wrecked car and into what looked like a park.

Steadying himself against the roof of the 4x4, he looked about him. To his left was a great expanse of playing fields and what he thought, with as much surprise as he was capable, might be a small herd of zebra.

There's something familiar about this place, he thought to himself as he continued to scan the horizon. In front of him was the shell of what had once been a Ford Fiesta, now empty. "Bugger," he grumbled lightly to himself, remembering the chase, then was distracted by a noise behind him.

Inspector Finnegan was crawling down from the 4x4 with an ungainly, spider-like movement. He looked back at the car in an emotionless way. He thought he might be a little concussed. He was about to turn and say this to Finnegan, when the tattered remains of a football net caught his eye and instead what came out was-

"I used to bring my kids here on Sunday mornings…"

Inspector Finnegan didn't seem to hear, but took a few faltering steps forward. Sergeant Horner looked back at the net.

"Not every Sunday…but I brought them…I brought them a few times. Judy's birthday I think it was. Not recently mind."

"They're getting away!"

For a moment Horner didn't know what Inspector Finnegan meant, but he obediently followed the line of her finger off to his right. There he saw, at some distance now, the two targets, an IC1 and an IC3 male. They were running as fast as the long grass would allow them in the direction of a playground full of small monkeys and a clump of trees.

"Move it, Tyrone. Move your arse."

"Why're we running this way? We could be in those bushes before they know what happened."

"Trust me - we do *not* want to hang around here. Make for the trees."

"But they'll see us."

"Doesn't matter. It could be anywhere."

"What could?"

"Hurry!"

Tyrone looked back at their steaming Fiesta and the hump of the black 4x4 behind it and then the side door burst upwards.

William trod in something foul smelling, but didn't stop, though he noticed that it was mucousy and had hard lumps.

They carried on past the play area.

"Are those monkeys?"

"Yeah…but there used to be a lot more of them…hurry."

William was panting hard, but Tyrone was now finding it difficult to keep up - after his time locked up, and the run across the rooftops, he just didn't have the strength.

Behind them the government agents were running too now.

Tyrone looked to his right and through the rain saw the statue of a dinosaur by the swings. He couldn't remember any dinosaur statues in the park. It was big - ten foot at least.

A bright yellow tongue flashed out of its mouth.

Sergeant Horner was covering the ground between himself and the two targets fast. He was in good shape for his age and his long legs gave him the advantage through the tall grass. But his suit was hot and airless; the extractor in his hood must have been damaged in the crash and now the condensation that he'd noticed earlier was building up fast.

Inspector Finnegan had dropped back but he could still hear her - barking orders as usual - as they continued the pursuit. He couldn't quite make out what she was saying; she just gesticulated angrily in the direction of the boys, the targets.

He'd never noticed quite how young they were before; perhaps it was seeing them next to the play park. When he'd been a beat bobby he probably would have had to move them along for loitering - smoking on the swings or some such. Then he saw it. Something greenish-brown and huge moving low and fast from the play park. He couldn't see clearly through the long grass but he had the impression of something powerful almost swimming along the ground. And then in an instant it had reached the boys. There was a scream and one of them went down. He saw something torn off with such force that it flew into the air.

Tyrone lay on the ground in shock. William had only had time to shout a wordless warning, so he didn't know what had hit him, only that something had grabbed him from behind. He'd felt something wrenched painfully away but he couldn't work out what had happened.

Suddenly William's face was above him.

"You OK?"

"What happened? Am I alright?"

"A Komodo grabbed you, ripped your bag right off your back." William hauled the stunned Tyrone to his feet. "Leg it - before it comes back."

They began to run for the trees again.

"What the hell was that? Never seen anything like it."

"Told you. Komodo dragon. Big friggin' lizard," shouted William. "That's the plan."

"*That's* the plan?"

"Didn't think it would find us first."

They reached open ground, the trees just a hundred metres away now. The grass to their left rustled, exploded, and a huge scaled muzzle burst from the green shadows. The yellow tongue whipped from a bright pink mouth and even in their hurried glance the boys saw the rows of serrated teeth and the shreds of Tyrone's bag hanging from them.

The dragon's squat, wrinkled legs powered it over the ground, much faster than either of the boys could run.

Neither of them looked back now, but ran full-pelt at the trees.

Their hands touched the wet bark, they reached up for branches, feet kicked off the tree, off each other, fingers clawing - anything to get higher.

Something slammed into the base of the tree right beneath their feet.

There was a low hiss and Tyrone felt a flash of pain across his calf as a claw tore through his jeans.

In desperation he kicked off the dragon itself and swung his feet up and out just as it snapped at empty space.

The two boys were clinging desperately to the lower branches. Blood trickled into Tyrone's shoe. They were safe - covered in sweat and trembling - but safe.

The Komodo hissed angrily up at them. It paced back and forth, once, twice, in a thick serpentine figure of eight, then, rearing up on its hind legs, it slowly began to climb the tree.

Sergeant Horner could see that the boys had chosen badly; their tree was isolated, the nearest alternative a good six or seven feet away - certainly too far to jump. They were trapped and at the rate the lizard was climbing they would be out of branches in a matter of seconds.

At first Sergeant Horner didn't even realise what he was doing; it was an automatic reaction to the danger. He was shouting - screaming at the lizard as he ran.

Behind, Inspector Finnegan shouted, "Leave it, Horner, it's doing our job for us. Leave it – that's a bloody order."

The lizard continued smoothly upwards after the terrified boys, its claws finding easy purchase. He shouted again and again, trying to attract the creature's attention, but his voice was muffled. Under his government mask his voice couldn't be heard. Again, not even realising what he was doing until it was done, he reached up and unzipped the layers of his protective hood. He tugged the mask off and shouted as loud as he could.

The lizard seemed to hesitate, then it brought its powerful head round away from the boys to look at the distant figure running towards it, unprotected in the middle of the long grass. Its tongue darted out, tasting the air. The Komodo turned and slipped swiftly down the tree.

Horner stopped to catch his breath. He knew that the creature would be on the ground again in a moment and that then he would have to run, and run hard. He inhaled deeply and for the first time in months breathed fresh air and felt the rain cold over his skin. He looked over at the boys and lifted one arm up in the breeze.

The Komodo was picking up speed in his direction. Sergeant Horner turned and prepared to sprint off. He never saw the second dragon coming.

High up in the tree Tyrone clung, terrified, to a spindly branch, William was just below him on the other side of the trunk. There'd been nowhere else to go; he'd tried to have the courage to let go and fall from the tree but something wouldn't let him. Tyrone had been sure he was about to die when the dragon had turned and gone after the government agent.

He'd watched in confusion as events unfolded; he knew that the government agents were ruthless, heartless adults and yet it seemed like the man had saved them, it even seemed, before the second dragon hit, like perhaps he'd even waved at them. It didn't make sense.

The man had been brought down in the long grass. They'd heard the brief scream and seen the violent movements in the tangle of pasture, but that was all. There was nothing they could have done even if they'd wanted to. Then Tyrone watched the other, smaller agent as she ran out of sight, two thin lines of disappearing grass behind her showing the rapid pursuit of the Komodos.

CHAPTER 38.

Down in the dark heart of London, beneath the rain-washed streets, Georgie and Sarah lay among the dead.

They kept still in the blackness, hearts pounding in their chests. Trying not to think of what the lumps and heaps that they were lying on might be, they listened for the sounds of returning feet.

Georgie didn't even know where Sarah was – she'd had a hold of her shirt when she pulled her down on the ground to hide, but now?... She wasn't certain what was Sarah and what was something else. She strained her eyes but it was so dark she couldn't tell the difference between when they were open and when they were shut. She might have gone blind for all she knew. She pushed her face into her forearm until red lights danced briefly in the black. Well, at least she wasn't blind.

Suddenly she saw outlines and then shapes stood out, differences in the density of the quivering black particles that constituted her vision. A shadow moved next to her, and taking the opportunity she reached out and grabbed Sarah's arm.

"They're coming back. No matter what, don't move."

The group of government agents burst back around the corner with a blinding dance of torch beams. Spots of light swept over the girls.

"They must have doubled back." It was the unmistakeable

voice of Dr Hubbard. "I'll take the service route and retrieve the night-vision equipment. Take the main tunnel, move fast and FIND THEM!"

A boot thumped down just inches away from Georgie's face. She didn't even dare turn her head to see who it belonged to. She was forced to stare at the disembodied leg, the scuffed plastic, the tracings of scratches and mud over the toe.

The quicklime began to sting in the creases round her eyes and in the numerous forgotten cuts on her exposed skin.

The enormous boot moved as, somewhere high above, its owner shifted his weight and then brought it down on Georgie's hand. She fought the urge to scream.

Next to her in the gloom, Sarah was also in agony. Hearing that voice again – harsh and full of scorn - brought it all back. Her betrayal; Donnie's death and Joanna - poor Joanna. How could she have got it so wrong? It was her fault, how could she? No. *They* were supposed to be the authority, *they* were the adults, how could *they*? She felt her anger flush her cheeks and was amazed that she didn't light up like a beacon in the darkness, that the loudness of the hatred in her head didn't bring them all running. She had never felt like this before; there was a pressing need in her to hurt them, to get revenge. It was all she could do not to jump up and tear at them, claw them to pieces, anything to get the bitter, bile-hot ache out of her chest.

When the echoing footsteps had dampened away to nothing and the flashes of light had receded to pinpricks in the darkness, only then did the girls dare to move. They got uncertainly to their feet and Georgie realised that she could still see. They'd lain there for so long that their eyes had become sensitive enough to pick up the tiniest glow of daylight. It was bleeding through into the chamber from somewhere beyond the curve of the tunnel.

"Let's go, let's head towards the light," said Georgie.

But Sarah hesitated.

"What's the problem?"

"Hubbard went down the right hand tunnel; she must have a key to open the door. She went alone."

Georgie didn't understand, but there was something new in Sarah's tone, something hard.

"I'll catch up with you," said Sarah.

"What the hell are you talking about? We need to head towards the light together, find a way out so we can meet the others."

"I'll catch up with you," Sarah repeated.

"But it's dark that way."

"If I hurry I can catch up with the light of her torch. Follow her." And with that Sarah disappeared into the deepening darkness. She'd made her choice.

Georgie called after her as loud as she dared but there was no reply, only her own voice bouncing back to her - small, strained and frightened. She had no option but to continue on alone and hope that Sarah came back.

* * * * *

Farran waded onwards, his arms flailing. If he paused, even for a second, he began to sink. Picked out by the lightning, he could see that the men were closing now, only a hundred metres behind him.

The rain pelted him, stinging his eyes.

He'd come to a collection of four or five burnt-out buildings huddled together like refugees in a storm, broken and without hope. They stood dark against the flashes in the sky. The men had reached the corner of a ruined warehouse where girders sprang from the brick like the fronds of a palm tree. Farran was only halfway along the same building, pulling himself laboriously forwards, fingers gripping the edge of breezeblock.

Through their rain-spattered visors the men saw their quarry and they knew they had him.

A bolt of lightning screamed into the remains of the iron girders, exploding in a shower of sparks. When their eyes cleared from the white streaks which had seared across their corneas, the boy had vanished.

* * * * *

Sarah didn't know what she would do when she caught up with Hubbard, or even what she *could* do, but something was drawing her inexorably into the gloom. She just had to get rid of the stone in her chest. The same numbness she'd felt after Donnie's death smothered her senses again like a shroud. She no longer cared about herself, she wasn't thinking rationally anymore.

Turning a corner she came upon a set of precarious steps that spiralled down to who knew where. Hubbard was just below her, moving slow and laboured in her suit.

Sarah paused briefly but the woman seemed completely unaware that she was there, and so she followed her down.

Sarah stalked in the shadows outside the bubble of light from Hubbard's torch. Slow step after slow step. Watching. There was a strange power in following her unobserved, being so close. The woman's backside stretched out the rubber of her bio-suit and gathered in painful-looking rings at the backs of her knees.

She ought to turn back, find Georgie, this woman disgusted her but somehow this was where she deserved to be.

"Are you just going to follow me all day like a lost puppy?"

The torch beam dazzled as it hit Sarah's eyes.

"I thought I heard someone. So, it's the little turncoat, is it? You were supposed to bring them to us in the car park, nice and simple. It was only sheer luck that we spotted you heading down here. No matter, I'm sure your other friends have been rounded up by now. They're probably being experimented on as we speak."

She moved up the steps towards Sarah.

"You were warned – but you were too smart, too smart and too stubborn weren't you, Miss Hobbes?"

"First Donnie, then Joanna. Why? What's wrong with you people?"

"You're just a child, you wouldn't understand. There's a bigger picture – there's *always* a bigger picture than our own, small lives."

Hubbard was up close now, her mask almost pressing against Sarah's face.

"Children don't have to make the hard decisions – you've never had to lock yourself away, lock out the people you loved and leave them to die. Because that was what was necessary. You didn't have to hold people together, to keep discipline – even when that meant taking lives to stop chaos spreading. I had to let go of the nice, simple morality a child like you thinks lies happily at the heart of everything. I had to get dirty."

She was holding Sarah, shaking her painfully, and Sarah was letting her.

"And if you think, in the middle of all that suffering, I could give a damn about the pain of you and a few children then you are very much mistaken."

Her face was a snarl, yellow and ugly. The control had gone, and Sarah watched with fascination as something mad and distracted broke through the calm exterior she'd shown before. She was pushing Sarah backwards, tipping her until her spine felt as though it would crack.

"You're just *meat*. A biological detail that might, just *might* contain the cure to all this...and I will get it out of you any way I can."

And with that she pushed harder – much harder, as though there were something in her that had forgotten any justifications and now just wanted to snap Sarah in half.

Sarah felt her spine wrench and in a sudden rush of fear and anger pushed back – flailed and hit and kicked.

Hubbard slipped, her feet flying out from under her, almost comic but for the sickening crack that resounded in the tunnel when her neck hit the step.

Sarah ran for a couple of steps before she realised that she wasn't being chased. Turning back she saw Dr Hubbard splayed-out on the stairs. Over the curve of the woman's belly Sarah could see her masked head turning groggily. That was the only part of her moving.

Sarah took a couple of tentative steps towards the body, a groan emanating from behind the mouth filter made her hesitate, but the rest of it remained unnaturally still.

The groan became a gurgling cough.

She moved closer until she was standing directly over it. Hubbard's eyes looked up at her from behind the plastic of her protective suit, wide and frightened.

"H-help me," she gasped, her voice muffled, "I…I c-can't move. I think I've hurt my neck."

Sarah looked at her for a moment and then made to move away.

"Damn you girl, don't leave me like this!" she screeched.

Sarah stopped dead in her tracks. She found it in her pocket, smooth and hard and sharp-edged – the stone arrowhead Joanna had given her.

She ran her thumb along its satisfying contours before turning it over on her palm. On the other side of the flint was a label –

**Stone Age, Thames Valley.
King's Cross Excavation.**

So, this had always been part of London – this struggle, this violence. She felt at once saddened and reassured that she was just one part of it all.

She turned back to the helpless figure on the floor.

Hearing the approaching footsteps, Dr Hubbard began to shout again.

"Good. That's it, help me. Hurry up. Hurry up."

Sarah knelt down beside her and using the keen edge of the flint, cut away the layers of Hubbard's mask with jagged slashes. The woman screamed and screamed.

"No! No! What are you doing you stupid girl? Stop, you'll infect me. Noooo!"

Sarah peeled back the layers so that at last she could stare directly into this woman's eyes. The front of the mask sagged at the side like a flap of skin. Without it she could see that Hubbard's face was the colour of over-cooked fish and that the pudgy folds of her features were all twisted up in equal parts fear and anger.

"What have you done? You've infected me."

"I know," Sarah replied simply, a detached look of fascination playing about her features. "But let's make sure." And with that she hawked and spat through the woman's open mask.

Hubbard shrieked in disgust. She tried to clear her mouth but the spittle just plopped messily back down onto her lips again.

"Joanna taught me to do that," said Sarah. Then she got to her feet and walked off.

It wasn't until she had walked for twenty minutes that she could no longer hear Hubbard screaming.

CHAPTER 39.

The air is so thick with static it hums. Rain pours and thunder rumbles from the belly of the darkened sky, rolling and echoing across the houses and skyscrapers of the storm-battered city.

Filthy streams plough along the gutters and spread outwards. The wide, cracked roads and high streets flow with water that has already risen ankle-deep.

Smaller cars begin to move and slide, carried by the growing force of the flood as it races along. The cold water churns and eddies, bubbling from the drains as they overflow so that streets begin to swirl with broken furniture and rubbish. Water cascades down steps and floods into basements and cellars.

It searches for every hole and crack to fill. Every tunnel.

* * * * *

Georgie was alone again in the dark. For a while the grubby orange fluorescents had been working, but it had only been a short section where an empty train sat like an elephant in a graveyard. She'd squeezed through the narrow gap between the train and the curve of the wall. Beyond that was the darkness again, the constant pressure of it was all around her now.

She stepped carefully, barely raising her feet, feeling her way, not putting her weight down till she was sure. She made slow, laborious progress but she didn't want to trip again.

In the dark her mind began to wander. She was alone and the need to find people was growing in her like an urgent hunger. She had to fight the instinct to run, to bolt for the outside. She tried to keep her mind focused but it wandered despite her efforts. She seemed to see the bodies of the dead before her. All of those poor people. It was as though her eyes, now blind, began to leak images. They flashed before her. Mouths open. *Flash*. Skin taut. *Flash*. Hair spread mermaid-like. *Flash*. Badges, handbags, glasses. *Flash*. Bodies now just discarded shells, empty trinkets; life departed like a hermit crab. *Flash, flash, flash, flash, flash.*

She couldn't keep hold of them as people, her sympathy putrefying, becoming horror and disgust. She imagined ghouls waiting in the inky blackness just beyond her touch. They could be anywhere about her. She imagined them leaning towards her whispering angrily, "Why us? Why not you?" Their fetid words tickling her ear. "You forgot us. You left us. You *left* us."

She whirled round, feeling their breath on her skin, heard a noise and turned again.

Nothing there, stupid girl. You're behaving like a child.

She breathed, making herself stand still, ignoring the creep at the back of her neck, knowing it was all in her mind.

Her heart began to slow. Control returned. *That's better.* Then she realised that in her panic she had turned so many times she had no idea which way she was facing anymore. A shiver went through her. She went cold. Her foot was cold. Wait, it wasn't in her mind - her foot *was* cold. And wet. It was the distant trickle of water she'd heard.

Now her left foot was wet too. Water runs downhill, so if she went in the direction the water was coming from, she could follow it above ground. She was saved.

That's when it hit her.

A great surge of water came gushing at her in the darkness. All Georgie knew about it was a cold force that took her legs from under her and brought the hard surface of the floor flying up to meet her. The blast span her around until she managed to grip one of the rails.

With difficulty she got to her feet in the rapidly rising water and tried to force her way upstream. The water was up to mid-thigh and her sodden clothes clung heavily to her, making her teeth chatter like a wind-up toy as she began to make her way slowly against the force of the oncoming water.

She hoped that Sarah had made it out. She felt terrible about letting her go but it had all happened so fast and Sarah had been so determined. It made no sense though, she just couldn't understand why Sarah had gone. What did she hope to achieve, disappearing after Hubbard like that?

She stopped and looked pointlessly back down the tunnel for a moment. Sarah had gone further down into the tangle of passageways, Georgie could only hope that she'd head upwards again as the lowest parts flooded.

Her hands were tight with cold and her feet were already dead. She looked ahead and realised, to her surprise, that the walls seemed to be resolving out of the darkness and she could see highlights on the water.

An apparition appeared, a diffuse yellow ball of light that bobbed and weaved before her eyes, accompanied by a strange gurgling. It seemed to be growing larger.

Georgie was shivering uncontrollably with cold, making her vision jiggle. This had to be a hallucination brought on by the cold and her desperate need to get out of the tunnels. Then she realised that it was a light, a light attached to someone underwater.

A head broke the surface, carried along by the torrent, bedraggled and young. It was Sarah.

Georgie couldn't imagine how, but it was definitely Sarah's face barrelling towards her.

She braced herself and stretching out an arm, managed to

hook the girl as she rushed by.

"What happened? What happened?"

Sarah spluttered and coughed, "The ceiling collapsed. I followed the side tunnel round, I was almost out, then the ceiling collapsed."

"How did you get ahead of me? What happened with Hubbard?"

"Don't know, just followed the track. Look we have to get out of here, I don't know what happened up there but the whole thing just came down on me. We need to get out of here fast. We need to get out of here or we're going to drown!"

"We have to keep heading upstream. The water's rising too quickly, we can't go back." Georgie couldn't bear the thought of trying to find some other passage leading them further into the tunnels. She knew King's Cross was ahead of them somewhere, even if there had been a collapse, she'd risk it - she just wanted out.

Sarah clambered to her feet. "We need to find another way."

"There *is* no other way, we *have* to follow the water."

Sarah looked about her exasperated. The growing stream was up to their waists by now. It seemed like a risk, but perhaps Georgie was right.

Leaning forward, arms held high, they began to force their way against the current, the water constantly threatening to drag them away into the dark and the depths.

"What's that noise?" shouted Georgie above a growing roar.

"I don't know, but it doesn't sound good."

The roar was now accompanied by a frightening rumble.

In the torchlight they saw a fist of white water come careening around the corner, rebounding off the sides of the tunnel and heading straight for them with terrifying speed. The two girls barely had time to take a breath before the water was upon them.

They felt themselves plucked from where they stood and twirled helplessly around like spiders down a drainpipe, all limbs and motion.

The water whisked them further and further back down the tunnel, flinging them mercilessly against the walls. All they could see was the thick green of the bubbling water and murky white froth.

Sarah's torch bounced about dangerously at the end of its cord, first smashing against the floor and blinking out, then smashing against her temple.

They no longer knew which way was up, roaring onwards in the terrifying black. Brackish water filled their mouths. What little breath the girls had in their lungs was quickly battered out of them and soon they were both aching for breath, clawing at the sides of the tunnel, anything to raise their heads above water and get a gulp of air.

* * * * *

Meanwhile, elsewhere, but closer now, much, much closer, the vast tidal wave boils and heaves as it charges towards London from the sea.

* * * * *

Farran pressed himself against the interior wall of the building, panting. He prayed that the men would assume he'd made a run for it and would carry on past the gap he'd squeezed through. Because there was nowhere else for him to run. If they found him now he was trapped.

The fire had eaten out the inside of the building, leaving only the jagged dog's tooth of a wall around the perimeter about eight foot high. The upper stories had collapsed inwards leaving a precarious tangle of debris.

Rain poured through the open roof and somewhere in the mess above Farran it pooled before running down a series of beams which funnelled the water straight down the back of his neck. But he didn't dare move because behind him, just the other side of the wall, came the suck and pop of heavy boots moving through mud. He tried to hold his breath.

His mind drifted back to another time hiding from authority: a car park late at night, excitement bubbling in his chest, the thrill of getting caught mixing with the drugs in his veins, making him dizzy. But this wasn't fun, this wasn't an adolescent game; if he was caught by these men, these faceless adults, they would kill him. He hadn't even done anything wrong this time.

He remembered trying to suppress a giggle, hidden in the shadows, as the police car drove by. He remembered the snort of laughter that burst from him and the car's exhaust turning red as the driver heard and slammed on the breaks. Farran snapped back, but he was still looking at that police car's exhaust. How could that be? No, something *was* there. Beyond the smashed window in the far wall of the warehouse, exhaust was rising - no, *steam*.

This was it, this was what he had been looking for.

He listened carefully. The sound of boots had gone. Still cautious, he made his way quietly over the slippery floor of the warehouse to the window. Two hundred metres from the end of the buildings, out in the middle of the flatness, there was a patch of rubble and the ground was definitely steaming.

He craned his neck out as far as he dared. The government men would be out there in no-man's-land by now. If he ran they would be sure to spot him, but that was exactly what he wanted.

He braced himself against the edges of the window; still no sign of the men. He counted one, two, three and leapt.

He missed the rubble and his feet powered into the mud, the weight of his body forcing them in like a pile driver. He looked to his right - no sign. He tested his legs. They were firmly stuck. He tried again – nothing.

A shout from his right brought his head whipping up. There they were, rounding the corner of the warehouse. They'd seen him and they'd seen that he was stuck. The larger man clapped the other briefly on the shoulder and then they started to make their way slowly towards him.

Sheet lightning clattered bright in the sky, throwing his frightened silhouette before him and illuminating the men's faces through the shadows of their facemasks. Farran thought he saw cruel smiles hanging from bearded cheeks, and hollow eyes sunk deep below ridged brows. They were the terrifying carved faces of grins on pumpkins.

He tried to pull his left leg up and then his right, but it was as though great shapeless hands were determined to hold him fast until the men could reach him. He tried the left leg again without luck.

The men continued their inevitable approach.

CHAPTER 40.

There was a harsh jolt and Sarah and Georgie felt something solid against their backs. Their movement down the tunnel had stopped but now they were pinned fast. As the water rushed over them both girls felt blackness begin to swirl at the edge of consciousness until at last the first ferocious surge began to subside and they could get air into their lungs.

The torrent continued to pummel and pick at them. Georgie managed to turn her head and saw that they were pushed up against the last carriage of a train.

"Help me get this window open, we have to get inside."

They pulled themselves around and with tired arms, pushed and pounded at the top edge of the window until it jerked reluctantly downwards.

One after the other they pulled themselves through, flopping onto the floor of the carriage where they lay gagging and twitching like fish out of a net.

For a few moments they enjoyed the luxury of breathing, listening to the rage of the water as it buffeted past the train.

Sarah sat up on her elbows, the cut on her head dripping a burning hot line down her cheek. "What the hell do we do now? We're never going to be able to swim against that."

Georgie's world was still spinning; she touched her forehead to the ground trying to steady it. "I know, I know." She looked despondently out to where she could see that the water level had now reached the bottom of the windows. It sparkled in the dirty haze of the caged lights above the train.

"This is crazy, surely we can't drown in the tube, there are miles of tunnel," laughed Sarah bitterly.

"They did in the war, people drowned in bomb shelters."

"OK then, we can," she puffed, "but I don't want to. We can't just stay here and do nothing." Her words hung in the frigid air.

Georgie looked again at the windows and the rapidly rising water. "Maybe that's exactly what we do. Look, if we go outside we're just going to get carried off, but if we close all of the windows and doors, this carriage might be pretty water-tight - we could just wait it out. I mean, we're not under the Thames or anything, it can only be a burst pipe or something. When it runs dry we can just walk out of here."

Sarah didn't look convinced.

"What choice have we got?"

Georgie had a point; in the complete absence of other options, it was a great plan.

The water was now at eye-level outside the carriage. If they were going to stay they needed to work fast. They dragged their cold, goose-bumped bodies off the floor and set about slamming all of the top windows closed and wedging them shut. Then they pushed the stiff doors completely together so that the rubber seals met, shutting out the spray of water. They finished not a moment too soon. The water bubbled up above the windows and they were completely submerged.

Light continued to filter down through the water, reveal-ing the eddies and undercurrents that sent bits of debris banging against the fragile glass on their journey down past the carriage.

The atmosphere inside the train changed, everything sounded deadened. Their ears popped, the air pressure in the carriage rising as the increasing weight of the water bore down on their makeshift submarine.

Aware of every creak and clank, their eyes darted from

window to door to window, searching for leaks. They hardly dared breathe lest the noise set up some catastrophic vibration that brought the glass shattering inwards.

But in the end that wouldn't be where the water got in.

*　*　*　*　*

Farran began to panic.

He pulled at his legs.

Every time he heaved at one it drove the other further in.

He tried rocking his body; his right leg gave a little but still the mud clawed at his feet jealously - *stay, stay with us* it seemed to hiss.

He looked at the men, close enough for him to read the name tags on their suits – *Bob* and *Larry*. How could they be the names of people he feared?

He looked back at the girder in front of him; if he could reach that maybe he could pull himself free. But it was just too far.

If he lay down he might reach it, but what if the mud sucked him down completely? He didn't want the men to catch him, but he didn't want to end up drowning in five foot of mud either. He imagined lying cold and dark, the pressure of the mud weighing down on him, like someone buried, like his family.

The men were only ten metres away from him, but the depth of the mud was hampering *their* movement now. They didn't seem to care, they knew they had him.

Farran leaned forward, lost his balance and the weight of his upper body brought him down into the ooze, his feet still stuck.

He had nothing to pull on, no leverage.

He pushed his hands into the mud but they met no

resistance, nothing to lean against to lift his face out of the suffocating sludge.

Foul smelling muck forced its way into his mouth and up his nose and in through the slits of his tightly closed eyes. Mud clogged all of his senses as it closed over his head.

He moved his arms out in front of him groping for anything, like a man panicking in slow motion. *This is it*, he thought. Then the palm of his hand felt a hot line drawn across it. He moved it back again in the same direction, fingers like feelers. There it was again.

Farran realised that he was cutting himself on a sharp edge. He stretched beyond the warmth of the blade and found that it was the point of a thick steel rod. Grabbing it he pulled with all his might.

Agonisingly slowly his body began to move through the blackness. His head wormed its way upwards and he felt the rain on his face once again. He still couldn't see, but snorted as hard as he could and breathed in. Air filled his lungs again, giving him the strength to pull once more. This time his entire upper body rose out and came to rest on top of an outcrop of rubble.

Suddenly, a hand shot up from the mud and snaked itself round his left ankle. It gave a sharp yank, pulling his arms from under him, slamming him down and knocking the wind from him.

He tried to shake his foot free but the hand was stuck fast.

He searched for finger holds in the rough concrete but it was only his right foot, wedged against the rod, preventing him from being dragged back into the mire.

He heard a noise - the smaller man was fighting with the mud and losing; every movement he made seemed to pull him downwards. Farran recognised the panic in his movements and almost felt sorry for him. The man was calling, crying, begging for help, his voice muffled by layers of mask and mud. Farran saw the larger man incline his head but he didn't move, didn't let go.

The cries for help became a bubbling scream, then there was silence except for the different tones of the rain - the deep plop on the surface of the bog, the high pitched *ting* against the large man's suit and the splatter Farran felt against his own skin.

"Why didn't you help him?" he heard himself shout.

In reply the man began to pull on his leg again. Farran understood. *He's not gonna let me go even if it kills 'im.*

His foot started to slip. He held on for as long as he could, feeling the tension build. Then he let himself go.

He went flying backwards but managed to bring his left foot down hard into the man's visor, using his own strength against him.

The plastic splintered and Farran felt his naked heel driving a piece of it into the face beneath.

The man screamed in pain, groping like a cyclops at the mess where his faceplate used to be.

Farran pushed off against his head, was up on his feet in seconds and pounding the metal path of the girders.

It was only a few moments before the man was chasing behind him. His weight made him ungainly on the tracks but pain drew him on.

Farran continued to make for the steam, finally coming to a straight length of metal that ended in the patch of boiling ground.

The man was just behind him, only feet away, hands outstretched.

Farran didn't hesitate. Feeling the ground grow hotter beneath his bare foot, he ran, launching himself into the air as he reached the end of the runway.

Gloved fingers momentarily touched the collar of his jacket and then the man's heavy boot went straight through the ground.

Farran's momentum carried him up and over the cellar

roof and he landed, knees and elbows, on the other side.

He looked back at the man. His weight had sent him through the weakened concrete and now he was wedged firmly up to his waist, just like Donnie had. Only Farran wasn't going to pull this guy out.

The ground around him still gave off thick steam, but there was a strange whining sound that grew with every second. The steam began to circle round and round, faster and faster, as though the man was obstructing a giant plughole, and just as the noise reached an unbearable pitch all went suddenly silent.

Through the shards of visor Farran saw an eye grow wide with fear and pain. Then, in a split second, the image of the eye was replaced by a pillar of fire that shot forth from the hole with the power of a geyser.

Heat blasted at Farran's hair and face, blinding him with its glare, then, just as suddenly, the fire was gone and so was the man.

Farran blinked and his mud-baked face cracked into a smile.

Something fell from the sky, landing with a soft *thunk*. It was a white boot. The foot was still inside it.

* * * * *

Water bubbled ominously against the walls of the submerged train.

"It doesn't seem to be subsiding. How long d'you think it can take this?" whispered Sarah.

As if in answer a shudder ran the length of the carriage. They both froze, hearts in mouths, waiting until they dared breathe again.

Georgie edged towards the front and looked out, but the

tunnel was quickly obscured by the swirling waters. Sarah was right, it was flowing just as hard, if not harder. What had she done? What if she'd condemned them to drown down here in the tunnels? Left here like the forgotten bodies of the other Londoners. Then she became aware that her greatest fear was being realised. The air vents above the windows were leaking.

At first there was just a gentle trickle that dribbled down the walls and onto the seats, but as the pressure grew and seals gave way, the trickles became sprays. In a matter of minutes they were up to their ankles in freezing cold water.

"We have to stop the water coming in." Georgie was gripped with fear.

"But the leaks are behind the grates - we can't get at them."

"We have to do something."

It was hopeless; grimy water continued to fill the small space. Georgie could feel the panic of claustrophobia beginning to tighten in her chest.

A high-pitched *clink* rang out and a fine network of cracks appeared in one of the windows.

"We have to do something!" Georgie shouted again in rising fear and frustration.

"There's nothing we can do but cross our fingers and wait." Sarah looked about her. "But we need to get out of the water. Stand on the seats or we'll die of cold before we even get a chance to drown." The muscles in her back were already aching from the uncontrollable shivering.

"No, no, we can't risk moving. We have to stay where we are."

But it was too late, as Sarah climbed up onto the seat the whole carriage moved under them.

"OK, OK," shouted Sarah as she hurried back down.

The carriage shifted again, an unpredictable bobbing motion that knocked the girls off their feet.

"What did you do?"

"Nothing."

"Well, what's happening?"

"I think we're floating."

The carriage continued to groan, the front end rising upward until it juddered against the roof of the tunnel, crushing the lights and plunging the front portion into shadow.

The whole carriage twisted queasily from side to side.

As the angle steepened the girls began to slide to the far end. They looked out of the connecting window. The rest of the train behind them was flooded and acting as an anchor for their carriage, though they were connected by nothing more than the rusted coupling.

The carriage bucked like a horse in harness, desperate to be free. The coupling made an agonised grinding sound, then an almighty *clank* as the connection snapped completely.

Instantly the back end leapt upwards. The girls had time to see the floor rapidly levelling before the roof smashed against the tunnel, destroying the remaining lights and steeping everything in blackness.

Huddled on the floor, Sarah and Georgie waited in terror for the ceiling to buckle and death to follow.

But what came was a scraping sound that the two girls felt as much as heard; it rippled in the darkness, it hummed somewhere in the walls and entered their bodies in a numbing vibration. It made their teeth ache and their eyeballs rattle in their skulls.

"I think we're moving," yelled Sarah.

She was right, it was unmistakeable now, the feeling of movement, a lurching in the pit of their stomachs. The roof was screaming as the train scoured the tunnel on its way upwards.

Faster and faster they went, picking up momentum like a bubble in a syringe. The girls could do nothing but cling on for dear life as they were thrown about inside.

Jonah-like they sped through the flooded arteries of the underground, racing round corners, slamming into walls, always moving onwards and upwards in the gloom until suddenly jagged lines of light sliced down into the murky water, kaleidoscoped through a dam of debris.

"Hold o-"

They crashed into the blockade, the front of the carriage concertinaing as they burst up through it and out into dazzling sunlight.

Like a whale breaching, it seemed to hang in the air shedding a tail of spray behind it, then crashed down in a violent and ungainly belly flop that sent sheets of water into the sky, giving birth to a thousand shattered rainbows.

Inside, the girls lay in stunned relief, bloodied but alive, as rain pattered down on the upturned wreck of the Piccadilly line train.

CHAPTER 41.

Besides the sound of falling rain, the roads of Westminster were quiet. The vines that covered the Houses of Parliament continued to creep silently upwards. Water trickled in great rivulets down the railings and pale buildings of Whitehall – now cracked and grimy – and nothing disturbed the growing lake which lay slick across the pavements and roads. Somewhere though, an elevator shaft hummed with movement, cutting its way hundreds of metres downwards beneath the rain-splashed streets.

Tired and bedraggled, the people in their bio-suits exited in groups and shuffled through decontamination, nodding to colleagues as they returned from the hunt, flinging their hated masks to one side and tending to injuries or empty stomachs. There were murmurings, anger and discontent.

Dr. Lightbourne sat in what served as his office now, his face grim in the harsh glare from the fluorescent lights overhead. The place had begun to show signs of decay. A dented filing cabinet stood to one side, several of its drawers buckled and scattered across the grubby carpet. A broken computer sat in the corner, its blank face gathering dust.

Lightbourne flicked carelessly through the folders strewn across his desk, ignoring the stocky figure before him. The man had a paunch and a good few days of stubble on his cheeks and although he was standing to attention it was clear it had been a long time since he'd seen any active military service.

Sounds of squabbling and the crash of moving equipment filtered in from the corridor outside. A walkie-talkie hanging at the man's belt gave a muffled squawk before its battery finally died. Eventually Lightbourne spoke.

"These children have proven more resourceful than we'd anticipated. I no longer believe that such a serious expenditure of time and manpower is our best course of action. Especially in light of Dr Hubbard's disappearance."

"You want to abandon the 'Search and Seize' sir?"

Lightbourne sighed. "Yes; in fact, abandon *all* Search and Seize missions with immediate effect."

"Your new orders?" asked the man, tentatively.

"We need a clean sweep, I think. Instruct personnel that the new protocol will be to terminate all vectors for the virus on sight."

"Very good, sir."

"And sergeant?"

"Sir?" he paused, turning back to Lightbourne.

"I want everything dead. Not one living thing left above ground in the whole city."

"Yes sir."

"Keep in contact. We'll continue to scan for the children on the remaining camera network."

"Of course, sir. We're currently in pursuit of two of the boys. They got away from us briefly but we have two motorised units chasing them and on course for intercept."

"Good. Finish them."

* * * * *

Farran's teeth chattered uncontrollably as he waded through the floodwater, hoping that he wouldn't tread on anything sharp and unseen with his already sore, bare foot. His salwar kameez clung to his shoulders in painfully cold drapes and he hunched, moving stiffly so as little material as possible touched him.

He'd seen what he thought was the Golden Hinde on the far bank but as soon as he'd stepped off the bridge into the muddle of narrow alleyways of Southwark he had lost sight of it. He prayed he'd find it soon; the water was rising fast and with it the current.

He'd stepped down from the bridge into the chill, rapidly flooding streets with a growing sense of fear – he'd never seen the Thames flood and it made the whole city unfamiliar and dangerous. In the water he felt connected to the terrible, indifferent power of the river. If he didn't get to the ship soon he'd have no choice but to find some safe dry ground and wait it out alone. If he stayed on the streets he'd eventually be unable to stand and he'd be washed away. Either that or he'd sodding-well freeze…one or the other.

He pushed on under a railway arch. Away to his right a passage led up to what looked like a market, abandoned stalls reverberating with the hard rain. Ahead the street drifted off to the left, back towards where he thought the river itself should be. A scum of crisp packets, cigarette ends, cardboard and leaves drifted past him on the surface of the murky brown water. The river must be up ahead.

Raindrops nestled in Farran's beard and caught on his long eyelashes, blurring his vision and surrounding the edges of things with smudged halos.

Rounding the corner he was struck by a bizarre sight. A sudden clearing opened up - a raised flood-wall on one side and high-rise offices on the others - and in the middle of this square sat an enormous galleon.

It looked like a pirate ship from an old film – three masts that stretched up half the height of the office blocks, steeply sloping sides of black wood patterned with red and gold stripes and a row of gun ports complete with cast iron cannons.

Looking across, Farran saw that the flood-wall here was so high that the Thames beyond was actually above the level of the ship's decks, and far above his head. The thought of the weight of all that water held back by a thin barrier terrified him.

As he looked on, the river began to cataract over the edge of the wall in a great curve of brown water - it splashed down onto the footpath, spread out across the decked area of a pub garden, knocking over wooden chairs, then flowed down the steps to join the knee deep water covering the square. The crow's nest topping the galleon's main mast began to bob urgently as the choppy water rushed down to fill the little inlet.

Georgie appeared on deck followed by Sarah. Both were running to the masts when they spied Farran. They looked as bedraggled as Farran felt, but there was a steely look of determination on Sarah's face that made him uneasy. He wondered what they had been through.

"Thank God you made it," Georgie called down. "Have you seen the others?"

"I thought they were with you."

"We got separated; Sarah and I took the tunnels, they ran off - we don't know what happened to them."

"Damn. It's alright, they know where to meet us, I'm sure they..."

The steel gangplank grated noisily against the rocking side of the ship, cutting Farran short.

"We need to get the lock lowered somehow so we can get out of here."

Farran followed Georgie's gaze to the lock set into the flood-wall, separating them from the rest of the swollen Thames. Down by his feet, water was now gushing out of the manhole in a dirty fountain instead of draining away.

"I don't think we're gonna need to, this place is flooding fast."

The two girls looked around at the rapidly filling square.

"You're right," called Sarah, her hands busy with ropes, "We'll be able to float out of here soon. I think the problem's going to be stopping the ship long enough to wait for the others."

Georgie noted the steep angle of the gangway, now jammed hard against the ends of the steps. "You'd better climb on board and help us get ready. Between the water and the government we need to be ready to push off the moment the boys get here."

As soon as the deck was under his feet Farran could feel the energy that throbbed through it, transmitted from the churning waters all around. The ship felt alive, straining at the leash, wanting to be free. He'd never been on a ship before and it made the hairs stand up on his neck.

Georgie came over and hugged him briefly, but Sarah was all business. "I've reefed the mainsail as best I could; I think we'll have our hands full without the jib and we've weighed anchor - it's only the docking ropes that're holding us in place now."

"I got no idea what you just said," said Farran, "but great, what can I do to help?"

"Look, Georgie and I have been practicing, so just do what I tell you, *when* I tell you and we'll be fine." And with that she began to climb the rigging to where the sail lay bunched up against the large crossbeam.

"Yes, *Sir*," said Farran, a little thrown by her fierceness. He looked towards Georgie for an explanation.

"I don't know…something happened…it's complicated." Georgie moved towards Farran and gave him a thin smile "There isn't time now. Sarah says the tide should bc turning soon and when it does it'll take us all the way out to sea. As soon as we drop the mainsail the ship'll want to move."

Just then the ship heeled over and they had to grab hold of the side rails to stay upright.

"What the hell was that?"

Lashed by the wind and rain, Sarah shouted down from the rigging, "The gangplank's wedged against the steps, holding the ship down and tipping us over. It was never meant to take a tide this high."

Farran and Georgie leant over the rail – at the prow the floodwater was continuing to gush over the dock, raising the ship high as its buoyancy fought for freedom.

"This thing was a museum - it isn't really ready to sail," explained Sarah.

"What?" Farran gasped.

"It's fine," reassured Georgie, "it's sailed around the world and everything…just not for a while."

Sarah continued from her perch on the rigging, "We need to get that gangplank off, otherwise we're just going to keep on heeling more and more and then she'll flood."

Farran dashed over and began kicking at the plank.

"What do we do about the others?" Georgie called to Farran above the rising storm. She could feel the urgency of the boat and she wasn't about to lose any more of her friends. Where were they? But she didn't have to wait long for an answer.

"There they are!"

Sarah was leaning out from the rigging, one arm pointing out towards the distance.

Farran and Georgie climbed up to the foredeck from where they could see the expanse of the river. It now ran swift and dark over everything, filling every crack between the buildings that used to flank its path. Through the slanting rain they could see Tower Bridge; the Thames had almost risen to the top of its arched supports and on the summit they could just make out a green car. It looked like it was being driven by a madman.

"How d'you know it's them?" Georgie shouted up to Sarah.

"I'd recognise Tyrone's driving anywhere."

Georgie smiled; the car was weaving drunkenly across the width of the bridge. It certainly seemed like Tyrone. She looked up, but Sarah wasn't smiling and her eyes were fixed intently on the distance.

"They're not alone."

Georgie hopped up onto the prow to try and get a better view. She could see now that the green car was being pursued by two battered 4x4s which had bounded onto the north end of the bridge.

"How're they going to shake them?"

"I dunno, but they're bringing the bastards right to us," said Farran.

They could only watch in horror as the silent chase played out. Georgie and Farran were braced against the port side of the ship, its angle increasing as the swirling waters rose about them.

"They'd better get here soon, we're not going to last much longer," said Sarah.

The 4x4s were gaining every moment. They saw the closest ram the back of the green car and Farran cursed as it slammed into the side of the bridge and sparks flew.

"What can we do to help?"

"Nothin'. Just hope they get here before they get trashed an' before the whole government turns up wiv 'em."

The vehicles disappeared for a moment behind one of the bridge's turrets. When they reappeared both jeeps were right on Tyrone and William's car, taking it in turns to smash chunks out of it like a couple of hyenas trying to bring down a gazelle.

Georgie saw one of the bridge's cables snap up into the air, followed a moment later by a metallic crackle that cut through the noise of the downpour.

The whole surface of the bridge twisted like a strip of paper, the cars sliding down towards the river as momentum kept them moving onwards.

The rear 4x4 dropped back to maintain control and a little distance opened up between the green car and its pursuers.

Another massive cable snapped. The top of the second tower began to collapse, sending debris hurtling down into the river and onto the surface of the bridge. The cable whipped out high into the air then sliced back down, crashing onto the roof of the closest jeep and cutting it in two. Only a muffled crunch reached the trio on the ship.

The rear 4x4 zigzagged around the wreckage and continued the chase.

Another cable came free, then another and another until the entire side of the bridge was dancing with cables like the headless necks of a hydra.

The section attached to the tower came away and plunged into the river with a silent crash.

Georgie screamed.

The weight of its descent tore the remaining cables free one after another, a chain reaction moving towards the south bank. It was a race between the collapsing bridge and the two remaining vehicles as the road was torn from under them.

A ripple moved along the bridge, as though the steel and tarmac had become liquid. The undulation caught the cars, flicking them up towards the bank just as the remainder of the bridge crashed into the river and disappeared like a calving glacier.

"What happened? Sarah, can you see? They went out of sight."

"Can't tell. Building's in the way."

The wave from the collapsed bridge reached the shore, drenching the ship and the children on it.

The level of the water around them had reached so high that the lowest parts of the main deck were now hidden by the scum that topped the floodwaters.

They heard the distant sound of at least one car engine

drawing closer, then a mighty crash and rattle as the green car bounced round the corner and splashed down into the flooded square.

In a second, Tyrone and William were pulling themselves out of the windows as water flooded in and the car began to disappear in a storm of bubbles.

Farran ran to the gangplank, "You boys alright?!"

"Yeah, yeah," Tyrone replied, spitting out dirty water as he and William swam to the steps. "Their car got trashed coming off the bridge, but those scum are still running after us."

"Bastards aren't going to be long," added William, climbing up after Tyrone onto the rain-soaked deck.

"We ready to go? I want to get the hell out of here," said Georgie.

Sarah was balancing high up on the yardarm, mainsail rope in hands, ready with the last knot. "We need to remove the plank so I can drop the sail-"

Just then there was a gunshot.

Two government agents stood at the entrance to the square, rain running down their white biohazard suits.

"Off the ship now!" came a flat, authoritarian voice.

"Sod that!" said Tyrone and began kicking at the gangplank.

A shot whistled through the air and a chip of wood splintered from the mast.

Tyrone ignored it and kicked harder, William and Farran joining him.

Another shot echoed through the square, closer this time.

Too close.

They all froze.

The suits began to work their way around the edge of the square towards the ship, all the time their guns trained on the group by the gangplank.

"Hold onto something," shouted Sarah.

"Eh?" grunted William.

"Just do it!" she yelled.

One of the men cocked his gun and raised it towards Sarah. "Don't try anything funny, young lady."

"Screw you!" came the reply and she dropped from the yardarm just as a bullet thudded into it.

She fell with the rope still in her hand, coming to a stop inches above the deck with a jerk that ripped the knot free and sent the sail tumbling down. It unfurled, flapped once before the wind caught it and billowed out taut as a pregnant belly. The ship wrenched away from the steps, sending the gangplank spinning across the square.

Finally free, the desperate ship righted itself, swinging too far, past the vertical and over the other way. The masts smashed through the glass of the office tower, scraping a line of destruction as the wind carried it grinding through the lock and out into the Thames.

The river rushed into the gap in a second, burying the government agents in an avalanche of water.

CHAPTER 42.

Floodwaters like cold, dark steel. They roll on – vast, unstoppable, a deluge steadily sweeping over London. The sea reaches the business district of the city and crashes against its skyscrapers in a gigantic wave. Spray flies, mixing with the rain; the waters drown the little streets below, rolling over the cars and cafés and expensive restaurants until only the battered sky-scrapers are left, marooned in this new ocean. They stand alone now, jagged black cliffs of steel and glass swept all around by swirling waters.

Soon the flood reaches the burnt wasteland; the cold waters meet the hot, smouldering ground, plunging down into the glowing red chasms without stopping. An ear-splitting hiss scorches the air. Grey steam and soot billow thickly upwards, spilling slowly out like a foul mushroom cloud above the city and making the sky darker and more forbidding than ever.

It tears through the city, following the path of the swollen Thames on which floats, tiny and insignificant in the distance, a single speck of a ship.

* * * * *

They were out on the open river. Wind howled uninterrupted across the vast expanse, blustering from first one direction then another and sending dark patches scudding across the surface of the water. The sail would billow out one moment and the next it would sag heavily. The ropes flapped around dangerously, making it impossible to steer. Despite all her best efforts Sarah couldn't control the ship and they were dragged relentlessly upstream with the tide, under a bridge and past the Houses of Parliament.

"It's no good with this wind, we'll have to wait for the tide to turn," said Sarah from her position at the wheel.

That sunny August day, tilling the land by the museum, seemed like a lifetime ago instead of three days. The fear, the anticipation of the attack and then the attack itself, each of them fighting and running for their life, had all taken a heavy toll on the group. They were tired and haggard, each aching and nursing their own scars. They thought about what they'd been through. They thought about Joanna. There was no discussion between them; they were glad that they were alive but there was a hollow feeling inside them all that they couldn't ignore.

Rain dripped persistently from the rigging and the ship creaked mournfully.

Something bumped under the keel. Georgie reluctantly dragged herself to her feet and went over to the starboard side. Sarah had guided them as best she could out of the fastest moving water and over towards the north bank, but it wasn't clear where they were. Georgie leaned over the side - they seemed to be at the edge of a weir, water rushing down to a street to create a new river below.

"I think we're up against the embankment. The rest of the city's flooding fast."

"Better keep clear. Farran, can you haul on that bowline... the big rope by you - maybe we can catch enough wind to pull us away."

William stood sullenly, looking eastwards towards the waiting sea. Through the rain he saw a new London; no longer the familiar neat curve of the Thames but a ragged mess stretching towards something dark and massive in the distance, something obliterating everything. The line seemed to shift and roll, as though the bruised, stormy sky were sweeping forward.

"What's that, Sarah?"

"What's what?" she asked irritably.

"That black line in the distance."

Tyrone was watching now too. "Hey, yeah, that *is* weird, it looks like the horizon's moving towards us."

Sarah turned to look behind her. "I...I'm not sure."

They were all looking now.

"Can't be the horizon, that don't move."

"What the hell is it?" said Georgie, "It's getting bigger."

"No," whispered Sarah, "it's getting closer."

"Whatever it is it's moving fast."

"Oh my god," said Sarah, "it's the tide."

"What do you mean the tide?"

"That's the sea."

The line was closer now, a band of water so huge it swallowed everything, its towering summit a wall of churning, spitting waves

"Ohmygod, ohmygod, what do we do?" William was pale with fear.

"I don't know," said Sarah, "but if that thing hits us it's going to smash us into matchsticks."

"Head for shore, we have to get off the river," shouted Tyrone.

"What shore?"

"Bring us up alongside a building or somethin'."

"No time," shouted Sarah.

But the decision was taken out of their hands, for just then the battered embankment finally gave way. The waters collapsed through the breach, sucking the ship backwards against the tide and into the flooded streets of London.

* * * * *

As they stood on the ship's deck they could hear the tidal wave approaching, a hissing rumble pushing the cold air along in front of it.

Georgie felt her insides shake with the noise; holding her hands across her stomach she sensed her heart beat faster and faster and her chest tighten. She could smell the damp and the electricity in the air. Around her she saw the others raise their heads, searching, aware that something vast was moving all about them.

To her side, William grasped a rope until his knuckles whitened; he sensed her glance and looked towards her, managing the faintest of smiles before he turned away.

The flooded road ahead became a jumble of grey rapids. Georgie saw a white van tumble forward like a pebble before it was submerged, whilst the road to the left of that was already a tube of galloping waters in which every shop and house had disappeared.

Then in a flash the waters finally smashed into them from every side at once.

Waves leapt and crashed over the deck, drenching them all and knocking Farran and Sarah off their feet. Sarah thudded into the cabin with a horrible crack but Farran flew across the slippery deck, spinning helplessly on his back as he skidded closer to the edge. The stormy waters below frothed and leapt, waiting to claim him. Blindly, he stretched out his arms, flailing for purchase until by chance he caught a dangling length of rope, his fingernails digging in as he struggled to hold on.

The planks of the hull groaned and creaked. The main mast swayed until it seemed as though it would crack and then the entire ship pitched backwards. Farran's feet dipped into the water – so dark and thick with muck that they seemed to disappear. Like a wild thing the ship bucked upwards again and he was flung into the air like a ragdoll, thudding back onto the slick deck so hard that the wind was knocked out of him.

Georgie was next to him in a second, William holding him beneath the arms and heaving him upright.

"You okay?" shouted Georgie through the howling gale.

Eyes bulging, Farran still struggled for breath but was able to nod.

"Everyone - grab something," she called, as William helped Farran to his feet and pinned the two of them to the rigging with both hands.

There was a shocking lurch as the whole ship rose suddenly upwards on a swell of water; trapped in the tunnel of buildings the ship bucked and strained on a foaming whirlpool.

Every creak of its boards made the group fear she was about to splinter and break in two but still the vessel held.

Finally, the influx of water built a current and decided on a direction. She was slowly pushed forward, splinters scraping from the sides of the ship as she squeezed past buildings and down the flowing street.

* * * * *

Deep in the government bunker eyes were fixed on the huge bank of monitors, images cycling rapidly as they searched CCTV feeds for any sign of the children. There had been reports from units five and six in pursuit of an IC1 and IC3 male in a green vehicle, but those had gone quiet. In their intense concentration, no one noticed the sound of trickling water.

On the surface, floodwaters had found the shaft entrance and begun to gush in like a waterfall down a pothole. With power diverted the place had been left weakened. Water rushed around the elevators and out through cracks, along corridors, between carelessly unclosed blast doors.

At first the grated floors carried away some of the water but the pumps were soon overwhelmed and the motors submerged. By the time the first of the government agents realised the danger it was too late.

Water flooded in at such a rate that it was impossible to push against the flow - exits were cut off, fates were sealed. Every possible route to the surface was now just a way for yet more water to get in.

The control room began to flood, becoming a scene of chaos: computers shorted and exploded, fires broke out, sparks ricocheted back and forth across the room. It was plunged briefly into darkness before red emergency lights flickered on. Only the watertight monitor banks continued to work.

The government agents screamed and clambered over one another in a frenzy but there was no escape. Soon the water was up to their knees, then up to their groins, then up to their chests, their necks, their mouths - and then it was above their heads and they were drowning. Eyes bulged underwater, hair splaying out like seaweed. Lungs felt like they were going to burst but the instinct not to breathe was stronger than the painful need for air; it was not until they were on the verge of unconsciousness – a minute, almost two – before they helplessly sucked in the murky water and drowned.

Under the failing lights and stillness of the sunken bunker, shapes floated like marionettes; one of the monitors, shortly before pressure cracked the screen and it blinked out of existence, showed a strange image: a galleon racing past the Houses of Parliament, almost directly above the base.

* * * * *

Meeting the freedom of the wider streets, the flow became a raging torrent. Powerless to control its course, the ship was carried, pitching and turning like a cork, spinning as the streets funnelled the water back east after the initial surge. Taken by the strongest current, the group found themselves moving with growing speed, swept down what had once been the city's main roads.

Oxford Street had been transformed into a man-made gorge of dark grey water and plate-glass windows. The tops of lampposts peeped above the surface, the rapids occasionally splashing over them as they jumped and swirled. Only the upper floors of the big department stores were visible now; as the ship was carried forward the group could still see the aisles full of bright clothes, racks of forlorn sporting goods, abandoned offices of empty desks and scattered paperwork.

Pulled by this current the ship was then turned and swept down the wide expanse of Regent Street. Georgie gripped the nearest rope, trying to keep her balance as they pitched and rolled amidst the screaming wind. The grand edifice of Hamley's slid by on their left side, its windows smashed. As she looked down she could see a forlorn teddy bear float past, face down amongst the debris. A little sea of coloured Lego bricks bobbed along - red, yellow and blue atop the filthy tide, eddying around footballs and drowning dolls. Everywhere she looked Georgie found the contents of buildings spilling outwards. Desks floated off with the stream like rafts, with old newspapers and rusty cans whirling around them like shoals of drab fish.

Here and there the grey steeples of churches rose above the new river and Georgie could only imagine the great spaces beneath – the ancient pillars and altars, the artwork and vaulted ceilings transformed into shadowy, drowned caves.

A statue passed as they emerged from Regent Street, its head and a forlorn arm visible above the rising waters, seeming to reach for the ship as it drifted out of sight and into a wider space beyond. The flow was a little steadier here and Georgie took the opportunity to climb some way up the rigging and scan the horizon. The maze of London streets had become a network of rivers - straight and cold like wide grey canals. Slanting rain battered the long wedges of rooftops, often all that remained visible of the submerged streets.

*   *   *   *   *

For what seemed like hours they were pitched and rolled through the flooded London streets at the capricious whim of the currents, Sarah doing her best to steer a course, avoiding half-submerged lorries and bus stops. More than once the keel of the ship struck hard against some unseen danger, threatening to tear open the hull and drown them all. All of them worked together, pulling ropes, heaving with all their might on the wheel to avoid being swept down a dead end or sucked into a whirlpool. Shop windows shattered underwater, pavements collapsed, and the rapids disappeared into basements threatening to take the ship down into the dirty drowned bowels of London.

Saltwater swirled and gargled and foamed around them, constantly soaking them with spray so that the group shivered and their clumsy, numbed hands could hardly hold onto the rigging.

Sometimes the prow of the ship would be driven down by an unexpected wave and the deck left awash with green water so that it was all the group could do to hold on and avoid being dragged overboard. All the time the sounds of the storm and the water boomed around them and the buildings groaned under the onslaught.

They were exhausted now, almost too tired to react to the desperate commands of Sarah, her voice hoarse with effort and raw with salt spray.

Finally they were thrown into a large junction where the water swirled round and round a single, central office block. Georgie thought she recognised it as Centre Point.

Once they circled in the whirlpool. Twice.

Shop signs crashed against the sides of the ship, shredding the mainsail, and at one point they heeled and bobbed up again so violently that the top of the mizzen mast crashed into the giant yellow 'M' of a McDonald's, destroying both. The mizzen shrouds flopped onto the deck like a torn spider's web, a tangle of rope and tarred wood.

Round they went again. Lower now.

It was as though they were now in the very eye of the storm, a terrifying vortex of debris, rain and rushing water. Sarah's arms ached with the effort of pulling down on the ship's wheel but it was no use - the ship no longer responded and she gave herself up to the mercy of the currents. They could only hold fast and pray - and she told the others so.

Assaulted by the spray, the group tangled their tired limbs in the rigging and gaped in helpless awe at the terrible forces that raged about them.

If they'd been trapped in the whirlpool much longer the ship would have been shaken to pieces - sunk by one of the cars that swirled with them or crushed by the falling masonry which splashed down - but London helped one last time. The flooded foundations of Centre Point finally gave way. Submerged concrete cracked and steel girders shivered apart and the tower fell in on itself.

Where once the depression of the vortex had been, now rose up a solid wall of water. They were part of the wave; dragged backwards up its slope they joined its crest, curling over, threatening to upend. The crest broke and for a moment the ship was completely submerged; the world became muted watery darkness and they felt the tug of the cold current all around them.

Then as suddenly as it had hit, they burst spluttering back

up into the storm.

The force of the wave hurled them through the streets and at last spat the ship out into the Thames where the strong, steady ebb tide took hold of them and the group collapsed in exhaustion right there on the sodden deck.

*   *   *   *   *

Georgie could remember very little of their journey along the Thames. The flood subsided and took them with it. She lay huddled on the deck cold and wet. Glimpses of broken cottages and fallen trees on the riverbanks slid by as she drifted in and out of a sleep that was so close to unconsciousness as to make no difference.

Once she half-woke to realise that someone had laid a rough blanket over her shoulders and she recognised the warmth of Farran next to her. Later she came-to just enough to look about her, anxiously jarred by some half-remembered dream into looking about the ship and reassuring herself that all of her comrades were still on board. That was the last time she stirred before she slipped away again into a long and dreamless sleep.

CHAPTER 43.

Georgie awoke to bright sunshine and a fresh salt tang in the air. She hauled her body upright; her limbs were stiff and her hands were pruned and sore, but the sun felt good on her skin.

She looked about the ship and her eye was met by nothing except an unbroken curve of gently undulating blue and an azure sky above it. They were out in the open sea. For a moment she was disorientated and a little concerned, but the rocking of the ship and sleepy caress of the sun had a lulling effect, and her concern soon blew away like spindrift.

Georgie turned and saw that Sarah was standing at the helm watching her. They nodded at one another but said nothing. It seemed wrong to break the calm of the wind and the rhythmic slap of waves against the hull with anything as crude as words.

Over the next hour the others stirred one by one, but they too did so wordlessly. There was too much to say and no way to begin. They let the sounds of the sea fill the void and were grateful for it.

High above the tattered mainsail and the battered tops a gull cried out in a sound like pain or anguish.

They all looked up to where it fluttered in the breeze.

Georgie smiled a sad smile, remembering, then she broke the silence, "I'd better go and check on our supplies." And with that she went down into the hold.

* * * * *

Georgie climbed the ladder from the hold to find the others sitting on the main deck, "What now? We don't have much in the way of food – less than I'd thought actually. Should we try to find somewhere along the coast that wasn't battered by the storm and stop to pick up supplies? Or should we just make straight for France?"

Sarah looked up, and very quietly said, "We go back."

Suddenly all eyes were on her.

"Back where?" asked William, confused.

"Back to London," said Georgie, still looking at Sarah, a smile starting to creep onto her face.

"But it's flooded."

"Some of it is, the bit by the river. Not the whole place, not our home," said Sarah.

"We don't just *live* in London," said Georgie, "that is, we don't just happen to live there because that's where our parents lived or because that's where we found ourselves. It's *ours*. We made it our home, we changed it – I mean, we made stuff *grow*, we made it something new."

"But it's more than that," said Tyrone. He hesitated. "Those bodies I saw when the government took me – the others. The children they cut up. I've only just realised something."

Georgie looked at him, watching his eyes move as he remembered. The pain – that deep well of hurt was still there, but this time there was something else.

"It means there have to be more like us," he said, looking quickly at each of them, "The government found them some-where - we weren't the only ones."

Georgie brightened, "Then they might be out there still, even now."

"Everywhere," said Sarah, gripping Georgie's hand, "in cities like Birmingham or Manchester. There might even be some stuck out on their own in the countryside or the middle of nowhere – thinking it's just them – waiting to be found."

"We can find them. Get them to join us," said William.

"We'll set up a signal," agreed Georgie, "we'll start a radio broadcast. They can come to us. And we'll help them."

"But what if there are any of those government men still alive?"

A shiver ran through the group, a cold dip in pressure. The sails flapped briefly for a moment as though the wind had dropped out of them.

Farran pulled the ship into the wind and the sails came taut again.

Sarah growled, "If the government are there and they want a fight, then we give them a fight." She looked at the arrowhead in her hand - *And God help them.*

* * * * *

Georgie leaned over the prow of the ship, balancing precariously out from the foremast. She felt the wind in her face and as the ship pitched, she felt spray splash against her skin. She had a sense of speed, of exhilaration, of freedom like she'd never felt in her life.

She looked down onto the choppy turquoise waters below and there, gambolling about in the bow wave, was not one, but an entire pod of dolphins, their bodies sleek and dark against the cresting foam. They swam together, despite the buffeting of the sea. Five of them. She smiled.

"Take us home, Mr Alkhaban," she called back with a laugh.

"Aye-aye, captain," came the response and they slipped between the white rocks of the coast of England, into the Thames Estuary, heading for London and home.

Acknowledgements

Many thanks to our friends, loved ones, and family whose support, understanding, and encouragement have helped to make this book possible. You know who you are, and if you're not sure, we'll happily tell you again.

Special thanks to Sue Reid, Leigh Carrick-Moore, Oscar Reid, Sos Eltis, Mark Daniell, David Low, and our editor John Hudspith for reading some of the many, many drafts and for giving us such thoughtful feedback over the years.

Printed in Great Britain
by Amazon